CROSSROADS

Awakening

T. Z. WITHERITE

ARCHWAY
PUBLISHING

This is a work of fiction. All of the characters, names, incidents,
organizations, and dialogue in this novel are either the products
of the author's imagination or are used fictitiously.

Archway Publishing books may be ordered through booksellers or by contacting:

Archway Publishing
1663 Liberty Drive
Bloomington, IN 47403
www.archwaypublishing.com
844-669-3957

ISBN: 978-1-6657-0527-1 (sc)
ISBN: 978-1-6657-0528-8 (e)

Library of Congress Control Number: 2021906982

Print information available on the last page.

Archway Publishing rev. date: 6/1/2021

A dark figure stood over the world it had conquered, admiring its work—the burnt villages, the mountains of corpses, and the rivers of blood. Only one man stood before it, but the figure did not notice because the rags the man wore were drenched with blood, blending in with all the land surrounding him. This creature, though miles away, still towered over all that stood. To it, mountains were hills, oceans were ponds, and every step it took pushed it farther and farther away.

The man did not waver, however, and brandished his sword, if for nothing but his own benefit. His life had been destroyed by this monster, and he had nothing left to lose. The man began to charge, and despite the distance, he was making gains quickly, covering miles in mere seconds. He jumped, raising his sword high, to slice through the nape of this horror's neck. But as the sword made contact, everything went black.

Then Derrek woke up.

He had fallen asleep at his desk, a result of spending the last thirty-six hours straight working on the arrangements for the company's next excursion to Germany. A lot had to go into it. Housing arrangements were made for upward of two hundred people, transport for several tons worth of equipment, and going through the bureaucratic hell that was Frostbyte's budgetary system.

Derrek Snowe worked for Frostbyte Incorporated, a philanthropic company based in New York City focused on environmental conservation and the furthering of humanity as a whole. The owner and CEO, William Shale, founded the company in 2003 with the intention of achieving immortality for everyone at a reasonable price. While they had thus far made little progress toward that goal, it remained the reason Shale kept the company alive. Most of the company's revenue came from their technological developments, namely their prosthetic limbs and artificial organs. The limbs were able to completely replicate their lost counterparts, down to artificial skin grafts that blended seamlessly with the patient's natural skin, and the organs fully integrated with virtually all recipients. Even for the year 2035, it was decades ahead of its time.

Derrek yawned and stretched his arms. This alerted his cubicle neighbor, Neil Jenkins—a kindhearted man with thick glasses in his midforties, who popped his head over the thin wall separating the two. He said, "Morning, sleepy head! Did you have a nice nap?"

"Fuck off, Jenkins," Derrek replied without opening his eyes.

Jenkins laughed, then perched his arms atop the wall, getting comfortable. "Every time you wake up from a late night, you tell me to 'eff off'—can always count on it!"

"And I can always count on your impeccable timing, annoying me as soon as I wake up."

Jenkins pulled his right arm back to his own desk, grabbed a mug, and gestured for Derrek to take it. "Hey, give me some credit; you can also count on me making your coffee exactly the way you like it."

Derrek accepted the mug and took a sip, "I drink it black. There's milk in this."

"Oh, well, if you don't like it, I'll gladly go dump it out," Jenkins said, reaching for the mug, which Derrek quickly pulled out of reach, sloshing the coffee around but not spilling a drop.

"Try to take it, and I'll send you home in pieces," he said with murder in his half-opened eyes.

Jenkins bellowed with laughter, falling back into his chair, "Like clockwork, I swear!" he continued laughing for quite a while, long enough for Derrek to chug over half of his coffee. After Jenkins managed to quell his laughter, he got back up on his perch and asked, "What had you up all night this time, young buck?"

"The GM wanted me to get the lodging arrangements set for the survey team we're sending to Germany next week. He said something about 'expanding my horizons,' so I think he thinks he was doing me a favor." He then took a long sip from his mug. "But at any rate, he's a total ass."

"Would you say he's a whole ass?" Jenkins asked, with a coy smirk and raised eyebrows.

Derrek caught on and replied, "No, but I'd say he's an asshole." Jenkins went into another laughing fit, while Derrek smiled faintly as he finished his coffee. "What time is it anyway? I have a meeting with him at nine, and you know how much of a stickler for punctuality he is." He pushed back his dark brown hair and checked the clock on his computer.

8:56 a.m.

"Oh shit!" he said in a hushed yell as he scrambled to gather his materials. He had papers he printed the night before, but he also needed to transfer the presentation he had spent so much time on to his flash drive.

He had everything he needed and was on his way to the conference room, after thanking Jenkins for the coffee. As he rushed past his busy coworkers, he caught a glimpse of the clock that hung above the west wall.

8:59:42 a.m.

I can make it! thought Derrek. This was right before he tripped over the service dog of his coworker Jerry, which he claimed was for his bum knee. He was sure Jerry didn't need it. He just wanted an excuse to bring his dog to work. But whenever anyone asked him about it, Jerry would just say, "Legally, you can't ask me that," until they went away.

The dog let out a loud *yip* as Derrek crashed onto the floor, breaking his fall with his left shoulder. His papers scattered across the floor. The cheap carpeting gave him a nasty carpet burn on his forearm; it was a bad choice to roll up his sleeves.

Jerry jumped out of his chair. "Hey! Watch where you're going!" He had no sympathy for Derrek, who was collecting his papers as quickly as he could.

He found all his papers but couldn't find the flash drive. His eyes darted across the off-gray carpet for it. It was between the legs of the dog, who was now growling at him. Derrek scooped it up in a quick motion while not breaking eye contact with the dog. He then turned to Jerry. "Remind me how this helps with your knee?" he asked as he went on his way to the manager's office.

"Legally, you can't ask me that!" Jerry called out.

Derrek turned his head back to Jerry, and right before he was out of earshot, he said, "Well, legally, you're a dick!"

He rushed his way to the conference room, running at a near-full sprint, and came to a stop only a few inches before he would have hit the door. He took a brief second to straighten his tie and brush the dust off his shoulders, and then he knocked. As soon as he heard, "Come in!" he opened the door and entered the room.

The first thing he heard after the door closed was his manager saying, "You're late." Derrek looked at the clock that hung above the projection screen.

9:02:24 a.m.

Crap, he thought. He knew this was going to be another fifteen-minute spiel about punctuality. "I'm sorry, Mr. Hanes. I tripped over Jerry's dog on the way—"

Hanes cut him off, "There you go, blaming your shortcomings

on others. Can't even take responsibility for your failures? I swear, if all my employees acted the way you do—"

Before he could finish his sentence, the door opened. Hanes was ready to chew out whoever was on the other side for having the audacity to enter without knocking before realizing it was William Shale standing before him.

He looked at Hanes and said, "Oh, am I interrupting something?"

"Um … no, Mr. Shale. I was just scolding Derrek here on his tardiness."

"Tardiness? The meeting was set at nine, right? It's only a couple of minutes past now."

"Well, yes, but being late by even one minute shows a certain lack of professionalism."

"I understand where you're coming from, but isn't it company policy to give a five-minute grace period for all meetings?"

"Well … yes, I suppose it is."

"And I think you should cut him some slack, considering he's late because he was up all night doing the work I had asked *you* to do."

"Erm … well, I had more pressing matters, so I delegated the task to Derrek."

Shale raised an eyebrow. "More pressing matters? Do you mean that new vampire romcom? What was it called … *Love Sucks?*"

Hanes's face turned bright red. He wanted out of this conversation, so he let out a forced coughing fit. Then he said, "Right, so the lodging. Do you have the arrangements, Derrek?"

Derrek flashed a thankful smile to Shale. "Yes, everything has been approved by the Schadenfreude hotel. I managed to arrange for a single flight for all our passengers with cargo space for our equipment. I rented a small warehouse for the month for storage. All the vehicle arrangements are in order, and we even came out six hundred dollars under budget."

Shale raised his eyebrow again. "Schadenfreude? What a strange name for a hotel."

"I thought so too, but they had the best ratings in our price range. Plus, the owner is apparently a huge fan of Americans. She jumped at the chance to have two hundred of us on her property. I have it all printed out and the charts mapped on this flash drive. I can pull it up right—"

Hanes interjected, "No, no, that will be quite all right. I trust your judgment. Now, if you gentlemen will excuse me, I believe I have to take a call." He left the room, putting his silent phone to his ear, pretending to have a conversation until he was sure they couldn't hear him.

Shale looked at his watch. "Let's see, the meeting was set to run until nine thirty, and it looks like we still have about twenty-five minutes left." He reached into his jacket and pulled out a rectangular wooden box with a checkered pattern. He shook it, rattling the insides. "Up for a game?"

Derrek grew a cocky smile, "Oh, you're on."

Shale set the box on the table, undid a latch on the side and emptied the contents onto the surface. Among them were two bags of chess pieces, one black, one white, a notepad with a score count and an attached pen, and a small trophy made of tin foil spray-painted gold. He then laid the box down checker side up, grabbed the white set of pieces, and began setting his side while Derrek did the same with the black pieces.

"I keep telling you, son, you really need to stop overworking yourself like this," said Shale as he put the last of his pieces in place.

"I can handle a lot worse. It was only a day and a half this time anyway. Remember a couple of years ago? I didn't go home for six days straight!"

"Even so, you know I worry about you. You haven't willingly taken a single vacation day since I brought you on."

"Oh, come on, I was an unpaid intern for the first six years. You know they don't get any vacation time."

"I would've had you a lot higher up a lot sooner, but you were twelve! There was legally nothing I could do there! But you still turned it down when I offered it."

"Hey, if the work never rests, then I won't either."

Shale let out a bellowing laugh. "I swear, you remind me so much of myself when I was young."

Derrek rolled his eyes, "You say that every time we talk."

"And it's true every time I say it."

"Yeah yeah, you're full of clichés. I know you're just stalling 'cause you know I'm going to win," Derrek said, brandishing a half smile.

"Oh am I? I'd better get things started then," Shale said as he moved his left-most pawn two spaces. "By the way, do you know what today is?"

"Thursday?" Derrek replied as he made his first move, getting his right knight out.

"It's Friday, actually, but that's not what I meant," he said, waiting a few seconds to see if Derrek could remember.

Derrek couldn't remember, which caused Shale to sigh loudly. "It's the anniversary of the first time we played against each other."

Derrek's eyes lit up with that revelation. "*Oh yeah*! Fifteen years ago today I whooped your ass and took your twenty dollars!"

"That's right! Really taught me a lesson about underestimating my opponent."

"Then you offered me a job."

"You looked like you needed it, considering you were hustling people in chess just to get food in your stomach."

"Wasn't my fault. The foster system doesn't work. I was bound to end up there one way or another," Derrek said with a grin as he pushed his bishop onto the field.

"Be that as it may, I knew there was something special in you."

"You said that then too, and let me tell you, it did not help your case."

Shale chuckled a little, moving to get his bishop onto the field. "But you still gave it a shot, and I'm glad you did, son."

"I was homeless, and you offered me hot food, a place to live, a paying job, and someone who could actually match me in chess. You gave me a second chance, Will."

"You were the first one to beat me in thirty years, and ever since you've been challenging me, making me want to be better than I am," he said as Derrek took his rook. "In fact, I'd like to make a little wager."

"Oh really? Want to lose another twenty dollars?"

"Not quite," Shale said as he moved his queen to take Derrek's knight. "I'm thinking something a bit more high stakes."

"Forty?"

Shale laughed. "No, not money. Something much more valuable than that."

Derrek couldn't imagine what he was going to wager but was eager to find out, "All right, let me hear it," he said as he moved his rook to defend his king.

"If I win, then you have to take a vacation."

"Come on, Will, where would I even go?"

"You said we were six hundred dollars under budget on the survey team, right? That's enough for the ticket, and I'm sure they'll let you get another room for the time with what's left. Plus, since you'll be on a business trip, you can satisfy your workaholism."

"That ... actually doesn't sound like the worst thing. It would be kind of nice to get some real field experience. But what if I win?" he asked, moving his queen to lure Shale's queen into a trap.

Shale smiled and said, "If you win, then the company is yours."

Derrek looked at him, eyes wide in surprise, not sure he heard him right. "The company?"

"That's right."

"Frostbyte?"

"Uh-huh."

"Mine?"

"Yours and yours alone."

A moment passed as Derrek realized what this could mean for him. He had spent the last fifteen years climbing the ladder, pushing himself harder and harder to be the best he could be, and this was the ultimate prize. He looked at his hands, which he had spent so long working to the bone, then looked at Shale and said, "You've got a deal."

Shale smiled and moved his queen away from Derrek's trap, taking his rook and cornering his king. "Checkmate."

Derrek jumped up and stared at the board, mouth agape, amazed he could have missed a move like that. He slumped back down into his chair and said, "You're a cruel man, Will. You knew what I was setting up the whole time, didn't you?"

Shale crossed his arms and put on a smug face, proud of his victory. "You've pulled the same move one hundred and forty-three times. You had to expect it wasn't going to work at some point. Would you please do the honors?"

Derrek grumbled comically, more for a gag than actually airing his grievances, as he grabbed the notepad and wrote the new score: 1532 to 1531, advantage Shale.

"I swear, I'm going to pull out ahead when this is all over with. You won't get me with that trick again," Derrek said as he gathered his pieces back into his bag.

"Trick? What trick are you talking about?" Shale asked as he did the same.

"Tempting me with the company. I knew there was no way you'd bet it if you didn't know you were going to win."

"I was serious, son."

Derrek could tell by looking in Shale's eyes that he was telling the truth. It was the same look he'd had when he'd first offered

Derrek his job. As he put the last piece in his bag, he said, "If you were serious about that, then I guess I was serious about my end as well."

Shale's eyes lit up. He was ecstatic Derrek was going to finally take a break. He put the pieces, notepad, and trophy back into the chess box and tucked it back into his jacket pocket. As he got up to leave, he said, "Wonderful! I'll have the personnel change put through immediately and have Hanes take care of your arrangements."

He put his hand on the doorknob, but before he opened the door, he turned to Derrek to say, "If you ever want to play for keeps again, I'd be happy to send you on another vacation."

"Do you really think I have what it takes to run Frostbyte?"

Shale raised an eyebrow. "Doubtful of my judgment? I wouldn't risk it unless I knew it was in good hands."

"I'm only twenty-seven. Don't you think it'll go over poorly with the board?"

"As long as you prove yourself, you'll be fine."

"But what if I can't?"

"Son, you proved yourself the first time you had me in checkmate." Shale left, leaving Derrek alone in the conference room.

He gathered his materials and headed back to his desk. He passed by Jerry's cubicle, avoiding eye contact and stepping around his dog, who was still lying down in the middle of the walkway.

When he got back to his little slice of life, he sat in his swivel chair and covered his face with his hands, exhausted both physically and emotionally. He looked at his desk to check his inbox but found something that wasn't there when he left.

There was a steaming mug of coffee with a note tucked underneath it that read, "Looked like you could use it. —N Jenkins."

Derrek smiled and took a sip. Afterward, he looked at the coffee with a puzzled look on his face, which shifted to one of annoyance.

Milk.

He smiled again and took another sip.

It was a long flight, almost nine hours, and Derrek was glad to finally be able to stretch his legs. He had to be at the airport at 4:00 a.m., but delays pushed the flight to 7:00, and he couldn't get much sleep the night before. Due to his last-minute booking, he ended up with a middle seat and had the misfortune of sitting between someone who snored like a bear and one with a bad cold. The in-flight movie was awful, some inaccurate allegory of fifties politics but with talking dogs. They were out of noise-canceling headphones, and every time Derrek got close to falling asleep, he was interrupted either by an impossibly loud snore or a sneeze of equal volume.

But he was finally off the flight and boarded a shuttle to the hotel. Each shuttle had a capacity for only sixty, so they split their group over the four they had rented, and to Derrek's delight, he was on the one with the least people and didn't see either of his seat-mates from the plane. It was another couple of hours to the Schadenfreude, so he decided to get comfortable.

Before he could even fashion a pillow from his duffle bag, a man popped up from the seat in front of him. He was bald but had a full beard, a large scar across his left cheek, and muscle mass for three. He spoke with a commanding but thoughtful voice.

"You're the last-minute add-on, Derrek, right?"

Derrek replied, "Yeah, that's me. And you are?"

The man stuck his hand out to shake Derrek's, and with a big smile, he said, "Major Jeffrey Reynolds. Pleasure to meet you."

Not wanting to be rude, Derrek shook Jeffrey's hand. His hand felt like it was almost all callous, but it was clear he wasn't squeezing as hard as he could so as to not absolutely shatter Derrek's bones.

"Major? I didn't know we had those rankings in Frostbyte."

He gave a small laugh and said, "You don't, but your CEO has done a lot of good for the government, so letting him take a few good soldiers in rough territory so he can do more good is kind of a no-brainer."

"Rough territory? I thought Germany was at peace."

"It sure is, which is why there's only eight of us here. Usually, the bigwigs send one soldier for every two Frostbyte employees."

"I guess that's a good sign," Derrek managed to say before he was interrupted by his own yawn.

Jeffrey realized how tired Derrek was and said, "You should get some rest. Jet lag can be a real pain. Plus, you'll need your strength. You've got orientation tomorrow."

"For the survey work?"

"Well, yeah, but I was referring to your weapons training. Gotta carry a sidearm if you're in the field, and you gotta be trained to carry a sidearm."

"I guess that makes sense. Never know what you might run into. Crazy world we live in."

"You know it, but get yourself some shuteye," Jeffrey said as he reached into his bag and pulled out a pair of headphones. "Here, these might help. They're noise-canceling, the good kind."

Derrek gratefully accepted the headphones and hastily said, "Thank you *so* much," before putting them on and almost immediately passing out with his head on his duffle pillow.

Jeffrey gave a slight laugh. "I swear, Shale, you'd better know what you're doing with this kid," he said as he turned to face forward, pulled out a well-worn book, opened it to the middle, and began reading.

Derrek opened his eyes and found himself in an empty warehouse. It was the dead of night, but the full moon lit the room well enough that he could see. He couldn't tell how large the building was, but he could see the floor around him was splattered with what looked like blood. His dreams were often strange, but they never as vivid as this felt.

He was fearful and confused but decided to investigate. There was a trail heading into an unlit part of the warehouse, and Derrek could hear noises from the shadows. Tearing. Slurping. Crunching. Growling.

He couldn't see what was making the sounds, but he caught a glimpse of a pair of eyes reflecting light. They were bright yellow. Whatever it was, he was sure it wasn't human.

Before he could react, there was a crash above him. He dove away from the falling rubble and by some miracle came out unscathed. The hole in the ceiling let in significantly more light, and Derrek could completely see not only the creature lurking in the shadows but the person who busted through the roof.

The thing lurking in the shadows was humanoid but clearly wasn't human, not anymore, at least. Its limbs were long and spindly, its fingers were as sharp as knives, its skin was tight, and the outline of every bone of its nude body was visible. The teeth of this creature were like needles, and its jaw opened much wider than it should. Its eyes were like cat eyes, except bloodshot and sunken in. The thing had no body hair to speak of, and even though it was crouched over, eating something that was too mangled even to tell what it was, Derrek could tell this monster would tower over him.

He couldn't get a good look at the person, but not from lack of trying. Even though they were in direct moonlight, the image was blurry and incomprehensible, and all he could make out was a large mass of the color red.

Despite the obstruction, the person's voice came through clear as day. It was a masculine voice but sounded young. Derrek heard the person say, "One fifty-two. Gotta say, those are rookie numbers for your kind."

The creature responded with an incoherent series of growls, snarls, and hisses, with a few clicks sprinkled in. Even though Derrek couldn't make out anything from it, the man behind the blob seemed to get the gist of it.

"Make all the excuses you want. Won't stop what's gonna happen next. Oh, right, I meant to ask last time: did you ever even actually eat anything? And I don't mean the cannibalism."

The thing gave a low growl, apparently in thought. After several seconds, it gave a loud bark and a short series of clicks.

"You got me there. I guess wolves do count. Shoulda maybe gotten one that wasn't quite as rabid though." Derrek wasn't sure, but it looked like the man put one of his hands to his head, which gave a loud *smack!* "Oh shit, that reminds me! Did you ever see *Old Yeller?*"

The monster started to growl as if it were giving an answer, but was cut off by a loud *bang,* quickly followed by two more. The sound caused Derrek to close his eyes for a split second, and when he opened them again, the creature's head was missing, along with its neck, and there was a large hole where he assumed its heart was.

He wasn't sure where the third shot went, but he was hopeful the thing was dead. With the creature out of the way, Derrek saw what it was eating, and although he couldn't make out many details, he saw it had a human hand.

The red man appeared to have his arm outstretched and was holding a large object, the shape of which resembled a handgun.

"Eh, probably good you didn't see it," he said as he spun the object and threw it into his belt. "You would've hated the ending."

Even though Derrek couldn't see what was happening, he had a feeling the man was showing off.

The shape turned and began to leave when the body of the creature began to convulse and undulate. The wound in its chest healed over rapidly, its head began to grow back, and its limbs were violently twitching.

"Damn it, I had twenty dollars on you not being that far gone," the man said as he moved his arms around, apparently looking for something. "But looking back on it, if eating even one person usually does the trick, a hundred almost definitely would. Oh, well, you know what they say, right?"

The creature was fully reformed at this point and was shrieking at the man, its teeth dripping with saliva and its claws raised.

"Hindsight's twenty-twenty."

The monster pounced at the man, but before it made contact, the room was suddenly filled with fire. Derrek felt intense heat, making him scream in agony. He could feel his flesh melting off his bones, every agonizing second as he felt his skin char and his clothes fused to his body. He felt his organs begin to liquefy. He felt pure pain as every nerve in his body melted away.

Then he felt nothing.

Derrek woke with a start, nearly falling out of his seat. He took off his headphones and rubbed his eyes, trying to get his senses back. The bus wasn't moving anymore, so he guessed they had reached their destination.

Looking around, he saw all of the seats were empty, including the drivers. Through the windshield, he saw bright lights and a grand entrance to a large building.

He began to gather his things when he realized there was a note taped to his shirt. He took it off, careful not to rip it. In the light from the entrance, he could that see it read, "Go on in whenever you wake up. They'll take care of you at the front desk. Oh, and keep the headphones. I stole them from the plane anyway. See you tomorrow, 600 sharp! —MAJ. Reynolds."

He checked his phone to see just how long he had slept; by his calculations, he had been alone on the bus for almost two hours.

He left the bus and took a second to appreciate the massive hotel before him. He had seen pictures when he made the reservations but wasn't prepared for how extravagant it looked in person.

It was twenty-five stories tall, more of a skyscraper than a hotel, and Derrek knew it had five layers of parking beneath it. The giant neon sign was at least a hundred feet up, and each letter was fifteen feet tall, reading in bright orange, "SCHADENFREUDE."

The entrance was decorated with huge marble columns wrapped with golden ivy in a perfectly symmetrical pattern. The doors were large enough to let people come in droves, and on each side, there was a small but fitting fountain, filled with coins from all around the world.

Derrek had never seen anything like this, spending the majority of his life in New York, leaving for only a month in Hawaii six years earlier after losing a similar bet with Shale. It was intimidating and awe-inspiring, clearly the result of someone who truly loves their work.

He caught himself staring at the building, standing in front of the entrance for longer than he should, and decided to go in. He was simultaneously greeted by the doorman and the smell of lavender. The lobby matched the entrance, with ample seating, several televisions with wireless headphones, a row of four elevators with glass doors, and a large roaring fireplace in the center of it all made from what Derrek could only assume was a hollowed-out pillar of solid marble, matching the ones he saw outside. It was open concept. Each floor had a balcony. The ceiling went all the way up and was capped with a pyramid-shaped window wrapped around the chimney.

He must have been standing there for a while, because the woman at the front desk waved him over.

"Kann ich Dir helfen?" she asked as he approached. Derrek didn't have time to learn much of the language beyond "Where is the bathroom?" so he searched his bag for his German-to-English dictionary. As soon as she saw the cover, she said, "Oh, don't worry. Most people here speak English."

"Really?" Derrek asked, questioning his purchase. "I guess I paid nine ninety-nine for nothing."

She laughed and started tapping some keys on her computer. "Do you have a reservation?"

"Yes, I'm with the Frostbyte party."

"I thought you all checked in hours ago. Did you get caught in traffic?"

"No, I've actually been asleep on one of the busses for a couple of hours. It was a really long flight."

She laughed again. "I totally understand, and what was your name?"

"Derrek Snowe, with two R's, a K, and an E after the W."

She typed for a few seconds, then said, "Ah, there you are. Room 719. Here's your key." She handed him a plastic card with the Schadenfreude logo and said with a big smile, "Enjoy your stay!"

"Thank you ver—"

He cut himself off and began flipping through the pages of his guide. Once he found what he was looking for, he said, "Danke schon," and hurried off to his room before he could hear her say how poorly he had pronounced it.

Behind him, however, the woman smiled, glad he put in the

effort, and waved to him once he got in the elevator. He waved back, embarrassed, and pressed the button for the seventh floor.

The ride was quick, and the glass doors were so clear, he wasn't sure if they were even open. Looking over the balcony, he could see the floor had a massive mosaic pattern of a flock of doves, with a ten-pointed star underneath the fireplace.

Every part of this hotel inspired awe in Derrek, and he only wished he was awake enough to truly appreciate it. He walked along the balcony, looking for his room, and found it after a minute or so of sauntering along, admiring his surroundings. There was a small sign hung on the doorknob, which read, "Reserved."

He smiled, knowing this was likely Shale's doing, stuck his card into the slot, and went inside. The room didn't quite match the lobby, but it was still the nicest place Derrek had ever lain his head. He booked everyone with single rooms, since they had enough rooms to accommodate them and it was surprisingly more cost-effective to do so.

The room was large, around four hundred square feet, with its own balcony and a view of the beautiful countryside, although he couldn't really see it at the moment. The bed was queen sized, with a comforter that resembled either a cloud or a pile of freshly-picked cotton and a matching nightstand on both sides, with ornate lamps. On the wall opposite the bed, there was a long dresser topped with a fifty-inch plasma TV, with the remote perfectly placed on one of the nightstands alongside the channel guide and a landline phone. In the corner aside the sliding glass door was a minibar, which he was sure he'd get to know on a personal level throughout his stay.

Derrek was too tired to worry about figuring out which shows were on which channel, and he just wanted to sleep in an actual bed. He tossed his bag next to the dresser and rummaged around in it until he found his pajama pants, into which he quickly changed.

They were his favorite pair, a Christmas gift from Shale years before. Blue plaid, covered with patches and near threadbare, but he wouldn't give them up for anything. No matter where he was, when he wore them, he felt safe enough to sleep. And sleep he did, almost immediately after climbing into the bed. It was softer than he could ever have imagined. The sheets underneath felt like silk, and the pillow made it feel like his head was floating on a cloud of pure comfort.

Derrek was awakened by the deafening sound of a trumpet in his ear, throwing him clear out of the bed, causing him to bump his head on the nightstand and knock the lamp over. He was dazed, and his ears were ringing, but he was sure he heard the sound of intense laughter.

A head popped over from the side of the bed, looking over him as he lay on the ground, rubbing his head. He couldn't tell who it was at first, but the shiny scalp gave it away.

"Morning, sunshine!" Jeffrey said with great enthusiasm. "Probably should've worn those headphones!"

Derrek was in a lot of pain, but he managed to say, "Jesus Christ, Jeffrey! How did you even get in my room?"

"I told the front desk that I needed a copy of your key so I could wake you up with a trumpet."

"And they just let you do that?"

"Of course not. I picked the lock."

"The locks are electronic," Derrek said as he managed to climb to his feet.

"They are, so I just threw a cup of coffee at it," Jeffrey said as he went to the minibar, got a cold bottle of water, and handed it to Derrek. "Put that on your head. You'll be fine."

"Those are like eight dollars a piece."

"First off, it's like eight *euros*. And don't worry about it. We've got full privileges."

"I booked the rooms. I know that isn't true."

"Then it's on me. Just take the damn water, dude."

Derrek reluctantly accepted the water and pressed it to the bump forming on the back of his head. He sat on the bed and took a second to get his bearings. He looked around for a clock; he couldn't find one, but he saw a few beams of light coming out over the horizon.

He remembered the note Jeffry left him on the bus. "Did you seriously wake me up at six a.m.?"

"I'm a man of my word," he said, tucking his trumpet under his arm. "Coffee's in the dining hall. Be down there in five."

Derrek was exhausted, but even though his rest was abruptly interrupted by an unwanted brass performance, coffee sounded like heaven to him. Taking the water bottle away from his head, he said, "Fine, I'll be down right away. But have a cup ready for me. I take it black."

"That's the spirit! Now, get dressed. Oh, and you might want to get someone to fix your door. Toodles!" he said as he exited, slamming the door behind him. But due to his method of entry, it didn't latch but bounced back open.

Derrek looked through his bag for something to wear and settled on a pair of khakis and a plain white T-shirt. He put on his shoes and headed for the dining hall, doing his best to close the door but to no avail. After getting to the ground floor, he made a quick detour to tell the front desk about his "defective" door, then went straight to the dining hall.

The doors were open, and even though the sun was barely up, the wafting smell of breakfast pastries and sizzling bacon filled the lobby. As was par for the course, the room was huge; there were buffet tables set up, filled to the brim with breakfast foods, pitchers upon pitchers of drinks, dozens of coffee machines, and seating for hundreds, with decor matching the rest of the hotel.

Most of the seats were empty, but across the room, at a table next to a window, Derrek saw Jeffrey sitting with two cups of coffee. After making the trek across the room, he sat across from him and reached for the cup he assumed was his. Jeffry started to speak, but Derrek put his hand up in a, "one-second" gesture, then took a long sip from his mug.

It was still some of the best-tasting coffee he had ever had. It had rich, deep, earthy tones, with a hint of hazelnut. From just that one sip, he felt ready to take on the world. He put his hand down and waited for Jeffry to start speaking.

"Feel better, sunshine?"

"Without a doubt. What blend is this, anyway?"

"I think they call it Deus Ex Coffeena or something like that."

"Well, it's pretty great."

"I'm glad you enjoyed it, because today's gonna be a lot tougher than it was gonna be."

"What? Why?"

"I told you to be down here in five. It's been at least six."

"Are you really fretting this much over a minute? Besides, the only reason I was late was that you decided to destroy my door!"

"Excuses, excuses. You'd best tighten up, soldier, especially if you wanna run the show."

Derrek was surprised by what he said and choked a little on his coffee, throwing him into a short coughing fit. After catching his breath, in a hushed tone, he said, "How the hell do you know about that?"

"Seriously? You thought Shale was gonna throw you into the thick of it with nobody to help you up?"

"I ... I guess I hadn't thought about it that way."

"And that's why he whooped your ass the last time you played," Jeffrey said as Derrek glared at him, "but it's also why I'm here."

"So, are you my coach now?"

"Closer to drill sergeant."

"Of course you are." Derrek took a look at the closest buffet table, his mouth watering at the sight of the piles of bacon and stacks of pancakes. "So, is this just a coffee morning, or am I allowed to eat?"

Jeffrey smiled and said, "Feel free. Might puke it up after our ten-mile run."

"Excuse me?"

"Oh yeah, you'll be joining me in my morning routine for the next few days: ten miles, fifty sit-ups, a hundred push-ups, and eighty jumping jacks. And don't forget about your firearms training."

"That sounds like a bit of overkill. I'm just trying to be able to run Frostbyte."

Jeffrey's smile faded, and he let a beat pass while he made an uncomfortable amount of eye contact with Derrek. When the tone was set to Jeffry's liking, he said, "You aren't *just trying to run Frostbyte.* If that's what you think all this is, you'd be better off booking the next flight back to the States and get real comfortable booking trips for the rest of your life. What I'm doing for you, what *Shale's* doing for you, is not just getting you ready to take his place. He thinks you can do a lot of good and wants you to be able to move it all further than he has. For you to do that, you've gotta learn discipline, both mental and physical. I'd trust that man with my life, but the fact that you don't get that gives me doubts."

Derrek stared at his coffee, feeling small. His appetite was suddenly gone, and the bump on his head began to throb. He looked up at Jeffrey, and doing his best to keep eye contact, he said, "I'm sorry. Will only told me about this two weeks ago, and I still have no idea what I even need to know how to do. I'm trying to be the man he wants me to be, and if you think this will help me be that, I'll take any order you give."

Jeffrey kept his composure, staring him in the eyes, waiting for him to waver. After several seconds passed, Jeffrey cracked a smile and started to laugh. He laughed harder and harder until Derrek felt awkward watching this mountain of a man slam his fists on the table with laughter.

After regaining his composure, Jeffrey looked back at Derrek and said, "Kid, you gotta learn to not take everything so seriously."

"What? You just told me I need to learn discipline."

"That I did, but you also have to learn not to take things personally. Business is a crazy thing, and people are gonna try to screw you over. But sometimes, you've gotta work with the same ones who do. I'm glad you're serious about this, but you gotta loosen up."

"I'm really confused."

"That's the spirit! Now you're in the headspace to learn. When you've got no idea what's going on, you try to figure it out, and even if you don't end up getting it, the fact that you're trying shows a lot."

Derrek still wasn't sure what he meant, but he felt better. His appetite had returned, and he resolved to eat a heaping plate of bacon and eggs, and to his delight, Jeffrey joined him to do the same.

The two returned to their table, plates piled high with pancakes, topped with butter and syrup, eggs cooked sunny-side up and bacon cooked to perfection, not too crispy to taste burnt and not too chewy to be inedible, the perfect balance.

As they ate, they shared stories of their pasts, Jeffrey starting it off lamenting his youthful years growing up in Virginia. "I had a pet raccoon. Patches, I named her. She would always hang out on my head, y'know, like I was Daniel Boone. She always cackled like crazy when she scared anyone who thought she was just a hat. I swear, my mom almost had a fit!"

Derrek shared how he first met Shale, playing chess in Central Park. "I was in foster care for as long as I could remember, and when I was eleven, I decided to run away. It went all right, aside from all the hungry nights, the unforgiving cold, and most of the other vagrants. A few were nice though. I was making good money hustling people—chess is my game—until I hustled just the right person. I pegged him as some rich fat cat and figured his ego was big enough to take on any challenge.

"I swear, the look on his face when I put him in checkmate was absolutely priceless. I wish I stuck around longer to see it, but I thought he'd catch on to my scheme pretty quick, so I bolted. I wasn't very good at covering my tracks then, so he found me about an hour later. He said he saw something in me, and I was convinced he was some weird pervert until he gave me his card. A few weeks later, I gave him a call, and the rest is history. He gave me an assistant job, clothed me, fed me, set me up in a decent apartment—the works—all from his personal funds," he said as he finished his coffee. "He's a good man. I'm proud to work for him."

Jeffrey, with his mouth full of pancake, decided to share his story of meeting Shale. "I was freshly enlisted in 2020, and right out of boot camp, we were shipped off to fight the Russians after they decided they wanted the EU. The beard didn't grow in full until a couple of years ago, so I swear I was a six-two soldier with a big ole baby face!

"We were deep in the Austrian countryside, doing our best to push them back to Hungary. They had some crazy tech we didn't know about, so we couldn't get shit for an idea of what they had with our satellites. Even without that, though, we thought we had the edge, figured they were too spread out to stop us.

"Found out we were wrong when the mortars hit our base. Totally blew us away," he said, beginning to laugh, then resumed a somber look on his face. "Lost a lot of good men that day. A lot more got sent home from the wounds, myself included. I caught a chunk of shrapnel in my right leg. Went right through the bone just above my knee, and a little bit hit my face, as you can probably tell. By the time they were able to do anything about it, it was unsalvageable, and they amputated.

"Sent me home with a Purple Heart and a fat check every month, and if I were anyone else, I'd probably be fine with that. But damn it, I still had a lot of fight in me. I went everywhere I could trying to find a way to get back into the thick of it, but all I could find were some admittedly stylish 3D printed prosthetics, nothing that could get me back on the battlefield.

"After a year of looking, though, I got a call from William Shale himself. Said he'd heard of my struggle and that he wanted to meet me. I figured he was just gonna offer me the same thing everyone else had, but he was paying for my flight, so I went along with it," he went on, smiling again. "First time I went to New York, if I weren't there on business, I probably would've enjoyed it more. I met him in his office, y'know, with that view of the whole city? Breathtaking, I swear.

"He gave the same spiel everyone else did, how I was brave for what I was trying to do, some such prepared statements on the strength of the human spirit—you know how he talks. I thought he was full of it, until he showed me the leg. I swear, it was perfect," he said, putting his leg up on a chair and rolling up his pants, revealing a sleek, fully articulated metal leg. "This bad boy literally got me back on my feet. The actual leg is removable, but the base has wires hooked up directly to my nervous system so I can move it just like if it were flesh and bone," he explained, rotating his ankle and bending his knee back and forth. "Hell, I can even wiggle my toes! This one's more for everyday activity, but he gave me one with armor plating, storage space for extra ammunition, and in a pinch, there's even a blade that pops out from the toes, and the whole thing barely weighed more than my old leg to boot!

"It took some convincing, but with Shale on my side, they let me back on the front lines, and I like to think I did him proud. I was up front when we stormed Moscow, and I celebrated with everyone that night, American and Russian alike. I tell you, it was magnificent. You ever drink one hundred eighty proof vodka? It makes for one hell of a hangover—I'll tell you that!"

The men burst into laughter. They had been sharing stories and eating breakfast for around half an hour, the sun was fully up, and other people were starting to fill in. Their plates had been empty for some time, and their food felt had digested enough to get to running. They got up, put their plates on a conveyor belt that took them back to the kitchen to be washed, and went outside. Jeffrey directed Derrek to a bright red, heavily rusted pickup truck double-parked close to the busses. The doors were unlocked, and the keys were in the ignition, so they climbed in and Jeffrey started driving down the road.

"I thought we were going for a run, why are we in a truck?" Derrek asked.

"It's a big-ass estate. The track is two miles away."

"My God. How much land does the hotel own?"

"Ain't the hotel. Just the owner, Mila Müller. I swear, she's got an absolute fortune."

"Where'd she get it all? Inheritance? Good investments?"

"Not sure, but I've got my own theory."

Jeffrey was silent for several seconds while Derrek looked at him expectedly. "And what might that be?"

Without missing a beat, Jeffrey immediately said, "Bitcoin."

Derrek said nothing for the rest of the ride but maintained a look that best expressed, *Seriously?*

They arrived a couple of minutes later. Derrek saw a full-kilometer circular track with Olympic-sized seating. In the center of the circle was a large assortment of exercise equipment, including weights, uneven bars, and an assortment of heavy objects, such as tires and thick ropes. The track itself didn't match the hotel's aesthetic, as it was made more for function instead of fashion, but it still seemed to be of high quality and very well maintained.

The two exited the truck and walked to the starting line. It was at this point that Derrek realized he was still wearing khakis. He turned to ask if Jeffrey had any exercise clothes but was taken off guard by the deafening sound of Velcro ripping. Jeffrey had torn off his pants and shirt, which before now, Derrek had not realized were tear-away. Underneath, he was wearing a plain white T-shirt and a pair of gym shorts.

Derrek was still stunned when Jeffrey pointed to the side of the seating where a door was. "Get some clothes from there. They wash them daily, so don't worry about that."

Derrek complied without saying a word and entered through the door into a large room full of labeled drawers. Each label had three words—the article of clothing, the size, and the color, except for a row by the entrance that was meant for leaving your clothes while you worked out. Derrek found a medium white T-shirt and a pair of black gym shorts to go with them, folded his clothes, deposited them into an empty drawer, and went to join Jeffrey at the starting line.

Derrek did his best to keep up but fell behind pretty quickly, with Jeffrey lapping him while he was only on his second lap. At that point, Jeffrey kept pace with him, and in the fashion of a true drill sergeant, he gave as much encouragement as he could, in the form of extreme deprecation, his favorite line being, "How do you expect to run a company if you can't even run ten miles?"

Despite his exhaustion, Derrek kept going, and he managed to finish his tenth mile, roughly the sixteenth lap, in just under two hours. He collapsed on the track while Jeffrey stood over him, brimming with pride. He got down on one knee and pressed a button on his leg, causing a section on the inside to pop out and produce a metal bottle of water, which he gave to Derrek.

After chugging the entire bottle, he felt almost completely refreshed, and said, "Jeez, that leg of yours sure is convenient."

"Hells yeah! It's got a cooler on this side. I keep my sidearm on the other, and I can charge my phone in the back of my knee. Things got crazy battery life too; a full charge gives about a month of full use."

"Wow, I didn't know Frostbyte even had prosthetics like that. I've gotta give it to the guys in research and development. They really know what they're doing."

"Enough chitchat. On to the rest of our workout!" Jeffrey said, heading toward the equipment in the center of the field.

They set up in an empty area designated for body weight exercise and started with the sit-ups. Derrek began to cramp after ten, but with Jeffrey's aggressive encouragement, prodding him about his "flabby" middle, which struck a nerve with him, he powered through. He rode the same wave of anger through the push-ups and jumping jacks, utterly collapsing and nearly passing out before Jeffrey splashed some water on his face.

"Damn, kid! I wasn't sure if you were gonna make it! You looked like hell until I poked fun at your flabby bits."

"Yeah, I guess it's a bit of a … soft spot."

They both burst into laughter, but Derrek was too exhausted to maintain it. Jeffrey grabbed him by the arm and pulled him to his feet, and Derrek went to change back into his clothes while Jeffrey struggled with his Velcro.

When they were both done, they rendezvoused at the truck, and Jeffrey started driving back toward the hotel.

"You'd best get yourself a shower. You'll feel like a new man."

"Don't I still have weapons training?"

"Yeah, but we can pick that up around noon. Get yourself some water and some protein. I'll get you when it's time."

"Think I'll have time for a nap?"

Jeffrey laughed and said, "Maybe a short one, but don't be surprised if I wake you with the business end of Ole Tootsy."

Derrek's face turned to the same one he had after Jeffrey shared his theory earlier, except he actually saw it this time. "Like you could do better," he said with a cocky grin.

Without thinking, Derrek said, "King Tootankhamun."

Jeffrey was silent the rest of the way to the hotel. He parked, killed the engine, and just sat there for an uncomfortable amount of time. After about thirty seconds, Derrek slowly exited the truck, keeping his eyes on Jeffrey, who was completely unresponsive.

He went back into the hotel, boarded the elevator, and went to his room. He tried to open the door, but it was locked. Derrek was impressed by how quickly they had fixed his lock, and he used his key. He immediately jumped in the shower, where he saw that the body wash, shampoo, and conditioner were all full-sized bottles, possibly the fanciest aspect of the hotel he had seen thus far. When he was done, he emerged from the bathroom, feeling completely revitalized but still exhausted. There weren't any clocks in his room, so he called the front desk to give him a wake-up call at 11:45, giving him a couple of hours to sleep while still getting ahead of Jeffrey.

He closed the blinds and climbed into his bed, quickly drifting off to sleep.

He found himself in a black void. Nothing around him. Nothing to see. No up, no down, no left, no right. He floated in the nothingness for what seemed like ages when suddenly, he heard what sounded like a door opening.

The scene shifted in an instant to that of a drab office, no furniture save for a plain wooden desk perfectly placed in the middle of the room. There was a window, but there seemed to be nothing on the other side, just a white void. He faced the desk, which was unoccupied but had a name plate which he couldn't read, along with a bird dipping into a glass of water.

"Is there a reason I opened my closet door and walked into here, or was there just something funky in my milkshake?" a voice behind him said. He turned around to find the same red blob he had seen in his dream the night before.

"There's a reason for everything, but that milkshake *was* from 2014, so I'd say it was pretty funky," said another voice from behind him. Turning again, he saw the desk now had someone seated behind it. The man behind the desk was adorned in a gray pinstripe suit and had slicked-back black hair. He had no scars, marks, or blemishes and seemed average, save for his eyes. He had no irises, just black dots with shockingly white sclera. His voice was firm, but he sounded a bit off, as if his voice wasn't genuine.

The man behind the desk continued, "I need something of you." The next word he said was incomprehensible, sounding like a series of guttural noises.

"You know damn well that isn't my name. Say it like a human," the red man protested.

"Fine, I need something of you, Kahli."

"Close enough, I guess. What do you need, my brother from another plane of existence?"

The man behind the desk smiled coyly. "I need you to accept this gift."

"A gift? I've been doing this shit for a long time, and I never even got a paycheck from you. What's the occasion?"

"I'm sure I gave you something here and there. I'm not a slave driver."

"The closest thing to you giving me something was when you offered me a mint the first time we met."

"See? I still gave you something."

The red man, whom Derrek assumed was named Kahli, gave a laugh as the other man reached under his desk and pulled out a plain shoe box, which he placed at the end of his desk. Kahli walked toward the desk, passing right through Derrek, who was standing between the two, prompting him to step aside to try to get a better look at what was going on.

The man behind the desk opened the box and pulled out a necklace. It had a long leather strap, letting the pendant sit around the solar plexus when worn, and the pendant was a stylized longhorn skull made of hand-carved dark wood.

"I've taken to calling it the Spirit of the West, but you're free to call it as you wish."

"Oh, damn. Really sprung for me, didn't you?" Kahli said as he accepted the gift, presumably putting it on.

"It did take a while to find, what with it belonging to Samuel Colt himself."

"I knew Sam. Dude never wore this. He had a gun on a string."

"I said it *belonged* to him. He never actually wore it, partly because of its properties."

"Properties, you say? Do tell, desk guy, do tell."

The man behind the desk rummaged around in the box, throwing tissue paper everywhere, and pulled out a small paper pamphlet. He flipped through a few pages. "Ah," he said, "here we are. For one, it soul-binds to whoever wears it, so it'll always be around your neck. I thought that would be pretty nice, considering your track record."

"Showering might be a bit of a pain, but I'm still liking it."

"It's also indestructible."

"Oh, great. I won't have to make up a story behind how I accidentally destroyed it."

"And that's pretty much it." He snapped his fingers, causing the box and the booklet to disappear but not affecting the tissue paper. He looked around and quietly said, "The universe at my fingertips, and I can't figure this stuff out."

Behind the blob, Kahli appeared to unsuccessfully try to remove the necklace as he said, "So, you just gave me a permanent chunk of wood?"

"And the strap, don't forget the strap."

Kahli was quiet for a few seconds. "Has anyone ever told you you're an asshole?"

"Nobody still living."

"Makes sense. Was that all you wanted?"

"There is still one thing; I wouldn't waste your time with just a small present."

"Then shoot your shot, space cowboy."

The man behind the desk leaned forward in his chair and said, "I need you to trust me."

There was a short bout of tense silence until Kahli broke it. "Seriously? I've been doing your dirty work all this time, following your orders to a T, and you only now need me to trust you?"

"I know you've been loyal thus far, but I need to make sure you stay loyal."

"Oh, come on. When have I ever been disloyal?"

"Ponce de Leon, for one."

"Hey! *They* turned on *me!*"

Kahli burst into laughter, and the man behind the desk smiled meekly. "That's all I needed to hear. Thank you, Kahli."

"No probert, Robert," he said, opening the door, "I'll see you whenever the next hungry boy shows up. And thanks for the jewelry."

He closed the door behind him, leaving the man alone at his desk. The smile faded from the man's face, and he turned to make direct eye contact with Derrek. The black circles grew, drowning his eyes in solid matte black, and he calmly said, "Count yourself lucky I had company. Otherwise, I would have cut this quite short."

Derrek, having never experienced anything like this before, tried to respond. He moved his mouth, but no sound came out.

"Interesting. I'm going to ask you a few questions. Shake your head for no and nod for yes. Understand?"

Derrek understood and nodded his head.

"Good, but know I can tell if you're lying. Do you know where you are?"

Derrek shook his head.

"Do you know who I am?"

He shook his head.

"Are you human?"

He nodded.

"Last one, I promise," he said as he stood up. He snapped his fingers, causing the desk and all of its contents to disappear, except for the tissue paper, which slowly drifted to the ground.

"Can you fight back?"

Derrek's eyes grew wide as the man snapped his fingers again, causing his hands to start dissolving away. He felt himself becoming completely obliterated, his very existence being undone. The last thing he saw before his eyes dissolved was the blackness in the man's eyes receding to a small dot in a sea of piercing white sclera.

Then he woke up

He opened his eyes, staring up at the ceiling, admiring the flock of doves painted upon it. He couldn't remember the dream. All he knew was his whole body ached deeply. He chalked it up to the workout and put it out of his mind.

Seconds after opening his eyes, the phone rang. Picking it up, still half asleep, he answered, "Hello?"

He was thrown out of his bed by the impossibly loud sound that came from the receiver, causing him to bump his head on the nightstand in the same spot as before. He scrambled to his feet, snatched the phone from where it landed, and angrily said, "How the hell did you get on this line, Jeffrey?"

Bellowing laughter came from the phone, followed by a short trumpet performance, which made Derrek wince away. He slowly put the receiver back to his ear, hearing another round of laughter and Jeffrey's gruff voice. "Thought you could get away from Ole Tootsy, did ya? The truck in five. Get a move on," he said, leaving nothing but a dial tone.

Derrek let out a groan and started to get dressed, wearing the same clothes he had worn that morning. Before leaving, he went to the minifridge, pulled out a bottle of water, put it to his head, and went to meet Jeffrey, who was leaning on the hood of his truck, staring at his watch.

"Four minutes, fifty-eight seconds. Cutting it close, aren't ya?"

"Do they even make pickup trucks in Germany? Because at this point, I wouldn't be surprised if you had it shipped with the equipment."

Jeffrey scowled at Derrek. "I'll have you know Volkswagen makes a pickup truck, so cut it out with your preconceived Teutonic notions."

"Sorry, I'm just a little peeved because I'm going to have to pay another eight *euros*," he said, gesturing to his water bottle.

"You know what? My bad. I'll cover that one too," Jeffrey said as he climbed into the driver's seat. "Now get your ass in gear! We got shooting to do!"

"Oh, right!" Derrek said as he hurried to the passenger door.

Jeffrey drove for several minutes before pulling into a dirt road leading into the woods. "You don't have hylophobia, right?" he said snidely.

"I'm gonna guess that's the fear of the woods. No, I'm good."

"Good, because we've gotta be pretty deep in the woods for this."

Derrek gave him a worried look. "We're allowed to be doing this, right?"

"Allowed as in are we supposed to be doing this or allowed as in are we allowed to have guns? Because the answer is no."

"How did you even get into the military acting like this?" Derrek asked, glaring at him.

"Mostly charm and intimidation with a little bit of bullshit sprinkled in."

Derrek rolled his eyes and said, "If we get arrested, I don't know you."

Jeffrey laughed and said, "Story of my life, sunshine!"

They drove deep into the woods until Jeffrey decided they were far enough in. They both got out of the truck, and Jeffrey pulled a plastic garbage bag out of the bed, which rattled as he handled it. They walked for a quarter of a mile until they got to a clearing that had a few trees. He grabbed the bag by the bottom and dumped the contents onto the ground, which were several discarded soda cans and a sealed pack of paper targets. He put his hand on his chin in thought. "Hmm ..." he said. "Gotta put them up somewhere."

He eyed a nearby tree. It towered over them and had a thick trunk but was visibly dying. Without saying a word, he approached it and looked at it for several seconds. He assumed a stance with his right leg behind him, closed his eyes, and brought his breathing under control. With one last breath, he opened his eyes, and Derrek watched in awe as he roundhouse kicked the tree, putting his leg clear through it.

It hit the ground with a loud *thud,* landing just in front of the pile of cans. With a satisfied smile, Jeffrey began placing several of the cans atop the tree, ten total, spacing them a few feet apart. He took a step back to admire his work and was pleased.

"All right!" he exclaimed. "Time to get started!"

He rolled up his right pant leg to expose his prosthetic and pressed a button just below his knee on the outside, causing a slot to pop open opposite to where he kept his water. Inside was an integrated holster with a handgun, which Jeffrey pulled out before popping the slot back into place. He laid it in his palm to show it off. "This is a Beretta M9, standard-issue sidearm for the army, navy, and air force. Holds fifteen round, shoots at 1,200 feet per second, and reliable as all hell." He pointed to a switch on the side of the gun. "This is the safety. Flip it down to prevent it from firing and up to shoot. If you see the red dot, it's good to go."

He held the gun by the grip, keeping his fingers away from the trigger. "You wanna line the wedge at the end of the barrel up with these two bits here, then squeeze the trigger. Don't jerk it back, though. You won't hit shit like that."

He pulled two small plastic bags out of his pocket and tossed one to Derrek, who saw they were foam earplugs. Jeffrey put his in and gestured for Derrek to do the same.

He cocked the gun, flipped off the safety, and pointed it at one of the cans, holding it with both hands. He kept both eyes open and focused on his target. Derrek winced back when he heard a loud *bang* and saw the can flipping around in the air. Without missing a beat, Jeffrey shot three more cans, sending them flying. He then took out the magazine, popped out the bullet in the chamber, relocked the slide, flipped the safety back on, and put the magazine back in.

"Your turn!" he said as he tossed the gun to Derrek, which he fumbled with as he tried to catch it, eventually getting a good grip on it, directly pulling the trigger. Jeffrey yelled, "Bang!" startling Derrek and throwing himself into an uncontrollable fit of laughter.

After he calmed down, he stood aside and let Derrek try his hand. He squared his feet, held his arms out as he had seen Jeffrey do, and pulled the trigger, forgetting there was no bullet in the chamber. Jeffrey stifled a laugh when Derrek gave him a sideways glare before getting the gun ready to fire. He held his breath and slowly squeezed the trigger.

The recoil took him by surprise, and he closed his eyes and

stumbled back reflexively, nearly falling over. When he regained his balance, he saw the can he aimed at was still standing. Jeffrey chimed in. "Hey, you didn't drop it, so I'd say that wasn't too bad for your first—"

He was cut off by another gunshot and saw a can missing from the lineup. He looked at Derrek and saw his expression. His eyes were completely fixated on where the can was. He didn't even react to the recoil, it was as if he were in a trance.

He snapped out of it when Jeffrey called out, "Hot damn! That's what I'm talking about!"

He shook it off, coming back to reality, and with a proud smile, he said, "Beginners luck, I probably won't make another shot like that anytime soon. It didn't even fly like yours did."

Jeffrey slapped him on the back in congratulations, and said, "Nonsense! You'll be good enough by the time you take the test. Besides, you gotta hit it just right to pull that off."

"Wait, test? You didn't say anything about a test."

"Yep. At some point this week, I'm gonna put up one of these targets, and you're gonna stand thirty feet away. You gotta take ten shots and hit with at least six of them. Then you're clear to carry that bad boy and you can get some fieldwork under your belt."

Derrek was suddenly filled with determination. He didn't get the chance to prove himself often but always jumped at the chance to do so. He readied himself up to keep shooting but missed the next four shots.

He didn't waver, however, and took out two more with the rest of his ammunition. Jeffrey tossed him a full magazine and gestured for him to reload. It took him a few seconds to figure it out, but he replaced the magazine, chambered a round, and took out the remaining cans with seven shots.

He gave the pistol back to Jeffrey, which he laid on the tailgate, and they both took their earplugs out. Jeffrey went back to the truck and lifted the passenger seat to reveal a cooler underneath. He reached in and pulled out two green bottles, calling out to Derrek, "Care for a Brewski?"

With a perplexed expression, Derrek replied, "Brewski? Has anyone called beer that since the '90s?"

"Whoever drinks this sure has," Jeffrey retorted as he tossed him one of the bottles. Catching it, he saw the label read, "Brewski" and watched as Jeffrey popped off the cap with his thumb and chugged half of his.

Derrek tried in vain to pop his cap. It appeared to be a twist-off. After taking a second to think about how Jeffrey popped his off, he decided to let it go and took a sip. The flavor left him speechless, and he physically could not find the words to describe what he tasted.

He racked his brain trying to comprehend the drink in his hand. He had never tasted anything like it before in his life—it was utterly unique. He questioned everything he had ever done, every choice he ever made, and found nothing he could connect to this beer, no part of it had ever reached him before. The smell was like no other. Even the way the carbonation tickled his nose was unique—softer than most but faster.

His eyes widened when he finally understood what he was drinking, and it hit him like a sack of bricks. He took his lips away from the bottle, stared at it for a few seconds, and calmly said, "This tastes like shit."

Jeffrey polished off his beer, let out a long belch, and said, "Yeah, it's more of a chugging beer. Helps you get past the taste."

"Why would you intentionally buy bad beer?"

"Because it's my favorite," Jeffrey said as he reached for another. "Plus, it's got a twelve percent alcohol content."

Derrek looked at the label again and was surprised to see that was true. "Jeez, that's a potent drink."

"Damn skippy," Jeffrey said before he began chugging his second Brewski. He downed it in ten seconds flat while Derrek choked his way through another sip. He grabbed his newly empty bottle by the neck and said, "Check this shit out," throwing his bottle high into the air.

In one swift movement, he grabbed the pistol and took three shots, the first blowing off the neck of the bottle, the second taking out the base, and the third completely shattering the remains. Derrek's ears rang as he covered his head to defend against the raining shards of glass.

Derrek snapped his fingers next to his ears, and as soon as he could hear them clearly through the ringing, he said, "Maybe a little warning next time?"

"Oh, come on. If I warned you, you would've been ready for it."

Derrek covered his face with his hands in exasperation, groaned, and said, "That's exactly my point."

"And *my* point. You won't always be ready for what happens. What matters is how you adapt to unfamiliar situations—for example, loud noises and glass falling at your face."

Derrek started to protest, but he understood the lesson and kept his mouth shut. But that didn't stop him from thinking of how to get back at him. With great conviction, he chugged his Brewski, struggling to force down every gulp but determined to finish it. After he polished it off, he gasped for air and grabbed the bottle by the neck.

"Think fast!" he shouted as he threw the bottle, aiming directly at Jeffrey, who was turned away, chugging away at his third beer.

Without turning or even opening his eyes, he used his free hand to catch the bottle just before it made contact with the back of his head. He finished his Brewski and glared at Derrek. With a cocky grin, he flipped both bottles back toward him.

Without thinking, Derrek dropped down to the ground prone, narrowly avoiding the bottles as they hit a tree behind him, completely shattering. He looked up to find Jeffrey standing above him, hands at his waist, with a wide grin on his face.

"Fast enough for you?" he asked smugly, holding out his hand, which Derrek accepted. Before he knew what was happening, he was pulled to his feet, practically weightless. Jeffrey put his hand firmly on his shoulder, leaned in close, and whispered to him, "If you're gonna get someone with a surprise attack, always go for the kill." This sent chills down Derrek's spine.

"Surprise attack. Go for the kill. Got it, sir," he stammered, flabbergasted.

Jeffrey let go of his shoulder and doubled over with laughter, slapping his knee, struggling to breathe. Derrek had no idea what to do, so he just watched as he continued his bout of laughter for another minute straight. When he finally snapped out of it, he took a moment to catch his breath and said, "Sorry, dude. It's just you looked so scared! It's like you thought I was gonna kill you or something!" He immediately started laughing again. Derrek, now knowing the joke, joined in.

Several minutes and another round of beers later, they went back to weapons training. After an hour, they had exhausted all the ammunition Jeffrey had brought, and it showed in Derrek's rapidly increasing skill. He took to it and was coming along nicely, now able to take out ten cans with eighteen shots, but he needed to do better to pass the test.

Jeffrey was proud of Derrek's progress and went to get a celebratory round of Brewskis, but he found his cooler empty; he had only brought a six-pack. Normally, this was when he would call it a day, but he had one more thing planned for Derrek. He closed the cooler, put the passenger seat back down, and asked, "Wanna learn how to throw a knife?"

Derrek was caught off guard. He thought it was just going to be firearms training, although he had to admit, it did catch his interest.

"Sure, sounds like fun," he said with a smile.

"All right!" Jeffrey said as he opened the inner side of his leg. He put his water bottle aside and reached deeper in, emerging with a black rectangular pouch. He put his bottle back in his leg and closed it, then reached into the pouch and produced three small knives.

"When it comes to throwing knives, stance is everything. Stand up straight, best foot forward, eyes on your target," he said as he got into the stance he described. He took one of the knives in his right hand keeping the other two in his left. "Hold it firm at the grip, tip pointing toward the sky."

He held out his right arm, pointing it at a nearby tree, his knife upward. He bent his arm, putting the knife next to his ear, "Focus on where you want it to go, reel back, and ..."

He whipped his arm forward, sending the knife spinning toward the tree, where it landed with a loud *thunk!*

"Let that bitch fly."

Without missing a beat, he threw the other two knives below the first.

Thunk! Thunk!

He had formed the three into a perfect equilateral triangle.

"Woah ..." Derrek said, impressed in Jeffrey's skills and eager to try it himself.

"Do me a solid and get those, will ya?" Jeffrey asked with a devilish grin.

Derrek approached the tree and grasped the highest knife but found it firmly stuck. He struggled with it for several seconds, doing his best to twist and pull to dislodge the blade. When it finally popped out, he fell backward, proudly wielding the knife, although his mood did drop after he realized there were still two more.

The other two weren't nearly as difficult, but Derrek wasn't sure why. Maybe Jeffrey hadn't thrown them as hard as the first one in an attempt to mess with him. The smile on his face strengthened that guess.

Derrek got into position while Jeffrey stood to the side, silently watching. He stood the same way he saw Jeffrey and quietly said to himself, "Focus on where you want it to go, reel back, and ..."

He threw the knife as hard as he could, but he missed the tree completely, sticking it roughly twenty feet behind it, in the ground. He took another knife and reeled back for another throw, repeating his quiet mantra, "Focus on where you want it to go, reel back, and …"

The second knife hit the tree, but the handle hit first, causing it to bounce back and land near Derrek's feet. He gave a sideways glance to Jeffrey, who was obviously holding back a laugh, but he just rolled his eyes and looked back at the tree. He took his final knife, and without thinking or repeating Jeffrey's words, he threw it.

Thunk!

Both men were surprised, and a beat passed before either did anything. Jeffrey looked at Derrek expectedly, and he knew what needed to be said.

"Let that bitch fly."

"Hells yeah!" Jeffrey yelled before moving to gather the knives. "I'd love to stick around and do this for another hour, but we're out of Brewskis."

"Fair enough. Do you want me to gather up the cans?"

"Nah, they'll be here tomorrow, we'll clean up when you pass the test. Why don't you go ahead and hang out in the truck? I gotta take a leak."

"You could have just said you needed a minute, but all right," Derrek said as he went to the truck.

Jeffrey walked away into the bushes and was completely out of sight. Derrek usually filled his downtime by fiddling with his phone, checking current events and crushing candy, but he left it at the hotel. He glanced around the cabin and found it to be well-worn. It didn't appear to be a rental.

There was an ashtray filled with cigarette butts, several hand rolled, leading Derrek to question its contents. The radio was fitted with a cassette player, not fitting the shiny exterior, and had several strands of tape sticking out. There was apparently a cassette stuck in there. On the dash, there were dozens of papers with important looking information covered in coffee stains randomly strewn about with candy wrappers of varying brands and several empty packs of Huff's Puffs brand cigarettes.

The console, however, was nearly pristine—no trash, no clutter, nothing at all aside from a book, perfectly placed in the middle. The book was paperback with a wordless, faded red color, and although it seemed to have been read several hundred times, it was very well maintained.

He decided to take a look and found an inscription on the cover page, in red ink. It read,

> We all go through our own personal hell at some point, but you were among the lucky. *You lived through yours.* We'll meet again someday, but until then, remember what you were taught, and never falter from your desires.

> —L

Just as he finished reading, the driver's door opened. Derrek scrambled to put the book back as it was, hoping Jeffrey didn't see him reading it. He climbed into the driver's seat and saw the look on Derrek's face.

"Were you reading my book?"

"Er … yeah."

"That's fine. Just be careful with it. It's a first edition."

A wave of relief washed over Derrek, but he left the book where it was, not wanting to push his luck. "I think I'll leave it be. I didn't catch the title, though."

"It's *The Inferno*, by Dante Alighieri."

"Wow, aren't the first translated copies worth thousands?"

"You misunderstand, young padawan. Not translated, *first* edition. As in it's in Italian."

"You speak Italian?"

"Not a word. I can read it, though."

"That's ... something I didn't know about you."

"There's a lot you don't know about me. For instance, I've got a buddy. He grows tomatoes. He killed eight people across the US."

Derrek was caught off guard by that. "Wait, what about the tomatoes?"

Jeffrey started at him with a confused look and said, "What *about* the tomatoes? I just said my friend's a serial killer."

Derrek had a blank look on his face for several seconds, until he realized he had indeed just said that. He raised his eyebrows and said, "Jeez, I really fixated on the tomatoes, didn't I?"

"You sure did. Now, stop saying tomatoes. It's starting to sound weird," Jeffrey said as he started the engine and began the drive back to the hotel.

The ride back was uneventful, until Derrek posed a question.

"Who signed the book?"

Jeffrey gave him a sideways glance for a brief moment. "Honestly, I'm not sure. I asked the same thing to the guy who gave it to me. All he did was get real quiet for a few seconds and then ham-fistedly changed the subject."

"That's pretty weird."

An awkward silence fell over the two, which persisted for the rest of the ride. When they arrived back at the hotel, Jeffrey grabbed the book, slid his seat back, and opened it to the middle. Derrek was unsure what to do, so he sat silently for several seconds until Jeffrey spoke up.

"Our day's done. You've got the rest of the day to do whatever you want. I'm just gonna chill out here for a bit. Might hit up a pub later if you're interested."

Derrek smiled. "That would be nice, but I've still got a good amount of sleep to catch up on. I'll tell you what, though, if you knock—and I mean *knock*, not break my door down—and I answer, I'm there."

Jeffrey gave out a solitary chuckle. "Sounds like a plan. Get some rest. We're doing the same thing tomorrow. Oh six hundred sharp."

Derrek jokingly saluted. "Aye aye, Captain!"

Jeffrey snorted. "Get out of my truck."

They both gave a decent laugh. Derrek went inside. Jeffrey watched as he entered the hotel, and as soon as he was out of sight, he opened the glove box and took out a package of cigarettes. He put one in his mouth and lit it, taking a long draw, filling the cabin with smoke.

He cracked a window, turned the air on low, and flipped the book to the cover, revealing the inscription. He read it several times, letting his cigarette burn, not taking a drag. He looked at it, seeing it was halfway burnt, and gave a loud sigh. He firmly held the book and put out his cigarette, pushing the embers directly into the blue words, burning a hole clear through the cover.

He held on to the crushed butt and stared patiently at the hole he had burned into the book. It was still smoldering, letting off some smoke of its own, spreading outward until it lost too much heat and fizzled out. The hole had spread to destroy no less than half of the message, but Jeffrey kept staring.

Just then, the book appeared to reverse the damage, healing from the burn. The words were coming back, closing in toward the center. In less than fifteen seconds, it was as if the book had never been damaged. The ink even looked freshly dried.

Jeffrey closed his eyes and took a deep breath, then opened them and saw it was still intact. He felt the same mix of panic, relief, dread, and control he felt every time he had done this before. He then shoved the butt into the ashtray, flipped back to the middle, and picked up where he had left off.

Derrek had an uneventful night. He had planned to do nothing but sleep as soon as he got to his room, but it wasn't even 2:00 p.m. yet. That, with the nap he took earlier, would have made for a restless night if he went to bed right then. Lunch services ended at one, and dinner didn't start until five, so he had very little to do. He could have gone out to a pub or take in the sights, but after the day he had, he really didn't feel like doing anything that would require him leaving unless he was dragged along.

With nothing else to do, he flipped on the TV and found it to be on a channel that constantly played bizarre game shows. Despite the huge language barrier, Derrek was enthralled with the pies and giant pretzels being thrown around, the ridiculous costumes, and the outrageously wide smile of the host, who he recognized from somewhere, but he wasn't sure where. He may have been a star from an old TV show or a movie, but he wasn't sure.

The phone rang. He answered, "Hello?"

"Ah, Mr. Snowe with an E at the end, right?" the voice responded, followed by a hushed giggle.

It was the woman who had checked him in the night before, in whose presence he had embarrassed himself. He meekly laughed and said, "Yeah, that's me. How can I help you?"

"Help me? Oh no, sir. This is the Schadenfreude! Where we aim to give our guests the gift of absolute relaxation!"

"Right. Sorry. Force of habit." He rarely got phone calls, and when he did, they were either business related or a recorded conversation trying to sell him insurance.

"I just wanted to inform you that dinner will be ready in ten minutes, since you missed the cutoff last night."

Derrek was confused. Last he checked, it was only two. There were no clocks in his room, so he checked his cell phone and found she was right.

4:50 p.m.

He had been watching this show for three hours! He didn't even know what it was called and could remember nothing but the pretzels and that vague celebrity whose name he still couldn't place.

"Oh, right. Thank you. I'll be sure to partake."

"Very good, sir, and please remember that if you have any questions, comments, or concerns, every one of our employees will be happy to hear you out! Goodbye. Enjoy your dinner!"

The phone played a dial tone, which Derrek listened to for several seconds, still distracted by how long he had been watching that show.

He eventually hung up the phone and got ready for dinner, realizing he could actually smell it from his room—the wafting scents of beef, pork, chicken, and several other meats he had never smelled before. His mouth watered before he even left the room, and his stomach growled like a roaring lion.

He took a seat at the same table he had eaten breakfast with Jeffrey, now seeing the beautiful view through the window. The sun hung in the sky, casting an amber glow over the fields surrounding the hotel and the forest bordering it. There were animals grazing, birds soaring above, and only the thinnest wisps of clouds floating high in the sky. He felt absolute bliss staring off into the countryside, until he heard a voice behind him.

"Good evening, sir. My name is Emmett, and I will be your waiter this evening. Would you like anything to drink?"

He looked away from the window to find a pristinely dressed waiter, his blond hair swept back, arms behind his back.

"Oh, yes, I'll just have a water, thank you."

He pulled his arms from behind him, a pint glass filled with ice water in his right hand and a menu in his left, and carefully placed them at Derrek's side.

"I'll be back soon to take your order. Please don't hesitate to ask if there's anything I can do for you."

"Oh, thank you," Derrek said as he left.

Derrek was amazed at the service of this hotel, a feeling that had not faded since he had arrived. As he looked through the menu, most of the food names were beyond his pronunciation, and because the descriptions were in German, he based his judgment solely on the pictures. He wasn't quite sure what was in any of the foods, but he was drawn to what looked like a type of roast. As soon as he looked up from his menu, he saw Emmett standing beside him. He jumped slightly but quickly recovered.

"Are you ready to order, sir?"

"Yes, I'll have the …" he said, leaning in close to be sure to say it right, "sour … braten?"

Emmett smiled widely and said excitedly, "Ah, the sauerbraten, one of our finest dishes! A wise choice, sir!"

"Well, thank you! But honestly, I can't read German. It just looked really good."

Emmett was confused for a brief moment, then understood what was going on. He calmly grabbed his menu and flipped it over.

With an understanding smile, he said, "We do have an English translation on the other side. With this new information, would you like a few minutes to change your order?"

Derrek's ears turned red with embarrassment, and he took a second to think, looking at the menu, which he could now clearly understand. After looking at a few other options, he decided he wanted to stick with the sauerbraten.

"No, thank you. First choice, best choice," he said with as much confidence he could muster, handing the menu back to Emmett.

"Very good, sir. Your food will be out momentarily. In the meantime, our live music will be starting soon. Tonight we have a very special guest, a very talented pianist visiting from France, Hadrian LaFayette."

"Oh wow, that sounds delightful!"

"I can assure you, sir, it is. Is there anything I can get you before I put in your order?"

"Hmm …" Derrek said. He wasn't partial to soft drinks and wasn't a wine snob. He rarely drank at all, and even then, it was usually with Shale. "I don't suppose you have thirty-year Steel Barrel whiskey, do you?"

Emmett pondered that for a moment. "We do have a very extensive stock, but I'll have to check. Apologies in advance. I do hope you'll bear with us."

"No worries at all. Take your time."

Emmett smiled and nodded, then shuffled off to the window to the kitchen, dropping off his order before entering an adjacent door.

Derrek took another look around the room and saw a stage to the left of the entrance. Atop it was a piano. A man dressed in a tuxedo and white gloves walked up a set of stairs to the side of the stage, approaching the instrument. He assumed this man was the entertainment—Hadrian LaFayette.

A voice came from the speakers integrated into the ceiling as LaFayette took his seat.

"Ladies and gentlemen, may I direct your attention to the stage, where our musical guest, Mr. Hadrian LaFayette, will be performing one of his original compositions. Please, be respectful of your fellow guests and Mr. LaFayette, and above all else, please enjoy your dinner!"

The lights dimmed, and a spotlight focused on the piano, giving a clearer look of the man. His hair was short, curled, and bright red. His tuxedo was freshly pressed and solid black, adorned with a bright blue bow tie.

He took his place on stage, sitting at the piano, and closed his eyes. He cracked his knuckles into his microphone, causing most of the audience to cringe, and put his hands in position. The room went deathly quiet. Derrek could almost see the tension in the air. The silence was broken by a single note, ringing like a bell tower, commanding everyone's attention. What followed was a one-man symphony. With his hands, for a brief moment, he completely shattered the audience's sense of individuality; everyone felt as one in this moment. With his instrument, he took the audience on an emotional journey. Derrek felt his past, those cold, hungry nights, his only comfort being his hope and his sheer determination. He saw that fateful game of chess, and he felt the move that claimed him victory and changed his life.

He felt those years of work, those sleepless nights he spent honing his skills, grinding to earn his position. He felt every single hardship he went through. He felt every good memory. He saw his family, the one he was too young to remember. Without realizing it, he was now crying, but his focus remained on LaFayette. He felt fire and impossible heat. He smelled burning wood and blood. He saw a demon, the same one he had seen in his childhood nightmares. This monster he thought he had locked away in his mind now stood before him in a burning hellscape, holding a bloody hatchet, staring at Derrek with its burning red eyes.

And with that, the song was over. Derrek snapped back to reality and looked around him to find every single person in the room doing exactly as he was: crying. Nobody was sobbing, for nobody was sad. They weren't bitter tears. Nor were they sweet. Those tears weren't from any single emotion but rather all the emotions they had felt in their lives, and Derrek felt the same. He tried his best to remember what he had seen but couldn't. In fact, he couldn't even remember seeing it. He wiped his tears away and stood, nearly knocking his chair over, and led the crowd in uproarious applause.

LaFayette had not opened his eyes, but when he heard the roar of applause, he gazed out into the audience to find every single person standing and clapping. The wait staff had stopped everything they were doing, some mid order. The chef staff had left their stations to get a better listen. Dozens of people from the lobby had come in. Several people had even come down from their rooms after hearing the beautiful sounds this man had played.

He stood from his seat and stepped to center stage, basking in the spotlight, absorbing the praise he was being given. He bowed, and the applause and cheers grew even louder, and when he came back up, Derrek saw his eyes.

They were piercingly gray, as if a storm brewed within his head. He saw the pride in this man's eyes and could tell how hard he worked to get where he was. He saw the same pain, love, anger, sadness, and joy he had just felt, but he saw no tears. He felt as if he understood this man and knew the whole world should.

LaFayette left the stage, shaking the wave of hands that reached out to him as he made his exit. Derrek wanted to join them, but he saw that the crowd that formed around him was completely impenetrable, so he took his seat and waited for his order. He saw Emmett squeeze his way through the crowd, holding a brown bottle and a short crystalline glass, nearly dropping both.

He hurried his way to Derrek's table. "I'm very sorry, sir. It seems I was caught up in the action!" he said, opening the fresh bottle, pouring his drink. "We didn't have the thirty-year, but I do hope fifty-year will do."

Derrek was intrigued, since he had no idea they aged it for that long. "Oh, that will be great. Thank you!"

He took a sip and immediately tasted the deep, earthy tones, giving him flashbacks to his twenty-first birthday, when he shared his first drink with Shale.

"My God, this is delicious!"

A wave of relief washed over Emmett's face. Apparently, he was nervous over this small compromise. He put on a big smile and said, "Very good, sir. Your food should be out soon. Let me know if there's anything you need." He left the bottle before hastily walking away, tending to some of his other tables.

Derrek took another sip and reminisced about the good times with Shale: His eighteenth birthday, when Shale had given him an official position in the company. He would have put him much higher up, but Derrek insisted he earn his way up. After starting as a paid intern, in nine years, he had worked his way up to the environmental department, establishing wildlife sanctuaries all around the world, promoting renewable energy, doing his best to make the world a better place. He proved himself again and again, grinding his way to the top of every department he moved on to, earning promotion after promotion, working his way through sales, marketing, customer relations, human resources, even the mail room.

He had been in environmental for three years but was being held back by Hanes, who saw him as an asset too good to lose. Every time a promotion came around, Derrek would apply, and Hanes would give it to someone else, always citing his lack of experience, whenever it was brought up. He never gave up, however, and kept working, knowing that one day, Hanes would have no other choice but to move him up.

That all changed when Shale made his offer two weeks prior.

"Here you are, sir, our famous sauerbraten, accompanied by roasted root vegetables and risotto a la Milanese.

Derrek looked up to see Emmett holding a plate that gave off a savory aroma, making his mouth water. He carefully placed the plate next to his glass along with a set of cutlery laid on a napkin.

He was shocked. "Is … are these gold?"

Emmett beamed and said, "Yes, sir. We used to use silverware, but those have an adverse effect on the taste of the food. Gold, in our opinion, is the only option for our dishes. We like to call it our 'gold standard,' if you will excuse the turn of phrase."

Derrek was amazed, not at the extravagance of this hotel per se but at how it continued to impress him over and over again. From the moment he walked through the front door, he had been bombarded with constant waves of luxuries and comfort.

"I'm honestly blown away," he said, staring at his food. "I had no idea there was anything like this anywhere! I haven't even tasted any of this yet, and I already want to send my compliments to the chef! And don't even get me started on the whiskey!"

Emmett's smile grew even wider. "I'm glad to hear everything is to your liking, sir! Here at the Schadenfreude, we strive for greatness in every single aspect of our guests' experience."

"I've noticed!" Derrek said, finally looking up from his food, making direct eye contact with Emmett. "Thank you, Emmett. I'm sure I'll remember this night for the rest of my days."

Emmett was taken aback. Most people weren't this outgoing about how much they enjoyed their stay. Most took it with a silent smile and a nod, showing their appreciation through their reviews when all was said and done, and even then, many still gave a poor review to leverage a refund. Finding someone who genuinely appreciated the work that each of the employees at this hotel put in was a fresh breath of air. It almost made him emotional.

"It's no problem, sir. We all do our best here, and I'm ecstatic our best is to your satisfaction! And I certainly hope you enjoy the rest of your night!"

"Oh, are you not coming back with a check?"

Emmett raised his eyebrows in confusion, then smiled and laughed. "No, sir, there won't be a check coming. The food is included with your room, along with our bar, pool, spa, sauna, exercise equipment, archery range, and golf course—caddy included, of course."

Derrek shook his head. He had forgotten about the complimentary meals when he booked the rooms. "Right. Slipped my mind. I doubt I'll get used to it, though!"

"Then it will be a pleasant surprise every meal!"

"I suppose it will."

With a silent nod and a smile, Emmett walked away, tending to his other tables, leaving Derrek with the delicacy before him and the bottle of nostalgia he had been sipping for who knows how long. He took a bite from the roast, which was so tender, half of it fell off the fork. He was hit with an intense torrent of flavor, utterly assaulting his taste buds. It was possibly the best thing he had ever eaten. The risotto was perfectly cooked, creamy with hints of white wine and Parmesan cheese. The medley was perfectly cooked, onions, carrots and radishes that seemed to have been mixed with the same marinade used for the roast.

Before Derrek could even comprehend what he was tasting, he was looking down at an empty plate and saw the sun had almost set. He felt full and thought it might be nice to watch the sunset from the roof. However, he also wanted some more whiskey, so he gestured for the nearest server to come over.

"Yes, sir," she asked. "How may I help you?"

"Is there any way I could get a to-go cup for this?" he asked, gesturing to the bottle.

"Absolutely, sir, but would you rather simply take the bottle and glass with you?"

A slightly intoxicated smile grew on Derrek's face. "That would be perfect, actually. Do I need to bring the glass back to the kitchen, or will it just be gathered whenever room service comes around?"

She smiled. "You can leave it anywhere, but I do ask you to not leave it in the walkways or on the stairs, as someone could get hurt!"

Derrek grabbed the bottle by the neck and raised it up in acknowledgment, grabbing the glass with his other hand, and walked through the crowded room, drawing as little attention to himself as possible. To his knowledge, he didn't see any prominent Frostbyte employees, so he figured he would be getting away from this scot-free.

He got to the elevator without any dirty looks and pressed the button for the roof. He danced to the dulcet tunes playing from the speaker on the ceiling and realized he had no memories of ever dancing. Thinking something was off, he looked at the bottle to find it had much more than a single glass worth missing in contents, down to about two-thirds full. He was sure it was a fresh bottle. He had seen Emmett open it!

He had been suspicious of the amount of lost time he was experiencing but figured he was just drunk from whiskey and the Brewskis, so he continued dancing until he reached the roof.

The door opened to a massive lounge area centered around the glass pyramid he had seen from the lobby, smoke billowing from the marble column rising from its peak, giving the distinct smell of a wood fire. There was a railing surrounding everything, tall enough to prevent falling over but still short enough that one could look over the edge with comfort. There were benches and several natural areas, rows of flowers and several trees, some even bearing fruit, with signs that read, "Pick as you wish," in English, and what Derrek assumed was the same in several other languages.

Despite the beautiful, unobscured view of the surrounding several miles, he didn't see a soul up there with him. His best guess was that everyone was hoping for an encore of that performance. He sat on one of the benches facing west so he could watch the sunset. Approaching it, however, he heard what sounded like angry French coming from behind a nearby hedge. He couldn't make any of it out, but it seemed to be one-sided, possibly a phone call. He took his seat on the bench and hoped whatever altercation was going on would pass so he could enjoy the view.

The voice got louder and angrier until Derrek heard what sounded like an object being thrown at the ground, making him fix his gaze on the hedge. A few silent seconds passed before he heard footsteps. From behind the hedge stepped a man apparently storming away, who stopped dead in his tracks when he met Derrek's eyes. They stared at each other for a moment, the man's face obscured by the shadow of the hedge, before Derrek gestured to his bottle, offering him a drink.

The man walked over to the bench and sat next to him, accepting the bottle and taking a huge swig, which Derrek tried to warn him against doing. The man cringed and went into a coughing fit, being careful not to spill the bottle.

Derrek chuckled slightly and said, "Yeah, it's more of a sipping whiskey."

He caught a good look at the man, noting his overly formal attire, pristine while gloves, and undone blue bow tie. He realized this was the man he had just seen perform, Hadrian LaFayette. Considering how enthusiastically he had attacked the whiskey that soon after getting offstage, however, Derrek figured it was a bad idea to bring it up.

LaFayette had regained his composure. "Thank you," he said with a soft voice and a faint French accent as he handed the bottle back to him. "I needed that."

"No worries," he said, reaching for a handshake. "I'm Derrek, by the way."

"Hadrian," he said, reciprocating the gesture.

They sat in silence for a few minutes, passing the bottle back and forth, taking sips, staring out into the distance. The bottle came back to Derrek, who saw it was down to a bit over a third left, and he decided to break the silence.

"If you don't mind me asking, what was going on behind that hedge?"

LaFayette glanced at him with a flash of hesitation in his grey eyes, but he looked back over the horizon, taking a second to find the right words. "My mother called me. You know how parents can be."

"Honestly, not really."

He looked at Derrek, confused, then realized what he meant.

"Oh, I'm sorry. I didn't realize—"

Derrek held his hand up and gestured for him to stop, "They

were gone before I could even remember them, and I've had well over twenty years to deal with it. Your wound seems fresh, so don't think this orphan doesn't care about your parental problems."

For the first time he had seen so far, LaFayette smiled. Derrek handed him the bottle, which he took a sip from before saying, "My father died when I was eight years old, leaving me with my mother, living off the life insurance she made him get. She always pushed me in my schoolwork, signing me up for extra courses, never giving me any free time. I was barely ever allowed outside the house, and even then, I was always chaperoned. The only escape I was ever given was my great grandfather's piano.

"She demanded I get lessons to make me a more desirable applicant for university, and I hated them at first, mainly on principle. But then I got the hang of it. I learned the notes, the harmonies, how you can express yourself with little more than a foot on a pedal and a finger on a key. I was beyond the instructors in a month, and my mother thought that was all that was needed of me, and told me to stop.

"For years, I left it behind, until I got into *lycée*, or high school, as I suppose you would call it, where I found there was a grand piano in the auditorium. I had a free class, and thanks to the school I was in, it was listed as Study Hall, so I never had to worry about her asking questions when I blew it off to practice. Every single day, perfecting this, the only outlet I ever had. Nobody ever said anything about it, the staff liked the music, and I was already at the top of my class, so my teachers paid it no mind, at least until the principal called my mother to praise my skills."

He took another sip and a brief pause before continuing, "She never said a word. I came home to find my room destroyed, the posters gone from my walls, all of my academic awards smashed, my sheet music torn to shreds, my door taken entirely off its hinges. She even confiscated the sheets off my bed. I asked her about it, and all she did was ignore me. For the rest of my days living there, I swear we didn't speak a word to each other, just crushing silence. After I graduated, I left. I just left.

"She never asked me why. She never tried to stop me, even when I told her I was going to America to play. I was dead to her. I didn't hear her voice again until I made a name for myself, and by then, all she wanted was money. I think that's all she ever wanted. Constant prodding from her, insisting she *deserved* the money I had made, that I wouldn't have gotten where I am if *she* hadn't pushed me.

"Every day she calls me, and every day, we argue about the same thing. When she isn't calling me, she's badmouthing me on social media, or texting me with the same verbal abuse she always uses. It's … it's a lot, sometimes."

Derrek wasn't sure what to say, and LaFayette could tell.

"I'm sorry. I didn't mean to dump all of that on you."

Derrek looked out at the sunset, and without looking at LaFayette, he took a deep breath and said, "When I was eleven, I ran away from my foster home and was homeless, wandering the streets of New York for a year and a half. I would have died on those streets, but I found what I was good at and held onto the hope that things would get better. With tenacity and an ungodly amount of luck, fifteen years of hard work later, I'm at the most luxurious hotel I've ever seen on behalf of my place of work, drinking the best whiskey I've ever had with the most talented artist I've ever met."

He turned to look at LaFayette with a serious look in his eyes and with the kind of confidence that only comes from a great deal of alcohol, he said, "Never let your past dictate your future."

This resonated with LaFayette, and even though he didn't say it, Derrek knew he appreciated what he had said. The bottle came back to him, and it was very low. He took the glass, which had been sitting next to him, poured half of the whiskey into it, and handed it to LaFayette.

"Cheers," Derrek said, raising the bottle toward LaFayette.

He raised his glass to meet it, causing a loud *clink* before saying, "À nôtre santé."

They both drank, taking big gulps of the whiskey, burning their throats and causing their eyes to water. It would have been much worse if it had not been the end of the bottle, but they both still reeled back from it. They laughed through their respective coughing fits, LaFayette letting go of his troubles, even for just a moment, and Derrek finally understanding how quickly a listening ear and a bottle of liquor could form a friendship.

When they both regained their wits, they stared at the sunset, which was almost over at that point. Minutes passed as the two watched the sun slowly drop over the horizon, leaving behind nothing but a sky of orange and a sea of stars in its wake. They saw constellations and galaxies they had never before seen, twinkling like roaring fires.

The hotel was built with an overhang on the roof, preventing light pollution and allowing this magnificent sight to occur. Moments passed, and the orange sky shifted to deep blue, then to midnight black, with more and more stars filling the sky with every new shade.

Derrek checked the time on his phone and found he had been on the roof for three hours. With the morning Jeffrey had planned, he knew he needed to get some sleep. He stood up from the bench, reached his hand out and said, "It's been a pleasure, Hadrian, but I've got a hell of a day ahead of me tomorrow."

LaFayette smiled and shook his hand. "I understand, friend. Get some rest. I'll be doing the same soon enough."

Derrek gathered the empty bottle and glass and headed toward the elevator. Before he was out of earshot, he stopped and asked, "Hey, why didn't you ever just block her number. You know, cut ties and such?"

LaFayette turned to face him and thought for a few seconds. The thought apparently had never occurred to him. He found an answer. "Because she's all the family I have."

Derrek flashed a smile and boarded the elevator, leaving LaFayette alone on the rooftop. Staring out into the night sky, he took a deep breath and pulled out his newly-damaged phone, calling the contact, "Mère."

When she answered, he said, in French, "Mother, we need to talk."

Derrek slept like a drunken baby, which was at least half accurate. He set his alarm for 5:30, hoping to beat Jeffrey's wake-up call before he drank two-thirds of that whiskey so he was safe on that front. He carefully set the glass and the bottle on the dresser beside the TV, confident room service would take care of it. He kicked off his shoes and fell asleep on top of the covers in his clothes, snoring like a bear, drifting peacefully off into sleep.

His dream, however, was anything but peaceful. He found himself in the middle of a battlefield with cliffs encompassing it, surrounded by bodies adorned in what looked like Roman armor, maybe Greek. Each one was beaten, mutilated, and bloodied, many missing limbs and even more missing their heads. Fires raged, some burning bodies, some burning what looked like siege equipment. Chariots and catapults were damaged and broken. The entire area was bleak and desolate. It reeked of death. And blood. Definitely blood.

The only break in the carnage was a single man standing in the center of it all, standing in the silhouette of the largest fire on the field. Derrek couldn't make out many of his details, but his left arm looked freshly amputated, pouring blood out from just below his elbow. His eyes adjusting to the light, he saw the man was drenched in blood, painting him solid red.

The air was heavy with heat and filled with ash falling like snow, but something was off about the air around this man. There were ashes around him, but they didn't seem to be falling. Rather, they were swirling around him, and they were bright red. They didn't seem to be embers but red ash.

The scene suddenly shifted, and what Derrek assumed was the same man was lying on a table, surrounded by people in white robes. The room appeared to be a mixture of an infirmary and a forge, with primitive medical equipment covering one wall and blacksmithing equipment covering the one opposite. Several people were pouring molten metal into several small molds, seemingly working to form them into a single piece.

The table was on the infirmary side of the room, and many of the people were focusing on the man's arm. The wound had been sealed through cauterization, leaving a massive burn mark on the newly formed stump. He couldn't see the man's face, but he did seem conscious, powering through the operation. Three of the people were apparently tattooing his arm in runic patterns, being extremely deliberate in their markings, lightly hammering bone needles into his skin, rubbing ink in after blood was drawn.

The scene shifted again, but the room remained the same. Most of the robed people were gone, save for three, and the man was now sitting up on the table, apparently having both arms once again. Upon closer inspection, however, Derrek saw the left didn't match the right; it looked like armor. One of the robed figures, a woman, who stood in the middle of the three, apparently the leader, spoke up. She spoke in a language Derrek didn't understand, Latin maybe, but he understood what was being said.

"We did the best we could," she said, gesturing to the man's new arm, "but you will not have the same range of movement ever again."

"That's fine," the man replied, staring down at the hand, which was clenched into a fist, obscuring his face, "the immortals are crippled, and Ormazd is dead—that's all that matters to me. I only wish my comrades had lived to see that fight."

The man to the left of the group spoke up. "There was no way victory could have been claimed. The fact that you survived is nothing less than a blessing from the gods themselves."

The man gave out a bellowing laugh, hitting his knee with his metal arm, causing him to kick violently. After the pain and his laughter subsided, he looked up, revealing a heavily scarred face, and said, "The gods owe me nothing—I learned that long ago. The only blessings I've ever received were curses in disguise. I survived, yes, but nobody else did. Had I been Persian, I would likely be the new leader of the immortals!" he said, laughing again, repeating the strike and the kick, both learning and regretting nothing.

The people were put off by this, amazed and horrified at how this man who had just lost an arm, who was still covered in the blood of friend and foe alike, who watched as his comrades were cut down before his eyes, was still able to laugh. Unsettled, they took their leave, the woman in the middle straggling behind.

Before she was out of the doorway, she turned to the man and said, "You have a home in Argos for as long as you wish. We and our people see you as a war hero and will treat you as such. There's an inn a few buildings over, we will cover your rent should you choose to stay there."

"Thank you. I accept your offer. I have to gather some supplies before I leave, namely, a new sword, a good pair of sandals, and your city's entire supply of wine."

The woman flashed a smile before leaving as her compatriots had, leaving this man alone. He stared at his metal hand, attempting to open his tightly clenched fist to no avail. He sighed and stood to gather his belongings, which were laid out beside the medical table. His clothing had been torn to shreds and his sword was broken, leaving a jagged piece of the blade and a heavily scratched hilt. The robed people had apparently provided some clothing: a simple tunic and a set of the robes they wore, which he was wearing.

He picked up his sword, which was now the length of a dagger, and inspected the damage. From where Derrek was standing, it seemed irreparable, which the man apparently also assessed. He put his scabbard at his side and sheathed it regardless, then started to adjust his robes to cover his metal arm.

Before he could leave, there was a voice from behind where Derrek was standing. He stepped aside to see the whole conversation.

"Another day, another war. How is your arm?"

Before him stood a tall woman, around eight feet tall, with swirling gray eyes, adorned in battle gear and a large helmet, holding a spear in one hand and a shield in the other. The man seemed unfazed, giving Derrek the impression that he either expected her or was far too used to this type of thing.

"Doing about as well as your spear."

The woman scowled. "Lost and replaced, then?"

"With a less useful replacement, yes."

"I *will* get that spear back from you, but that is not why I am here."

"Then speak, god of wisdom. The Sumerians were boring, but at least their gods got to the point."

The woman thrust her spear toward the man, who didn't flinch as the point pierced his neck, barely breaking the skin but still drawing blood.

Unshaken, the man said, "I would have thought your father had taught you better. Threats have no effect on me. State your business. I have copious amounts of wine to imbibe."

She pulled back the spear and put it back at her side, her scowl never fading.

"Despite your efforts, the war is lost, drifter. Sparta will fall."

"What a shame," the man said, pocketing a few odds and ends

from the medical table—several small blades and a few bottles with what Derrek assumed were some kind of tonic. "If only I cared."

The woman was taken aback by his nonchalant attitude. She gripped her spear tightly and said with anger in her voice, "How *dare* you? Hundreds of your allies were killed, the city will be razed, and the people will be slaughtered! Yet, here you are, bothered more by your arm than the result of your failure!"

The man only turned his head, barely even looking at her. "If you were that troubled by it, perhaps you should have stepped in, since I obviously didn't meet your expectations."

"I did *not* come here to be lectured by you, of all people! I should smite you where you stand!"

He turned, fully facing her. "Then have at it. I have no solid plans for the night. It might be fun. I do ask that you spare the city, however. They have been very hospitable, and it would be a shame to burn them in another of your tantrums."

The woman was fuming with rage, her shield and the tip of her spear now glowing dimly, her face red and her eyes shifting to a darker gray. Her voice was filled with anger, but she remained restrained. "You forget yourself, *mortal*. You may have my brothers and sisters fooled, but I see what you *really* are."

The man slowly approached her, death in his eyes, and even though she was at least two heads taller than him, his presence seemed much larger. He was inches away when he finally spoke, and his tone chilled Derrek to the core.

"Ironic, is it not?"

"Excuse me?" she asked, confused and still furious.

"Is it not ironic that you, the god of wisdom, seem so keen to anger the one mortal capable of killing you?"

Derrek could feel the tension in the air. Neither of them said anything for several seconds. They just stood there, staring at each other, refusing to be the first to flinch. The man eventually cracked a smile and gave a small laugh, turning away from her and heading toward the door.

"You will regret this, drifter," the woman said. "The time will come soon enough."

The man laughed. "This empire will not stand forever, and when it falls, so will you. For what is a god with no followers?"

"Is that a threat?" the woman asked through clenched teeth.

"No, I only speak from experience," the man said, his good hand on the doorframe, ready to leave. He turned and gave one last look before saying, "As the Sumerians fell, as the Mesopotamians fell, so the Greeks will fall. Those gods are now scattered in the winds, so will you someday. But life will go on, and so will I."

He exited, leaving Derrek and the woman behind. She stood for a brief moment, staring at the empty door frame before vanishing without a trace, leaving him alone.

The scene changed once more to an aerial view of a burning city. Derrek was floating above it, feeling the heat and choking on the smoke. He saw carnage—people being murdered indiscriminately, blood-soaked streets, limbs and corpses littering the roads. He heard a sick mixture of screaming, burning, and laughter.

Among the violence, he saw a single man calmly walking through, sword drawn, cutting down the citizens of this town as he passed. Effortlessly, he sent heads rolling with a casual swipe, seemingly in no hurry. The heat grew more and more intense with every passing second, the fires raging as the city burned.

The man stopped in his tracks and looked up. It was the same man from earlier. The man was looking directly at him, or maybe through him. There was a look of boredom on his face, and he appeared to sigh before a large wave of smoke temporarily blinded Derrek. He rubbed his eyes, but when he regained his vision, the man was gone.

The heat grew, but it felt like it was coming from behind him. He struggled for a few seconds to turn around from his suspended state to see what was going on and was stunned at what he saw. A volcano towered above the city, massive amounts of ash spewing from the top, lava running down the side, bellowing deafening roars as it erupted over and over again. How he had missed it before eluded him, but he saw it now. He saw the destruction it was causing. The riots were out of desperation. The fires stemmed from the molten rock that slowly engulfed the town.

Those revelations rushed through Derrek's mind as he stared at the mountain, completely unaware of the giant flaming rock heading toward him. He felt the impact along with brief excruciating pain, then felt nothing at all. He was still partially aware of his surroundings and felt as if he were falling rapidly, but he felt no pain. In the few seconds before he hit the ground, he wondered why these dreams always ended with his painful death and why he could never remember the dream when he awoke, but the thought was cut short by a sudden impact.

Derrek opened his eyes to find a trumpet pointed at his face and Jeffrey behind it, in the middle of taking a deep breath.

"Don't you dare," he said before Jeffrey could finish his breath.

Noticing he was awake, he let out his breath with a loud, exaggerated groan. He lowered his trumpet and gave Derrek a chance to wake up. He turned on the lamp and thought his drunken slumber had made him miss his alarm, but one look at his phone told him that Jeffrey had, in fact, beaten him to the punch, since the time showed 5:20 a.m.

"What happened to six sharp?" a groggy Derrek asked as he rubbed his eyes.

"Gotta keep you on your toes, element of surprise and whatnot."

Derrek got up from the bed, his head throbbing in pain. He had a rough time getting his footing, and his stomach burned. He tried to speak, but his mouth suddenly filled with saliva, and he ran for the bathroom. The sounds he made as he violently vomited into the toilet were enough to make Jeffrey shudder, reminding him of his high school days as a self-described alpha party animal.

While Derrek was expelling his bile, Jeffrey took a look around and saw the empty bottle on the dresser, confirming his suspicions. He went to the minifridge for a water bottle and put in two antacid tablets he had in his pocket, shaking the bottle to help them dissolve.

Derrek came out a couple of minutes later, as white as a ghost, eyes puffy and red, completely exhausted. He slumped back onto the bed, covering his face with his hands. Even the low light from the lamp was enough to make his eyes burn.

Jeffrey held out the water toward him and said, "Drink. You'll feel better."

Derrek accepted and began to drink, meaning to take only a few sips. However, he was extremely thirsty and quickly chugged the entire bottle. When he finally stopped for air, he put the cap back on and tossed it to the trash basket beside the dresser, missing by almost three feet. Jeffrey didn't laugh, even though he thought it was very funny, since he knew the pain he was going through. He walked over and put the bottle in the basket for him.

"Did you have a fun night?"

"Yeah, had some saur … something. Some kind of beef or something, I don't know. Had some whiskey too, but they let me leave with the bottle. I think I was on the roof too. And I think there was a piano involved, but my head's killing me."

"Then don't worry about it. Just take it easy. Take yourself a quick shower and put on some fresh clothes. I'll be in the dining hall. Be there by six."

"Sure," Derrek said as Jeffrey started to leave. Before he got to the door, however, he asked, "How'd you get in? Did you seriously break another lock?"

"Didn't have to. The door was open," Jeffrey said, prompting Derrek to look at the wide-open door. In his drunken haze, he had apparently forgotten to close it.

He nodded slowly, seeing that it was his fault, and let Jeffrey leave without another word. He took a few minutes to just sit before he went to shower. He spent a solid ten minutes just standing under the water until eventually the antacids kicked in and he finally had some relief from his nausea. By the time he got dry and dressed, he had only five minutes to be in the dining hall, so he put on his shoes and a pair of sunglasses he had in his duffle bag and left the room.

Jeffrey was sitting in the same spot he was in the morning before, the only one in the room save for the cook staff. There were two coffee cups and two plates of food on the table; he had gotten breakfast for Derrek, who took his seat.

On his plate were two scones topped with ham and poached eggs drizzled with a yellow sauce with a side of bacon. The smell made his mouth water and his stomach rumble.

"Eggs Benedict. Eat up," Jeffrey said as Derrek did just that. The plate in front of him was already empty, but the leftover sauce made it obvious he'd had the same. The plate was clear before either of them knew it, and they both felt satisfied.

"That was delicious," Derrek said as he began to sip his coffee.

"Hells yeah," Jeffrey said as he stacked their plates and placed them on the side of the table. "Some Wall Street bene-dick made it as a hangover cure about a hundred and forty years back, and I'll be damned if he didn't nail it on the head."

Derrek tried to laugh, but it made his head throb, so he did his best not to.

The rest of the day went similarly to the one before; the two ate another plate each, sharing stories and jokes over their eggs. Eventually they loaded up and went to the track, Derrek having a rough time but feeling much better thanks to his breakfast. He even managed to stay on his feet when they finished their workout. The weapons training went well; he was hitting the target consistently at four and five times out of every ten shots, even getting six once, and was getting better with his knife-throwing extracurricular.

He wasted the same couple of hours on that game show, the name of which he finally caught: *Kuchenparty,* which he took to mean, "Cake Party."

Dinner was similar to the one before, but he was joined by Jeffrey, to whom he recommended the sauerbraten with risotto, while he had a delicious dish of spaghetti squash and sausage. The entertainment was a standup comedian who left everyone in stitches despite a fifteen-minute tangent about horses, or perhaps because of it. After their meal, they stuck around for a few drinks, Jeffrey ordering a full six-pack of Brewskis and Derrek getting a large mug full of a sweet ale, which he had refilled twice. People filed out after 8:30, and they did the same, turning in to their respective rooms.

That was how the next few days went as they continued Derrek's training. His dreams took a more mundane turn, most being the same level of nonsense to be expected from a dream, with a staggering amount of chickens speaking English, but in reverse. He got better every day, finishing his workout faster each day. He was even able to keep pace with Jeffrey on the first mile and a half on the fourth day.

On Friday, the fifth day of training, Derrek earned his certification, hitting eight out of ten on his exam. As a graduation gift, Jeffrey gave him his sidearm and his pack of knives. He said it was legal to open carry the knives there, but Derrek took that with a grain of salt. That night, they decided to embrace their manliness, ordering twenty-four-ounce steaks and a bottle of whiskey, valiantly consuming the slabs of meat before them, immediately regretting their decision and continuing anyway. Jeffrey did his best to maintain his composure, but he utterly failed and looked like a full tick—too engorged to move.

Derrek claimed victory that night, stomaching his entire steak and his fair share of the bottle of Steel Barrel he insisted they drink with hardly a sweat. He was feeling the pain, but still riding high from getting his certification, he played it cool for the entire dinner. When he got back to his room, it was another story; he completely collapsed and writhed in the agony that came from eating a pound and a half of steak along with half a bottle of whiskey. He was visibly bloated and unable to make many vocalizations beyond pained grunts and groans.

He eventually fell asleep watching *Kuchenparty*, which was either running a marathon or on a constant loop, but he was certain he hadn't seen any repeats. He had no dreams and slept like a hibernating bear, snoring like one as well.

Every aspect of the Schadenfreude had surprised him, but the biggest surprise so far was waking up without Jeffrey standing over him. He was groggy from the night before and was confused for a solid five minutes before he remembered his training was finished. Since Derrek had passed his certification, there was no reason to drag him out of bed.

However, he had grown accustomed to the early morning workout and decided to meet Jeffrey at the same spot they always met and joined him for the usual breakfast.

The next two days were a challenge for Derrek. Orientation didn't start until Monday morning, and very few of the activities provided by the hotel appealed to him. There was a chess tournament, but very few people signed up, a total of twelve, including Derrek, all of whom he mopped the floor with. The prize was a prepaid debit card, roughly forty US dollars, which Derrek used to buy a cool hat online to be delivered back home.

Little else happened that weekend. He went out with Jeffrey to a bar on Saturday night, but that was the only time he left the hotel grounds. He was nearly dragged into a fight after someone poked fun and the reflectivity of Jeffrey's head, which Derrek did his best to mediate, buying a drink for everyone to cool everything off. It didn't calm the perpetrator, but it did make it clear to him that the patrons of the bar were now on Derrek's side, prompting him to take his drink to go.

Monday had rolled around, and Derrek was up bright and early for his morning routine. He got back to the hotel before nine, not only giving him enough time to freshen up before orientation at ten but also setting a new record. It was a special class; since he was the only one who arrived without their open-carry qualification, he was the only one who missed the initial orientation.

It was taking place in the hotel conference room. Derrek entered to find a large ovaloid table in the same white-marble-with-gold-trim style with which the rest of the hotel was adorned. At the head of the table were two people, a man and a woman, along with assorted presentation materials, including several piles of papers, a laptop, and a laser pointer. The woman had black hair tied back in a bun and glasses and a red blouse, while the man had short, matted brown hair and appeared to be wearing pajamas.

"Ah, you're here," the woman said, shuffling through some papers. "Derrek Snowe, right?"

"Yes, ma'am. That's me."

"It says here you had Major Reynolds your weapons instructor. I can imagine that was a challenge."

Derrek was confused. "What makes you say that?"

The man spoke up with an English accent. "Because he has a habit of pushing too hard. Let me guess: he had you run a mile at the crack of dawn?"

"Ten, actually. And a lot of sit-ups, push-ups, and jumping jacks."

Both of them stared at Derrek in disbelief. He didn't have the form of someone who, in the past week, had run a cumulative seventy miles, but they saw no reason for him to lie.

"Right," the woman said, "I suppose introductions are in order—"

The man interrupted, "Wait, are we really just going to scroll past that?"

"Yes, we are."

"What the hell? I've got questions!"

"And *I've* got a schedule to keep. Ask him on your own time."

The man grumbled with minimal coherency. The only word that could be made out by the listeners was "breakfast."

The woman coughed to regain Derrek's attention. "Anyway, my name is Dr. Rebecca Shepherd, and this is my"—she paused as the man yawned loudly, still trying to continue his grumbling—"my associate, Professor Lewis Philman."

"My friends call me Syler," Philman interjected, reaching out to shake Derrek's hand. "It's my middle name."

Derrek shook his hand and said. "I don't believe that one bit."

Shepherd smirked at Philman, looking at him with eyes that said, "Ha-ha, he called you on your nonsense."

"Ha-ha, he called you on your nonsense!" she said, pointing and laughing at him.

"Shut up!" Philman said. "It says so on my birth certificate!"

"You know perfectly well that *I know* that's bullshit."

"Oh yeah? Prove it!"

Shepherd didn't break eye contact with him as she reached under her chair and pulled out a briefcase, which she dramatically placed on the table. She opened it and produced a single piece of paper, which she slid in Derrek's direction.

"Do me a favor and read that out loud, will you?" she asked, still maintaining eye contact with an increasingly nervous-looking Philman.

Picking it up, he saw it was an official document and did as she asked.

"Lewis Shelby Philman."

"OK, that's enough of that," Philman said as he snatched his birth certificate out of Derrek's hands, throwing his compatriots into a fit of laughter. He tried to tuck it into his waistband before realizing how bad of an idea that was. Then he placed it on the table, guarding it with his life.

After her laughter subsided, Shepherd coughed loudly to reestablish the professional air. She opened the laptop and tapped away at the keys. Across from them, at the foot of the table, a narrow rectangular slot opened in the ceiling. From the slot, a screen slowly unfurled, and from behind the "professionals," another slot opened. From that slot, a projection began, shining on the screen with an image clearer than anything Derrek had ever seen.

The screen showed the beginning of a slideshow, which read, in Comic Sans, "Frostbyte for Goobers: Environmental Scanning and You!"

"There we are," Shepherd said, eyes fixated on the laptop screen. "Let's get started, shall we?"

Philman groaned and said, "God, you're pretentious."

"Says the man with the fake middle name," she said, looking up at him from her screen for a brief moment before gluing her eyes back in place.

Philman grunted and reverted to another bout of grumbling, albeit much quieter than his previous one. All the while, Derrek stood uncomfortably just inside the doorframe, debating whether he should sit.

Philman took notice of his internal struggle and ceased his grumbling fit to say, "Please, take a seat. This'll be a little while."

"Thank you," Derrek said as he sat in the middle seat on Shepherd's side. Philman slid him a folder that was akin to a dictionary, absolutely brimming with forms, documents, and a clipboard, for some reason. Taking a look at several random pages, it seemed to be full of several hundred waivers.

"We're going to need those signed and initialed by tomorrow

morning, just so you're aware," Shepherd said, glaring coldly at her colleague. "And I would recommend that you actually *read* them; it's important to know what rights you're signing away, *Philman.*"

"Oh, get over it already! If I didn't blindly sign that contract, I wouldn't be here now, would I?"

"Exactly my point."

Derrek could feel the tension between these two and thought that changing the subject might help them not kill each other.

"'Frostbyte for Goobers'—I actually had to make one of these for the policy they put in about the flu last year," he said with a jovial tone. "Although my boss did put his name on it and passed it off as his, but that's work, right?"

The two looked at him with blank faces, neither of them sure what to say, but it was clear that they had forgotten they were in the middle of an angry staring contest. Eventually, Shepherd cracked a smile, and Philman let out a short laugh.

"You've got that right," Philman said, "At the university I used to teach at, my department head would always put his name at the reports I wrote! Ended up being what got the bastard fired. Well, that and how creepy he was to the coeds."

"Every time my team's research gets published, they put our names in fine print at the bottom," Shepherd said with an exasperated tone that didn't fit her smile. "But first page? Center print? In bold? The damn pencil-pushing bigwig bureaucrat who green-lit our budget."

The three had a hearty laugh, which Shepherd cut short so they could get to work.

"We should really be further ahead. You're supposed to be in the field tomorrow."

"Right. Sorry, ma'am," Derrek said.

"Don't apologize," Philman said. "I needed a good laugh."

"He has a point," Shepherd said, half-glaring and half-looking at Philman, "but I will ask that distractions are kept to a minimum. Feel free to ask questions, though."

"Yes, ma'am."

She looked at him for a moment before fixing her gaze on a sheet of paper with Derrek's full name printed on top. She wrote down, "Oddly formal," matching the header perfectly, leaving him amazed at her handwriting. She looked up and tapped a key, changing the slide.

"Let's start with the purpose of this operation. As I'm sure you're aware, our main reason for being here is to lay the groundwork for Frostbyte's one hundred twenty-seventh wildlife sanctuary, our first one in Germany. But our secondary objective is to add the DNA of the flora and fauna to our ever-expanding database of genetic code. William Shale and many of our scientifically inclined professionals, myself included, believe this may reveal the key to lengthening the human lifespan, possibly indefinitely.

"Over the course of the past two decades, we have already mapped approximately thirty-eight percent of the global genome, mostly due to our highly efficient equipment," she said as she changed the slide to a picture of a large rectangular machine and let Philman take over.

"The genetic screening and recording machine, or as I like to call it, the GENRAM," he said, prompting Shepherd to roll her eyes, "the way this bad boy works is you put either a little critter or a small sample, like a leaf or a patch of hair, in that there slot."

Suddenly a red dot appeared at what Derrek took to be the side of the machine, centered on a small square-shaped slot, about a foot wide. Philman was now holding a laser pointer, and it was clear that Shepherd was not happy about it.

"The machine then works its magic, performing deep scans and effectively obtaining around ninety-nine percent of the genetic code of whatever was slapped in. Whatever was put in then comes out the other side, completely unharmed. Don't know how it works personally, but that's not in my job description."

The red dot moved from the screen to the center of Shepherd's forehead, unbeknownst to her, as she was focused on her notes. She turned to the next slide which was a large chunk of text with the header, "Dress Code and Safety Regulations."

"Obviously, opened-toed shoes are not allowed," she began, "along with shorts, graphic T-shirts, and extravagant jewelry—although we do allow wedding bands—and no primary use of the color red-orange."

Derrek raised his hand for a question, which Philman acknowledged with a nod, still pointing the laser at Shepherd's forehead.

"Why is that particular color banned?"

Shepherd looked up from her notes, catching the laser in her eye. She fought the urge to scream while Philman fought the urge to laugh, but she got over it before him, giving her the time she needed to snatch the laser pointer from his hand. She put it in her briefcase, which she promptly locked. She then gave Philman a murderous glance before facing Derrek to answer his question.

"Frostbyte just doesn't want to get confused with our competitor, Spitfire. I think their CEO and shale have been fighting since the company's inception."

Derrek had never heard about this feud, but he figured if it were important, Shale would have told him, so he brushed it off. However, he would be sure to ask about it when he got home.

"That makes sense. Sorry for the interruption," Derrek said as Shepherd nodded, appreciating the apology. She quickly went back to her notes to underline, "Oddly formal."

"Anyway," Shepherd continued, "you will be provided with a uniform. It's very thin, durable, and breathable, so feel free to wear whatever you want underneath. Just don't dress for winter. If you have long hair, you have to tie it back, and we work with a lot of powerful magnets and moving parts, so piercings must be removed before going out in the field.

"Unless it's an absolute emergency, your sidearm is to be holstered with the safety on and the chamber empty. Normally, the biggest threat we face on these missions in terms of wildlife are bears, but seeing as they were hunted to extinction here in 1835, the boars are a bigger worry. And the snakes. There are snakes. Venomous snakes. However, there is also the possibility of a more … human threat.

"In the past, there have been ecoterrorist groups, crazed civilians with conspiracy theories, militias who didn't get the memo, and one time, there was a confused old man passing by who thought we stole the refrigerator in his front yard."

"Although," Philman interrupted, "there haven't been any major militias in Germany since the 1940s, they're not at war, and nowadays most of their population is reasonably mentally sound. Not to mention, we've got ample supplies of the antivenom for both the European adder and the asp, the dangerous snakes Becky mentioned, so I bet you'll be fine."

Shepherd glared at him, then shook it off, apparently letting it slide. "That's pretty much it as far as regulations go. There are several smaller ordinances, but they mainly line up with standard Frostbyte practices. Last week was almost entirely set up, so all the machines are in place and calibrated. You'll get the tutorial when you're out there."

"So," Derrek began, confused at the brevity, "is that all?"

Philman began to speak, but Shepherd seemed to kick him under the table and said, "Yes but also no. While I'm sure you're familiar with said ordinances, we do legally have to go over them." She glared at Philman; Derrek got the impression she thought he was going to try to get out of it.

The next forty-five minutes reminded Derrek of his eighteenth birthday, the day he was officially hired full-time at Frostbyte. They went over appropriate banter, sexual harassment, rules against horseplay, and their very hard stance on forming unions: in favor of them but adamant that terms be negotiated with union heads and corporate. He got the feeling it would have taken substantially less time were Shepherd and Philman not constantly at each other's throats.

When all was said and done, Derrek shook both of their hands and went back to his room with his folder full of waivers. As soon as he was out of the room, he heard yelling from inside and was impressed that they were able to not kill each other for so long. He thought about trying to break it up but decided that they could handle it. They were adults, after all.

It was only eleven, but he got the feeling the rest of his day was going to be dedicated to those waivers. Each and every one of them detailed different ways he could get injured, maimed, crippled, killed, and in one case liquefied, and he had to read and sign well over a hundred of them. He surmised that at a rate of one every five minutes, he could spend every hour of daylight he had that day just signing them.

He got comfortable on the bed and used the clipboard as a backer. He thought about turning on *Kuchenparty*, just for some background noise, but he was certain it would eat up all of his time before he even realized it, so he decided to just hunker down and get it done.

He had hoped the time would pass the way it had with the rest of the hotel, but it did not. He felt like he was back on the flight, wanting to sleep but unable to, the only difference being he had to actively keep himself awake. He agonized for hours, reading in great detail every way he could potentially be killed on this innocuous excursion, taking note of every stipulation, condition, and exception, making sure he wasn't signing away his life rights.

He finally signed the last one well around eight, which he couldn't tell until he opened his blinds to a pitch-black landscape. He had skipped lunch, so he made up for it with a big dinner—a massive plate of linguine Alfredo with the juiciest grilled chicken Derrek ever had. The cheese was rich but not overpowering, and the perfect consistency. He tried to think of a word to describe it and ended up with "carbolicious."

He was bloated and devoid of regret, but he still managed to lug himself back to his room. The thought it was nearly a week since the first time since he first went to sleep in that lavish bed with a belly full of luxury food ran through his head, but he was too tired to think more on it. He changed into his pajamas and slipped off to sleep as soon as he closed his eyes.

"Wake up, sunshine!"

Derrek woke with a start to find Jeffrey hovering over his bed. He hadn't woken him up like this since he got his certification, but that didn't impact him much.

He rubbed his eyes and said, "Mornin', Jeffrey."

Jeffrey looked disappointed but also impressed at how calm he was.

"Well, damn, not even an ounce of surprise. You're fixing to be a regular hard-ass!"

Derrek sat up and stretched, revealing his toned figure. He had quickly adapted to his new exercise regimen quickly and was now devoid of the "flabby middle" Jeffrey had poked fun at only a week earlier.

"Not sure if I'll ever be able to beat a cyborg in a foot race, but I'm getting there," Derrek said as he put on a shirt.

Jeffrey frowned quizzically. "You must have a kick-ass

metabolism, because you really shouldn't be this built after just a week."

"What do you mean?"

"You're halfway to me, and I've been building this temple of a body since 2015."

"I guess so. Might have something to do with the massive portions here."

"Even still, it's weird," said Jeffrey as he started toward the door.

"That's all? No trumpet today?"

"Just wanted to make sure you're up, first day in the field and all. Get dressed. I'll have coffee waiting."

Derrek took note of his change in tone but decided to brush it off. "All right. I'll be down in five," he said as Jeffrey nodded and left, closing the door behind him. He wasn't quite sure how he managed to get inside this time, as there was a distinct lack of signs of breaking and/or entering.

He made his way downstairs to find Jeffrey solemnly staring out the window at their table, sipping his coffee. He took his seat and took a sip from the cup waiting for him.

"Everything OK, Major?"

Jeffrey had only just noticed Derrek was sitting with him, "Huh? Oh, yeah, everything's fine. Just thinking about what I'm gonna eat," he said, slowly putting on the grin Derrek had grown accustomed to.

They had a relatively light meal: a half dozen waffles each with a side of bacon. The two told stories and jokes, as they had every morning before, but Derrek could tell something was off. Jeffrey wasn't laughing like he usually did, and every few minutes, he would lose all expression and stare blankly into the distance before snapping out of it, trying to brush it off with a joke about needing more coffee. Derrek continued to brush it off, confident that if he wanted to talk about whatever was bothering him, he would be the one to bring it up.

About twenty minutes had passed, and both men had cleaned

their plates and emptied their cups. They got up to take their trays to the conveyor belt and began to walk to the front door until Jeffrey stopped halfway through the lobby. Derrek was following him and nearly bumped into him.

"Is something wrong?" Derrek asked.

Jeffrey didn't face him, only turning his head enough so Derrek could hear. "Sorry, I forgot to mention, I've got some business to handle, so we're gonna have to take a rain check."

"Oh, all right. No worries. Are you going to join me for dinner after work?"

Jeffrey paused for a moment. "No, actually. I'll probably be gone for the rest of the week."

Derrek was confused. "Don't you have to help with the fieldwork? Stand around and look threatening? Order the other soldiers around?"

Jeffrey turned around, now facing him, "No, my only task was to get you ready to carry a gun. I've basically got the rest of the month off. And since I'm the highest-ranking uniformed individual here, I don't have anyone to report to or anyone to yell at me for taking off."

He was oddly cold and serious, completely out of character for him. Derrek got the impression that whatever he was going to do, it was of grave importance, at least to him.

"I understand. Good luck on whatever you're off to do," Derrek said, reaching out for a handshake.

Jeffrey shook his hand and realized he hadn't done so since the bus ride. The hand he felt was no longer that of a desk jockey but one that reminded him of his own drill sergeant years before. He was half-surprised, half-impressed, but he felt he shouldn't have developed this much this quickly.

Without saying another word, Jeffrey nodded and exited the hotel, heading toward his truck. Derrek could swear he saw someone leaning against the hood, but after Jeffrey passed through his field of vision, he saw nobody there.

Derrek wasn't meant to report to the parking lot until 8:30, so he filled the time browsing his phone, catching up on the latest news. Another US senator was impeached for a sex scandal, a plane had crashed into the ocean, prompting an extensive investigation, and a small town in North Dakota had elected a well-known stray cat as their mayor. People were outraged about his newly instated policies involving a citywide ban on all forms of animal euthanasia, regardless of how sick the animal was, legalization of recreational catnip, and making all spaying and neutering of animals a form of second-degree assault. He was fairly certain it was satire, but it was very detailed.

Before he knew it, it was time to go. He laced his shoes, grabbed his sunglasses and the massive pile of waivers, and headed for the lobby.

He saw a flood of faces, some familiar, but only because he shared a plane with them. He caught a glance of the man who snored beside him through the entire flight, but he quickly lost him. Many were grouping up, apparently assigned as such, as they left the building. He followed, almost getting swept away with the crowd that was now forming around the busses. Over the heads of everyone in front of him, he saw Shepherd. She was holding a clipboard and apparently standing on something.

"All right, everyone, listen up!" she shouted, getting the crowd's attention and causing it to fall silent. "You've all been given your assigned groups and tasks. You all should know what to do. Just do your job, meet your quota, and don't set any fires. Dismissed."

The crowd split off, but to Derrek's surprise, nobody went to the busses. As the crowd thinned, he saw there were many more vehicles, all suited for off-road travel. He remembered that he was the one to arrange for these vehicles to be there in the first place, making him embarrassed. He then realized he was the only one who knew he forgot about the vehicles and got embarrassed about being embarrassed.

He did put it out of his mind, partly because he thought it was pointless but also because he knew he needed to get the forms to Shepherd before he was allowed in the field. She stood atop what Derrek recognized as a cooler, Philman standing beside her, arms crossed, visibly grumpy. Derrek got the impression that Philman was not a morning person.

He weaved his way toward them through the quickly dispersing crowd, eventually catching her attention. She waved him over, and he made his way to them as fast as he could without losing all of his papers.

"Good morning, Mr. Snowe. Did you manage to get them all signed?"

"Yes, ma'am," he said, handing the folder to her.

"How long did it take?" Philman asked, clearly impressed he had gotten it done in a day.

"Almost nine hours. Did someone really get liquefied?" Derrek asked, knowing it had to happen at one point for there to be a waiver explicitly mentioning it.

Shepherd and Philman looked at each other nervously. Then she said, "Yes. Someone got liquefied."

She made it clear she didn't want to speak further on the matter, and Philman did the same. An awkward silence fell over the three, despite the ruckus of the hundreds of people surrounding them.

Philman eventually nudged her with his elbow, gesturing toward the vehicles.

"Oh, right," she said, stepping down from the cooler. She flipped through several pages on her clipboard until she found the right page. She scanned the page until she found what she was looking for, "It says here your team head is Dr. Amir Rathod. That would be him over there."

She pointed to her left at a man of Indian descent. He was standing with his back to an SUV, addressing his team of around ten people. He had long black hair tied back in a ponytail and didn't seem much older than Derrek.

"Might wanna join them," Philman said, reaching into the cooler and pulling out a frosty-looking can of Krazy Kola!, made by Kline enterprises. Derrek distinctly remembered a major debacle when it came out, partially due to the extremely problematic nature of the name and partially due to the fact that it was found to be directly linked to breast cancer. He was sure it had been discontinued years before, yet here Philman was with an apparent cooler full of them.

Derrek had scores of questions, but there was no time. He thanked them for their time and headed toward his team. Behind him, he heard Philman open his can, followed by Shepherd saying something that Derrek assumed was either a criticism of the soda, commentary on the moral implications of drinking it, or her calling him an idiot for drinking something proven to cause cancer. In response, he heard Philman loudly say, "Oh, come off it. Guys can't get breast cancer!"

This was followed by several people around him, Shepherd included, saying in unison, "Yes, they can."

He approached Dr. Rathod's group and caught the tail end of the speech he was giving. He spoke with a distinct Indian accent and had a deeper voice than Derrek had expected.

"And Gary has made turkey sandwiches for everyone, so feel free to have one come lunchtime."

Derrek filed in with the rest of the group, quietly saying hello to the person next to him. Rathod took notice of him and smiled.

"Ah, I am glad you were able to make it. Derrek, correct?"

He hoped he wasn't in trouble for being late to join the group.

"Yes, sir."

Rathod put his hand up in a *stop* gesture. "Please, call me Amir. I prefer to work on a first-name basis. You did not miss much, if you were worried. I was just making sure everyone was aware of everyone else's dietary restrictions come lunchtime. Do you have any dietary restrictions, Derrek?"

He was caught off guard by that question, but he answered, "I have a minor shellfish allergy. Nothing that could kill me, but it messes my stomach up whenever I eat it."

"Then we will take it easy with the king crab," Amir said, prompting laughter from the team. "But in all seriousness, we should really head out. Daylight is burning."

With that, people began to load into the SUV behind him, and the one parked behind it. They were six-seated, allowing for even dispersal of the ten people he counted, himself included. Amir gestured for him to join him in the middle seats of the front vehicle after he allowed the man carrying the cooler, presumably Gary, to get into the back seat. Derrek couldn't be sure, but he swore he saw him buckle up the cooler.

"This is your first time in the field, correct?" Amir asked as everyone strapped in for the trip.

"That's right."

"I noticed your application went in only a week before the flight. May I ask why that is?"

Derrek scratched the back of his head. He rarely talked about his relationship with Shale with his coworkers, as it tended to breed jealousy, so he decided to play it cool.

"I lost a bet that I couldn't back out of. I just made it in under the wire."

Amir raised an eyebrow. "Lost a bet? I am not sure that is the best reason to put your life in danger like this."

"In danger? Isn't Germany one of the safest places on earth nowadays?"

"No place is truly safe, Derrek. Even here there are risks. Herds of boar, ecoterrorists, meteorites—any number of things could happen."

"Couldn't those same things happen sitting behind my desk—aside from the boars, of course?"

Amir smiled and patted Derrek on the shoulder. "Ah, sharp as a tack, I see. You will be a fine addition to the team. Allow me to introduce everyone."

He pointed to the woman driving the car. "This is Aubrey. She has been with Frostbyte for nearly twenty years. She is a candidate for a PhD in ecology, she is the best billiards player I have ever met, and she is one of the best drivers among our ranks."

"You flatter me, Amir, but it isn't my fault you suck at pool," she said as she started the engine.

Pointing to the man in the passenger seat, Amir said, "Here we have Steven. He is a good man. He has two beautiful children and breeds horses on the weekend, and he is also our team's security director."

"Served six years in the navy. Best choice of my life. The benefits are great. I even met my wife there."

He pointed to the man behind them, confirming Derrek's suspicions about the cooler being buckled up. "And this is Gary. He makes really good sandwiches."

Gary gave a thumbs-up and smiled warmly. Apparently, that was enough for him. Derrek was suddenly looking forward to lunch.

The fleet of SUVs began their departure, leaving in a single-file, color-coded line, some groups having eight or nine, some, like theirs, having only one or two. As Derrek recalled, he had rented sixty of the same model, and based on the lack of complaints, the efficiency of the color coded system, and the ample amount of lumbar support he felt, he thought he had made the right call.

Amir leaned in and whispered to Derrek, "I saw your name all over the requisition forms. Were you the one to set this all up?"

Derrek was impressed. He knew for a fact that his name had intentionally been put in the fine print, Hanes's name being bolded as the project head for the budget. If he saw Derrek's name, he was clearly a man who paid close attention to detail.

He whispered back, "Yes, actually—although my boss took most of the credit."

"Ah, a story as old as time, my friend," he said, now speaking at full volume. "How did you manage to get us all individual lodging at that hotel—if you do not mind me asking, of course?"

"Weirdly enough, they gave me a deal that made it more cost-efficient that way, as opposed to having bunkmates. They charged about five hundred dollars a month for singles and twelve hundred for a double. I don't really understand their business model, and I can't think that five hundred dollars covers all the luxuries they provide."

"It could be them trying to establish a working relationship with Frostbyte. Or maybe they are in their offseason and need all the customers they can get. But regardless, I would say you did a great job, Derrek."

"Thank you, Dr. Ra … Amir. Thank you, Amir."

Amir smiled. "Are you not used to informal interactions?"

"Almost my entire life has been business. Formality is just second nature to me now."

"I understand, friend, but please feel comfortable! I believe a professional environment is good for business, but when working with a small team, the anonymity that comes with it can get in the way. It is easier to work with one's equals than with one's superior."

That thought had never occurred to Derrek, but he was willing to see how it played out.

The ride took almost an hour and a half, with everyone sharing stories except Gary, who was focused entirely on keeping his cooler safe. Steven told the story of how he met his wife and how they bonded over cinnamon gruel and complaining about their commanding officer. Aubrey reminisced on her childhood working on cars with her dad, racing lawnmowers, and working as an EMT driver for a Frostbyte subsidiary for a low-income area without proper funding. That job not only fit with her skill set, but honed it nicely, allowing her to put herself through college, studying her passion for the environment.

Amir told of his childhood in the slums of Mumbai, struggling alongside his family until his parents were finally able, after more than fifteen years, to move to the UK. He studied there, eventually getting his PhD for his thesis on the global impact of the privatization of environmental sanctuaries, getting the attention of William Shale.

Derrek didn't share how he met Shale or anything about his younger years, fearing the former may make them think differently of him and worrying the latter would kill the mood. He told stories of his workplace antics, shared some stories Jenkins had told him, namely the one where he won $50,000 in Vegas and bought a sports car, which he instantly crashed. He told them about his weapons training and intensive exercise regimen, surprising even Steven that he was able to keep up. Before anyone knew it, they were at the site.

They had been off road for about twenty miles by Derrek's guess and arrived in a clearing roughly a hundred feet wide. In the center of the clearing was a Conex for storage, and what he recognized as a GENRAM, partly because of the presentation he sat through the day before and partly because it was printed on the side of the machine in large, bold letters. He had thought Philman wasn't the one to make up the nickname, and now he was sure of it. The car that was following parked behind them and all four doors opened at once. Out stepped the rest of the team, three men and two women.

"All right, let's get going," Steven said, opening his door. The rest of the passengers followed suit, and Derrek stepped out into the pleasant warmth of the German woods. The whole team gathered in a circle, and Amir spoke up.

"Everyone, if you have not been introduced, this is Derrek, our last-minute addition. I would love to give the same level of introduction we had on the ride here, but time is of the essence, so I would like the five of you to give your name and something interesting about yourself."

"Like kindergarten?" one of the women said.

"Exactly like kindergarten. Whoever wants to go first, please go ahead."

One of the men, who had dark skin and thick, round glasses, spoke up. "Hi, my name is Fredrick, and I raise bees."

The woman next to him, with short, purple hair said, "I'm Hanna, and I have a black belt in taekwondo."

One of the men who towered above the rest by at least eight inches said, "Hey there, my name's John. I play golf."

The last man left was roughly five feet tall but extremely toned. He said, "What's up? I'm Joey, but you can call me Jojo, and as you can probably tell, I do CrossFit."

The remaining woman was of Asian descent. Standing at attention, she said, "I'm Ann, and I spent eight years in the marines in IT."

Derrek felt a bit overwhelmed at the rapid-fire round of introductions, and Amir took notice of that. He leaned over and quietly said, "Do not worry. You will have plenty of time to get to know everyone."

Derrek nodded and put on a smile. He looked at the line of people in front of him and said, "Hello, everyone. I'm Derrek, and this is my first time doing any fieldwork."

Amir smiled, happy that it didn't freak him out too much. He clapped his hands loudly to get everyone's attention, and with a booming voice Derrek had not yet heard from him, he said, "OK, introductions are finished! Let us get our uniforms on and get to work!"

Everyone raised their fists in the air and cheered. Derrek had never seen anyone this enthusiastic about working. Without saying a word, Gary opened the trunk and brought out a box, which he set down in the middle of the group. Amir opened it and started handing out the contents, which Derrek saw were the uniforms Shepherd had mentioned the day before. He was given his and found it looked rather comfortable. Everyone else was already putting theirs on, so he did the same. The uniform was a one-piece that went over the clothes they wore. They were white with deep-blue trim, matching with the company logo. It seemed too small to even fit over Derrek's feet, but he found it was exceedingly stretchy but still comfortable. It went up to his neck and included built-in gloves and a hood, which Amir pointed out to him was optional to wear. It also had an exterior belt, on which everyone affixed their sidearms.

After everyone was suited up and ready to go, they started grouping up and splitting off, leaving him standing next to the cars with Amir.

Amir nudged him and said, "Ann and Hanna are going to calibrate the GENRAM. How about you join them?"

Derrek nodded and followed the two. They got to the GENRAM mere seconds before him and were already typing away at the display screens, data rolling down the screen at rates he could barely comprehend. He stared at the screen, eyes wide, trying his best to understand what was going on but to no avail.

Ann noticed Derrek was standing behind them, mouth agape, and instantly assumed the worst. She was ready to give him a piece of her mind before she realized he was staring at the screen. Upon closer inspection, she saw that his eyes were not stationary but were darting across the display, following bits of data. He was trying to make sense of it all.

"It's a lot to take in," she said, snapping Derrek out of his trance.

"The GENRAM takes every piece of genetic code and assigns it a twenty-eight-digit alphanumeric code based on its sequence. It then stores it all and compares its accrued list and compares it with the main database at Frostbyte HQ, deleting previously recorded sequences and adding the new ones. And because all GENRAMs use the same algorithms to produce their code. The worry of duplicates is infinitesimal, with a practical success rate of 99.999978 percent."

"Wow," Derrek said, looking back at the screen with his new perspective, "that's pretty amazing. So, what's it doing now?"

Hanna spoke up. "Right now, it's running through all we recorded yesterday, setting a filter so it doesn't record anything it already has fully mapped. Don't think that doesn't mean you need to get multiple samples of a species, though. Genetic variation is as prevalent in everything else as it is in humanity."

"OK," Derrek said, putting his hand on his chin, the pieces coming together in his head. "So we can't just sample one tree; we have to get the whole grove?"

Hanna snapped her fingers, transitioning into her pointing at him, and said, "Bingo. You're a natural."

A high-pitched *ding* came from the GENRAM, and the screen that until then had been filled with a seemingly random series of numbers and letters now had a light bulb in the center of a bright green background. Ann grunted positively and tapped several keys, bringing up a simple window resembling an empty text document with the word "ready" printed at the top.

"I'm guessing that means it's ready?" Derrek asked sincerely.

"That's right, Captain Obvious," Hanna said with a smirk. "Now the real work begins. It looks like the rest of the team is already hard at work gathering samples."

Looking around, he saw every member of the team. John, Aubry, and Joey were removing individual leaves from the surrounding trees, making sure not to damage the branches. Fredrick and Gary were scouring the grass looking for insects, placing them in small plastic containers. And Amir and Steven were setting up nonharmful traps for larger animals, mostly cages fit for catching squirrels.

Hanna slapped Derrek on the back and said, "We'd best get to it. Ann knows how to work that thing. We just gotta get stuff to feed into it."

Derrek smiled and nodded. "Right. So, what are we going after?"

"When we were setting up last week, I saw a boar. That orientation thing said there were a bunch of them around here. Getting some of that fur would look great on our reports."

Derrek looked at her with a mix of confusion and shock. "So, just the two of us are going after the only actually dangerous wildlife out here just so it'll look good on paper?"

Hanna looked disappointed. "Well, when you put it like that, everything sounds like a bad idea. If it's too much for you, I'm sure Gary and Freddy would love the company."

"Oh, I'm on board. I just wanted to make sure I had the plan right," Derrek said, instantly lifting Hanna's spirit. "Do you have some snares or something to set up? Maybe some bigger cages?"

Hanna smiled and slapped him on the back again. "You're all right, dude. We don't have cages big enough, and snares would hurt them too much. Company policy won't allow them. However …"

She led him to the rear SUV and popped the trunk, looking around for something. After several seconds, she found what she was after.

"There's nothing that says we can't tranquilize them."

In her hands were two small tubes that seemed to be made of a combination of PVC piping, rubber, and metal bands, along with hefty amounts of duct tape. She handed one to Derrek, who accepted it, then handed him a clear plastic container containing several darts with orange feathers for tails.

"All you really need to know is to make sure you don't breathe in when you're ready to shoot. Otherwise, you're gonna have a real bad time. The rest is just like firing a gun, and you're packing, so you clearly figured that one out."

Derrek examined the blowgun and found it heavier than expected, around two or three pounds. It had a very intuitive design, one end having a mouthpiece. The only thing that threw him off was that there appeared to be a rail along the side of it for mounting a scope. She handed him a satchel with a holster for it and adorned one herself.

"Ideally," she said, "we'd be able to tag one of them in this clearing, but with all the activity, there's no chance in hell of them coming around here. You ever gone hunting before?"

"No, but I used to be top notch at tracking stray cats."

Hanna looked at him quizzically. "You must have had a weird childhood."

Derrek raised his eyebrows and shook his head. "You have no idea."

The two checked with Amir to let him know about their hunting trip, and he gave the go-ahead, advising they keep their wits about them before going back to arming his cages.

Hanna led him into the woods in a seemingly random direction, heading in a straight line for almost half an hour, silently moving through between the trees and through the bushes. They came to a small clearing, and they thought it was a good chance to catch their breath, as there was a minimally rotted log they could sit on. Their satchels had been packed with water and trail mix, and they both took several swigs from their bottles of water.

Hanna noticed how quiet Derrek was, and found it odd, since almost everyone she meets asked about her hair within the first five minutes. He agreed to come out there with her with no resistance, so she knew he didn't have any apprehensions about her presence. It seemed to her the silence was more respectful than awkward. Regardless, the quiet was starting to get to her, so she decided to break the silence.

"When I was growing up, I would go hunting with my dad every chance we got," she said, setting down her water bottle. "Most weekends, he and my mom would fight, so that's what we did to cool off. I'll never forget my first buck, an eight-pointer. We tracked him down for hours!" She started to laugh. "We eventually caught him, and I got him right in the heart. We got him stuffed, and I still have him hanging in my living room back home." She turned to him and said, "Tell me something about your childhood."

Derrek's eyes flashed with sadness, and he hesitated before saying, "There really isn't that much to tell."

"Then tell me something. I just gave you a grade-A hunting story. It's your turn."

Derrek took a deep breath and said, "I don't have any memories of my family. All I know is they died in a fire. I was told I survived because my mother dragged me out of it before she collapsed. I can't even remember what she looked like, and none of the pictures survived. Lucky me, right?" he said, chuckling meekly. "The foster system was awful. Too many kids moving around way too much, and I just wanted some … consistency, I guess. So I ran, and homelessness was just as bad."

He stopped, but Hanna got the feeling that he was still reliving it, and only stopped saying it out loud. She was stunned but felt it would be rude to try and change the subject.

"Well, it looks like you got yourself out of that struggle. Maybe you're luckier than you think. I mean, it seems to me you got the shitty part of your life over with early on."

Derrek looked at her and smiled. He was glad she didn't just go silent. He could tell she could at least understand his pain.

"I hope so," he said, the sadness draining from his eyes. "After all, I've got this fulfilling job, and I've met so many interesting people over the past few days. Maybe I am in the upswing."

She slapped him on the back and said, "There you go! Eyes up, young buck. We got a boar to find!"

Derrek laughed. "That's funny. My desk neighbor calls me that too."

She stood up and stretched. "Sounds like they've got good taste in nicknames! Now, come on. I want to get back for lunch," she said, reaching out her hand, which he accepted, and she pulled him to his feet. "Now, where do we …" she said, trailing off and fixing her gaze on a particular spot on the ground. She approached it and squatted, examining the dirt, smelling a small portion of it. "One was here. These tracks are pretty fresh, maybe fifteen minutes old, heading north. Its den might be around here somewhere."

"Wow, you really know your tracking."

"Why, thank you. I can find just about anything. One time, my friend flew me in from three states away to help find his cat. Had it back and pooping in a box within the day!"

The two shared a laugh and headed in the direction of the tracks, Hanna taking the lead and Derrek following close behind, both brandishing their blowguns—loaded, of course. They went back to their silence, but there was no tension, just the silence of hunters.

They were following the tracks for several minutes until they heard a rustling from a few feet away. They both froze in their tracks before slowly moving into a nearby bush, concealing themselves. Coming out from the surrounding brush was a large boar, snorting and grunting loudly, sniffing the air. Its tusks were relatively small, but they were both in awe of the size of it.

Hanna nudged Derrek and whispered, "I'm gonna count down from three. When I say go, we both shoot."

"Both of us? Isn't that a bit overkill?" Derrek whispered back.

"Look at the size of her. I'm sure only one dart would just piss her off. Just use both hands and keep it trained on her."

Derrek nodded, agreeing to the plan. They readied their blowguns, steadying their breath, focusing on the boar.

"Three …" she whispered as the boar started looking around, apparently picking up a smell.

"Two …" she continued as Derrek narrowed his gaze, staring directly at the boar's flank, marking it as his target.

"One …" she whispered as Derrek took a deep breath and the boar noticed the smell was coming from them.

"Go!" she said at full volume, leaving only a split second between her words and her shooting the dart. Even though she took the extra time, she still landed the dart before Derrek could shoot, but he managed to land it on the boar as well, not quite hitting the flank but making the target.

The boar squealed, rearing slightly before running into the bushes it came from, leaving a trail of broken branches and trampled grass behind her.

"So, was that good, or did we just royally screw up?" Derrek asked, having no frame of reference.

"It's real good, all that running around will get the tranquilizers working faster. Really gets the blood pumping. If we were actually hunting, it'd be a bit of a problem. You wanna get the kill on the first shot when it comes to deer; otherwise, the meat might go bad if it runs too much. We want her tired though, make her take a nice nap."

"So, it's female? How can you tell?"

"The females have smaller tusks, and she's big enough that her being young is out of the question. She might be running back to her den if it's nearby, and if that's the case, she might have piglets, which means more samples for us. Odds are we won't even have to tranquilize them."

Hanna led him through the bush where the boar had run, following the path of broken branches and trampled grass. They followed the path a little more than minutes before coming to what Derrek thought looked like a small cave, which is where the trail ended. They kept quiet so as not to startle what might be inside.

Hanna crouched down low and looked into the dirt cave, smiling at what she saw. Derrek heard what sounded like snoring and high-pitched noises coming from inside.

"This is her den," Hanna said. "The darts last for about ten minutes once they set in, so we'd best get to work."

She pulled a small flashlight out from her satchel, turning it on and putting it in her mouth. She then lay prone and crawled into the den, Derrek following suit. The space inside was much larger than he expected, and he was able to sit up without having to crane his neck.

In the center of the den was the boar, snoring loudly while around ten piglets nuzzled her, trying to wake her up. Hanna was already holding one of the piglets in one hand and a pair of scissors in the other. She held it over a small plastic container, snipping a few hairs off, making sure they fell into the container.

"Try to get all of them. All we need is a few hairs from each. You've got some containers in your bag," she said as she labeled her container "Piglet 1" and moved on to another piglet.

Derrek rummaged around his bag for the tools and began snipping the hairs off of the piglets, marking the containers as he went. He got to his fourth one when Hanna got to her fifth, and they were out of piglets, left only with the boar. It was sleeping on its side, the darts sticking directly upward, which she removed carefully and placed in a container labeled "used darts."

They worked together, getting the sample they had sought for the past hour. They finally sampled all the members of the den and were ready to head out, but Hanna stopped before they left.

"Hold up," she said quietly, pulling a camera out from her satchel. "I want to get a picture."

Derrek smiled and nodded, thinking it would be nice. She gestured for him to get in frame, crouching next to the sleeping boar next to her, and snapped a selfie, flashing brightly, partly blinding both of them. When they came to, they both looked at the camera to see how the picture had turned out. Hanna seemed satisfied with the results, but something caught her eye.

She looked closer and her eyes grew wide as she saw the boar's eyes were open, reflecting the light from the flash. She turned to see an awaking boar, slowly crawling to its feet.

"We gotta go, now!" she said, heading toward the entrance with Derrek following close. They heard an angry squeal coming from behind them as they exited the den, and they ran in the direction they came from, hopeful that the boar was too groggy to follow them.

They finally slowed down when they got to where they tagged the boar and made sure they couldn't hear it behind them. They were in the clear, and they got everything they were looking for. They caught their breath and started to laugh, happy they got out of it unscathed.

"That went well," Hanna said. "Those tusks could have done a real number on us!"

"I don't doubt it. Orientation said a lot about how dangerous they can be, especially when we're neck-deep in their territory!"

They laughed and took a few more swigs from their respective bottles of water, resting up for the trek back. Derrek considered eating some of the trail mix, but Hanna advised him that Gary's sandwiches were top-notch and lunch would roll around soon after they got back, so he held off.

They made their way back to the small clearing they found themselves in earlier, allowing Hanna to get her bearings and lead them back to base camp. Along the way, Derrek saw that she had marked the trees as she passed them earlier, establishing the route back. He was just amazed he hadn't noticed it earlier. They joked the whole way back, making an unprecedented amount of pig-related puns, their favorite being "hog wild."

When they finally regrouped with the team, the sun hung high in the sky, signifying it was around noon. When Amir saw the two of them emerging from the woods, he called out to everyone, "All right, everyone. Let us break to enjoy the lunch Gary made for us!" to which everyone responded with cheering.

Derrek and Hanna stopped by the GENRAM to drop off their samples, then joined the rest of the team around the cooler, where Gary was handing out sandwiches in little plastic baggies. The people who were working in the dirt took their suits half off, freeing their hands. Ann, who had been working on the GENRAM the entire time saw no need, as her gloves were still relatively clean.

When Derrek got his sandwich, the first thing he noticed was the smell of smoked turkey that wafted from the baggie as soon as he opened it. Everyone was several bites in before he sunk his teeth into it, but as soon as he did, he was struck with the deep, smoky flavor of the turkey, the rich, but not overwhelming mayo and mustard, the crunchy, tangy pickles, and the potato bread that wrapped it all together. It was possibly the best turkey sandwich he'd ever had.

He saw everyone laughing and enjoying themselves, praising Gary on his remarkable sandwich craftsmanship, comparing notes and telling of interesting finds, including Fredrick finding an albino beetle. He had never seen as many people who loved their jobs as much as they did. Even Ann, whom Derrek gathered was normally cold, was smiling and laughing with everyone else. He decided to enjoy the moment, joining Hanna in telling the story about the boar, chiming in whenever she exaggerated a bit too much.

"And I swear, that boar must have been three hundred pounds! With tusks out to here!" she said, holding her hands as far in front of her face as possible.

"She wasn't that big—two hundred, maybe," Derrek said, laughing along.

Hanna glared at him, then smiled and said, "Either way, I don't see anyone else … *bringing home the bacon.*"

Everyone stared at her blankly, Joey stopping midbite to stare. The forest was deadly quiet until a loud snort broke the silence.

Everyone turned to face the source, and they were all surprised to find it to be Ann.

"Was that you, Ann?" Steven asked.

She coughed lightly. "Yes, I thought it was funny. Her *ham*-fisted attempt at a pun, I mean."

The silence persisted for a full beat, then the clearing roared with laughter. Ann sat still, smiling while everyone else writhed in laughter, Derrek keeled over, and Hanna just sat, clearly angry her joke didn't land as well as hers did.

The tone was set for the rest of the lunch break, which was a half hour to give everyone a chance to rest their minds and bodies alike. Everyone was finished with their sandwiches in the first ten minutes, and they spent the remainder of their time carrying on with their jokes and stories, reminding Derrek of the ride that morning.

When lunch was over, everyone went back to work in unison, Ann jumping right back into processing the samples Hanna and Derrek collected and everyone getting back to gather samples. Hanna wanted to go on another hunting trip for another boar, but Amir didn't want anyone straying too far off, as they were in the back half of the day, so she settled on setting additional traps.

Amir instructed Derrek to work with Joey on collecting plant samples, and he did, with only a mild apprehension that the rest of his day would be filled with him talking about CrossFit. It was mentioned a handful of times, but the majority of the time was spent properly training him on collecting leaves and severing small branches. Derrek learned of Joey's background, a master's in botany and a minor in physical therapy, and it showed in the way he gently and respectfully collected samples that were the least viable. He made sure not to harm any plants as a whole and even removed several diseased and dying sections from smaller plants, as the DNA remained intact. Even once the samples were progressed, he planted the branches he took, allowing them to take root, and sprinkled the leaves and petals around them as fertilization.

It was clear to Derrek that nature was important to him, and he was proud to work with someone with such a passion for what he did. He felt the same could be said for everyone on the team. He could see it in the way Hanna enjoyed tracking the boar. He could see it in the way Ann attended to the GENRAM. He could even taste it in Gary's sandwiches. Seeing all that passion fueled him to strive for greatness and pushed him to go all-out for the rest of the day.

Amir called everyone back to the cars around five, praising everyone on their progress, especially Derrek. He gave the day's report, bringing everyone onto the same page on what they gathered and pointing out specific insects and plants to be on the lookout for, Fredrick and Joey whispering to each other, apparently betting on which of them could bring in more of the high-demand samples in their respective groups.

After the debriefing, everyone loaded up their materials in the Conex, and Ann shut down the GENRAM while Gary and Steven wrapped a tarp around it for protection. When all was said and done, they all took off their uniforms and headed back to the hotel.

Derrek was glad to be back to work; even though he had been training for the past week, he still wanted to be productive. The ride back was similar to the one that morning, everyone talking about the day, talking like friends, having a good time. It caught everyone off guard when they were back at the hotel. Even though they had been driving for an hour and a half, it felt like almost nothing.

Everyone split up and went back to their rooms, almost all of them agreeing to have dinner together, the only ones sitting out being Amir, who had to give his report and Derrek's fieldwork evaluation to Shepherd and Philman; and Gary, who simply shook his head no and gestured to his cooler, implying that he had more sandwiches to make. They all shook hands and made their way back to their rooms.

Derrek showered and changed into nicer attire, and with still forty-five minutes until dinner, he decided to check his phone for the first time since that morning, as it had been inside his suit all day. He was disappointed to have not heard anything from Jeffrey, but it wasn't a surprise, as he didn't see his truck in the parking lot. The thought hadn't occurred before; that truck must have been his personal vehicle, but Derrek saw nothing about a truck on the requisition forms.

He spent the rest of his free time playing a fantasy hero collecting game Steven had recommended on his phone, and although he was initially bombarded with "deals" for new players, he found it was pretty fun. Before he knew it, it was time to go to dinner.

He met everyone just outside the dining hall and they managed to get a table big enough for all of them. The standup comedian he had seen with Jeffrey almost a week before was performing again, this time with much less material about horses. Joey heckled him but made sure not to make everyone hate him, keeping it PG for the sake of Frostbyte's public image.

Everyone got different dishes, but the aroma from all the different meals mixed into something truly remarkable, a true symphony of delicious smells and mouth-watering scents. As they ate, they joked and laughed, telling stories of the best food they ever had, barring anything they had since visiting the Schadenfreude. There was a slightly heated argument between Joey and Hanna about who was the better arm wrestler, but a quick, two-out-of-three match made it clear that Hanna reigned supreme. He seemed disappointed, but that quickly faded when he gave her a sporting handshake.

Derrek rarely ate with groups of people, despite being invited to several formal functions by Shale, which he usually turned down in favor of work, but none felt as comfortable as this. He didn't see coworkers or employees of Frostbyte or a group of well-versed scholars. He saw people he was quickly considering to be friends. He wondered if this was how all gatherings of friends went, as he had very few friends outside of work, but he enjoyed it.

Derrek felt at peace, and part of him hoped to have dinners like that with a family of his own someday.

It was Friday, and the team was short-staffed. One of the other teams working farther south was falling behind, and since Amir's team was so far ahead, Philman decided to send Aubrey, John, Joey, and Gary with them. They still took both cars, as they needed the equipment, but they were significantly less crowded than the rest of the week. The time was nearing 2:30, and Amir called everyone together.

"If I may have your attention. I would like to propose something I believe everyone will enjoy. Studies show that Friday is the least productive day of the week, and I am sure we have met our quota for the week, not to mention our current lack of staff, so I would like for us to take the rest of the day off."

Everyone got excited and started murmuring to each other, talking about what they planned on doing with the extra two and a half hours. Amir put his hand up to get them to stop, and they did.

"But company policy states that we cannot leave the equipment unattended until five passes, so somebody will have to stay behind. They will be paid for their time and will essentially have to just keep guard until then. If there are no volunteers, we can draw straws, or we can all stay behind if you feel this would be unfair."

The murmuring began again, this time more nervous than excited. They were all deliberating with each other when Derrek raised his hand.

"I'll volunteer to stay back."

Everyone looked at him in shock and awe. Then they all erupted into thanks and slaps on the back.

"Very good," said Amir. "Let us get everything locked down, and we will leave you to your alone time with nature."

Derrek smiled and nodded, then joined everyone who was already working hard to wrap everything up. After the GENRAM was shut down, everyone worked together to move it into the Conex, keeping it safe for the weekend. They got all of their materials in order and everyone aside from Derrek loaded into one of the cars, leaving the other for Derrek to have a ride back to the hotel.

Before leaving, Amir told him that the directions back were already programmed into the GPS, and handed him a fifty-euro note, winking and thanking him for staying behind. He waved as they drove off and immediately went to the cooler, grabbing a bottle of water for himself, happy to find there were sandwiches left, since almost half the team was elsewhere.

He decided the best use of his time was to take inventory, and so he did—three times. He grew bored quickly but remained upbeat and did his best to entertain himself while still trying to be productive. He started to take some plant samples before thinking that sitting for the whole weekend may have an adverse effect on the DNA, so he ultimately decided against it.

Boredom began to truly set in around 3:30, but then he remembered he had downloaded a podcast about genetics on his phone. He intended to study up on it as well as botany, entomology, and information technology over the weekend in hopes of being better equipped for the work ahead.

He put in his headphones and decided to clean his sidearm. Jeffrey had taught him the proper technique along their training and gave him a set of tools to work with. He laid out a plain cloth and began disassembling his handgun. He hadn't taken it out of its holster since getting his certification, and he was glad of that.

Time passed as he cleaned and oiled the gun, listening to three people share their knowledge on genetics, laughing at their own jokes and telling a lot of stories from their college days. The podcast wrapped up around the same time he finished reassembling the gun, but he hadn't downloaded another episode, so he wrapped up his headphones and put his phone away.

He only had another forty-five minutes before he could leave, and he thought he might have a fourth go at inventory. Before he got to the Conex, however, he thought he heard a distant rumbling. He went to the edge of the clearing, facing the seemingly endless woods, listening to the sound. He could tell it was getting louder, or possibly closer.

He drew his sidearm, having no idea of what it could be. His palms began to sweat, and he started breathing heavily. Adrenaline filled his veins, and he stared into the unknown, ready to fight for his life, despite not even being sure it was in danger.

The noise had grown from a low rumble to what sounded like a roaring stampede. He was about to start firing blindly, hoping to hit whatever was heading toward him, when the forest suddenly went deathly quiet. He looked around and listened intently for a full minute and heard nothing, concluding that whatever it was, it had gone around him. He holstered his handgun and started walking back to the car to get another water.

Halfway back, he heard some movement from behind him, prompting him to turn around. He saw a deep-red vaguely human shape streak past him and did his best to keep his eyes on it. The shape stopped close to the other end of the clearing, looking behind it at Derrek.

"Ohshitduck!" it yelled out at him in a booming, commanding voice.

Derrek tried to turn around to see what it was yelling about and suddenly felt as if his entire skull had caved in. He felt every nerve send every pain signal it could, and his perspective suddenly shifted an entire ninety degrees to his right, making the world look sideways to him. He felt himself hit the ground with his still-skewed perspective, then felt nothing.

Over Derrek's body, which was twisted beyond survival, with half his spine pulled out of place along with his head, somehow not breaking the skin, each vertebrae pressing against it, making clear outlines of every bump, stood two figures. The first was a man in a red coat that hung down to his shins, leaning over to check his pulse before realizing he might have more luck checking his wrist. The other figure towered over him, around ten feet tall, wearing a black cloak that seemed to be emitting black smoke out of every opening. The man in red let go of Derrek's arm, which slumped onto the ground with a dull *thud*.

"Well, bud, you really screwed the pooch this time," the man in red said.

"Me? This is all on you!" the towering figure replied in a deep, ghastly tone.

"Hey, I'm not the one who broke the most basic of rules."

"It is not *my* fault that you've been cheating me for thirty years!"

"And it's not *my* fault that you never provided the coin for the flip. Besides, I know damn well you can't collect, even if I did lose."

"*Quiet!*" the figure yelled, apparently intimidating the entire forest into a state of silence. They heard Derrek grunt, as if he were dreaming. The two figures stepped back and watched as the body's limbs straightened and began to move to get the body standing again, despite a complete lack of central structure. He rose slowly, slumped over backward, defying gravity and coming to his feet. His torso straightened out despite his spine being in his neck and his eyes opened, the right eye, as always, was a dark brown, but the left was a bright, glowing green.

The two figures stood in silence and watched as he rose to its feet, the green eye moving independently and switching between both of them rapidly.

The man in red nudged the towering dark figure. "See, Boyd? You done goofed for real this time."

"By the eternals, Grim is going to have my ass over this," Boyd said, looking up into the air in confusion.

"It's your own fault man, I mean—"

"Did you just make the narrator call me Boyd?"

"Shut up, Boyd. You've got bigger problems than your name. How hard did you hit him?"

"Hard enough to kill you."

"All right. Real bad day for you then," the man in red said. Then, cupping his hands to amplify his voice toward Derrek, he added, "Hey! Deadhead! You all right?"

Derrek turned his body toward the man, then put his right hand to his head, which was still skewed. With one swift motion, he pushed his spine back into place, sounding like a thousand joints popping at once, causing both the man and Boyd to cringe visibly despite the black cloak. He was suddenly back to his normal self; his eye remained green but had stopped glowing and he started rubbing his neck, as to him, it hurt slightly. He looked up to see the two standing across from him and jumped back in surprise, stumbling backward and falling on the ground, crawling backward away from them.

The man in red tried to follow him and called out as he went, "Kid, that was honestly metal as hell, and I know all this crazy shit you're seeing is all way too new and way too weird to accept all at once. I mean, look at this crazy tall dude behind me. Dude looks like a goth circus tent. You may be afraid of him, but right now, you and I can kick his ass if we work together." He was standing over Derrek now, offering his hand, and with a warm smile, he said, "I just need you to trust me."

Derrek looked up at the man. He couldn't tell how he knew,

but he could tell he was telling the truth. Looking at Boyd, he saw he was taken aback by what the man in red said and was readying himself for battle. Without another thought, he grabbed the man by the wrist and was pulled to his feet.

"Ha-ha! Now things are gonna get interesting!" the man yelled, turning to face Boyd and then asking Derrek, "You know how to fight?"

"I got into a few scraps when I was a kid, but none in the past fifteen years. I've got a gun, though," Derrek said, drawing his weapon.

"Oh, you're American. I just took a shot in the dark with that English, and unless you got some real specific runes carved on your bullets, that'll just piss him off. Do use it, though. Might buy you a few precious seconds to do what you gotta."

"Then I might not be of any use," Derrek said, remarkably calm. "If a gun won't stop him, what am I going to be able to do?"

The man chuckled. "You don't know it yet, but your punches are about to be stronger than just about any gun."

Derrek was about to protest, but the man said loudly, "Shush," then pointed to Boyd, who was now opening his robe. As the cloth moved away, his emaciated form was revealed. He had very little flesh, looking more like a skeleton than a man. He was holding a scythe as tall as he was, ready to attack at any moment.

He stared in awe as this creature, which completely challenged everything Derrek thought about the world slowly started stepping toward him. How his heart wasn't pounding out of his chest was beyond him, but he felt more aware than usual. He could see every falling leaf, every passing ant. He could even feel the exact direction of the wind, all of which he chalked up to adrenaline.

He broke his gaze when he saw the red man move, and when he looked at him, he saw he had a sword in each hand. His left held what looked like an ordinary katana, albeit with a serrated back to the blade. The sword in his right hand, however, was made of black metal, double-edged, and seemed taller than Derrek was from tip to pommel, almost a foot wide and at least three inches thick down the center, with two semicircle outcroppings halfway along the blade next to each other on both sides, forming spikes as long as spearheads jutting out beyond the width of the blade. Along the blade he saw seemingly endless carvings, some of which hurt to focus on. He got the feeling there was no earthly way anyone could hold something like it, let alone use it in a fight.

"Take this. You're gonna need it," the man said, handing the katana to Derrek. He was reluctant at first, but something told him it was the right thing to do, so he took the sword, holding it at the ready with both hands. He had never held a sword before, aside from a few fencing lessons he took with Shale when his usual partner broke his leg, but he felt right holding it.

The man in red grinned. "Follow my lead, trust your body, and for the love of whatever god you might worship, don't … get … hit."

Derrek nodded and narrowed his gaze onto Boyd, who had taken another few steps toward him, covering a lot of ground due to his gait. The man in red got into a crouching stance, holding his sword high, effortlessly rotating it like a slow propeller. Boyd stopped in his tracks, and the three of them stood in tense silence, each side waiting for the other to strike first. A stray leaf floated into the middle of the clearing, and all their eyes fixated on it as it slowly floated down, swaying back and forth as it drifted to the ground.

Just before it landed, the man in red yelled, "Now!" and sprang into action, lunging forward, almost floating above the grass, never taking a step until he was just in front of Boyd. When he jumped up to eye level with him, he brought down his sword in a one-handed downward strike, giving him only a split second to deflect it with his scythe. The man stayed in the air for several seconds, slicing and slashing in a blinding flurry of strikes with a single hand, which Boyd struggled to defend against, causing him to fall back as the man landed gracefully on the ground, propping his sword on his shoulder, clearly taunting him.

Derrek realized he should do something, as standing there watching might be even worse for his health. He took a deep breath and thought of what Jeffrey would have said.

"Come on, Derrek. You have one job right now! Keep the GENRAM safe. That skeleton is a major threat to not only that but the whole damn forest! Now, get your ass in gear and go mess that up freak's life!"

Jeffrey's voice rang in his ears as he started running into battle, caught off guard by his own speed; after only a couple of seconds, he had already almost caught up with the man! He moved ahead, passing him and slashing at Boyd, catching him off guard and tearing off a large portion of his cloak. Boyd retreated even further back, clearly cautious of the situation he was in.

His cloak was in tatters and would serve only to hinder his movement, so he tore it away, exposing his skeletal face. Glowing green lights floated in place of his eyes in empty sockets, he wore a permanent rotting smile, and his armor looked old and worn. He went in an instant from an enigma to an imposing threat, worrying Derrek and making the man in red smile even wider.

Black smoke poured out of Boyd's mouth as he yelled, his words matching with the jaw movements, "Damn it! Why the hell is this happening now? I should be gone by now, or Grim should have at least sent support! Where is everyone?"

"If I were a betting man, I'd say someone caught wind of your little scheme a loooooong while back and is letting you pay for it. Although, odds are you're just having an off day," the man said, stabbing his sword into the ground and letting it stand. He reached into his pocket and pulled out a silver coin, which he began to flip absentmindedly, infuriating Boyd and causing his eyes to glow more intensely.

The man flipped the coin high as Boyd charged at him, scythe raised, screaming at the top of his lungs, assuming he had them. Just before he made contact, the man leaned back entirely at his knees, completely avoiding the attack. He stood back up straight and caught the coin, which he slapped onto his opposite wrist, covering it with his hand as Boyd turned around, eyes glowing even brighter.

"Hey, kid, call it," he said to Derrek nonchalantly.

"Seriously?"

"Yeah, man. Heads or tails?"

Derrek looked back and forth from him and Boyd, who also seemed baffled at the casual way this man was handling the situation. He threw his empty hand up in a *whatever* gesture and said, "Heads, I guess."

The man uncovered the coin to show it had, in fact, landed on heads, which made him say, "Nice one! Have at it."

"What?"

"You won, it's your go," he said, leaning against his sword and crossing his arms.

Derrek was baffled, but a part of him said to do as he said and have at it. He lunged at Boyd who was holding his ground and began slicing wildly, occasionally firing his pistol to throw him off much faster than he could have ever imagined. Boyd struck back, but he was able to dodge the blows almost unconsciously, deflecting several attacks and leaning completely into some, giving him the chance to catch the towering man off guard. He thrust his sword into Boyd's leg, catching the serrated edge between his tibia and fibula and pulling back, completely shattering both bones, causing him to collapse under his own weight.

He never knew he could do anything like this, but he felt powerful, as if he were playing a video game. His reflexes were beyond anything he had seen from anyone, and he had never experienced even an ounce of the strength he felt at that moment. He felt like he could take on the world if he wanted to.

Boyd screamed in agony to the surprise of both Derrek and the man in red, who were under the impression he didn't have nerves, let alone could feel pain. He tried to prop himself up with his scythe but was completely unable to do so and ended up falling again. He tried once more, but before he could maintain his balance, something came over Derrek and he did the same to Boyd's other leg, causing him to collapse.

Boyd seemed to be breathing heavily, clearly in intense pain, his scythe just out of reach as he tried to grab it to no avail. The man in red winced as Boyd's bones shattered, and he held back laughter as he tried to fight back in vain, eventually giving up, lying on the ground, conserving what little strength he had left. Black smoke poured out from his broken bones where marrow would have been, and his breathing began to steady.

"Damn … you …" he struggled to say, staring at the man in red. "You … should have … lost …"

"Bud, you never had a chance. I mean, look how things turned out. The hands of fate are clearly not in your favor."

"Go … to hell."

"Sure, I'll meet you there," he said. Then, looking at Derrek, he said, "All right, he's had enough. You can back off now."

But Derrek didn't hear him and clearly wasn't listening. He stuck his sword into the ground, walked around Boyd's body, and was now standing between him and the man in red, looking down at his skeletal face, not saying a word. He crouched down and put his hands at the sides of Boyd's skull and stared into his eye sockets.

The man in red was confused and called out, "Hey, what're you doing? The fight's over. We won." But Derrek continued to ignore him.

Boyd began to panic, trying to fight back, but was completely unable even to lift his arms. The space around the two began to glow the same shade of green his eye had been earlier, completely blinding the man, who couldn't see what happened next. He felt his existence unravel. Derrek's mouth opened inhumanly wide, sucking the life right out of him. His screams of agony echoed across the entire forest, causing flocks of birds miles away to fly into the air and herds of deer to bound away. He began to completely disintegrate, forming into a bright orange stream of light, tapering off as he was seemingly being eaten by Derrek.

The scream persisted until there was nothing left of Boyd save for a burnt outline of his form on the grass and his scythe lying several feet away. Derrek stood, the light fading, allowing the man to get a look at the situation. His eyes grew wide after realizing what he had just witnessed, and he immediately reached into his coat, pulling out a large revolver, which he pointed at Derrek.

Derrek turned around and faced him, his left eye glowing green and his right one completely unresponsive. The glowing stopped, and he came to all at once, rubbing his eyes and temples, experiencing a very painful headache. When he opened his eyes and saw the man holding a gun, they stared at each other for a full beat, after which he slowly put his hands up.

"Please, don't shoot," he said with no idea what else to say.

The man had a puzzled look on his face. He lowered the gun slightly, no longer aiming for center of mass. He let a few more seconds pass before saying, "Is that really all you have to say?"

Derrek shrugged his shoulders, still keeping his hands up.

The man's face went from confusion to one of intense thought. Still keeping the gun up, he said, "So, let me get this straight. You, some completely ordinary dude, just killed what I wouldn't blame you for thinking was the Grim Reaper, something that isn't supposed to be able to die, I might add, and then fucking ate him and just turned around, put your hands up, and asked me not to kill you?"

"I ... ate him?" Derrek asked with a surprised expression on his face.

They stared at each other for another few seconds before the man began laughing intensely, doing his best to catch his breath, struggling to stand up straight as he keeled over, howling with humor. Derrek watched for a full thirty seconds before thinking it was all right to put his hands down back at his side.

After the man caught his breath, he twirled the gun, tucking it back into his coat. "You're a riot, man!" He pulled his sword out from the ground and stuck it into his coat as well, defying logic and confusing Derrek immensely. He walked up to him and held his hand out. "The name's Discord, by the way."

He reached his hand out to shake Discord's, which he grabbed at his wrist in a Spartan handshake. "I'm Derrek, Derrek Snowe."

Discord shook his head and said, "No, no, I wanna hear your warrior name."

"What's that?"

Discord looked shocked. "Seriously? That trend fizzled out?" he asked as Derrek shrugged again, clearly having no idea what he was talking about. He sighed loudly. "All right, you've got your real name, the one you use pretty much every day, the one everyone knows you by, but then there's your warrior name. That's what they call you on the battlefield when you wage war, when you're with your comrades. That's pretty much what anyone you've either fought alongside or crossed blades with knows you by, what your brothers-in-arms chant whenever you have a victory drink."

"I think I get it. It's like a nickname."

Discord snapped his fingers. "Exactly, the only difference being you can pick your own without seeming like a total wang. So I'll ask again, what's your name?"

Derrek looked down for a second, thinking.

"Don't overthink it. Just say whatever feels natural."

He looked Discord right in the eyes and said, "Havok."

Discord grinned and said, "Now that's a badass name! Let me guess: with a *K* at the end?"

"How'd you know?"

"Because I can read."

"What?"

"Never mind. We got bigger fish to fry now that we're properly introduced, namely, finding a place with enough booze to serve us for a couple of hours. Shouldn't be too hard, us being in Ukraine and all."

"Ukraine? We're in Germany."

"Really? Damn, Boyd chased me a long way. But that's much better. The taps flow with beer here!" he said, fists at his side, laughing deeply.

Derrek hadn't gotten a chance to look at Discord clearly before now. He had an imposing presence, standing at approximately six and a half feet tall, with black hair that fell past his shoulders and parted at the center. His olive-skinned face was devoid of blemishes or scars, aside from a small portion of what he assumed was a tribal tattoo reaching up the base of his neck, and he had a small patch of hair directly under his lower lip, covering his chin, resembling a goatee without a mustache. Under his coat, he wore a plain black shirt that had been stitched and repaired many times and a pair of dark blue jeans in similar condition, with a belt buckle that had a symbol on it resembling an X, with a line drawn connecting the top and bottom left corners.

Discord began walking toward the car before stopping at the scythe, which was still lying on the ground. He picked it up halfway up the handle and began sliding it into his coat, not affecting the fabric despite being about ten feet long, then grabbed the katana and did the same. Derrek was in awe for a brief moment before realizing that might have been one of the more normal things he had seen that day. He brushed it off and made a mental note to ask him about it later.

"C'mon, I know a great pub nearby."

"You only just found out what country you're in. How could you possibly know what's nearby?"

"I always know a good pub nearby. It's one of the first things I look for whenever I get anywhere."

Derrek laughed and joined him on the way to the car. After making sure the Conex was secure, they both climbed in with Discord at the wheel. After realizing he was still wearing his uniform, he got out to remove it and caught a look at himself in the mirror. He was absolutely shocked by what he saw. His hair had turned stark white, and his left eye was now green!

It didn't seem dyed; it was as if his natural hair color had completely changed. He got back in the car and said, "When were you going to tell me about my hair?"

"After we got to the pub. There's a lot to fill you in on that's gonna totally rock your world view. I've found that having a drink in your hand helps the truth go down easier."

Derrek nodded, still fixated on his hair, which he focused on for the entire ride.

Discord pulled into the parking lot of Brier Faust's Bierhaus, which Derrek recognized as the place he had gone to with Jeffrey over the weekend, and the two entered to a warm greeting from the jolly-looking man at the entrance. The interior was dimly lit, and there were few patrons, but everyone there was clearly familiar with the staff based on how casually they interacted with each other. The walls had license plates from every country in the EU, as well as a good amount from States, and over the bar, on the rear wall, hung a long wooden sculpture of a briar patch.

"Guten tag! Deutsch oder Englisch?"

"Either's fine. We're fluent in both," Discord said, leading Derrek to a booth along the wall, turning down the menus the man offered.

"What did he ask?" Derrek asked as they took their seats.

"He was asking if we wanted a German- or English-speaking barmaid, but I know exactly what we're getting: four metric gallons of their microbrew."

Derrek looked worried. "I don't think I could physically drink that much."

"Trust me, bud, your metabolism is working a whole hell of a lot harder now. You might get a buzz, but I doubt it'll be enough to get you loopy."

Again, Derrek had no reason to believe him, but something told him that Discord was being truthful. A barmaid came to their table wearing a blue frilled dress and holding a notepad and a pen. With a thick accent, she said, "What can I get for you gentlemen?"

"Two pitchers of the house special and a bowl of assorted nuts, if you would be so kind," Discord said, winking at her.

"Coming right up," she said after writing it down on her notepad. She went behind the bar and started filling pitchers.

"This place has the fourth best microbrew I've ever had and the eighth-best beer overall," Discord said, trying to break the silence between him and Derrek, who just raised his eyebrows and nodded.

The barmaid came back after an uncomfortable moment with a tray. She placed the two comically oversized pitchers, two large mugs, and a big bowl of nuts on the table, then went to another table without saying a word. Discord filled the mugs, giving one to Derrek and taking large gulps of his own.

After taking his first sip, Derrek was struck with a mixture of sweetness and spices, with undertones of hazelnut and the faintest traces of apple.

"Wow, you weren't kidding! This is great!"

Discord had emptied his mug, which he slammed down on the table. He took a breath and said, "Told you. If there's one thing I know, it's booze." He refilled his mug and went back to drinking, barely making a dent in the pitcher.

Derrek took a few more sips and Discord finished another two mugs, and after his third, he put a plain expression on his face. He was clearly in thought for several seconds before he spoke.

"All right. Where do you wanna start?"

"Excuse me?"

"We've got a lot of ground to cover, and this place closes in, like, six hours."

"That sounds like a lot of time to me. Is there really that much to explain?"

Discord looked at him with a sideways glance for a few seconds. "Your hair turned white before you ate a reaper. There's a lot to cover."

Derrek looked up at the small tuft of hair he could see. "Fair enough."

"We could start with why your hair and eye are weird now, what Boyd was, why he was trying to kill me ... the possibilities are endless."

"I guess let's start with what Boyd was. That feels like a good place to start."

"Good choice, starting basic. So, you know how people die, right? Whenever that happens, they go to whatever afterlife best reflects their life choices, along with their beliefs and values. For instance, an alcoholic with no strong religious beliefs would fall under the jurisdiction of Dionysus, the Greek god of getting schwasted, so when they die, they go to the Greek underworld."

"OK, the afterlife is real. Kind of a mind-blower, but what does that have to do with Boyd?"

"I was just about to get to that. Some people die without going to any afterlife, usually in sudden freak accidents. A lot of these deaths are the result of the reapers. They exist beyond our plane of existence, as do all forms of the afterlife, but those they kill go to none of them. There are only a few of them, fifty-eight now that Boyd's out of the picture, and they basically eat the souls of who they kill as a form of payment. They're all given lists of who needs to die.

Nobody writes them. They just pop into existence. Real weird shit if you ask me, but they follow their rules. Except Boyd. Boyd was kind of power-hungry and wanted the position of Grim, the reaper head honcho, and the only way he could do that was by collecting souls. Their rules state that they can only kill who's on their list, but big, bad Boyd wanted a bigger fish. He wanted my soul.

"I don't like bragging, but I'm kind of a big deal, and the reapers know that. They're allowed to make deals with those on their list if they're unable to die in an accident, like if they're not human or they're immortal or some such tomfoolery. Oh, people can be immortal too, but that's not the point at hand.

"So, thirty years back, Boyd comes to me and demands that I make a deal with him or he'll take my soul. Now, unbeknownst to him, I know damn well I'm not on any of their lists, but I love messing with people, especially when they're dimension-traveling bringers of death and destruction. It's fun. You should try it."

He poured another mug and drank half of it in a single gulp, then continued, "So I went along with it, and we settled on flipping a coin. If I get it, I get another year of life. Then we flip again. If he gets it, he gets to try to collect my soul. I didn't tell him, but my coin's kind of weighted."

He pulled out the coin he flipped during the fight and spun it on the table. "This thing may look like an ordinary old-ass coin, but it's actually the physical reincarnation of an ancient being."

Derrek stared at him, confused, as the coin continued to spin with no signs of stopping or even slowing down. He was struggling to comprehend what he had been told so far, and that past sentence had been a bit much, even considering the circumstances.

Discord noticed the wheels spinning in Derrek's mind. "Don't worry. It'll make sense by the end of the night. All you really need to know about it for now is that it heavily influences probability around the user, making it effectively a working good-luck charm, which is how I won the coin toss thirty years in a row. How it works exactly is way too complex to get into. Just know I've got luck on my side as long as the coin decides it so."

"Wait … what do you mean by decides? How can a coin decide anything?"

"Like I said, it used to be a living thing, and it still has thoughts, feelings, a sense of humor—the works. Hell, it'll even decide to stop working entirely if it thinks it'll be funny. I don't blame it, though; it usually is pretty damn funny. Like this one time, I was playing cards with some mobsters and bet my left pinky finger, and I totally lost. I swear, the looks on those guys' faces after I chopped it off and bet the rest of my hand for the next pot! Priceless."

He started laughing and finished his mug, which he refilled, giving Derrek a chance to see that Discord was still in possession of all his fingers, but he still got the impression that the story was true.

"Anyway, a couple of hours ago, we met in Chernobyl for our usual flip, except this time, he actually decided to check the coin out once all was said and done. Reapers are hypersensitive to things like this, but Boyd was more on the dull side, if you catch my drift," he said, winking. "So he gets all mad and stuff, and just to see where it goes, I start running. After, like, five minutes, we ended up in that clearing, where he punched you so hard it dislocated your spine."

Derrek was in the middle of a sip and immediately spat it out. "My spine did *what?*"

Discord laughed. "Don't worry. You're fine now. You got super lucky. You see, when a reaper touches any human in any way, one of two things happen: they die instantly or their hair goes white and their eyes—or eye, in your case—turn green, and they get super powerful. That's called having the 'reaper's touch.' The way it works and the reason reapers have to be so careful not to kill those not on their lists is It speeds up your physiology without actually aging you, kind of putting you in a state of yourself later on in life, in most cases ending with instant death but super rarely ending with, well, you. If fate decides it so, it'll just give you a hell of a boost in spiritual energy."

Discord sighed and fished around in the bowl of nuts. "I know, I have to explain spiritual energy now." He pulled a cashew out of the bowl and ate it. "So, there are three types of energy that living beings can harness: physical, mental, and spiritual. Physical energy is essentially your overall physical capabilities, how hard you can hit or how much you can lift, and it's the only one you can hone with physical training. Mental energy measures your ability to perform what you might know as magic, from telekinesis to pyromancy. It all falls under this category. Spiritual energy, however, is the most fluid of the group, able to be directly converted into physical or mental energy at the user's discretion. For the most part, it acts kind of like a pool. You can take as much as you need from it, but it will shut off if you overexert yourself and use too much and will gradually refill itself based on several factors.

"All these are pretty versatile things and can be used in as many ways as you can think," he said, reaching into his coat and producing a small knife. He laid his left hand flat on the table. "For example, if I were to stab myself in the hand, I could channel my physical energy to harden my skin or have it exert an outward force equal to that of the attack to completely negate it. Or …"

He plunged the knife into his hand, pinning it to the table without so much as blinking.

"Holy shit!" Derrek said as Discord casually sipped his mug, his giant pitcher nearly half-empty. Several patrons and staff glanced at them briefly before turning back to their respective tables. He was doing his best to hold down his lunch while Discord continued to not acknowledge the knife in his hand.

He pulled the knife out and tucked it back into his coat, holding his hand up, palm facing Derrek, showing off the wound. He could see light shining through the hole, slowly oozing blood. Suddenly, the blood stopped, then started flowing in reverse. After all the blood returned to his hand, the flesh began to heal, rapidly closing up without leaving behind as much as a scar.

Derrek watched, mouth agape, as Discord nonchalantly dug around the bowl of nuts. He grabbed his mug and chugged the remaining half of his beer, refilling and emptying the mug and refilling it again.

"Yeah, it's a lot to take in," Discord continued, "but it's all about figuring out how to work the energy. You're taking it pretty well. Last guy I showed all this puked on the spot!"

He pulled his hand out from the bowl, holding another cashew, which he offered to Derrek. He accepted and ate it, noting that it was perfectly salted. "I appreciate it. This … this is a lot."

"You don't know the half of it."

Discord took a big gulp of his drink, then put on a serious face and said, "What do you remember from killing Boyd?"

Derrek thought hard. The whole situation was a blur for him, but he did his best to piece it together. He took a sip from his mug then said, "I remember breaking his legs, then standing over him. It's kind of fuzzy after that, but I think I remember … orange? The color, everywhere, and the taste of … peace? What? That doesn't make sense."

"No, you've got it right. That orange was you consuming Boyd, and I've heard reapers taste like the peace of death, with a hint of oregano."

"I think I remember that. Is that something everyone with the reapers' touch can do?"

Discord took a deep breath. "No, it isn't. That ability belongs to something known only as the Devourer, this crazy, ancient thing. There have been countless incarnations, stretching as far back as life has existed. Buckle up. This part is a doozy:

"Long ago, before time and space, there existed nothing—no atoms, no matter, and no mass. Within the nothing, there existed an endless number of beings known as the primordials, each and every one giant beyond belief and wise beyond years. They knew all and filled their time with experimentation, creating matter from nothing, using their nearly endless wells of spiritual energy to create worlds and minerals and elements, everything they could conceive of, but never life. There was so much empty space, they all lived in solitude, minding their own business, and that worked for countless eons.

"Then, one day, a being showed up. None of them had created it. Nor did they know its origins. They only knew it was consuming them one by one, growing stronger with each one it devoured. They eventually found that the being was leaving their creations alone, completely ignoring physical matter and eating the near-pure energy that was the primordials. Using that information, countless primordials opted to transform themselves into pure forms of metals and gemstones, becoming primordial relics, and like my coin here, they all have unique abilities. Some of them banded together and became larger relics. In this case, the original silver relic was a statue that the Spanish conquistadors found in modern-day Brazil, which they melted down into an indeterminate amount of these," he said, gesturing to the still-spinning coin.

"However, some of them tried to fight back, and although they were unable to do it themselves, they believed they could create something that could. A bunch of them got together and created something they never had before: reason. They found that fighting for a particular reason could produce an unheard of amount of spiritual energy, so they created a being and gave it all the reason they could. This thing had every single reason to fight that could exist, from greed to family, rage to joy and everything in between, and with it all together, it produced an actual shitload of spiritual energy. They called it the Warrior. They weren't the most creative namers.

"With all the Warrior's reasons, though, one overarching reason shone above the rest: killing the Devourer. They met and fought, ending with them both doing what they did best, the Warrior warring and the Devourer devouring. The Warrior got eaten, and the primordials mourned as their last hope faded, until something amazing happened.

"Turns out, eating Warriors makes for some crazy indigestion, and immediately after consuming it, the Devourer started to hurt like crazy. You see, for whatever reason, the Devourer can't consume reason, so it was left with an ever-increasing amount of spiritual energy within it that it was completely incompatible with. That ended up making it collapse in on itself, creating a single point of infinite density and infinite mass. Sound familiar?"

Derrek thought for a second, despite the information overload he was experiencing. "The big bang?"

Discord snapped his fingers. "That's it. The plane of the primordials has real messed-up time, so when the universe was created, it split off, multiverse style, into countless branches, our particular branch being known as the Crossroads," he said, looking into the distance and conspicuously winking. "Whatever primordials were left behind either perished in the explosion or embraced it, coming into the physical world, going completely insane and losing most of their power in the process. The relics survived, floating around in the newly created space until they found a place to land, a good amount of them ending up on earth.

"Now, the Devourer didn't perish; it just completely lost its corporeal form and was unable to devour. When life sprouted up, however, it was able to take a host. It couldn't make its host do anything. Nor could it communicate with them. It only allowed them the power to consume without informing them to it, aside from a few vague dreams. For the first few million incarnations, it was fish, dinosaurs, the works—all too instinct oriented to ever discover the power they had. Whenever the host dies, the Devourer kind of just floats around in the ether for about fifty years, until it finds a new host. And it takes a host at birth, gravitating toward those with bright destinies with no actual ability to read into them.

"The Warrior survived as well, but not in one piece. It broke off into as many different parts as there are reasons for fighting, now known as warrior spirits, taking root in whatever beings embodied their reason the most, the first known of which being a determined fish that wanted to walk. Whenever a being is the host to a warrior spirit, they have limited access to the spiritual energy they generate through their reason, making them crazy effective on the battlefield and fierce competition.

"However, whenever a host is on the brink of death, if they keep fighting despite being in the process of dying, they might combine with the warrior spirit, becoming one with it and giving them full access to the entirety of their capabilities. At that point, they're known as a fused warrior spirit, usually shortened to just warrior spirit, and yes, I know that's confusing, but that's what they're called.

"When it comes to warrior spirits, they have one thing in common: their shared desire to kill the Devourer. All warrior spirits have a kind of internal GPS leading them toward the current incarnation of the Devourer, and whenever they meet, they have a crazy-strong urge to murder the absolute shit out of them. Now, let me ask you: what did you glean from that multiple-page monologue I just spoke at you?"

Derrek was overwhelmed, for throughout his entire life, he hadn't put much thought into the origins of the universe, but never thought a battle between ancient beings to be it. He stared down at the coin, which was still spinning as fast as ever, trying to compose his thoughts and piece together whatever he could. He started talking it out. "So, I guess I'm … the Devourer? And you're a warrior spirit? I ate Boyd, and you were going to kill me?"

Discord raised his eyebrows, clearly impressed. "Spot on! Oh, and I didn't mention, but whenever a devourer consumes something supernatural, like a reaper, they gain some of their abilities. So, you've got some reaper powers now, probably something along the lines of being able to summon a scythe or something like that. Now, I wanna test something. Can you tell what my reason is? Take note of how I fought earlier."

Derrek still felt overwhelmed, but he decided to comply, thinking about the way he effortlessly swung his sword, doing more to show off than to effectively fight. He remembered the smile that was seemingly plastered on his face. "Entertainment?"

Discord clapped his hands and pointed at him. "Hot damn! You're a perceptive one! I would have also accepted bloodlust or the liberation of Wales," he said, merging Derrek's confused look. "Whenever a fused warrior spirit kills another fused warrior spirit, they gain their reason, and those are the biggest ones I've gotten over the years."

Derrek was still trying to wrap his head around it all. As he rubbed his temples, he said, "I've got a lot of questions."

"Have at it. I'll answer whatever questions you ask to the best of my abilities."

He took another sip from his mug, using it as an excuse to find the first question to ask, until it hit him. "What's up with your coat? How can you store multiple swords in there?"

"I'm actually glad you asked," he said, showing off his coat's interior. "There are things called pocket dimensions, and most of them are effectively worthless, usually just being pants with one pocket that's extra deep. It happens with no real explanation or reason—just the randomness of life. This one, however, is the shit. It's got an effectively endless amount of space so I can store whatever I need, and I can pull out whatever I need just by knowing what I need when I reach in. I've got swords and guns galore, a whole lot of money, a motorcycle, and enough nonperishable food to feed both sides of a war for months stored away in this bad boy. Plus, whenever it gets damaged, it heals itself. It's pretty awesome."

"OK, that one's been bugging me. You mentioned that there were supernatural things. How far does that go?"

"About as far as you might think. Werewolves, vampires, demons, gods, angels, wendigos—pretty much everything from every mythology is based at least partly in fact. Except for the Norse.

Reality was a whole lot different than the stories and fables. The draugurs are real though."

Reality was finally starting to set in with Derrek. He chugged the rest of his mug and ate a few peanuts. He took a deep breath. "All right. OK. All right. All right, all right. OK." He refilled his mug and drank half of it.

"Take your time. It's a lot of crazy stuff."

Derrek suddenly had a realization. He looked back up at Discord and asked, "Are you going to kill me?"

All expression drained from Discord's face. It was the first time Derrek noticed his eyes. They were dark brown, almost black, and he saw a mixture of anger and longing in them.

Suddenly, his eyes seemed to brighten to a lighter shade of brown, then, with a half-smile, he said, "I was going to, but nah."

A wave of relief washed over Derrek, along with a wave of confusion. "Why not?" he asked, uncertain if he even wanted the answer.

"Because you're the first devourer I've ever found that I was able to sit down and have a beer with. Every damn time it's just senseless blood and violence, and yeah, taking them out was for the greater good, but it pisses me off when I'm a slave to fate."

Derrek smiled, now confident that his life wasn't in danger. He lifted his mug and said, "I'll drink to that."

Discord raised his mug to meet Derrek's, and said, "*Prost*," and they both drank. The men had nearly finished their respective pitchers, but to Derrek's surprise, he didn't feel a drop of it. He figured it had something to do with everything he had just learned.

Discord polished off his beer. "All right, I've answered your questions. Now I get to ask some. Sound fair to you?"

"Sure, go ahead."

"First off, what were you doing out in the woods alone? I can tell you're with Frostbyte due to the uniform you were wearing earlier, so I'm guessing you're on a survey mission, but those usually have fully stacked teams, so why were you out there solo?"

"Oh, my team took two cars, and we're ahead of schedule, so everyone took off early, and they needed someone to stay behind."

"So you got the shit end of the stick? That sucks, man."

"Not really, I volunteered for it."

"Oh really? Why's that?"

"Well, it's my first time out in the field, I just want to make a good impression. Besides, I wasn't able to help set up last week since I had to get certified to carry my gun. It just seemed fair."

Discord laughed. "Nothing's fair in this world, Havok, but your heart's in the right place. I like that. Hey, you had some weird dreams over the last month or so, right? Three of them?"

"Yeah, actually, except it was four."

"Huh, it's usually three. It's like a subliminal introduction to being a devourer, showing you the enemy, you know, the warrior spirits. Do you remember any of them?"

Derrek thought for a few seconds. "The first one I can remember was in some burning hellscape with a giant creature standing over it all. Then a guy drenched in blood sliced him in the neck, and then I woke up."

"Yep, that was Humbaba. Have you ever read the epic of Gilgamesh? Dude took credit when I cut his head off. Doesn't bother me, though. Never been one for being center stage in history."

Derrek thought about that a moment. He had read the book in his youth when Shale had him schooled and remembered it was written well before 2000 BCE. He asked, "Gilgamesh? Exactly how old are you?"

"Very, but don't worry about that right now. Tell me about the rest of your dreams."

"Right, sorry. There was another one—I think it was in a warehouse. There was something eating what looked like a person in the shadows."

"And a guy crashed in from the ceiling, made an *Old Yeller* joke and set the building on fire?"

"Yeah, I'm guessing that was you?"

"You guessed it. I'm just glad someone got to hear that joke. Man, that fire was huge. It was awesome. The devourer then was a wendigo, he never consumed anything big, but he physically ate a whole bunch of people. What else you got?"

"Well, a few nights ago, I had a dream that I think took place in Greece … Argos?"

"Oh damn, you saw that one? I swear, that fight with the immortals was fun, even though I lost an arm."

"So that *was* you. But how'd you get your arm back?"

"Now that's an interesting story," Discord said as he poured another mugful. "So, around 1500 something, Ponce De Leon and his crew went to the Bahamas looking for the fountain of youth, and I thought it'd be fun, so I tagged along. I went by Kahli Ironfist back then, since my left arm was an iron prosthetic from the elbow down. We searched and searched, eventually coming to a small island off the main Bahamas.

"After we landed, I stepped away to relieve myself and went a bit further in than I needed to. After doing my business, I heard running water and followed it. There I found this pond full of the most refreshing water I've ever had, and I didn't stop drinking until the whole pond was empty!

"Apparently, I took a lot longer than I should have, and Leon came in after me with the bulk of his men. I thought he was worried, so imagine my surprise when they all start pointing their rifles at me! Turns out, the Spanish king had a hefty price on my head, and they didn't even intend to find the fountain of youth. They just wanted something to entice me into tagging along. They lined up, I said something along the lines of, 'What a Spain in my ass,' and they fired. Most of my chest was blown out, the whole left half of my head got removed, and they even blasted off my iron arm.

"So there I was, lying on the ground, bleeding like crazy, thinking, *Damn, I always thought I'd die drowning in the ocean,* when all of a sudden, the pain starts to go away. My wounds start healing—even the arm and my thousand-year-old scars. But I didn't think about that. I was focused on slaughtering those traitorous Spaniards. Without a second thought, I rushed at them, grabbing one of their muskets, making a Spanish shish kebab!

"By the time his men were over and dealt with, Leon was in shock, baffled that his ambush didn't work. I made sure it was clear that he'd end up like them if he tried that shit again and made him lead the rest of his crew back to the mainland, letting me get away scot-free. All in all, it was a pretty fun trip. I do wish I grabbed my old arm, though. It was a part of me for nearly two millennia. Hell, I still only use one hand attacks when I fight."

"With that giant sword? That thing *has* to be made for two hands."

"Indeed it was, but I decide what I do with my hands. If I can use one hand, I will, even with guns. I usually stick with handguns, but I got a couple of shotguns, a sniper rifle, a few submachine guns—you name it, I probably got it floating around in my coat," he said, pouring the rest of his pitcher into his mug. He took a sip, then snapped his fingers and said, "Right! Almost forgot, you had a fourth dream."

"Oh yeah, my bad. That one's a bit fuzzy, actually. All I really remember from it is a plain-looking office and a necklace shaped like a cow skull. Actually, I think there was something to do with tissue paper too, but I'm not sure. Does that ring any bells?"

Discord had fallen silent, eyes wide, barely even breathing. He picked up his mug, slowly drinking the entirety of it in one sip, carefully setting it down before looking Derrek in the eye. He slowly reached into his shirt, pulling out a necklace he was wearing, holding the pendent tightly in his palm.

"That one shouldn't have showed up," he said, letting go of the pendent, revealing a wooden longhorn skull.

Derrek's eyes grew wide before he remembered he had just

described three dreams that were actually pieces of Discord's past and that a fourth wasn't really that surprising at that point.

"I don't get it. What's the big deal about that particular memory?" Derrek asked.

"It isn't the memory that's the problem. It's who was in that memory."

"Well, who was it?"

"The closest thing to God—with a capital G."

"With the day I've had, that isn't exactly the craziest thing you've said."

"No, you don't get it. The fact that you were in his office means he saw you. The fact that he saw you means both of us are in some hot fucking water."

Derrek realized the gravity of the situation, as he had barely seen this man without a smile, even when he was ready to put a bullet in him. He didn't have the same look in his eye now.

"I still don't understand. What's so bad about this?"

"What's so bad about this is that he specifically recruited me to hunt down and kill any devourer that pops up. You ever hear about what happens when you disobey God? It sure as hell didn't work out well in Exodus!" he yelled, slamming his fists on the table, alerting several patrons and the bartender, who all quickly went back to what they were doing, paying them no mind.

Derrek looked around, surprised they got away with that. When he saw the coast was clear, he asked, "What does that even mean?"

"Jesus Herman Christ, what don't you get about this?"

"Mostly the part about you freaking out."

"What?"

"Didn't you just say you hated being a slave to fate?"

Discord sat, absolutely dumbfounded. His expression shifted rapidly—anger, despair, confusion, and constipation all shifting across his face. After nearly a full minute of that, he cracked a smile and started laughing once more.

"Son of a bitch, I knew you were something special! First, you've got the reaper's touch, then you're a devourer. Now here you are, hoisting me by my own damn petard! Barmaid! Another round! And one for everyone! We're celebrating friends, new and old!" he exclaimed, met immediately with uproarious applause.

Even though he had just met this man, Derrek was glad to have this side of him back. Every friend he had made since meeting Shale was a coworker or work related, it was refreshing for him to meet someone completely out of his wheelhouse.

The barmaid came back to their table with two more pitchers. Discord put an oversized twisty straw into one and began quickly drinking it. The mood had been renewed, and Derrek thought it would be a good time to pry.

"Hey, do you mind if I ask what that was all about? I get it if you don't want to talk about it," he said, refilling his mug.

"It's no problem at all. I kinda flipped my lid back there. That's on me, not you. This whole thing is new, not only for me but for literally all of existence. Do you have any idea how rarely a warrior spirit gets to even talk to a Devourer, let alone have a shitload of beer with them? It's totally crazy!"

Derrek was happy to see he had a new outlook on the situation. He was doing his best not to show it, but he had been flung headfirst into an entire world that had been right under his nose his entire life, and having Discord there was a big help for him.

He couldn't help feeling that he wasn't reacting correctly to the situation, however, and thought Discord may have some insight.

"Can I ask you something?"

"Have at it, ask away."

"So, in the past couple of hours, I killed and ate a reaper, learned that pretty much every crazy piece of folklore is true, and discovered that what is basically God personally wants me dead."

"That about sums it up."

"My question, then, is why am I not freaking out? I feel like my mind should be imploding right about now, but I'm just so … calm."

"Oh, yeah, that's a reaper's touch thing. Keeps you cool as a cucumber pretty much all the time. Keeps you alert, keeps you focused, prevents panicking—the works—something about settling down with age. And considering how hard he hit you, you're probably gonna be as stoic as a monk."

"So … does that mean I've lost my emotions?"

"Far from it. You just won't show as profoundly as you used to. Makes you look like a real badass."

"Huh. That might actually be helpful."

"Especially since you've got a future in business."

Derrek was surprised to hear this, and he raised his eyebrows. He leaned in close and in a hushed tone, he said, "How do you know about that?"

"C'mon man, I've got a brain. You said it's your first time in the field, and I've got a pretty good idea of what goes on in Frostbyte, so I gotta think you work at corporate. The rest just kinda falls in with your new hairdo."

"Oh … right."

"But it sounds like I'm missing something way more specific," he said, looking at Derrek with suspicion.

Derrek wasn't sure if he should tell Discord about his relationship with Shale, as historically, it tended to complicate things, and considering how much he seemed to know, it may be unwise to confess.

"Um … well … you see—"

Discord cut him off, "You can either tell me or I can figure it out. Either way works for me. Like a puzzle. Actually, don't tell me. Wait until it comes out naturally with some stronger narrative significance. Get some drama set up," he said, laughing and drinking his pitcher with his straw.

Derrek smiled, glad he let it go. He took another sip from his mug and looked at the rest of the pub, surprised to find how much it had filled since they took the booth. Everyone was having a good time, drinking from the pitchers Discord ordered for them, aside from a group of five that had just walked in, and were walking toward them. They were standing next to their table when the one in the middle slammed his hands down, almost knocking over Derrek's mug.

"You must be tourists or confused, because this is our booth," he said, leering over the two. He had short blond hair and a patchy, wispy beard. He was shorter than the rest of his friends, but clearly spoke for the group. Derrek instantly recognized him as the one who gave him and Jeffrey trouble the weekend before.

"And you must be mistaken, my friend," Discord said, "because it looks like we're the ones sitting here."

Derrek gave Discord a look, trying to say not to instigate anything before realizing he could handle himself.

The thug frowned and snapped his fingers, and the rest of his group got close to the table, crowding around them. Discord smirked and continued sipping his straw as the men tried to look intimidating, to apparently no avail. The head thug narrowed his gaze on Derrek, recognizing him.

"Well, look who it is! I almost didn't recognize you with that stupid hair."

"You should leave before things get bad," Derrek said, trying to match Discord's energy, casually sipping his mug.

This angered the thugs. The leader leaned in close and said, "How about you make me, freak?"

Discord looked at Derrek, then nodded. He took his pitcher and downed what was left, then took it by the handle and smashed it over the lead thug's head, knocking him to the ground as the other men stood in shock. In an instant, Discord was out of the booth, standing in front of the remaining four men. He cracked his knuckles and stretched as the men pulled out weapons—two with knives, one with a small metal rod, and one with a pair of knuckle-dusters.

"Fellas, there are two ways this can go," Discord said. "Either you all walk away, or my friend and I are gonna make you look real dumb in front of everyone."

The men were clearly individually debating whether they should fight before they all remembered they were armed. They got their assorted weaponry at the ready, and Discord smirked.

"That's what I thought," he said as the man with the chunk of metal came at him. He swung the rod aiming for Discord's ribs, which he effortlessly caught and pulled out of his hands, giving the man a swift punch to the gut, throwing him on the floor. He quickly examined it and found it to be very sturdy, made of rebar. He grabbed it by both ends, twisting it into a pretzel and tossing it on the ground in front of the rest of the men.

They took a step back before thinking it must have been some kind of trick, and the man with the knife and the one with brass knuckles charged at him. He stepped out of the way of the knife, grabbing him by the arm and bending it backward at the elbow, catching the knife and causing the man to scream out in pain. The one with knuckle-dusters tried to punch him in the face, which he leaned into, taking the hit on his forehead and knocking the thug off balance, hitting him upside the head with the butt end of the knife.

He threw the knife at the feet of the last man standing, sticking it into the stone floor, cutting into his left shoe, sticking between his toes and narrowly avoiding cutting him. The rest of the men were starting to get up, aside from the one whose arm bent backward. Their fists were raised, and they were clearly not ready to give up. The leader was standing again and pulled out a knife of his own, and the one who was pinned to the ground took his shoe off, freeing him.

Derrek decided to join in even though he was sure Discord could handle it. He stood back-to-back with him as the men surrounded them, and he put his fists up. The one with brass knuckles ran at him, reeling back excessively for a punch aimed at his nose. He ducked out of the way at the last second, grabbing the man by the wrist and twisting, completely flipping the man onto a nearby empty table, causing it to collapse under him.

Discord laughed as he had the other two goons under his arms in headlocks. He jumped and fell forward, smashing their heads into the floor and giving himself a badly broken nose. He stood up and looked at the leader, setting his nose back in place so it would heal faster. He looked back and forth from him and Derrek, furious as to how things played out.

"You ... you freaks! I'll kill you!" he said, throwing the knife at Derrek. Without thinking, he caught it by the handle just before the blade went into his eye. Discord nodded in approval, clearly impressed, and Derrek tossed the knife aside.

When the two looked back at the man, however, he was now holding a pistol, which he was pointing at Discord, his hands shaking violently.

"Get the *fuck* out of my town!" he yelled, causing several patrons to leave at the sight of his gun, some seemingly calling the police.

"Put the gun down before you get yourself hurt," Derrek said with confidence, which caused Discord to smile even wider.

"Listen to him, kid. A booth isn't worth your life," Discord said, unfazed.

"*Fuck you!*" he yelled, pointing the gun at Discord's head.

In a split second, the gun was out of his hand and into Discord's, which he used to pistol-whip the man, slamming him to the floor with a loud *thud,* splattering blood onto the floor. He tucked the gun into his coat and pulled out a stack of bills, which he tossed onto their table. He took his pitcher, which was half full, chugged what was left, and took a handful from the bowl of nuts and shoved it into his coat.

He then grabbed Derrek by the shoulder. "We should probably

go. Cops are gonna be here soon, and I'm low on favors with the German government."

Derrek nodded and led him back to the car, narrowly avoiding the fist of the jolly man at the front as he tried to block their path. Discord took the wheel and peeled out, leaving skid marks in his path. He drove at full speed, deftly weaving through traffic and avoiding any crashes, not even putting a scratch on the paint job.

"I'd take us to one of my safe houses, but the closest one I've got is in France. Where are you staying?"

"The Schadenfreude Hotel. Do you know where that is?"

Discord looked over at him in surprise. "Do I know where that is? Of course I do! It'll be nice to visit. I haven't seen Mila in years!"

"Mila? As in Mila Müller? You know her?"

Discord looked at him with a cocky grin. "I know everybody."

He turned on the radio, flipping through the channels until he found one playing what sounded like German covers of popular songs from the '90s, and sang along the whole way to the hotel.

Discord parked alongside the rest of the fleet of SUVs, about in the middle of the acre-sized parking lot. The time was nearing 8:30. The initial dinner rush had subsided, and many of the guests had turned in for the night, making the exterior a very quiet place.

"Is here all right?" Discord asked.

"Yeah, and you can just leave the keys in the visor. It's fully insured."

"You know what? I've never gotten insurance on anything."

"Really? Haven't you owned a house or rented somewhere?"

"Nah, technically speaking, I'm homeless, but I got shacks all around the world. Actually, I should really get one in Germany."

"Lots of woods. I'm sure you can find a good place for it."

Discord laughed. "I like the way you think, kid."

The men then left the car and made their way to the entrance. On the way, Derrek noted that Jeffrey's truck still wasn't there. He'd said he would be back by the end of the week, but he might have meant Saturday, so Derrek put it out of his mind for the time being, instead focusing on whatever misadventure Discord was going to drag him into as he was leading the way.

After entering the building, Discord inhaled deeply, taking in the smell of the lavender and the burning wood. It reminded him of fond memories past, which saddened him, as those he shared them with were long gone. His smile never faded, however, as he chose to focus on the good times that were, not those that could no longer be.

He headed for the front desk, where the woman who had checked Derrek in his first night was typing away at her computer, inputting data. She looked up at Discord and saw Derrek was with him. She smiled and asked, "How may I help you, sir?"

"Yeah, I need to talk to Mila Müller as soon as you can get her."

"I'm sorry, sir. You need to book an appointment to speak with Frau Müller, but I can take a message for you if you wish."

Discord leaned in close and spoke with a hushed tone in an effort to keep Derrek from overhearing. When he leaned away, the woman's eyes were wide, and the smile that was seemingly plastered on her face had faded. She pushed a button on her phone and spoke into it in hushed German. She then directed the two to a hallway left of her desk and said, "Last door on the right. She's expecting you."

"Thank you very much," Discord said, grabbing a handful of complimentary peppermints and shoving them into presumably the same pocket he put the nuts in earlier. Derrek mouthed, "Sorry" to her as he walked past, to which she responded with silent glare.

Derrek stopped Discord halfway down the hall and asked, "What did you say to her?"

"Just the truth."

"And what might that be?"

"You'll find out soon enough."

"What is 'soon enough' to you?"

Derrek was clearly displeased with how he had handled it with the woman at the desk, so to try and quell him, Discord said, "In this case, soon enough is the minute we walk through that door. And don't worry about her. That little fangless has been through a lot. She'll be fine."

"What did you just call her? Fangless?"

"It'll make sense. Trust me," Discord said, looking Derrek in the eye.

Derrek nodded, reluctant but trusting of Discord's judgment. After all, it was that same judgment that allowed him to live. They continued down the hall, coming to a stop at Mila's door.

Discord knocked, then entered without waiting for a response. "How's my third favorite mogul doing?"

The office was immaculate. No clutter or mess. Not even a wastebasket to be seen. There was a long filing cabinet behind a desk topped with a small collection of knickknacks, with two chairs set in front of it. Mila sat behind her desk, standing up as soon as he barged in, yelling back, "Du widerlicher Hurensohn! How the hell are you, old friend?"

She walked around the desk and gave him a firm embrace, picking him up several inches off the ground despite being a full foot shorter than him. She wore a long skirt with a thick sweater and had flowing blonde hair. Her skin was flawless and white as porcelain, and that, paired with her small frame, made her seem frail, but her lifting Discord told a different story.

"I'd say I'm doing all right. I've been eating my kale, getting into the stock market, and young-looking ladies keep picking me up, so life's good. How about you, *mein fraulein?*"

She let him down and gave a chuckle. "Business is booming, the guests are happy, and *Kuchenparty* has the highest ratings in the country! Life is good!"

The two shared a laugh until Mila noticed Derrek standing just outside her door. She looked him over, taking note of his hair and eyes, and ushered him in, closing the door behind him.

She glared at Discord and got in his face, grabbing him by the scruff of his shirt. "You brought a Hauch Von Tod to my hotel? You might as well have shot up a flare! He'll bring every poacher in the EU breaking down my door! I want him out!"

Discord raised his hands in defense and tried to inch away from her. "Hey, hey, *he* brought *me* here! Besides, if any poachers showed up, you know I'd be here as soon as you called! At least hear me out, and if you're still mad at me, I won't blame you."

She stared him down for a few more seconds before letting him go in a huff. She took her seat behind her desk and gestured to the two seats in front of her for the men to sit, which they did. Mila held her hands in a pyramid and leaned forward, making Derrek uncomfortable while Discord did his best to act casual.

After several seconds of tense silence passed, Discord tried to speak up until Mila interrupted him.

"So, explain to me why you thought it was appropriate to bring one of his kind here?" she said, staring daggers at Derrek.

"Now, you're gonna think this is hilarious," Discord said, which got a frosty look from Mila, "but this dude here has actually been staying here for a while."

Mila's eye was visibly twitching; she was clearly not amused.

"*But,*" Discord said, "he's only been like this for a few hours and had absolutely no idea about any of the weirdness of the world."

"Weirdness?" she asked with a scowl.

"Oh, come on, you know what I mean, the stuff not everyone

knows about. You should've seen his face when I told him there was an afterlife!" he said with a big smile, trying unsuccessfully to change the mood.

He sighed deeply and dropped the smile. "Look, I've got a lot riding on this kid, and I need to make sure he stays somewhere safe until he can get his jazz under control. Plus, you owe me one. Remember that problem you had a few years back?"

Mila slammed her hands on her desk. "Exterminating a few feral deadlings does *not* equate to putting my entire staff in danger! Give me one good reason to allow him to stay, or so help me, I'll have you both banned!"

"All right," Discord said, leaning forward. "He's the Devourer."

Mila leaned back in her chair, her hands falling down into her lap, her eyes wide in shock. After several seconds of staring at them in silence, in a stern tone, she said, "Get out."

"Now, hold on—"

"Get out now."

"He's with the Frostbyte party. Don't you think it'll look suspicious if you kick him out for no reason?"

"Don't you think it'll be even more suspicious that he suddenly has white hair and a different colored eye?"

"Fair point, but think about it—having him around would make for some good protection if anything happens while we're here."

Mila raised her eyebrows. "We? Are you intending to stay here as well?"

"For as long as he does," Discord said, gesturing to Derrek.

"You sure have been quiet," Mila said to Derrek. "What do you have to say about all this?"

Derrek had been sitting quietly the entire time, feeling uncomfortable being talked about while still being in the room. He took a moment to compose himself. "I'd hate to impose, Ms. Müller, and by the sounds of it, having me around would be dangerous. If you think it's best, I'll talk it over with my boss and make arrangements for the soonest flight home."

Discord and Mila sat in stunned silence, staring at Derrek.

"What?" they both said in unison.

"It just seems like I'm a danger now, and I'd hate to be the reason anyone got hurt."

Mila and Discord looked at each other, until Discord spoke up.

"You see how much he cares? I'm not bringing you a blind devourer. He actually has a conscience. I would never bring a threat into your home, but I know you have a lot at stake, so whatever your decision on letting us stay, we'll respect your judgement."

Mila reformed her finger pyramid and stared them down for a full moment before loudly exhaling. She looked Derrek in the eye and said, "Fine, you can stay." She then looked at Discord. "But you have to actually pay for a room."

Discord jumped up from his chair and extended his arm. "You've got yourself a deal, Ms. Müller! But I'm gonna eat and drink your entire inventory, really get my money's worth."

She sighed and reluctantly shook his hands. "Fine, but you have to keep an eye on him at all times, and I swear, if he lays a finger on any of my staff, I'll mount both of your heads over my door. Understood?"

Derrek was terrified, and Discord looked no better. In a shaky tone, they both said, "Understood."

"Good. Now, was there anything else?"

"Yeah, actually," Discord said. "I wanted your blessing to fill him in on what goes on around here."

"Absolutely not."

"Come on, he's a lot smarter than he looks, and I'm pretty sure the reaper's touch supercharged his thinker. He'll figure it out on his own if we don't let him know now. Plus, I already gave him the whole gods and monsters spiel, and he took it pretty well. I assure you, Fräulein, he can be trusted."

Mila stared him down, and she saw the sincerity in his eyes. She looked at Derrek, groaned, and said, "Fine, but my threat of taxidermy still stands if either of you let it slip." This renewed his terror and made Discord excited.

"Can I tell him?" Discord asked, jumping up and down in his chair.

"Fine, but you're on thin ice."

He pumped his fist in excitement. "All right!" he said, then turning to Derrek. "So, you know something's off about this place, right?"

Derrek thought for a moment. "Well, I thought the pricing was weird—single rooms costing less per person and all. I've got a lot of holes in my memory. Now that I think about it, I haven't seen a clock since I got here, and I have no idea how this place stays afloat with everything included for five hundred dollars for the entire month."

Discord nodded in approval. "Now, I'm gonna give you one guess as to what's really going on here."

Derrek thought for several seconds. All he could come up with were ideas of embezzlement or the use of the hotel as a front for something shadier, but something told him that whatever the truth was, it wasn't that.

"I have no idea," he said to Discord's delight.

"Vampires!" Discord exclaimed.

"What?" Derrek asked, not sure he heard him correctly.

Mila spoke up. "The majority of my staff, myself included, are what your people refer to as vampires."

After saying that, she opened her mouth wide, revealing a normal set of teeth. She then flexed her jaw, and a second set of needle-like teeth slid out through her gums, covering the first set. They were jagged and filled her smile, causing Derrek to jump back in surprise, although he did manage to keep silent.

He took a moment to compose himself, then asked, "Do you … feed on your patrons?"

She flexed her jaw again, instantly retracting the sharp set of teeth, allowing her to say, "Yes, but not in the way you might think." She looked at Discord, who was still jumping with glee.

"Vampires can be split into three major groups," he said, "the Black Hand, the White Hand, and ferals. The ferals are just that—mindless blood-seeking creatures. The Black Hand are like classic vampires, living in secret, coming out at night to feed on human blood. The White Hand, however, finds ways to live without feeding, some living on the emotions of others, as our friend Miss Müller here can attest to."

"We give our guests the time of their lives," she said, "and we sustain ourselves on their memories of their individual experiences, which you know as having holes in your memory. They still get the experience as well as remembering it as pleasant. For instance, if they eat from our dining hall, they will have memories of the taste and texture but will not have specific memories of eating the meal. You may find it immoral, but this way, we are able to live in comfort and peace and provide luxurious relaxation for all who walk through our doors."

Derrek was baffled, but he understood where she was coming from. He pieced together that his memories had been fed on the entire time he had stayed there, from the meals to the hours he spent watching *Kuchenparty*. After that realization, he took several seconds to compose his thoughts.

"I understand that the memories are the main reason you're open, and since, according to you, it's a peaceful alternative to hunting humans, I don't see any problem with it," he said to the relief of Mila. "But I do have some questions, if you don't mind my asking."

"That depends. What kind of questions?"

"Mostly about the logistics of the hotel, but a couple about vampires. I understand if you don't want me to ask them, though."

"No, feel free. I'll let you know if I prefer not to answer."

"Thank you. Now, I was the one who booked the Frostbyte party, so I'm fully aware of your low rates, especially for a single room, getting a month where the same price elsewhere might get a couple of nights' stay. My question, then, is how do you stay open with such small profit margins?"

Mila was taken aback, as she hadn't expected such a concise, thought-out question, especially after revealing her vampiric nature. "Our rates are calculated to be able to cover our human staff's wages, as we fangs are ill-suited for daytime work. Contrary to popular belief, sunlight doesn't kill us, but it can lead to extreme irritation after just minutes of exposure, so having humans around who are able to cover the day shift is very useful. As for the rest of the expenses, I have many investments and a diverse portfolio, including stocks in all major international companies and many different cryptocurrencies, and the interest on all of them combined is more than able to cover it."

"That makes sense, and that's been bugging me since I saw your prices," Derrek said. He then remembered what Discord said in the hallway and asked, "What does 'fangless' mean?"

Mila was surprised he knew the word but didn't seem to be offended. "We call ourselves fangs for obvious reasons. With our lifestyle, our true teeth get little use, but some among us still made the decision to have them removed to take away any temptation of feeding. They are known as fangless."

Derrek nodded, then looked to Discord, who had his arms crossed. "Told you it'd get explained."

Derrek looked back at Mila. "I've only got one more question: Did you say you had something to do with *Kuchenparty*?"

For the first time since she noticed Derrek, Mila smiled. "Yes, actually, it's a bit of a passion project of mine. It also helps the feedings, as one can gather a lot of joy from watching it, which I'm sure you're aware of."

"Absolutely! I lost three hours on that show in the blink of an eye my first day here!"

"I'm glad you enjoy it, I don't get to speak to many fans about it, as I opted to keep my name out of the credits for the sake of secrecy."

"I can see how that would make things difficult," Derrek said, glad to see her mood had finally lifted.

Mila spoke to both men. "Well, Cordy, you and your friend may stay, as long as you adhere to our conditions."

Derrek wasn't sure he heard her right. "Cordy?"

Discord looked at him with the same smile he always wore. "Hey, what can I say? I love nicknames. Ain't that right, Milly?"

Mila narrowed her eyes at Discord, and in a flash, grabbed a letter opener off of her desk, and threw it, hitting him in the center of his forehead, embedding it to the hilt. He hadn't so much as blinked, and with the blade still lodged in his skull, he said, "That's fair. You warned me this would happen if I called you that again. This is on me." He casually yanked it out, and the wound closed seconds later.

Derrek was taken off guard by the attack but remained calm aside from an initial jump. After wiping his blood from the letter opened, which blended in perfectly with his red coat, Discord placed it back where it once was, perfectly in line with a row of pens.

"Hold up. My noggin still has some damage. Can't wiggle my toes," Discord said, gently hitting the side of his head with his palm. "Gotta make sure it heals right. Last time my head piece messed up I was stranded in Alaska, totally convinced I was a lumberjack."

He hit himself hard on his right temple, making an audible *crack*. His body fell limp. His eyes glazed over, and he began to drool before coming back to his senses all at once.

"There we are, a quick reboot and we're good to go!"

Mila sighed. "You know I hate it when you do that. It's weird."

"Said the vampire to the reincarnation of an ancient being created to kill another reincarnation of another ancient being, whom he was sitting next to."

"Nobody asked for your sass, Cordy," Mila said, fighting back a smile.

"Nobody ever does."

The three of them shared a hearty laugh, after which Mila looked as if she realized something. She opened a desk drawer and rummaged around in it, eventually pulling out a small white container.

"Here," she said, handing the container to Derrek. "I think those will come in handy."

He held it and recognized it as a container for contacts, as Jenkins had been through a phase a year prior where he thought his glasses made him look old. Opening it, he found a pair of color contacts in a shade of brown similar to his own, aside from his newly green eye.

"They may not match perfectly with your natural hue," Mila said, "but it should help avoid suspicion. I'm not sure what to do about your hair though … maybe we could dye it?"

Discord spoke up. "Won't work. Reaper-white consumes all color. You'd just be wasting perfectly good dye. What's your opinion on hats?"

"I literally cannot think of a time I've willingly worn a hat," Derrek said.

Discord leaned forward in his chair. "Plan C it is then. As far as the story goes, after you left the site, you stopped for a beer, met some eccentric weirdo, drank a lot more beer, and ended up getting your hair dyed whilst you were wasted."

Derrek thought about the story, committing it to memory. "Easy enough to remember, and most of it's true, just in a different order of events."

Discord perked back up and slapped him on the back. "Atta boy! See, Mila? Like I said, smarter than he looks!"

"Smart, yes," Mila said, glaring at Discord, "but even the smart ones can do stupid things."

He smiled. "If I were anyone else, I'd probably take offense to that."

Derrek chimed in, "If you were anyone else, you probably would've died three times today."

Everyone laughed, and when it subsided, Derrek decided to have a go at putting on his new contacts. As he never had the need for them before then, he had a bit of difficulty getting them lined up properly. After some prodding and a lot of blinking, he got them lined up and could see just as well as he could before. Mila opened a drawer and pulled out an ornate mirror and handed it to him.

It was the first time he had taken a good look at himself since his transformation, aside from a few glances in the side view mirror of the SUV, and was surprised to see how natural they looked. Upon closer inspection, he saw a very faint shade of green from his left eye, but figured it would suffice, as very few people would be close enough to tell, and it could easily be explained away by saying it was a trick of the light.

"What do you think?" Mila asked.

"They look great. Thank you, Ms. Müller."

"Oh, please, call me Mila. Any friend of Cordy is a friend of mine."

"All right, thank you, Mila."

Mila smiled warmly, then looked at a clock hanging on the wall opposite to her and her eyes widened.

"Scheiße! I've got a meeting two towns over to get to!" she said as she hurried to her feet and gathered several of her belongings on her way to the door, including her coat, her purse, and a dagger she strapped to her calf so it would remain covered by her skirt.

"I keep telling you, Fräulein, a gun would serve you better. I even picked one up on the way here if you want it," Discord said, producing the gun he claimed as a trophy from the fight earlier.

"Put that away," Mila said. "I've said it before, and I'll say it again: not every problem can be solved by shooting at it. Besides, I have to keep my nose clean if I want this hotel to stay afloat."

"Suit yourself," Discord said, tucking the pistol back into his coat.

"I've got to be off. See yourselves out and keep our agreement in mind. If all goes well, I'll be back before morning," she said, halfway through the door.

She put her hand on the door frame for a moment and looked back at Derrek with a look of suspicion, which shifted to a faint smile as she left. She had protected the staff of the Schadenfreude for so long, and she wasn't sure if letting him stay was the best move, but she was sure that she trusted Discord's judgment.

Back in her office, the men remained in their respective seats, Derrek still looking in the mirror, making sure the contacts stayed in place, and Discord fiddling with a bird that dipped into a glass of water.

Suddenly, Discord shot up from his chair. "All right, let's get some grub!"

Derrek looked up at him and nodded his head silently, then carefully set down the mirror on Mila's desk. The two made their way to the dining hall, Discord overtly waving to the receptionist who responded with an evil glare. It was clear she was no longer a fan of either of them.

As soon as they entered the dining hall, Derrek realized more time had passed than he thought, as the room was nearly empty. Discord picked out the same table Jeffrey had for every meal he ate there. Apparently, it was universally ideal. The two took their seats and they were quickly met with a familiar face.

"Good evening, gentlemen," Emmett said. "Is there anything I can get you to drink? Perhaps an appetizer?"

"How's it hanging, choir boy?" Discord said.

Emmett was confused as to how he knew his name but quickly

realized who he was talking to. "Ah, Herr Discord! It's been quite a while since your last visit. Might I ask what the occasion is?"

"Same old life. Just happened to bring me around these parts. How're you doing? Adjusting all right?"

Emmett looked at Derrek suspiciously, then back to Discord. "Does he …?"

"He knows, bud, and Mila knows he knows, so we're on the level."

Emmett seemed relieved. "Well, it's been a difficult few years, but the people here are so accommodating! Every step of the way, Frau Müller has been by my side. The transition to this lifestyle can be … hard. But I've settled in nicely."

"I'm glad to hear it, bud. Any chance me and my friend here could get a couple of bottles of liquor?"

"Setting in for the night, huh? Any preference?"

"Dealer's choice. As long as it's good, it'll tide us over while we look at the menus."

"Right away, sirs," Emmett said as he went off to fetch their drinks.

Derrek looked over at Discord. "You really do know everyone, don't you?"

"Damn right. What're you hungry for?"

Derrek stared at the menu, weighing his options. Discord chimed in. "You should get the *Sauerbraten*. It's one of their best dishes."

"That's interesting. I actually had that for my first meal here. It was really good."

"True, but they were sapping your memories then. Imagine how it would be with your brainwaves intact."

"Humph," Derrek said. "You make a good point."

Just then, Emmett returned, holding two bottles of Steel Barrel whiskey, placing one gently next to each of them along with a single crystalline glass he was balancing on his forearms.

"Have you decided on your orders?" Emmett asked as Discord had already chugged a third of his bottle.

Derrek took one last look at his menu, then up at Emmett. "I think I'll go with the *Sauerbraten*."

Discord came back up for air and slammed his bottle down on the table. "I'll take one of everything off your dinner menu thrown into a giant bowl. Oh, and a diet cola. I'm trying to watch my figure."

Emmett smiled and wrote down "Discord special" underneath Derrek's order. It was at this point Derrek realized Discord hadn't even looked at his menu, which Emmett collected before walking away.

Discord went back to drinking his whiskey, polishing it off and placing the empty bottle on the corner of the table to be collected. Derrek looked at him for a few seconds, impressed that he could drink an entire bottle of whiskey in less than a minute even though he saw him drink at least three gallons worth of beer not an hour earlier.

"How can you drink so much?" he asked as he poured himself a glass of his own whiskey.

Discord belched loudly. "My metabolism works almost instantly, and my liver processes it so quickly I have to either drink enough to literally kill a lesser man to feel any of it, or I have to destroy my liver before I go out."

"You're immortal, right?"

"Far as I know."

"Do you even need to eat, then?"

Discord gave a slight laugh. "Pretty much all my biological functions are optional. I don't need air, food, water, sleep, shelter, clothing, heat, or any amount of my biomass at any given time. Really pisses people off when they can't kill me after cutting my head off. Man, you should've seen King Louis! His face when I kept talking while my head rolled around!"

Discord then started laughing intensely, slapping his hands on the table, causing his empty bottle to shake and jump, nearly knocking it over. After several seconds, he collected himself. "Eh, I guess you had to be there."

"I suppose so."

Immediately after Derrek spoke, the two saw Emmett standing before them, a plate of *Sauerbraten* in one hand and a comically large bowl in the other, which he placed in front of the men. After setting the food down, it was revealed he was also carrying a glass of iced cola in the crevice of his elbow, which he gingerly placed next to the bowl.

"Can I get you gentlemen anything else while I'm here?"

Derrek looked to Discord, who shook his head no, then said to Emmett, "I think we're good for now, but thank you very much."

Emmett smiled and silently nodded, bowing slightly, then hurried off to another table; he was apparently the only waiter working at the time.

Derrek looked around his surroundings to see if anyone was in earshot, and when he saw the coast was clear, he leaned in to Discord and whispered, "So, is he a vampire too?"

Discord replied in his normal speaking voice, "Yeah, but they generally prefer to be called fangs. Vampire is kind of a slur to them."

"I'll be sure to keep that in mind."

"But yeah, Emmett's probably the youngest fang here, and the freshest face. In fact, I'm the one who got him here," Discord said as he turned to watch Emmett work.

"Every fang has unique abilities. Choir boy here can get into people's heads, make them do what he wants or figure out what they want. As far as it goes, it's one of the stronger fang abilities. He was a victim, as many of the fangs here once were, of the greed of others. Some piece-of-shit pastor was using him to get his congregation to pour their life's savings straight into his pockets. Kidnapped him and kept him hidden from the world in the church basement. I don't make a habit of defiling religious sites, but I feel no remorse for burning that church to the ground."

"Huh …" Derrek said, looking at Emmett the same as Discord was.

The idea of every fang having a unique power, for whatever reason, resonated with Derrek, and a thought suddenly struck him.

"Do you know what Mila's is?"

Discord looked at him with a raised eyebrow and a flat expression. It was clear he wasn't sure if he should answer the question at all, but he didn't want to just brush Derrek off entirely.

"Honestly, I do know, but it isn't my place to say. Maybe you could ask her the next time you see her."

"You're right. That would probably be more appropriate."

Discord clapped his hands together, regaining Derrek's attention. "Enough chitchat, lets dig in!"

He then unwrapped his goldware and dug his fork into the bowl, pulling out an entire ribeye steak which he ate in a hardy three bites, then reaching into his mouth and pulling out the bone he had stuck in his throat. After gnawing on the bone and getting all the meat off, he dug right back in, going through entire feasts worth of food faster than Derrek could watch.

He eventually shook it off and decided to start his own meal and was immediately struck with the symphony of flavors and the tenderness of the meat. It was cooked to perfection, and brought Derrek back to his first meal, except he was able to experience every single bite. In a flash, he was done, but he remembered every bite, and finally had a full understanding of how, and why, the hotel was the way it was.

When he took his last bite, he looked to see Discord holding his bowl up, slurping up the juices that had accumulated at the bottom of his pile of a feast in the same way one would drink the broth from a soup. After several seconds and several sideways glances from others dining, he finished his meal, slamming down his bowl and letting out a belch that, despite him doing his best to stifle it, had enough force to cause the table to visibly vibrate. Derrek caught a glance of the inside of the bowl and found it completely empty—not a speck of food to be seen.

"Satisfied yet?" Derrek asked Discord, who was slumped back in his chair, patting his swollen stomach.

"For now, but now that we sit with full bellies, we have something to discuss."

"Then by all means, lay it on me."

Discord then sat forward, straightening his back, his stomach visibly retracting to its original size. He leaned over the table and spoke with a serious tone.

"I know I've been unhelpfully vague in general, brushing off what seems like important info, telling you to wait for it to reveal itself, and I might've dropped more on you all at once than I should've. I know I haven't even really explained why I'm sticking around you, and I really appreciate you going along with it. But I have a reason for it all, and I have a plan, but I needed to know you were willing to go along with it before I proposed it to you. I want you to guess what my plan is."

Derrek pondered the question. From his perspective, Discord was acting as a guide into the world he had lived in his entire life but had never known. To him, reality stopped seeming real immediately after his hair turned white.

He took a sip from his glass and thought of Shale. He thought of the man who took him from nothing and molded him into the hard-working man he was. He thought of Jeffrey, who only days before had taught him the value of training not only one's mind but one's body. He looked at Discord and realized just how much of them he saw in the man sitting before him.

He still wasn't sure of whatever plan Discord could have come up with, but he collected his thoughts and put forth the best he could come up with.

"My best guess is you want to train me to not be overcome by the Devourer."

Discord smiled. "You keep impressing me, you know that?"

Derrek was surprised by that and replied, "Excuse me?"

"Everything you've done. I'm certain anybody else in your position would have either turned tail and ran away or gone absolutely power-mad after the whole reaper thing. You weren't in control when you devoured Boyd, but you snapped back into it once it was said and done. You did your best to stop the fight back at the pub, and even though it didn't work, we still managed to take them all down without killing them. And I swear, if you didn't make such a good impression on Mila, we wouldn't even be sitting here right now.

"At every turn, you've made the right choice, and by the looks of it, everything lined up perfectly so that the right person was standing on the right spot on the right day at just the right time. The universe isn't just a place, Havok. It's a living, breathing thing. It thinks and feels just as we do, albeit on a much bigger scale, and it pushes events to happen when they're supposed to happen. I wholeheartedly believe we were pushed together so we can finally bring an end to the constant cycle of death and destruction that comes with the whole devourer/warrior spirit feud—to stop some otherworldly evil from popping up every fifty odd years and to stop me from hunting them all down.

"You may not fully understand it yet, but it seems to me you're destined for something great, and even though I hate being destiny's lackey, it seems I'm destined to lead you down the right path. So now I ask you: Do you feel the same way?"

Derrek looked out the window, briefly catching a glance of a snow-white owl perched on the other side of the huge field. Despite the vast distance, he saw it clearly, and he looked into its eyes. In that instant, which lasted less than a second, he understood what Discord meant.

"Yes, I do," he said, looking back at Discord with a smile.

Without saying a word, Discord grabbed the remaining bottle of whiskey and poured his own glass, raising it toward Derrek.

"To a new future and a better world," he said with conviction.

Derrek raised his glass to meet his toast, and they both drank. They slammed down their glasses in unison, getting the attention of Emmett, who made his way to their table.

"I see everything was to your liking. Would you like me to bring your bill?"

"Bill?" Derrek asked. "I thought meals were complimentary."

"Oh, they are, Herr Snowe, but I just received a phone call with explicit instructions from Frau Müller to charge Herr Discord for every expense he partakes in."

Discord sighed. "Can you just put it on my tab?"

"I'm afraid not, sir. Frau Müller was very particular with her instructions. 'Cordy is to pay for every penny he costs us as soon as he finishes partaking,' and I don't believe a tab would suffice. And if I remember correctly, you have a hefty unpaid tab with us already, which I was also instructed to collect," Emmett said with his arms behind his back.

"Shit."

Derrek leaned over the table and whispered, "I can cover you if need be."

"Nah, I got hella cash, and besides, I doubt you've got one point two mil on you."

"Huh, one point two million? How do you even accumulate that much debt?"

"Gold-flake milkshakes."

Derrek decided not to ask further, as he was already rummaging around in his coat, presumably for money. Emmett has been holding a platter behind him, which he had set on the table, and Discord was producing several stacks of bills and piling them up in a pyramid shape.

"That's one point four million in five hundred euro bills so I can get ahead of myself. Make sure you put on the invoice that I said, 'I thought killing the deadlings would cover this.'"

"I will be sure to, sir," Emmett said as he pulled out a large handkerchief from his pocket, using it to cover the pile of money. He balanced it on his right palm, collecting their plates and glasses with his left. "I hope you have a pleasant evening, gentlemen," he said, and he walked away.

Discord looked upset but not angry as he stared out the window. It was clear to Derrek that he had been aware of the debt and was likely avoiding it, and it was possibly the reason he hadn't visited in so long. He figured a change in the subject may help his mood, and he had a new question to ask.

"So, what are deadlings?"

Discord quickly shifted his gaze to him and put on a fresh smile.

"Deadlings are the most common form of undead and occur when some kind of external force causes one's soul to be bound to a body, regardless of how alive the body is. They're usually caused by some low-level necromancer trying his hand at some more advanced stuff, but they have been known to pop up due to some supernatural strain of a disease, a high level of spiritual energy mixed with some industrial waste, or someone just having so much willpower that they refuse to fully die. Usually they're just some mindless zombies like you see in movies, just wandering about aimlessly, but sometimes, they remain sentient.

"A few years back, a herd of about fifty of them started hanging out in those woods over there," he said, pointing out the window, "but they don't usually come out during the day. Makes them rot. Some of the fangs wanted to deal with it themselves, but Mila wouldn't have any of it. I swear, she considers her entire staff family."

Discord had a smile on his face, but it was different from his usual cocky grin. It was warmer and caring.

"So, she gave me a call, and I wiped them out in about an hour. They aren't too much trouble. The hardest part about fighting them is making sure you get them all, because if you let even a single one live, they can get the whole damn herd back up to numbers in a week. If you shoot them just right, they pop like a balloon! It's great."

He stared out the window, looking longingly at the woods. He eventually looked back and poured himself another drink from Derrek's bottle, drinking it down in one gulp. He stood up and grabbed the bottle, signaling for Derrek to follow.

Discord led him to the lobby, and they both did their best to avoid dirty looks from the receptionist, and Derrek made a mental note to learn her name. They went up to the roof and took a seat in the same bench Derrek had shared with LaFayette several nights before.

They passed the bottle back and forth, taking sips and admiring the stars. Once Discord threw back the final gulp, he looked at the bottle, then back at the stars. Then the bottle. Then the stars.

He stood up and threw the bottle high in the air, pulled out a suppressed pistol, and fired a single silent shot. Derrek was surprised but didn't flinch as the shards of glass rained down around him, as he could clearly see he was in no danger: Discord had somehow shot it so precisely, the glass formed a perfect outline of a circle around them.

"Did you have to do that?" Derrek asked.

"No, but if I didn't, they'd win."

"They? Who are they?"

"*They.*"

Discord gave him a look that said, *I dare you to question this,* and Derrek decided to drop it. The two leaned back and stared up at the stars, the infinite expanse of empty space and lights. Derrek had done this before in the exact same spot, but he had a newfound appreciation for the unknown that surrounded the planet he called home.

He remembered he had access to seemingly all the knowledge

of the universe through Discord, the only man he had ever met who claimed to speak to God and gave a solid reason to believe him.

"Discord, can I ask you something?"

"Go for it."

"What's the meaning of it all?"

"What do you mean?"

"Well, earth, humans, monsters—everything, I guess. Is there some grand plan beyond mortal understanding, or is it all just truly random? Are we all born with meaning, or do we pave our own paths? Humans have spent thousands of years looking for these answers, and I figured you just might have them."

It was too dark for Derrek to see, but his words made Discord smile wide. He let a few seconds pass as he formed his sentences and tried to find a satisfying answer.

"There isn't anything predetermined. Even things that destiny pushes toward are not set in stone. They're more like suggestions from the universe. You already know how it all began, with you eating me billions of years ago, but as far as I know, there was nothing further behind it. And personally, I think humans spend way too much time looking for an answer when there isn't even a question to ask. They totally consume their lives in pursuit of a higher power or some kind of vindication for their very existence when all there is for them is a shrug and a middle finger."

He turned to make eye contact with Derrek. "Don't worry about the big answers; they're never gonna make sense. Look for what makes you happy—that's all you need for an existence that goes for a max of one hundred thirty years."

Derrek saw sincerity in Discord's eyes, but he also saw a flash of sadness before he turned away and looked back at the stars.

"Although," he resumed, "I've gotta give it to humans: no other creature on earth would ever do as they did. No fang would ever build an empire. No *jiangshi* would ever invent the car. No Lamia would aspire to something larger than their base needs. None of the species on this planet could ever compete with the raw ambition that is synonymous with humanity."

He paused as a meteor passed over the two, sending a streak of light across the sky.

"You may not be human anymore, but you know what it's like. A lot of things used to be human too, but they tend to lose their humanity pretty quick. Keep your head and keep yourself, and I'd be willing to bet anything you'll do great things."

They sat in silence, letting the time pass and dwelling on the events of the day. Derrek wasn't sure if he could have stayed as calm if Discord hadn't stuck by his side, even with the reaper's touch. He would have been blindly stumbling around, with no idea what had happened to him and no idea he was able to control his powers, even though he couldn't yet.

Discord had shown no sign he was going to leave, and he made it clear he was going to stay for as long as he was needed. Derrek got the feeling that he truly cared not only about him but about everything and everyone on some level. Despite knowing him for only a few hours, he was proud to call him a friend.

After about thirty minutes, Discord stood up.

"It's getting pretty late, and I've got some business to attend to. You should probably get yourself some sleep. You might actually need it."

"What? You don't know if I need to sleep?" Derrek asked.

"In your case, not one bit. Hosts of the Devourer have the same biological needs as any other member of their species—since, for all intents and purposes, that's what they are—but you ate a Reaper. I've never seen a devourer get one, and I have no idea what kind of effect that could have on a normal human, let alone one with a reaper's touch. We're in uncharted territory. Gotta play it by ear."

"Fair enough. I'll set in for the night," Derrek said as he stood and extended his arm for a handshake.

"Nope, not my style," Discord said as he embraced Derrek,

lifting him a full foot off the ground, pinning his arms to his sides and crushing his torso. He didn't remember the pain from having his entire spine dislocated earlier, but he assumed it felt something like that.

As suddenly as he had picked Derrek up, he dropped him, and he just barely landed on his feet. He took a moment to stretch and reset his shoulders as Discord stood before him, hands on his hips.

"I'm a hugger."

As Derrek realigned his spine, Discord had climbed atop the railing, the toes of his boots hanging over the edge as he balanced himself perfectly on the inch-wide surface.

"Training starts tomorrow. Get whatever rest you can," Discord said, his coat swaying in the breeze.

"All right. See you then," Derrek said, unfazed by his choice in places to stand.

Discord smiled one last time, then turned around to face Derrek. He saluted and took a step backward, free-falling to the ground.

Derrek looked over the ledge to find exactly what he expected: nothing. As he suspected, Discord was long gone. He smiled and went to the elevator, making his way back to his room to set in for the night.

Discord sat under a tree, just out of sight from the roof, as his mangled legs bled, shards of bone sticking out randomly, the legs themselves looking akin to a broken accordion.

He grabbed his ankles and pulled them straight outward, setting the major chunks of bone that remained roughly in place. Within seconds, they were as good as new. He sprang up and was on his feet as soon as he was sure he could walk, shaking off the lingering pain.

"Note to self: next time you break your fall with your legs, bend your knees."

He looked around, as he knew the only way to get her attention was to be at the site of the crime and he needed to get his directions right. He knew the hotel faced exactly cardinal west, and he took into account where he was before, and once he was sure which way to go, like a sprinter, he got ready to run, lining up on the proverbial block.

In an instant, he was gone, almost unnoticeable by the naked eye save for the wave of force that followed in his wake. Such was the reason he went through the woods, as well as going at a lower speed than he would have preferred so as to not disrupt the trees too much and give away his location to anyone who might be hanging around.

He ran for about three minutes before coming to a stop at the clearing where he had met Derrek only hours before. He took stock of his surroundings, the Conex where he assumed the Frostbyte equipment was kept, the outline where Boyd once lay, and the silhouette of a robed figure stood over it, slightly shorter than Discord.

Just who he wanted to see.

"You've been ignoring my calls, drifter," the figure said with a cold, feminine voice and a mild English accent.

"Sorry, I get bad reception out here in the boonies."

"You know that's not what I mean. I've been speaking to you for hours."

"And I've been busy."

"With the new devourer? Honestly, what do you think he will say?"

"Doesn't matter. I've got it covered. Besides, there's other matters we need to discuss."

"Obviously there are," she said, gesturing to the burnt outline of an oversized skeleton.

"I'm sorry about Boyd. I tried to get Havok to spare him, but his instincts took over, and he finished him off. We're gonna start training tomorrow to get that under control."

"No worries. Boyd was on his way to the Ether anyway. I knew about all of his 'deals'—that's why I let him perish."

"I thought it was weird you didn't step in. Figured you were busy with a contract."

"No, I haven't had to deal with a contract in decades. Delegation and whatnot."

"Right, right. So what's it like being the big boss?"

She glared at him, revealing her piercing green eyes. "There's no need for small talk, drifter. I'm only here on business."

"Then let's get to it."

She turned to face him, her features still hidden by her robe, save for her eyes.

"The devourer has the reaper's touch, which makes him a bigger threat than other incarnations and also puts at least part of the burden that comes from the destruction he causes on my shoulders. Since you did me a favor by taking Boyd out of the picture, I'll allow you amnesty from the slew of regulations you broke tonight."

"Well, I sure appreciate that, Grim."

"But …"

"Aw, shit."

"If this turns bad, I want your word you'll take responsibility and kill him."

A tense silence washed over the two, and they stared at each other, unblinking. The deafening quiet roared over the forest. Even the wind has ceased rustling the leaves.

Discord finally spoke, with one of the most serious tones he had ever taken in his long life. He said, "If he can't handle it, if he loses control, if he goes crazy, I won't hesitate to snuff him out. I'd think you of all people would know that."

"Yes," Grim said, "but I needed to hear you say it. Desk guy will hear nothing from me, but your Havok will—once he gets settled, of course."

"Seems fair to me. Give him a few months or so."

Grin silently nodded and turned toward the burnt grass that once held Boyd. She knelt and waved her hand, which glowed with green light, over the patch. Gradually, the burn began to shrink, condensing on a single point, until it too was replaced with the living grass it once had been. She stood, clearly proud of her work, and walked toward the tree line, then stopped just before she was out of sight.

She turned her head to Discord. "What a shame. It seems Boyd's scythe was lost in the chaos. Oh well."

She disappeared into the trees, and the ambient sounds of nature started anew.

Derrek awoke in his room with the aid of neither light nor alarm. Despite drinking almost as much as Discord had, he felt right as rain. He climbed out of bed and took a shower, surprising himself briefly with his hair and eye when he looked in the mirror. He realized it would take a while to get used to, and put in the contacts Mila had given him.

He got dressed and opened the curtains to find sunlight just barely poking out over the horizon. By his estimates, it was about 5:45. He checked his phone to find he was right. He also found roughly two hundred text messages of animals wearing human clothes, sent from a phone number with no area code and only four numbers: 7924.

He scrolled through a few, then decided to go through it in depth later and put his phone away. He had a good idea of who sent them anyway. The thought occurred that he had been staying at the Schadenfreude for two weeks at this point and had never opened the glass doors to his balcony, so he decided to do just that.

The experience was breathtaking—the wildlife grazing in the field, the smell of the dew, the gentle breeze that rolled over him, all as low sunlight made the clouds overhead into beautiful shades of orange, reminding him of the skin of a peach for some reason.

Suddenly, there was a firm hand on Derrek's shoulder.

"Yeah, the view is pretty awesome."

He turned to see the bushy beard of Jeffrey and the body it was attached to standing beside him, staring at the scenery. He looked at Derrek, and the peaceful face he had been wearing up until was quickly replaced with one of confusion.

Derrek remembered his hair. "I had a bit of a crazy night. Want to grab some coffee?"

"Yeah … coffee sounds good right about now."

As they left the room for the dining hall, Derrek saw that his door handle had been removed and the lock tampered with. As they entered the elevator, he leaned over to Jeffrey. "You're gonna get reception to fix my lock."

"Aw, come on. You got the last ones fixed."

"I'm pretty sure they'll start charging for property damage if I come to them with any more. Get it fixed."

Jeffrey was surprised at Derrek's newfound confidence. He had been no pushover before, but he could tell there was something different about him, aside from his hair.

After the elevator came to a stop, the two of them made their way across the lobby to the dining hall. They went to the buffet table and each poured themselves a mug of coffee. Jeffrey led the way to their usual table, and the two took their seats. After several sips in tense silence, Derrek broke the ice.

"So, the hair."

"Yes, what's up with the hair?" Jeffrey asked, glad Derrek had brought it up first.

"Last night, I went out and had a bit too much to drink. I met this weird guy, and we got into a fight with those assholes from last weekend. After that, I thought it would be fun to dye my hair. That's pretty much it."

"Well, all right then. Did I miss anything else while I was gone?"

"Not really, aside from that it's been business as usual. Actually, we're ahead on our quotas. If we keep going at this rate, we might be out a week early," Derrek said, pausing to take a long sip from his mug. He narrowed his gaze over his mug on Jeffrey, and after he set his coffee down, he said, "And where have *you* been?"

"Eh, just trying to buy a couch."

Derrek wasn't sure why, but he could tell Jeffrey was lying.

"That's the best you can come up with?"

"What're you talking about? There was an antique couch for sale in Bulgaria, first come, first serve. Almost had to drag race two other couch enthusiasts the whole damn way there."

"Did you get the couch?"

Jeffrey paused for a moment. "Yeah, I rented a storage unit to keep it until we ship out. Hey, have you been keeping up on your workouts?"

Derrek glared at him for a split second but decided to let the lie slide and replied, "Yeah, managed to get my time down to forty-six minutes on the ten-mile."

"Good. Cardio is real important."

Just then, a voice came from the side of the table. "I'll second that. Who wants pancakes?"

Standing next to the table was Discord, balancing no less than six plates stacked high with pancakes, topped with butter, in and on his arms. He straightened his arms out and deftly slid the plates so that two ended up in front of Jeffry, two in front of Derrek and two in front of Discord. He sat down in a chair that the other two men were sure had not been there a second earlier.

Jeffrey was stunned, staring blankly at this man in the least first-thing-in-the-morning attire he had ever seen. However, he was not one to turn down pancakes when offered. "I don't know who you are, but these pancakes smell so good, I don't really care."

Derrek, who had already started digging into one of his plates, chimed in, "This is Discord, the guy I met last night."

"Ah," Jeffrey said, extending his right arm and sticking his fork into one of his plates. "Major Jeffrey Reynolds. It's a pleasure."

Discord shook his hand and said, "Double Colonel Dis H. Cord. The pleasure's all mine."

"Double colonel?"

"Yep," Discord said, opening his coat, revealing a slew of medals and insignia. He pointed to one that was two eagles, each holding a bunch of wheat, with the United States crest on their chests, connected by one bar behind their heads and one behind their respective supply of wheat. He then said, "They wanted to promote me. I wanted to stay in the field. This was the middle ground."

"Huh?" Jeffrey said. He knew there was no such rank, yet his badge seemed legitimate. Had this man not brought copious amounts of pancakes, he might have questioned further, but he chose to chalk it up to the weirdness factor Derrek had mentioned earlier.

"Good morning, Discord," Derrek said. "How'd you sleep?"

"Like a bat, my friend—not at all. How's that hair treating you? Did it surprise you when you woke up?"

"Totally," Derrek said, digging into his own plates. "I didn't even think about it until I got out of the shower. For a second, I thought it was a trick of the steam."

The three shared a laugh, stopping to engorge themselves on the feast of flapjacks before them. After nearly five uninterrupted minutes of this, Discord was nearly a quarter into his second plate, while the other two were only close to halfway done with their first. He stopped and faced Derrek.

"Hey, could you do me a favor and grab a couple of bottles of syrup for the table?" he said, pointing his thumb over his shoulder across the room at a table with a plethora of syrups, jams, and butters.

"Yeah, sure thing."

Derrek got up and made his way toward the table. As soon as he was out of earshot, Discord faced Jeffrey.

"How long have you had that book?"

"Come again?" Jeffrey replied, confused by the question.

"The inferno, Latin, signed by L, the cursed one."

Jeffrey was stunned, then very angry. He was about to reach for his gun, but Discord put up his hand.

"Hold your horses, partner. You've got nothing to gain by killing me and nothing to lose by letting me live. I'm very discreet, and I doubt shooting anything here would go over well with anyone."

He was right—Jeffrey knew that. Whoever this man was, Derrek trusted him, and that would have to be enough for him.

"About fifteen years."

"And who gave it to you?"

Jeffrey was silent for a moment, then hesitantly said, "One of my squad mates, Arnold."

"And how much do you know about it?"

"Just that the day after he gave it to me he was killed by the same mortar that took my leg."

"Yeah, luck in exchange for misfortune. Real weird concept. You know, it actually works retroactively too."

"What do you mean?"

"It causes misfortune, yeah, but it brings fortune to those who have been unfortunate in their lives."

Jeffrey suddenly realized something. "How did you know I have the book?"

"It's your aura."

Jeffrey looked at him like he was stupid, to which Discord simply raised an eyebrow.

"Look, I knew you had the book, so I'm obviously not bullshitting you."

Jeffrey dropped the look and stared down at his pancakes.

"It's like a sixth-sense thing, except it's really closer to a thirty-fourth sense. It's intuitive. It's not like reading the colors around you and they say this or that. It's more like having a deep understanding of someone you've never met. Some people can get the same effect just from body language. Besides, I've always preferred syrup with my pancakes."

Jeffrey looked up at him in confusion, then saw that Derrek was only a few feet away, coming toward the table, two bottles of maple syrup in tow.

"I got the syrup. What were you two talking about?" he said, noticing Jeffrey's worried expression.

"Nothing much, just debating on whether syrup or butter is better for pancakes. Personally, I prefer both, but I'd go with syrup if I had to choose."

"Yeah ..." Jeffrey said, rolling with Discord's lie, not wanting to drag Derrek into the conversation. "My dad was really conservative and saw buying maple syrup as supporting the Communist Canadian bastards, so butter was always the go-to."

"I don't mind either," Derrek said as he took his seat. "Plain is even fine by me."

Discord slammed his hands on the table, causing his plates to jump nearly a foot high. They landed perfectly where they once lay and yelled, "Blasphemy!"

They were silent for a brief moment. Then Derrek began to chuckle. Pretty soon, all three men were laughing. After regaining their senses, the men began to smother what pancakes they had left in syrup and dug into the sweet, fluffy pile of goodness before them.

Over the next few minutes, none of them spoke a word, as they were enthralled by the hypnotic combination of the sweetness of the syrup and the smell of the pancakes. Once they were all finished with their meals, they sat there satisfied and overstuffed, even Discord. The next few minutes were quiet, aside from occasional grunts and gurgles from their stomachs dealing with their contents.

About ten minutes had passed, and their stomachs had settled. Discord stood up. "All right, Havok, let's get a move on!"

Jeffrey was confused and asked, "Havoc? His name's Derrek. And where are you off to?"

"It's Havok, with a K," Discord replied. "It's a nickname. And as of today, I'm taking this snow-haired corporate drone under my wing and putting him on my strict physical training regimen. It's how I achieved the level of confidence I proudly possess, and I think he'll benefit from it immensely."

"Huh. Are you good with this, Derrek?"

"Yeah, we agreed on it last night. Sounded like a good way to fill the weekends while I'm here."

"Well, all right. Got room for one more?"

Derrek looked at Discord with a worried look on his face, but Discord calmly said, "Sorry, no can do."

"And why the hell is that?" Jeffrey asked, slightly annoyed.

"I was taught this training technique by an extremely secretive society of monks. I took an oath to never reveal the secret to anyone save for those who prove themselves worthy. And I'm sorry bud, but you're ineligible."

"What does that even mean?" Jeffrey said, clearly getting more annoyed.

"I mean, look at you. You're buff. Your muscles are too developed. There's just no way."

Jeffrey was visibly unsatisfied with that answer but realized there was no way he was going to be able to tag along.

"Fine," he said. "Let me know how it goes. I've gotta meet with the project heads anyway. Apparently, they didn't approve my week off, so I have to deal with that shit show. See you around."

Jeffrey left with his hands in his pockets and a sour expression on his face. Derrek wanted to let him come along, but he knew there was no way he could find out the truth, not yet, at least, but that didn't mean he didn't feel bad about it.

Discord nudged him. "Don't worry about it too much. He's a grown man. He'll get over it."

"I know. I just don't like lying."

"That's good, but you'd better get used to it. It kind of comes with the territory."

"Yeah, I guess you're right."

"Besides, the monk thing wasn't entirely a lie. I just used it creatively. The secret they shared was actually just a recipe for a vegetarian paella, but I'll be damned if I'm breaking that promise."

Derrek cracked a smile and began stacking the plates for the ease of whoever cleaned them up. Discord told him it was time to get to it, and the two got up and made their way to the parking lot.

Derrek started walking toward the SUV they had used the day before, but Discord stopped him.

"Nah, we're taking *those* beauties."

He pointed to a pair of sleek-looking motorcycles, one red with black trim, the other white with blue trim. Discord was already mounted on the red one, which surprised Derrek, as he had been standing next to him just a second earlier, and the bikes were easily fifty feet away.

"You ever ride one of these?" Discord asked after Derrek closed the distance.

"I never even rode a bike as a kid. I don't know how well this will work out."

"It'll be fine. All you've got to do is keep your balance and keep up with me."

"I really don't think this is a good idea."

"Nonsense. It's the *best* idea. Just give it a shot."

Derrek sighed and climbed onto the white bike, and Discord tossed him a helmet, which he put on and strapped tight, while Discord left his own head uncovered. The key was in the ignition. Nervously, he turned it, causing the engine to spring to life with a roar.

Discord was visibly excited and cranked his own bike, revving his engine and burning out, leaving marks on the pavement under him. He popped a wheelie and circled around Derrek for a lot longer than he expected he'd be able to.

Goddamn it, Derrek said to himself as he lifted his kickstand and revved his engine and took off at fifteen miles per hour, beginning his crawl down the road.

Discord got back down on two wheels and rode alongside him, calling out over the roar of their engines.

"You gotta go faster."

Derrek shook his head no, to which Discord responded by leaning over and twisting his throttle, sending him shooting through the parking lot.

Derrek was terrified. His heart was racing, and he could feel sweat dripping down his forehead. Suddenly, a wave of calm washed over him. He felt his speed, and it was simpler than he expected. He kept his balance, leaning into his turns, weaving his way down the road with Discord by his side.

Discord took charge and led him down a side road still on the hotel property leading into the woods. The road was narrow and unpaved, likely meant for walking or bicycling, but the two continued for several minutes. They eventually got to a fork in the road. One path continued the one they were one. The other chained off and didn't seem to have been used in years.

Discord got off of his motorcycle and undid the chain, signaling for Derrek to move forward while he walked his bike behind the chain, which he replaced once his bike was on the other side. They went down that path for another ten minutes before arriving at a clearing. It was a big clearing and not unlike the others Derrek had seen, save for a large white circle along its border. They parked their bikes at the entrance and approached the circle. Discord waved his hand above the line, revealing a shimmering dome covering the area, giving Derrek a sinking feeling deep within. He wasn't sure why, but he felt unwelcome there, like the clearing itself wanted him gone.

"Don't mind it," Discord said, snapping Derrek out of his fixation on the dome. "It's a Null Dome. Nothing gets in, nothing gets out, at least not without someone like yours truly's say-so."

Looking at him, Derrek saw he had his arm extended into the dome, creating an opening the size of a door, which Discord waved him into. Entering it, he saw it was exactly the same as it looked from outside the dome on the surface, but he couldn't feel the wind or he hear the sounds of nature, save for immediately behind him. Suddenly, even that sound was gone, and Derrek knew he was trapped within this silent prison. The grass beneath his feet was the only thing he could feel, and he took a moment to crouch down and run his fingers between the blades. That managed to ground him and snap him out of it.

"Yeah," Discord said, "it can be a lot to take. Something about the sudden sensory deprivation mixed with the dome's repulsion of spiritual energy makes adjusting to it a real pain in the ass."

"You don't say?" Derrek said, still petting the grass, gradually restoring his composure. Discord stood aside and let him take however much time he needed, and after a minute and a half, he stood again and brushed some dirt from his knees.

"Ready?" Discord asked.

"Yeah, I'm ready."

"Good."

He reached into his coat and threw a blade at Derrek's feet, giving him only enough time to jump back and narrowly avoid getting stuck between the toes. He was about to give Discord a piece of his mind before he realized what was stuck in the ground in front of him was the sword he had used the day before.

"Pick it up," Discord said.

Derrek hesitated for a moment, then grabbed it by the grip and pulled the sword from the ground, finding it was more than a foot deep in the dirt. He took a few seconds to brush the clumps of dirt from the serrated side of the blade, being careful not to get his shirt caught on it.

"I've had that bad boy for a long time," Discord said. "A Japanese village had a bit of a problem with some minor trickster god turning their crops to worms, and they gave me that sword as payment. Damn thing wasn't even worth a thousand yen, so I took it to some temple or another and got that baby blessed, so now it can hurt spectral shit, including reapers. I call it Oni's Tooth. Treat it with respect."

Derrek nodded, then asked, "So, when do we start?"

Discord held up a single finger. "We just did. Lesson number one: Weapons have a history, just as people do. Treat yours not as a tool but as an ally. You and your weapon must be in sync, or you're dead."

Derrek looked to the sword, then back to Discord, then back to the sword, then finally said to Discord, "I get that, but I mean … it's still just a sword."

Discord dropped his smile and sighed, then waved Derrek over. "Come over here."

Derrek approached, and Discord reached his hands into his coat in a crisscross manner, producing two perfectly identical handguns covered with eldritch carvings and flecked with small drops of blood.

He raised the gun in his right hand. "This is Sue." He raised the opposite gun. "And this is Mary. They may seem to be regular old satanic looking 1911s, but the girls I'm addressing are souls trapped within said guns."

Derrek blinked a few times, trying to process the information, all while rapidly looking from each gun to Discord, until eventually, he found the word he was looking for.

"What?"

"Yeah, should've seen that coming," Discord said. He looked at his guns as if he were listening intently to someone speaking. "That might work."

He deftly tossed both guns to their opposite hands, flipping them as he did, then caught them by the barrel, Sue now in his left hand and Mary in his right. He extended both guns toward Derrek, grip first. "Hold them. You'll get it."

Derrek was hesitant, as was to be expected, but he stuck his sword into the ground and slowly reached for them, carefully grabbing both, avoiding the triggers at all costs. He examined them, taking note of the intricate carvings and etchings as well as how well-maintained they looked as a pair.

Like what you see?

The voice was feminine, and seemed to originate from within Derrek's head, confusing him immensely. He looked around to try to find the true source, but stopped once he heard a second female voice.

Look all you want, but you already found us.

What Discord had said seconds earlier finally set in, and he looked down at the weapons in his hands.

So, the first voice said, *I guess introductions are in order. The name's Susanne Bates, but everyone calls me Sue.*

The second voice spoke up. *And I'm Maribelle Bates. It's a pleasure to finally meet you, Derrek.*

Derrek was silent for several seconds and was certain that if he didn't have the reaper's touch, he would have been on the ground, catatonic from the sheer overload of weirdness. He eventually found his words, and spoke thusly.

"OK."

Sue and Mary lacked the facilities to show expression, but Derrek felt if they did, they would've blankly stared at him, as did Discord, who was disappointed he hadn't freaked out.

I guess underreaction is better than over, Sue said. *Probably didn't help we're a bit late.*

Mary said, *We would've gotten a better reaction if we met before Mila, I'm sure.*

So, got any questions, or did this pretty much cover it?

Derrek looked at them in thought for a few seconds. "I think I get it now, but do you mind if I ask a question or two?"

"Knock yourself out," the two said in unison.

"How did you two end up like this?"

They fell silent, and Derrek could feel the discomfort the question caused. Discord stepped forward and whispered into his ear.

"Yeah, they really don't like talking about that. I'll fill you in later, but I think it'd be best if I take them back."

"I'm sorry, I didn't realize."

"It's all good. Just hand them over and pick your sword back up. We need to get to training."

Without saying a word, Derrek handed Sue and Mary back to him. Discord twirled them, flipping them into the air and deftly catching them before slinging them into his coat, which rippled and flapped as if wind were blowing, even though that was impossible.

Derrek did as he was told and retrieved his sword after Discord put on his display. After he cleaned the dirt from the blade, he heard a near-deafening shot ring out and felt a burning pain in his left arm. He winced from the pain and jumped nearly ten feet away from it. He looked to Discord, the only other person in the dome, and saw him holding the same oversized revolver he had pointed at him the day before.

"What the hell was that?" Derrek asked.

"Reflex test. Yours are pretty good. You even managed to halfway avoid it. Could be better though."

Derrek groaned and remembered he didn't have too much say in the matter. "What was I supposed to do, then?"

"Dodge it, deflect it, catch it—doesn't matter to me—just do your best to not get hit."

"Well, could you at least give me some warning beforehand?"

"Nope," Discord said as he fired another shot.

Time slowed for Derrek, and he saw the bullet heading toward him, heading for his right shoulder. He moved on instinct alone and rolled to the left, avoiding it completely. He landed on his feet and stood with his sword at the ready. He caught a flash of Discord's face before he could train another shot on him, and he looked impressed before shooting another toward his calf.

He jumped, spinning midair as a large chunk of earth was dislodged beneath where his feet were. Amazed at his newfound acrobatic prowess, he twisted his body, allowing him to see where Discord was in order to anticipate his next move, but he saw nothing but grass where he should have been. A brief moment of confusion washed over Derrek before he felt the wind leave his body and a deep pain in his stomach, followed by a sharp decline. As he fell, he saw Discord, floating with his fist pointed toward the ground.

He hit the ground and bounced four feet into the air, then came to rest as he tried to catch his breath. Discord landed gracefully next to him and briefly examined the damage he caused. After seeing Derrek was still breathing, he put his fists at his side and looked down on him.

"Second lesson: Never take your eyes off your opponent. The moment you blink is the moment you lose."

Derrek gasped for air, struggling to breathe. He managed to pull himself to his knees, and through his deep breaths, he let out a strained, "No ... ted ..."

Discord reached out a hand, which Derrek accepted, and pulled him to his feet. He took a few more breaths, and soon enough, the pain in his stomach was gone, and he was ready enough for round two.

Discord allowed him to fall back, reloading his revolver to full and pointing it at Derrek, who stood with his sword raised and his eyes fixed on Discord. For a brief few seconds, the two stood motionless in anticipation of the others' action.

Suddenly, the gun was lowered to Discord's waist and he fan-fired three shots, all aimed for center of mass. Derrek knew he didn't have enough time to avoid the bullets, so he gripped the hilt of his sword tightly and focused on his timing.

He swung the sword at an angle, deflecting the first shot over his head, doing the same for the second with a slash in the opposite direction. He wasn't so lucky with the third shot and was only able to take the force of the bullet just above the cross guard, violently launching the sword out of his hands, which were stinging with pain.

Another shot rang out as he reeled from the last hit, so he rolled, retrieving his sword along the way, and a chunk of dirt was blasted away some ways behind where he stood and readied himself for the next attack. Before he could prepare, however, he was greeted by Discord, standing inches away from him, with his right leg lifted high over his head.

He dropped his leg down, giving Derrek no time to react as the back of Discord's foot crashed in between his neck and shoulder, dropping him instantly to the ground.

"Lesson *número tres*: Predict your opponent while leaving them guessing. Works every time. And hold your sword a bit looser. You've got crazy strength, but if you hold as tight as you are, you've got no wiggle room when you take a straight hit."

Derrek was unable to move his limbs and his entire body was numb but somehow also exploding with pain, but he was breathing normally, so that was a plus. He lay flat on his back, splayed out along the grass, trying with all he had to move any part of himself. He could wiggle his toes, but for the time being, that was about the extent of his abilities.

Discord saw the state he was in. He knelt down next to his shoulder and gently pinched the spot where his foot had slammed into, and Derrek instantly regained full control of his motor functions, albeit with some definite stiffness.

"Sorry about that," Discord said. "There's a pressure point there, and I guess I overloaded your nervous system. Basically rebooted your whole body."

Derrek pulled himself to his feet and began stretching, alleviating the stiffness and limbering him up. As he rubbed his neck, he said, "So, is there an end goal here, or are you just having fun kicking my ass?"

"A little bit of both," Discord replied, grinning widely. "You can't get stronger from fighting someone you can easily beat. It's like chess; the only way you can get better is by going against those better than you."

Derrek started to protest, but he knew it was a good point.

"I guess that's fair," he said, picking his sword back up and raising it in his best estimate of what a dueling stance was, "but don't think I won't get in some hits of my own."

After hearing that, Discord's grin grew to a full-blown smile. He reached into his coat and slowly pulled out the sword he had used the day before, gripping it with his right hand, pointing it toward Derrek.

"Come and try, then."

Derrek rushed forward, closing the gap with a wide, leftward slash, which Discord braced for with the flat of his sword. He then hit Derrek with an open-palm strike, throwing him back several feet, but he remained standing.

Without missing a beat, he jumped forward, thrusting his sword toward Discord's chest. Just before the blade made contact, however, he was flung forward from Discord, kicking him in the back. He turned as he moved, digging his feet into the ground, leaving two trenches in his wake.

Discord rested his sword on his shoulder, beaming with pride. "You've got good form, but you're staring at your targets. I could tell exactly where you were going for. Try visualizing where you wanna strike instead while keeping your eye on me as a whole."

"Huh. All right, I'll give it a try," Derrek said as he dug his feet out of the ground. After kicking a large portion of the earth from his shoes, which he was sure were going to be ruined by the end of it, he rushed at Discord, staring him down as he readied his sword for an upward strike.

Discord jumped back as the slash cut through the air where he once stood, catching a portion of his coat's fabric, leaving a large gash across it. After landing, he looked at Derrek and readied his sword as threads began to launch from one end of the damage to the other, rapidly pulling itself together until the fabric was fully restored.

"Hells yeah! That's the spirit!"

As Derrek ran at him with his sword raised, Discord did the same and their blades clashed in an explosion of sparks and a shockwave that flattened all of the grass within a ten-foot radius. The two men pressed their swords against each other, moving back and forth as they fought over the upper hand, but Discord had the clear advantage. At least, that was until Derrek head butted him, shattering his nose in a shower of blood and a sickening crunch.

As he reeled from the pain, Derrek capitalized on the opening he had created and swept his leg, throwing Discord off of his feet and onto the ground. After his nose healed, he opened his eyes to see the point of a sword in his face. A few seconds passed before either of them spoke, and it was Discord to break the silence.

"You gonna go for the kill or what?"

Another pause fell over them, and to Discord's surprise, Derrek stuck his sword into the ground next to his head and reached out his hand.

"We're only sparring, right?"

Discord was shocked. He had planned for everything in case Derrek wasn't able to control himself. He brought him to a place where he couldn't escape should he need to be contained. He did everything he could to drag the power out of him, from a surprise attack to a complete bodily shutdown, but this was something he never expected from anyone, especially a host of the Devourer.

Mercy.

It was indeed only meant to be a sparring match, albeit an extremely intense one, but even still, Discord expected him to at least try to kill him. They both knew even if Derrek landed a fatal blow, it wouldn't take, but not once did he go for a lethal strike. Even with all this shared knowledge between the two, Discord could tell by the look in his eyes that were he not immortal and were they true enemies, Derrek would have done the same thing he had done then.

Discord's face changed to a smile, but one unlike his usual cocky grin. This smile was warm and knowing. He accepted Derrek's hand and used it to pull himself to his feet, and the two met eyes. They didn't see ancient foes or strangers, but they both saw friends in the other.

After a few seconds, Derrek was lifted off of his feet, lifted into the air in a narrow arc, and slammed flat on his back. He opened his eyes to see Discord, still holding onto his hand with his grin returned.

"Fourth lesson: Mercy is a damn good thing, but never forget that some will use it against you."

Derrek groaned and used Discord's hand to pull himself up. "I should have stabbed you in the face."

"You're welcome to try again. Arm up, we're going for round two."

Derrek nodded and pulled his sword from the ground, shaking the dirt from the jagged back of the blade and preparing himself for an attack. He had his doubts, as anyone in his situation would, but at that moment, in that split second in time, he knew that this was not only what he was meant to do but who he was meant to be. He lunged forward with his sword raised, a smile on his face and conviction in his heart.

A week had passed since that fateful day. Aside from Derrek's hair, nearly everything stayed the same. He started his days exercising with Jeffrey, now fully able to keep pace with him and even able to completely lap him several times over, but he consistently opted to keep pace to avoid raising suspicion. Discord joined them on Monday, but after five minutes of running (in his normal clothes, no less) he got bored and said he would catch up after Derrek got back from work. He didn't join them again.

Work had been going smoothly, aside from the expected questions about his hair. Luckily for him, however, everyone bought it, although Derrek was suspicious that Gary wasn't fully convinced, but considering he hadn't heard a single word from him in the two weeks they had been working together, he was confident it wasn't going to be a problem. His team had met their quota for the entire trip by Thursday, which they were expected to meet on Wednesday of the following week. Despite this, nobody saw it as an excuse to slack off, and they resolved to keep their productivity up despite meeting their goals.

He spent the majority of his time outside of work with Discord, mainly at bars or training in the woods. His reflexes were improving, and he was getting used to using a weapon. His wounds healed quickly, even when he slipped up and took a slash full force over his arm, he was back and swinging in minutes and healed over with nothing but a scar over the next couple of days. Even though he was getting acclimated to his new enhanced physical capabilities, he still wasn't able to control his Devourer abilities. He had tried several times over the week, mainly trying to absorb trees and small insects with limited success to say the least. But at this particular moment, Derrek was helping pack up the GENRAM for the weekend. He had just secured his corner of the tarp they wrapped around it when he felt a slap on his back.

"Feeling all right, young buck?'

He turned around to find Hanna standing before him, concern on her face.

"Yeah, why?"

"You've been different, and I don't just mean the hair. You're kinda distant. You aren't talking as much. I dunno. You just seem off lately."

"Oh, well … I've been on a new diet."

He knew it wasn't a great lie, but he hoped it would work. He didn't like having to lie, but there was no chance he could be honest.

"Diet, huh? Is paleo making a comeback?"

"Don't know, mine is all about, uh, portion control. Yeah, reducing intake by half, it's supposed to extend cell life."

Hanna eyed him over from head to toe, not seeing any indication he had slimmed down. However, according to him, he had just started the diet, and since he already had a slender form, a diet might not show right away. She didn't fully believe him, but the story made enough sense that she accepted it.

"Well don't go overboard with it, I've heard horror stories of people who get way too absorbed in their diets."

"Thanks, I appreciate your concern, but I think I've got a handle on it."

Hanna smiled and began to walk off before turning back around and saying, "Oh yeah, Amir wanted to talk to you. Said something about the hotel—I don't know."

She then went to help Joey and Ann, who were in the process of wheeling the GENRAM away, and Derrek made his way to the cars, where Amir was going through a large stack of papers on his clipboard. He hadn't noticed Derrek for several seconds after he walked up and continued to remain ignorant of his presence until he let out a short cough.

"Ah, Derrek, just the man I was looking for."

"Yes, sir. What did you need?"

"Apparently, there was an inquiry made about how long you will be staying at the Schadenfreude, and I just wanted to make sure I give the right answer."

"Oh? Who was it who asked?"

"I probably should not say, but ..." He leaned in close to Derrek and whispered, "It was Mr. Shale."

Derrek was suddenly nervous. Up to that point, the only person he was sure knew about his relationship with Shale was Jeffrey, and he wasn't sure how much Amir knew.

"Oh, what did he say?" he asked, remaining calm.

"He said you had yet to take any vacation days for this period and that if you were to extend your stay, there would be no complications on corporate's end. You would simply have to get your arrangements in order with the hotel and inform either Ms. Shepherd or Mr. Philman."

Derrek thought about it for a few seconds, and realized it might be a good idea to take some time to commit himself to training. He had the vacation days, and it could be dangerous to go home before getting his powers under control.

"Huh," he said, "I'll have to give that some thought."

Amir nodded. "Be sure to make your decision before we leave next Friday." He looked over Derrek's shoulder near the Conex, where he saw Joey and Steven struggling to close the doors. "Could you be so kind as to give them a hand? I need to get these sorted out," he said, gesturing to his papers.

Derrek nodded and went to help them. The GENRAM was sticking almost a foot out from the Conex, preventing the doors from being closed. Realizing it must be pushing into something, Derrek took the initiative and pulled the GENRAM out singlehandedly, surprising Joey and Steven, who had used everything they had to get it in there.

In the back of the Conex, there was a heavily dented cardboard box directly in the path of the GENRAM, labeled "Nets." Derrek, assuming they were the nets used in their traps for small mammals, picked it up and set it aside, clearing the way. He effortlessly pushed the GENRAM back up the ramp and into the Conex, closed the doors, and locked it as Joey and Steven stared at him in awe.

Derrek still wasn't sure what the extent of his new physical abilities were, but he knew the GENRAM took a minimum of two people to move; the company handbook dictated four. He looked over at the men who were staring at him and slowly raised his arms in a victorious pose, which was met with uproarious applause from the two.

"Damn, dude," Steven said. "What do you lift? Elephants?"

"Yeah man," Joey said, "you gotta tell us your routine. If I can make gains like *that*, I'll be a friggin' beast!"

"Well," Derrek began as the two men scrambled to find something to write with, quickly finding the markers in their uniforms pockets and writing directly on their gloves, "I start every morning with a ten-mile run. After that, I do a hundred push-ups, eighty jumping jacks, and fifty sit-ups."

The men hung on his every word, surprised that was where he stopped talking.

"Is … is that all?" Joey asked.

"That's all I've been doing."

"For how long?"

"About three weeks now."

Steven chimed in. "So, you got this strong in that short a period just with that routine?"

"Well, everybody's metabolism is different."

Joey and Steven started nodding and agreeing, completely convinced. Derrek didn't feel too bad about what he said, as it was technically the truth, even if he didn't add that he had more than just his metabolism working for him in that department.

"Hey," Derrek said, interrupting their quiet pow-wow, "I haven't been working out on the weekends, but you guys are welcome to join me Monday morning."

Without so much as a moment of hesitation, both of them exclaimed, "Yes!" and began slapping Derrek on the back, giving him high-fives and going on about how he was a true bro.

After locking up the Conex, everyone put away their uniforms and loaded up for the ride back to the hotel. Aside from Joey and Steven insisting that they ride with Derrek, pestering him all the way with questions about his workout, the drive had gone the same as the previous dozen. When they arrived, everyone did as they normally did: split off and spend the night their own way. Derrek went to his room, half expecting Discord to be inside, raiding the minibar and watching *Kuchenparty*, but when he opened the door, he was met with a pristine room. Ever since Mila arranged for his continued stay, her staff had been paying special attention to him and his room, and it seemed housekeeping would step in every time he stepped out. He didn't mind too much since they always left a mint on his pillow.

He sat on his bed and heard a crinkle from underneath him, prompting him to stand. He saw a freshly crumpled sheet of paper at the foot of his bed that read as follows:

Ate all the chocolate almonds in your fridge. Meet me on the roof when you can. I got my hands on some pretty cool stuff.

—DC

Underneath the message was a crudely drawn picture of what Derrek gathered to be a dog wearing sunglasses riding either a skateboard or a surfboard—he wasn't quite sure—but he didn't want to keep Discord waiting. He quickly changed his clothes, made his way to the elevator, and rode it to the roof. As soon as the doors opened, he was hit with a wafting stink reminding him of a skunk. After reacting to the initial stench, he looked around to find a man in a red coat with his back to him leaning over the railing, smoke billowing from in front of him.

"Jesus, Discord, what is that stench?" Derrek asked as he made his approach, covering his nose and mouth with his shirt. After getting a better look, he saw Discord was holding what looked like a rolled cigarette, except it was the size of a cigar, which he was in the middle of taking a long drag from.

After finishing his inhale, he held up a finger, gesturing for Derrek to wait. A full ten seconds passed, and Discord let out his breath, releasing a wave of smoke as a dragon would release a rush of fire. He coughed slightly, which surprised Derrek, who had seen him take a knife to the forehead without so much as flinching.

"Grade-A Algonquian kush," he said, reaching toward Derrek with the joint. "Want a puff?"

"I think I'll pass," Derrek said through his own coughs, as he was now downwind of the smoke.

"Come on, Havok. You don't have any idea how long you've got. Your life could end at any second in a million different ways, from undiagnosed brain aneurysms to rogue space trash making its way through the atmosphere. Humans—or former-humans, in your case—owe it to themselves to give everything that comes their way a fair shake, especially in your case. I mean, if you ever lose control, I'll have to put you down, which is a threat very few people have to worry about. Give it a try."

Derrek was suddenly reminded of the scores of waivers he signed the week before that had told him the hundreds of ways he could die and how prepared for his death Frostbyte was. Especially now that he knew alcohol had practically no effect on him now, he decided to heed Discord's advice and accepted the unwieldy cigarette.

Discord cracked a half smile. "Just make sure you actually inhale. It won't do jack if you just hold it in your mouth."

Derrek slowly put the joint to his mouth and inhaled, feeling the burning-hot smoke within his lungs. He held it for as long as he could, then released it all in a violent coughing fit. He handed it back to Discord and keeled over, holding onto the railing for support.

"Yeah, it has a bit of a kick to it," Discord said before taking another drag. "That might just be the sage, though."

Between his coughs, Derrek managed to ask, "Sage?"

"Yep, that was about half sage."

His coughing worsened, and he felt himself getting lightheaded. His field of vision was beginning to narrow, and he fell to his knees, still gripping the rail, trying to pull himself up.

"Funny thing about sage. It's great for clearing bad juju out of wherever it's being burned but practically toxic to spectral beings when inhaled."

Derrek was dry-heaving from his coughing but had nothing to expel and continued to suffer through his lack of air. The world around him was getting quieter and blurrier.

"Ghosts, banshees, and especially …"

Derrek looked up at Discord, seeing the cold look in his eyes, the complete lack of empathy chilling him to the bone. He felt a rush of emotions; anger, betrayal, sadness, and rage washed over him for a brief moment before everything faded to black, leaving nothing but a voice.

"Reapers."

Derrek was awakened by a loud yell, his eyes met with intense darkness. His lungs and throat ached, but he could breathe again, although his stomach growled and he could feel his lips were chapped from dehydration. He scrambled and felt around, finding his surroundings to be cool to the touch, and hard as rock.

"Wakey wakey!"

A familiar voice echoed around him. He couldn't tell where the source of it was, but he could tell it was Discord speaking. He felt a rush of anger, but got the feeling it wouldn't do him any good, so he put those feelings aside and called back out to him.

"Where am I, Discord?"

It took a moment for him to respond, likely due to the echoing nature of their conversation.

"Some cave—not sure what it's called."

Derrek put his face in his hands, exasperated and beyond annoyed.

"Why am I here?"

Discord's hearty laughter echoed through the cave, gradually growing louder and louder, to the point where it was nearly deafening.

"Cause that's where I put you, silly!"

Derrek groaned and came to the conclusion that Discord would be no help. He felt his way to his feet, which, due to the damp, uneven ground, was harder than it should have been. It was pitch black, and he couldn't see past his nose.

He could see a faint outline of the cavern surrounding him, growing clearer by the second. Soon enough, he saw the cavern clearly. He found an exit standing before him, although the green tint to it all was unusual. He waved his hand in front of his face, finding a light source coming from his left eye.

This had not happened before, even in his room at the Schadenfreude with the curtains closed, so he assumed it was his body's response to needing a light source. He took note of his newfound ability and trudged forward through the rocky opening before him, heading into a hallway-like tunnel, leading on as far as he could see.

"It's kinda funny," Discord's voice echoed. "Reapers are pretty much immune to poison, venom, bullets, knives, even nukes, but a little bit of sage in their lungs, and they're practically dead for half a day."

Derrek did his best to ignore him and pushed onward, and he found himself in a larger cavern with another door-like opening fifty feet away. He walked toward it, but after a few feet, he found the ground underneath him to be absent suddenly, and he began to fall.

He managed to catch himself on the ledge he just slipped off of, and he pulled himself back up. He was shaken but quickly got over it and peered over the edge. Saw that the light from his eye could not show the bottom, and as the light reached from one end of the chamber to the other, he decided that falling was out of the question. The crevice stretched over the majority of the cavern—thirty feet, by his estimate—and he was certain he couldn't jump it.

"You alive in there?" Discord called out. "Thought I heard some slipping and falling."

"I'm fine—asshole."

"OK, good. Thought you fell down that pit for a second there. The bottom is absolutely riddled with stalactites."

"Stalag*mites*. When they rise from the ground, they're stalagmites."

"Oh, yeah. Thanks, buddy!"

Derrek groaned again and looked around, trying to find a way across. There were no materials to work with on his end aside from a pair of wood posts with scraps of rotten rope tied to them, telling him there was once a bridge spanning the gap. He brushed it off as useless, as he was fairly sure he couldn't travel back in time to the point when the bridge once swung, and continued to scan the room, looking for anything useful.

He saw a small stretch across the gap along the wall left to him. It was maybe a foot wide, but it bridged the gap completely, and it was crossable as long as he stayed close to the wall. He spread his body out against the wall, making himself as flat as possible, and inched his way across the seemingly bottomless pit beneath him. He was almost ten feet across when he heard Discord's voice again.

"I always get those confused, you know, like conscience and conscious? Always trips me up."

With those words, Derrek's foot slipped, giving him only a split second to regain his balance. He stayed in place for a few seconds, allowing him to steady his hands and calm his pulse. After regaining his composure, he kept moving along, making it almost halfway across.

"What do you think about hitting up that Italian place in the village when we're done? I could go for some Alfredo right about now."

Derrek continued to ignore him and finally came to the end of the ledge. He carefully stepped onto the solid ground, getting down on his knees for a moment, in appreciation of the ground he always took for granted. He got back on his feet and continued through the tunnel.

"This actually reminds me of Orpheus and Eurydice. You ever heard that one? Real sad story."

After walking for several minutes, Derrek began to wonder just how far the tunnel went. At some point, he picked up a foul stench coming from ahead, smelling of rotting meat with faint traces of roses. He wasn't sure he wanted to continue and looked behind him, contemplating turning back. He couldn't be sure, but he could have sworn he saw something at the limit of his vision retreat, swallowed by the endless darkness. He turned back around and continued on his way, picking up his pace.

"It's all about these two lovers, and like any good love story, it starts with death. Eurydice got bit by a snake, and she bit the big one, but Orpheus, son of Apollo, the other half of this couple, wasn't gonna let her go without a fight."

After some time, Derrek found himself in a smaller cavern, and the stench nearly overwhelmed him. He coughed and dry heaved, and for a brief moment, he was glad his stomach was empty. After acclimating to the smell, he took a look around and found the source in the center of the room.

There was a mutilated corpse in the middle of the room in an advanced stage of decay. It lacked any identifying features, such as a head or skin, but based on the scraps of clothing and the partially intact backpack alongside the vaguely torso-shaped mess of bone and dried blood, he could only assume it was human.

"So, what he did was he went to the underworld, a big no-no for mortals and an even bigger one for demigods. He just played his lyre all the way through, putting Cerberus to sleep, and even swaying Hades's heart on his strict no-exceptions policy with letting souls escape."

Derrek did not want to stay in this room, and he hurried along, staying close to the wall to avoid the smell. As he passed through the next tunnel, he thought he heard scratching along the floor behind him, and he quickened his stride. He continued for a few minutes, eventually outrunning the smell and apparently only keeping pace ahead of whatever was following him. As he continued through, he felt around his person, trying to see if his knives were still on his belt just in case the sounds behind him weren't just his imagination, but it seemed Discord had disarmed him.

"He let Orpheus leave with his love, but on one condition: he could not look at her until they were back in the mortal world, or else she would eternally be the property of the underworld."

He felt a slight breeze blow across his face, and he was filled with hope as he thought this was a sign he was close to escaping this subterranean hell. Before he could finish that thought, however, he found himself in yet another cavern. The first thing that caught his eye was a massive stalagmite, stretching over a hundred feet into the air. Surrounding it were countless smaller ones, covering the entire floor, save for a path that had been cleared along the large stalagmite, which he started to follow.

"And to his credit, he made it pretty far—way farther than anyone else could have. But at the last stretch, he stole a glance and saw her beautiful face one last time. Of course, she wasn't so beautiful after her skin fell off."

Derrek stopped dead in his tracks halfway around the stalagmite. He didn't know what it was, but he suddenly felt a deep feeling of dread. He knew he could not go forward; nor could he turn back. He had no idea what, but he knew something was watching him, and this time, he knew it wasn't his imagination.

"A lot of people see the moral of that story as *If you love someone, you have to have patience with them*, but personally, I always saw it differently."

Derrek's heart raced. He knew something was close.

"*Never … look … back.*"

He turned his head slightly and caught a brief glimpse of the emaciated figure behind him, sparing him only enough time to start running along the path. The creature, whatever it was, began to screech in a high-pitched tone, hurting Derrek's ears and preventing him from keeping track of it as it jumped around the cavern. He managed to get to the next tunnel and ran through as fast as he could, trying to outrun the thing chasing him, which was clawing on his back, catching his shirt a few times, prodding him to go faster.

The tunnel suddenly opened into a wall of trees surrounding a small clearing, the moon hanging low in the sky, and a brief wave of relief washed over Derrek, which was soon replaced with the sensation of claws digging into his back. He was thrown to the ground, and he only had time to flip himself right side up before he was met with a withered figure.

It was humanoid, but its limbs were long and slender, and its hands ended in four knife-like appendages. Its skin was pale and pulled taught across its skeleton. Its eyes, or rather, where eyes should have been, were grown over with skin, apparently an adjustment to life without light. Its teeth were long and jagged, and its jaw stretched further than it should as it screamed in Derrek's face.

Without thinking, Derrek swung his fist at the creature's face, making contact with its jaw, even breaking off a tooth, which unfortunately got stuck in the meat of his right hand. He scrambled back to his feet and looked around for anything he could use as a weapon, quickly settling on a heavy-looking branch right next to him. He gripped it with both hands, gushing blood from his wound, and getting ready as the creature recovered and jumped at him.

He swung the branch, shattering it in a shower of splinters over its head, leaving nothing but a short chunk of wood in his hands. He threw the splintered piece at the creature, annoying it but having no other effect. He tried to find another makeshift weapon and set his eyes on a large rock nearby but was tackled by the creature before he could reach it.

It scratched and clawed at Derrek's chest as he tried to fight it off, punching and kicking wildly, breaking bones that never seemed to stay broken and shattering teeth that seemed to keep growing. He was losing the struggle, and the creature continued to tear chunks from his flesh, trying to bite into him, just out of reach but quickly getting closer. He knew he couldn't hold it off forever. It was just a matter of time before he became this thing's next meal.

Suddenly, he felt a surge of strength from deep within him. He had felt an adrenaline rush before and knew that wasn't what this was. He grabbed the thing by the throat and managed to flip it, pinning it to the ground as it continued to claw into him, slowing as its airflow was cut off.

When it stopped clawing, Derrek suddenly felt a deep, intense heat, as if his insides were on fire. His mind became foggy, and he could not think of anything save for the creature before him. He placed his hands on both sides of its head and stared into where its eyes would have been. He opened his mouth, letting out an orange beam of light, followed by one from each of his eyes, burning into the creature's face. It began burning from the inside out, visibly deflating its form as its body burned an outline into the barren earth beneath it.

Once nothing was left but a charred skeleton in a misshapen form, Derrek closed his mouth and eyes, stopping the flow of light. He reopened his eyes, which were back to their usual, heterochromous state. He pulled himself to his feet and stared out into the woods, where Discord slowly emerged.

"I was never a fan of the ending. If I had my say, I'd have it end a bit more like this."

Derrek glared at him. "So, did I pass your fucking test?"

"I wouldn't call it a test. Tests have answers. This was more of a challenge, and you passed it with flying colors!" Discord said, smiling widely.

"What was that thing?"

Discord walked over to the charred remains and picked up the skull, then began clearing the soot from it. "It's got a stupid name: 'cave monster.' They're like wendigos, except they live in caves, but because of semantics and cultural differences, they're considered different things."

Discord now held a clean skull filled with jagged teeth. He tucked it into his jacket and his hand came out holding a bottle of water and a protein bar, both of which he handed to Derrek. He accepted and quickly downed the water and tore into the bar.

"I'm sure you guessed it," Discord said as Derrek took another large bite from his protein bar. "But what you just did was *devouring*. That's what you did to Boyd."

Derrek took a break from eating, and took his first breath since he started. He then said, "You could have just—I don't know—*asked* me to come down here. I don't see why you had to poison me for this."

"I needed you weak, confused, and angry—that's always the best combination for something caused by pure desperation. And do you have any idea how dramatic that shit was? Had a whole parallels thing going, not to mention some OG Greek tales."

"And what if that thing killed me? What then?"

"But you didn't die, did you?"

"That is not an excuse."

"I get that a lot."

Derrek finished his protein bar and stared at the burnt earth where the creature once lay. He couldn't remember devouring Boyd, but he knew it meant his body had changed in some way. And if he somehow became like that creature …

"You won't turn into one of them."

"Huh?" Derrek asked.

"The devourer integrates only positive physical traits, like sharper senses or tougher skin."

"What about my sage allergy then?"

"Weaknesses don't count as physical traits, but they're nowhere near as potent. That puff of sage you took would have sent a full reaper into a coma for a month. This thing probably gave you better hearing or something like that, maybe its regenerative abilities—I don't know. I never had the chance to study how it chooses, just how its hosts fight."

Derrek took a seat on a nearby rock, exhausted as his adrenaline wore off. He examined the wound on his hand, which was already swollen and was starting to turn purple around the tooth. Hesitantly, he grabbed it as far up as he could and jerked it out, causing blood to spurt from the hole in his hand. It hurt more than he thought it would, but he kept his cool. Discord approached him and gently grabbed his wrist, assessing the damage.

"Getting bit by a wendigo, or cave monster, is like getting bit by a dozen corpses. The amount of bacteria that builds up on those teeth is just straight bonkers," he said, pointing to the tooth Derrek was holding.

Discord put his hands around the wound and closed his eyes, concentrating deeply. A warm light began to glow within his palms, and the pain slowly began to fade. Within seconds, the pain was gone, and Discord removed his hands, revealing that the wound had healed perfectly, leaving little more than a circular scar halfway between the base of his pinky and wrist.

Derrek was stunned, and after several seconds of looking at his newly-healed hand, he asked, "How did you do that?"

"I didn't really do much. Most of that was all you. It's like jumping a car."

"What?"

"I used a bit of my spiritual energy to draw yours out, allowing your body to take it from there. You've got a shitload, especially after eating that thing," Discord said, throwing his thumb over his shoulder at the burnt remains.

Derrek looked at his hands again. He didn't know just how strong he was. Nor did he have any idea what he was capable of, but in that moment, he felt strong. He had fought for his life, and he had survived. He wasn't sure how long it would be until he could call upon his ability to devour at will, but he could control it, and that meant progress. He was still mad at Discord, but he decided a beer on him would be enough for him to set it aside.

Discord set his hand on Derrek's shoulder, and before he could look up from his own hands, he was back in his room. He looked around, confused, and rightfully so.

"So, was this all some weird dream, or did you drug me again?" he asked, exasperated.

Discord laughed. "Neither, I just figured you'd rather get here quick than make the whole walk."

"But how did you do that? Did we just teleport?"

"Nah, I just kicked it into eighteenth gear and dragged you across a few dozen miles."

Derrek stared at him for a few seconds. "Huh. All right."

He sat on his bed and immediately lay back, sprawling onto the mattress, allowing the comfort to wash over him. Discord saw the look of exhaustion on his face. "Your phone and knives are in your nightstand. Rest up. We're taking the day off, but we're going back into it on Sunday."

He walked toward the door. Derrek grunted in the affirmative, then closed his eyes and fell right asleep. Discord looked back at him and decided to drape his blanket over him and take off his shoes, as he knew just how much he had gone through. After getting him in order, he left the room and went to the neighboring one, using his key to open the lock.

He had rented the room, as per his agreement with Mila, but he had barely spent any time in it. He did as he usually did for hotels when he showed up—draped the curtains, installed an extra lock, and put up whatever maps or charts he needed at the time. He had one map that was on the wall which marked the cave he dropped Derrek in. He no longer needed it, so he folded it up and stuck it into his coat.

He had a white cloth laid over the bed, atop of which were no less than seven guns he had been working on, cleaning the ones he collected, carving runes on the ones ready to go. The pistol he took during the pub scuffle the week before was among them, now unrecognizable, as it was finally given the attention it needed. Nothing irked him quite like poor weapon-maintenance habits.

He stood in front of the wall and scanned the maps, looking to see which lead he should follow next. There were reports of Skinwalkers in Washington state, which wasn't unusual, but the numbers were worrying. There was an online listing for a statue made of solid platinum, possibly a primordial relic. He made sure to keep placing bids, but tracked down the IP address of the seller just in case he was outbid at the last second. It was what was happening in France, however, that worried him the most.

Several known poachers were seen congregating at a cabin in the French countryside. Discord hadn't had the chance to check it out, but he worried they may have caught Derrek's scent, or worse—they were targeting the Schadenfreude.

It's always something, he said to himself as he pulled an open beer from his coat and took a sip. Still cold.

He heard a knock on his door. He didn't bother with the peephole since he already knew who it was. He undid the locks and opened the door and was met by a man with a bald head, a bushy beard, and a gun in his hand.

"How's it hanging, Jeffy?" Discord asked nonchalantly.

Jeffrey's face was serious, and his hand was steady as he rested his finger on the trigger. He didn't say a word, just gestured with the gun for Discord to go inside his room.

"All right then, won't you come in?" he asked, bowing and gesturing for Jeffrey to enter, which he did, closing the door behind him. He went to his minifridge and pulled out a Brewski, which he handed toward Jeffrey. Continuing his silent streak, he just stared at Discord, who eventually set it down on the dresser next to him.

"Nice piece. Looks like you clean it regularly. Oh damn, you even put a coat of polish over it? Classy."

"Shut up," Jeffrey said, pointing his gun in Discord's face. "Something about you has been bugging me all week, so here's what's gonna happen. I'm gonna ask some questions, you're gonna answer, and if I don't like your answer, I'm gonna shoot you in the mouth."

"Could you do me a favor and aim for my forehead? I was planning on getting some Italian this weekend, and I'd rather have it taste right."

"Shut up."

Discord put his hands up and mimed zipping his mouth closed, then locking it and throwing the key over his shoulder.

"Who are you?" Jeffrey asked. Discord began to pretend talking, keeping his lips pursed and mumbling with a muffled voice in incomprehensible words. Jeffrey rolled his eyes. "I'm not in the mood for this, open your damn mouth and tell me what I want to know!"

Discord laughed. "Sorry, couldn't resist."

Jeffrey groaned. "I'll ask again: Who are you?"

"How long you got?"

"All the time in the world."

"Won't be enough. I'll keep it simple: I'm Discord."

"Elaborate," Jeffrey said, pushing the gun in Discord's face.

"Odds are more will come out with the other answers. Asking me who I am is like asking a historian about the social impact of the Ottoman Empire: there's a lot more to it than you'd expect."

"Fine. Who sent you?"

"Nobody, I'm here of my own volition."

Jeffrey didn't believe him, but nothing about him pointed to him lying, so he opted to continue.

"What's with all the guns and maps? Are you some kind of fucking terrorist or something?"

"First off, I doubt anybody would admit to being a terrorist. As for the rest, I collect guns, and the maps are leads on some real weird stuff."

"What kind of 'weird stuff'?"

"Monsters, artifacts, magic boots—you know, stuff like your book."

"How do you know about that book?"

"What, you think you're the first to ever carry it? I've met probably a dozen people who carried it, and the end result is always the same."

"And just what might that be?"

"A fiery death."

Jeffrey's face went from anger to dejected, and he lowered his gun. He walked over to Discord's chair, which was left empty, and slumped into it, leaving his gun in his lap and burying his face in his hands. He continuously cursed under his breath, slowly shaking his head back and forth.

"Could be worse," Discord said, "You could've been fated to freeze to death—that's, like, ten times worse."

Jeffrey jumped out of the chair and pressed the muzzle of his gun under Discord's chin, to which he responded by maintaining eye contact and taking another sip from his beer.

"Here's a question for you," Jeffrey said through his teeth. "What, on God's green earth did you do to Derrek?"

"Well, I didn't kill him, for starters."

"What, were you going to? *Are* you going to?"

"I was supposed to, but I decided not to. I thought it'd be more fun to keep him alive."

"What the fuck are you planning with him?" Jeffrey yelled as quietly as he could.

"Nothing. His fate is his own, and I'm just sticking around for the ride." Jeffrey pushed the gun further under his chin, causing him to choke for a brief second. "Could you put the gun down? It really isn't doing you any favors."

"You're talking, aren't you?"

"Just back up a few feet and let me demonstrate, will you?"

Jeffrey wasn't sure what he was doing, but aside from the several guns on the bed, he seemed to be unarmed. He gave Discord some space, still pointing his gun between his eyes.

Without saying a word, Discord produced a knife from his coat, almost prompting Jeffrey to shoot until he buried the blade into his own neck. He pulled the knife forward, chopping out his Adam's apple and pouring blood onto the floor, splattering some onto Jeffrey's shoes and much more onto his pants.

All the while, Discord stood, not reacting to the immense pain he must have been in. He took another sip from his beer, which flowed through the hole, onto the carpet. He set the beer down on the dresser and maintained eye contact with Jeffrey as the hole quickly began to close over, completely healing within seconds.

As soon as he could talk, Discord said, "See? You can put the gun away. It won't do you any good."

Jeffrey stood before him, absolutely dumbfounded, staring slack-jawed at him, and dropped his gun to the ground, raising his hands in a surrendering manner, shaking like a leaf the entire time.

Discord, in an annoyed tone, said, "Oh, come on. You were talking that good shit just a second ago. Put your hands down and just talk to me."

Jeffrey slowly lowered his hands and was now very aware he was at a severe disadvantage.

"Do … you mind if I sit?" Jeffrey sheepishly asked.

"If it makes you more comfortable, have at it."

Jeffrey slowly made his way back to the chair, doing his best not to step in any more blood, and lowered himself into the chair. He was avoiding looking at Discord and was caught off guard when a towel was thrown over his head. He flailed around, thinking a sack was being pulled over his head but calmed down once he saw it was just a towel.

"Sorry about the mess. I would've shot myself, but even with a suppressor, odds are the bullet would've gone into the next room, which is some attention I just cannot afford bringing."

Jeffrey was still for a moment. Realizing there was blood all over his boots, he started to clean them off.

"There's a lot you don't understand, Major, and that's not me ripping on you. There's way more than a book that won't stay damaged, and there's way more than me."

"How deep does this go?"

"I just had this conversation, like, eighty pages ago. It goes real deep, man, and Havok is real deep into it. He didn't choose to be as he is, but fate has chosen him. I have no intention of really hurting him. I just want to be sure he can handle himself."

Jeffrey was still terrified. He had been through the hell that is war and went back and asked for more, but this man who stood before him was beyond anything he had ever seen. He considered bolting, running through the door as fast as he could, but then he spoke again.

"He talks very highly of you and thinks even higher. You matter to him, and he matters to me, so killing you was never an option, if that's what you're worried about. You can relax. If you want to leave, you're totally free to do so."

Jeffrey looked up to meet his gaze, and saw sincerity in his eyes. He felt relieved but wasn't sure from what. He took a deep breath. "I guess we're on the same page then."

Discord smiled and tried to hand him the Brewski once more. He considered turning it down, but as a show of good faith, he accepted but didn't open it.

"Glad to hear," Discord said. "Anything else you wanna know?"

Jeffrey considered all the questions he could ask, but he quickly realized he wasn't sure he wanted to hear the answer.

"I think I'm good," Jeffrey said, standing up from his chair. "Thanks for the beer. I think I should go."

Discord nodded. "It is pretty late—or early—at this point. Take care, Major."

Jeffrey nodded back at him and walked toward the door. He had his hand on the handle when he was grabbed by the shoulder. He turned around, terrified that Discord had changed his mind, and seeing him holding a gun didn't help.

"Wouldn't want you to forget this," Discord said, handing back Jeffrey's gun.

Jeffrey had completely forgotten. He took his gun back, quickly rolled up his pant leg, and stored it back in his prosthetic.

"Thanks," he said as he left. "Take it easy."

He closed the door behind him, leaving Discord alone in his room, fresh blood on the carpet mixed with a good amount of beer. He looked at the puddle and decided to leave it for room service. He was paying extra, after all.

He went back to his wall of maps and examined the one in the center. There was a suicide doomsday cult in Idaho—thirty-four dead and two in critical condition. He had been keeping up with them, believing them to be a blood cult, but once he was sure they weren't, he took them off his radar, thinking they were just another group of fanatics. Looking further into it, however, he found they had grown not only in numbers since he stopped paying attention but in their extremism. They had performed ritual sacrifice of animals, carved into the flesh of their members, leaving deep, intricate markings, and had even sacrificed members among them who had doubts. He was still sure they weren't at any time a blood cult, but something about them just wouldn't sit right with Discord even though they practically wiped themselves out. Maybe it was their name.

The Children of Ragnarok.

It was the final day of Frostbyte's excursion. All the equipment was packed and was already on its way back to its proper location, one of the dozens of warehouses under Frostbyte ownership. Everyone was scrambling in their own way to get everything settled and ready to leave.

The corporate workers, headed by Shepherd and Philman, were giving closing interviews to every employee involved to gather input and find any improvements on future trips. The research teams were all compiling their information, as well as settling their individual bets as to who would log the most information—Amir coming out on top thanks to his crack team. Derrek, as the one who organized the project, was meeting with Mila in her office to square away any extra expenses they had accrued in the past month.

"What I don't get," Mila said, "is how nobody, save for you, even so much as opened their minibars the entire time you were here."

"Company policy dictates that each employee is given a one-hundred-dollar stipend per week when traveling abroad, but it is made very clear that minibars are excluded from that and must be paid for with personal funds. If I were to guess, it's second nature for them to ignore them entirely."

Mila groaned slightly. "I know, I know. I just have profit margins to worry about. This place essentially hemorrhages money."

"Yeah, I can see that. Maybe the gold-trimmed fountains weren't the best investment."

"I stand by them," she said without hesitation.

The two had a laugh. Mila said, "So, do you want to get your debt squared away while we're here?"

"Actually, I've been meaning to talk to you about that."

"Let me guess, Discord was the one who ran up your tab? Doesn't surprise me. He always attacks other people's minibars."

"No. Well, yes, but that's not what I meant. I actually wanted to extend my stay."

"Oh? For how long?"

"I put in a request for a month of vacation time, but if you'd rather I leave, I completely understand."

Mila leaned back in her chair, laced her fingers over her desk, and looked at Derrek for several seconds in thought. After releasing her hands from each other, she sighed. "You've caused no trouble since coming here. Discord said he would stay for as long as you do, and as long as he's here to keep an eye on you, I guess you can stay as long as you like."

"If you honestly don't want me here, I don't mind leaving. I'm sure my mailbox is about stuffed full of junk mail by now."

Mila laughed. Then, smiling, she said, "It's fine, I trust him, and I have no reason not to trust you. Just keep your nose clean, and we won't have any problems."

Derrek smiled. "Thank you, Ms. Müller. I'll do my best."

"With that out of the way and the bills figured out, is there anything else I can help you with?"

Derrek gathered the receipts they had been going through and stood up from his chair. "I think that covers it. Thank you for your time, and have a nice day!"

Mila narrowed her gaze and scowled at him. "Mighty bold of you to say that to a vampire."

Derrek's eyes widened in realization of what he had said. He tried to search for the right words, but after a solid five seconds of staring blankly at her, Mila laughed, reached over the desk, and slapped him on the shoulder.

"I'm just messing with you. Have a nice day, Derrek."

He smiled back at her, relieved, and turned toward the door. The lobby was packed with Frostbyte employees buzzing about, working as fast as they could to get everything in order. There was a flood of faces that Derrek vaguely recognized carrying thousands of pounds of luggage and equipment to the shuttles and just as many packing the conference rooms, trying to get their forms and GENRAM results compiled.

It was total controlled chaos, yet it filled Derrek with determination. Seeing all those people doing this work, along with each and every one of them truly believing they were making a difference in the world, gave him hope. He had his doubts, but at that moment, he knew if the people kept their resolve, he'd be able to keep the vision that Shale had worked so hard to craft.

"Something to behold, isn't it?" Said a raised, gruff voice from beside him, which Derrek saw belonged to Jeffrey.

"I've never seen anything like it," Derrek said, "even after that turmoil in '31, it still doesn't compare in my eyes."

"It's like this at the end of every trip, everyone running around like headless chickens trying to tie up all their loose ends. Always reminds me of boot. Good times," Jeffrey said with a nostalgic smile.

"So what's the plan for your truck? Do you have an exporter lined up?"

"Yeah, I've got a few favors lined up at Sigonella, so I'm just gonna hitch a ride back to the states from there."

"Got room for your couch?" Derrek asked coyly.

"Huh?" Jeffrey said with a confused look on his face.

"The couch. The one you bought in Turkey. Antique."

Jeffrey suddenly remembered his story from before. "Oh yeah, gotta swing into town to get it from the storage place. They're cool with me bringing it."

"Good to hear," Derrek said, stone-faced.

Jeffrey looked around the crowd nervously, apparently looking for an out, until Derrek spoke up again.

"When're you planning on heading out?"

Jeffrey's nerves suddenly calmed, and he responded, "Probably in about a half hour. How about yourself? Gonna ride in those sardine cans? I'm sure you could get a taxi if you got the cash for it."

"Actually," Derrek said, "I'm staying for a little while longer. I just came from setting up the arrangements with Ms. Müller."

"Oh really?" Jeffrey said, putting his hands on his hips and smiling. "Derrek Snowe taking a vacation? Now I've seen it all!"

The two shared a brief laugh. Derrek said, "It had to happen sometime, right? I just think some time off will help to get me into the right headspace for what's ahead."

Jeffrey put his hand up. "You don't have to explain anything to me. I'm just glad you're taking some time for yourself. You're one of the hardest-working sons of bitches I've ever met. You're gonna do Shale proud, Derrek."

He extended his hand, which Derrek grabbed without hesitation and shook. Jeffrey took notice of how firm it was, but he could tell he was holding back. He wasn't sure what was going on with him, but he could tell whatever Discord was doing was helping.

Jeffrey let go of Derrek's hand and checked his watch. After seeing the time, he said, "Shit, I gotta pack."

"You're leaving in a half hour and you still haven't packed?"

"What can I say? I work best under pressure."

"Well, if I don't see you before you leave, hopefully I'll see you around."

"You'll be seeing me all right. I head to HQ every month or so for a tune up, so this ain't the last you've seen of me, bucko."

Derrek smiled. "Glad to hear it. I'll be seeing you, Major."

Jeffrey smiled back and gave a halfway salute before heading toward the elevator, fading away into the ocean of people. Derrek still needed to meet with Shepherd and Philman for an exit interview since it was his first time in the field, so he weaved his way through the crowd and made his way toward the conference room where they met before. He entered to find Shepherd and Philman speaking with Amir and was unsettled when they all fell silent upon seeing him.

"Ah, Derrek," Shepherd began, "right on cue. We were just talking about you."

Philman turned to her and gave her an annoyed look. "Snitch."

She turned back. "Asshole." Then he turned back to Derrek and continued, "I take it you're ready for your closer?"

"Yes, ma'am—if I'm not interrupting anything, of course," Derrek said, referring to Amir, who raised his hand in a *stop* gesture.

"It is no worry at all," Amir said. "I was simply catching up with old friends. The three of us were actually part of the same research team several years ago."

"Oh, really?" Derrek asked. "Where did you go?"

Philman grinned. "Somalia, China, Nepal, Canada, Brazil—it might actually save time if we just tell you where we didn't go!"

"It was just those five," Shepherd chimed in, glaring at him.

Philman conspicuously rolled his eyes and under his breath said, "Buzzkill."

There was a brief moment of tension, which was shattered by Amir's hearty laughter. He walked up behind the two of them and put a hand on each of their shoulders. "Just like old times! It always amazes me how much the two of you get done—even at each other's throats!"

Shepherd cracked a smile, which Philman met with a renewed grin, and the three shared a laugh. The moment hung for a few seconds before Amir let go and began to walk toward the door.

"I should go. There is work to do and people to meet. I will see you two next time. And Lewis, I do hope you will bring some of your famous peanut brittle then."

"Peanut brittle?" Derrek asked.

"That's right!" Philman exclaimed triumphantly. "Best brittle in Manchester eight years running!"

Shepherd looked like she was going to dispute him, but she quickly decided against it and instead said, "It's pretty good."

Derrek was surprised to hear anything positive about Philman come from her, and he made a mental note to try it someday. He turned to say goodbye to Amir, who already had his hand extended.

"You did an excellent job, Derrek. I hope to work with you again someday."

Derrek shook his hand. "I hope so, too. It's been a pleasure, Amir."

After letting go, Amir went to the door, gave one last smile to the three, and left, briefly letting in the noise coming from the lobby, which was quickly muffled by the thick walls. Derrek decided now was a good time to take a seat, and he sat across from the two with his hands laced on the table.

"So," Shepherd said, rifling through some papers, "were you at any time during work hours injured in a way that affected your ability to do your job?"

Derrek was instantly reminded of his scuffle with Boyd and how his spine had been, according to Discord, dislodged. He hadn't experienced any pain, though, so he said, "No, I haven't."

Shepherd nodded. "Have you had any altercations, verbal or otherwise, with any of your coworkers?"

"No, ma'am."

"Did you encounter any hostile wildlife or forces?"

"Aside from a couple of boars, no, ma'am."

"Oh, yeah," Philman interjected. "I forgot you had that in your report. Nice work. Not many would have the balls to try something like that."

Shepherd didn't say anything in response, but she did nod. "Last one: Is there anything you can think of that you believe would improve efficiency in future operations?"

Derrek looked up and scratched his head in thought for several seconds, leaving Shepherd and Philman in suspense, until it hit him.

"One of my teammates, Hanna, had these homemade blow guns with tranquilizer darts. That's how we got the boar samples. I was thinking these could be used for the same purpose for a variety of animals, instead of relying on loose fur and droppings for analysis."

Philman chucked at the word droppings and was swiftly kicked under the table by Shepherd, who was intently listening to Derrek's suggestion.

"I believe," he continued, "that providing these to all teams, as well as classes teaching how to use them, could increase productivity by a noticeable margin."

Shepherd shifted her glance to straight ahead of her, looking past Derrek, staring at the wall, unmoving except for her eyes rapidly darting around, following something only she could see. After several seconds, during which not even her breathing was discernible, she grabbed a pen and a sheet of paper and began scribbling formulas at a lightning pace.

Once she was satisfied with her results, she looked up at Derrek. "I'll bring it up with our superiors, but I think I can make a good case for it. This sounds very promising, and I'm confident it'll look great on your portfolio."

"Oh," Derrek said, "I don't want to take credit for it. Hanna was the one who had the idea. She deserves it."

Shepherd and Philman shared a look, then looked back to Derrek.

"Are you sure?" Philman asked. "You've got a lot to gain here."

"Nothing bugs me quite like someone taking credit for something they didn't do. I'd much rather stay where I am now than be a hypocrite."

Philman was taken aback, but after a brief moment, his lips spread in a smile. "Understood. Your name will stay off the proposal, and Mrs. ..." He paused and looked over a paper Derrek took to be a list of names, then continued, "Hammel will receive full credit."

Shepherd looked at Philman with surprise, or perhaps admiration, at this singular moment of humanity. She briefly smiled, then turned her attention back to Derrek. "That's all we had to cover. You're officially off the clock and free to start your vacation."

Derrek stood to leave and shook both their hands. "Thank you very much. I look forward to working with you both in the future."

"Considering how you rocked your first field mission, I'd bet money on it," Philman said. "See you round."

"I hate to say it," Shepherd said, "but I agree with him. You did a great job. I'm sure you'll do great things."

Derrek nodded knowingly, then left, leaving Shepherd and Philman alone in the conference room. They stewed in silence for almost a full minute before Philman decided to break it.

"So ... wanna grab a drink?"

Shepherd glared at him. "You realize we're leaving the country in about four hours, three of which we'll be spending on a shuttle, don't you?"

"Yeah ... I guess you're right."

Shepherd collected her papers and headed toward the door. She had her hand on the doorknob when she stopped in her tracks. She sighed deeply. "After we give our final report in New York, *one* drink."

Philman smiled. "Sounds like a plan, Becky."

She groaned, then quickly left the room, soon followed by Philman as they loaded up onto their shuttle.

Derrek had his affairs in order and was set to meet Discord for an early lunch in the dining hall, which was staggeringly empty. He was used to being the only table for breakfast, but the entire room was almost always packed past noon. He saw Discord sitting calmly at their usual table, sipping what looked like espresso, staring out the window. He approached the table and took his seat across from him, who was still fixated on the landscape. Half a minute had passed before he spoke.

"Beautiful, isn't it?" he finally said. "A hundred years ago, if you told me I'd be sipping coffee across from the Devourer in a hotel run by fangs, I'd probably break your arm giving you the best high-five ever heard."

"The only part of that I find hard to believe is that you're drinking coffee."

The two laughed as Emmett came up to their table, holding a bottle of Steel Barrel.

"May I top you off, Herr Discord?"

"Greatly appreciated. Thank you, choir boy!" Discord said as Emmett filled his cup.

"Called it," Derrek said as Emmett handed him a menu.

After Discord finished downing his cup, he said, "He'll take the chicken schnitzel and the *pommes frites*, same as me."

Derrek gave Discord a sideways glance, before handing his menu back to Emmett.

"Whatever it is, I'm sure it's delicious, and if it's no trouble, I could go for some coffee as well—the same way he takes his," he said, gesturing to Discord.

"Right away, Herr Snowe, half decaf, half fifty-year Steel Barrel."

After Emmett walked away, Derrek looked at Discord. "Decaf, really?"

"Eh, caffeine mixes weird. It's more about the coffee taste than the coffee pickup."

"That sounds pretty good, actually."

"Well, duh, I've got impeccable taste," Discord said, grinning widely.

Emmett returned, Derrek's drink in hand, which he placed in front of him.

"Here you are, Herr Snowe. Your meals will be out shortly. Is there anything I can help you gentlemen with?"

"No, thank you," Derek said, "I appreciate it."

Emmett warmly smiled and nodded, then quickly walked away. Derek took a sip from his cup and was hit with the rich coffee with the earthy undertones of the whiskey dancing on his taste buds. He was delighted by the taste and proceeded to sip it alongside Discord as the two stared out the window for a few minutes.

Derek eventually broke the serene silence and asked, "How long do you think it'll be until I can return to regular life? I've only got so many vacation days."

"Dunno," Discord said, finishing off his cup. "As I keep saying, uncharted territory and whatnot. You can already control yourself when you devour, which I'd argue is a damn good step, but you still can't summon it by will. We might be able to get you there in the next week, or you might never be able to do it when you want. We'll only really know when we know, y'know?"

Derek looked slightly disappointed, which Discord took notice of. He set his cup on his saucer. "Don't worry, Havok. Even if you never get the hang of it, you'll be fine. And I'll be around in case you aren't."

Derek looked him in the eye. "To kill me?"

"To talk you down. I don't want to kill you."

"But you will if you have to, right?"

"Yep."

A silence fell over the two that hung in the air for several seconds, until Discord spoke again.

"The first devourer I killed was human—when she was born, I mean. I happened to be staying in the village where she lived for a few years, mostly waiting for the next war to come around, when farm stock and pets started to die, their corpses charred beyond recognition. The villagers thought it was a god taking its own sacrifices, but I think you can guess what it actually was.

"I don't know what caused it, maybe she got careless, maybe she was getting ballsier, but she ended up consuming a human, and that was all she wrote. She went crazy that night and went hut to hut, devouring everything that moved. Unfortunately, mine was on the outskirts, so I didn't know until it was too late.

"She couldn't have been older than fifteen, but she gave me no other choice but to put her down. She couldn't be reasoned with, and there was no way to take her out without killing her, so I did my best to be swift."

"Why are you telling me this?" Derrek asked.

"Because she lost control after eating a single human. You ate a reaper, something infinitely stronger than a human, and just kinda shook it off. I genuinely believe you'll be fine."

Derrek met his eyes and saw sincerity, and he felt better. He cracked a smile as he was hit with a wafting scent of chicken, and he looked up to find Emmett holding two plates, which he placed before them. Atop their plates were two large portions of fried chicken fillets, alongside a pile of perfectly golden fries.

"Our chicken schnitzel, a simple dish but an effective one, especially when paired with our *frites*, made from only the finest potatoes. Will you gentlemen require anything else?"

"I think we're good, choir boy. Thank you kindly."

Emmett smiled and nodded, then left their table, leaving the men to their meals.

Derrek picked up one of his fries. "*Pommes frites* ... French fries?"

"Yep, fresh-cut too, not those frozen ones."

"You could've just said fried chicken and French fries."

"And da Vinci could've called the *Mona Lisa* 'Mildly Happy Woman.' Art deserves respect, my friend."

Derrek didn't reply but did nod his head, understanding where he was coming from. He bit into the fry he had been inspecting and was greeted with the perfect amount of crunch along with the hot potato middle. It was perfectly salted, and he immediately understood why Discord respected them the way he did.

"Pretty good, right?"

"Yeah, you were right."

"Try the chicken."

Derrek took his advice and cut a piece off of his filet with his fork and knife. He was struck by how tender it was, along with the subtle lemon zing basted into the crispy shell.

"I have to give it to you," he said. "You do have impeccable taste."

"Glad to hear it," Discord said, picking at his plate. He ate a few fries of his own. "I hate to ruin it, but there's something you should know."

"Huh?" Derrek asked in the middle of chewing a bite of schnitzel. After swallowing he said, "What is it?"

Discord took a deep breath, then asked, "Do you know what poachers are?"

"Probably not in the context you mean."

"Fair point. Poachers in 'weird' terms, are people who hunt down and destroy anything supernatural just because it's inhuman. They're huge racists in the most literal of terms."

"Damn," Derrek said, "so that's what Mila was worried about. Do you think they're coming for the Schadenfreude?"

Discord shook his head. "I'm not sure. There's at least eighty of them congregating in France. They could be rearing up to attack the hotel. They could be having their annual jackass meetup. Hell, they all could have just been separately following the same lead—it's too early to tell. For a bunch of eugenic asshats, they're really good at covering their tracks."

"Do ... do you think they're after me?"

"I doubt it. You've been maintaining a low profile, and I haven't caught their scent around these parts. Mila's been careful too. She's been off their radar for years. You never know, though. Those shitstains are like damn bloodhounds."

Discord silently ate another handful of fries as Derrek looked upon him with a combination of worry and fear for the safety of the hotel. He gathered his conviction. "Then we'll keep doing what we're doing, staying safe and quiet. And if they catch on, we'll fight them off."

Discord looked up from his plate and saw the seriousness in Derrek's eyes. He grinned. "You're goddamn right. I'll keep my ear to the ground. We'll keep whipping you into shape, and we should be golden."

Derrek raised a fry for a toast, which Discord met with one of his own.

"To the Schadenfreude," they both said before eating their respective fries.

They continued their meal, discussing their plans for training, Discord leaning heavily toward throwing boulders at Derrek and hoping for the best. They went back and forth with ideas, dropping the subject once the dining hall began to fill for the lunch rush. They laughed as they ate, and Emmett kept their mugs filled with coffee and whiskey.

Derrek could tell he was going to enjoy his vacation, even with all the training.

Two weeks had passed since Frostbyte left the Schadenfreude, and Derrek had been working hard to control his powers. He trained with Discord for more than ten hours every day and was growing more and more confident in his abilities by the minute. They had explored countless acres of the forest in those weeks, mainly sparing but also dabbling in survival training.

At this particular moment, however, the two were weaving through the trees, chasing a giant, chicken-like reptilian monster.

Discord was holding onto it by the neck as it charged through the forest, smashing trees into splinters as Derrek jumped from branch to branch, doing his best to keep pace with the rampaging creature.

"Get ahead of him!" Discord yelled as he was flung around the monster's neck, barely holding on as it slammed him into a tree, completely uprooting it in the process.

"Right!" Derrek yelled. He picked up his pace and managed to hold his place fifty feet ahead of it. Still jumping along branches, he drew his sword and watched for an opportunity. As soon as he saw his chance, he jumped in front of the beast and readied his blade as it closed the distance.

He moved to the side and slashed his sword, leaving a massive gash along its left side, severing its wing and making it tumble for another several feet. Discord had been flung upward into the trees, and he managed to grab hold of one of the branches and steady himself before gracefully returning to the ground, slowly approaching the injured creature alongside Derrek.

"Don't look it in the eyes," Discord said as he pulled his revolver from his coat. "It'll turn you to stone, like Medusa."

"Noted. You called it a cockatrice, right?"

"That's right. A huge one too. Half chicken, half lizard, all angry. Keep your guard up."

The creature lay curled into a pile, breathing heavily. Its green scales reflected the rays of light that shone through the leaves, the fresh blood glistening in the midday sunlight.

They were roughly fifteen feet away when Derrek stepped on a stick, snapping it loudly. The cockatrice immediately shot up to its feet, facing the men and raising its remaining wing, shrieking out a piercing wail from its razor-sharp beak, lined with countless jagged teeth. Derrek averted his eyes as Discord closed his, still facing the beast. Without looking, he fired his gun at the creature's face, hitting it in the right eye, leaving a hole in the side of its head.

"We're good for a few minutes," he said, opening his eyes. "It needs both eyes for the whole petrification thing."

Derrek uncovered his eyes and readied his sword, facing the cockatrice head-on as it cried out in pain, its newly empty socket gushing blood. It scraped the ground with its clawed feet, preparing to charge as Discord replaced the spent bullet in his gun.

"It's got crazy strong neurotoxin in its claws and teeth. It makes you feel like you're melting. Then it kills you, and then you actually melt. It's pretty unpleasant, so try to avoid getting hit."

Derrek grunted in the affirmative and stared the monster down, watching as its remaining eye darted back and forth between the two. It let out piercing roar as it ran at them, claws and teeth bared, aimed for their necks.

Discord casually leaned away from the talons that slashed at him and slammed the butt of his revolver into the back of the cockatrice's neck while Derrek ducked away from the remaining wing and severed it near, to his closest approximation of, the creature's shoulder. This combination of attacks slammed the creature to the ground, unable to properly stand up, flailing randomly, and rapidly slowing down.

Derrek laid his sword on the ground and approached the creature, reaching for its head while it ineffectually tried to bite him. He locked eyes with it and watched as it began to shine with a bright orange light from the inside out. Within seconds, the monster was nothing but a scorched skeleton on a burnt patch of grass.

Derrek stood and brushed the dirt off his knees as Discord swiftly scooped up the Cockatrice's skull.

"What is it with you and skulls?" Derrek asked.

"I've never seen one of these buggers bigger than two feet, beak to tail, so there's no way I'm leaving without a memento. Plus, the venom in these teeth sells for twenty grand a drop."

"It's that potent, huh?"

"It's like injecting hydrochloric acid right into your bloodstream. Crazy suffering, a one hundred percent mortality rate, and total liquefaction make it pretty sought after by those government assassins—and damn if they don't pay well."

"Wait, you sell poison to the government? Isn't that kind of unethical?"

Discord gave him a sideways glance. "Ethics are for humans, Havok. We do what we have to. Besides, I don't sell anything if I don't know who they're using it against, and I keep most of it for myself, so I don't really see a problem."

Derrek glared at him for a brief moment, then sighed. "Just don't sell to terrorists."

"Are you kidding? Fuck those guys."

The two shared a laugh as Derrek retrieved his sword, wiping away the blood with a cloth he kept in his back pocket. He put his sword back into the scabbard he wore on his back and examined the remains as Discord finished cleaning the skull.

"You're getting better," Discord said as he put the skull in his coat. "I'd dare to say you've almost got it under control."

"Thanks. I owe it to all this training."

"The training wouldn't do jack if it wasn't for your raw ambition. Give yourself some credit. It'll serve you—"

Discord put his hand up, gesturing for them both to be quiet as he fixed his gaze westward. He gestured for Derrek to follow him as he leaped into the trees and they both took point in sturdy branches.

Beneath them, Derrek heard rustling in the bushes and watched as a group of five people emerged from them, armed to the teeth, wielding large rifles. From what he could tell, there were four men and one woman. They surrounded the charred corpse while scanning the woods around them.

"Was denkst du hat das getan?" one of the men asked another of the men, who wore a flashy hat, adorned with feathers and teeth, whom Derrek assumed was their leader. Although his stout, pudgy physique made him wonder.

"Speak English, you damn Kraut. You know the rules," he said with a gruff voice and a thick British accent.

The man who spoke before let out an exasperated sigh. "What do you think did this?"

"That's more like it," the leader said. "And if I were to guess, I'd say a phoenix, but considering they haven't been sighted outside Greece in well over eighty years, I'd say it's unlikely."

"Could be an elemental," the woman chimed in with her Russian accent.

"Maybe," the leader said, "but I've never known elementals to take the skulls of their victims, not to mention the body is the only thing burnt."

"What even was this thing?" another of the men, an American, asked.

"*Caverna reguli gigantus,* the giant cockatrice," the leader replied, pointing toward the severed wings. "And whatever killed it did this after the fact, probably where that gunshot came from."

Derrek looked to see Discord, silently slapping himself in the forehead, apparently regretting his firearm use. He had been intently watching the people below, seemingly trying to decide their next move.

"I didn't think there were any hunters in this area," the German said.

"Aside from us, there aren't supposed to be," the leader said, looking around, "but it seems that what or whoever did this is long gone. Cut off the feet and talons and gather as many feathers as you can. An ounce of that venom can bring an elephant to its knees. Imagine what it could do to the fangs."

The people all went to work, two of them swiftly plucking the feathers from the severed wings as the rest collected the feet of the charred remains, placing them in containers and putting them into their respective backpacks. After they were done, they worked together to cover the rest of the cockatrice with dirt, just enough so anyone who stumbled across the bones might think it was a long-dead bear or something along those lines, and left in the same direction they came from. Almost a minute later, Discord jumped down from the tree, followed closely by Derrek.

"Son of a bitch," Discord said.

"Were those poachers?" Derrek asked.

"Yeah, and that was one of their higher-ups, Reginald Shit-Eating Bernmore VIII. That asshole's killed more fangs than Van Helsing."

"He mentioned fangs. Do you think they're after the Schadenfreude?"

"Don't know. Not enough to go on. But Reggie showing his fat face doesn't bode well anywhere, especially here. We'd best be on our way. Come on," Discord said as he jumped back into the trees, followed by Derrek. They traveled for several miles, eventually arriving at the Null Dome, where they left their motorcycles.

Fifteen minutes later, they were back at the Schadenfreude. They quickly put their bikes up and hurried into the lobby, heading toward Mila's office when Discord put up his arm to stop Derrek.

"Get yourself a shower. I've gotta talk to Mila one on one about this."

"No, I'm coming with you. I'm not going to let anyone get hurt."

"And neither am I, but if I know Mila, she'll jump to the conclusion you're the reason they're here. It'll be easier for both of us if I talk to her first. Besides, you smell like shit."

Derrek was confused, but after taking a sniff of his shirt, he saw what Discord meant. Some of the cockatrice's blood had gotten on his clothes, and it reeked of rotten garbage.

"Yeah ... you're right. I'll catch up with you later. Good luck."

Discord gave his signature half smile. "Thanks, Havok. I'll come to get you in a few."

They went their separate ways, Derrek heading to his room, Discord toward Mila's office, which he entered without knocking, of course, interrupting a phone call, which she quickly hung up on.

"Cordy, how many times do I have to ask you to knock? That was an important call."

"Not as important as this," Discord said with a grim expression as he walked over to a shelf where a bottle of gin and a set of glasses were. He made two drinks, one of which he handed to Mila as he took a seat across from her.

He took a long sip from his glass and took a deep breath. "We ran into some poachers. Bernmore was with them."

Mila looked at him, slack-jawed, as her glass fell from her hand, shattering on her desk. She slowly pushed a button on her telephone. "Emmett, please come to my office. Bring a dustpan. And a towel."

She didn't wait for a reply; she got up from her desk and went straight for the bottle of gin, which she started chugging. She stopped when the bottle was near half-empty and took her seat as Emmett knocked on the door.

"Come in," she said.

Emmett entered and immediately saw the mess, which he wasted no time cleaning up.

"Frau Müller, if you don't mind my asking, what happened here?" he asked as he finished sweeping the broken glass into the pan.

"Discord, would you mind explaining?" she said, panic in her eyes.

Discord finished his glass and set it down on the desk then said, "Havok and I were hunting that chicken lizard you've been talking about, and right as we put it down, five of them came through, led by Bernmore."

Emmett stared at him with the same expression Mila wore seconds earlier, spilling the mix of broken glass and gin onto the hardwood floor. As soon as he realized what he had done, he went straight to cleaning it up, quickly dumping it into the trash can behind the desk before taking a seat next to Discord, burying his face in his hands.

"They didn't see us, thankfully, but they mentioned the fangs. I don't know if they're coming for the hotel, but I came here as fast as I could."

"Why didn't you just kill them then and there?" Mila asked.

"Could you imagine the shit storm that would have raised? Bernmore is one of their top guys. They'd launch a crusade across the whole country if he turned up missing, and you know better than most how brutal those people can be."

Mila formed her hands into a finger pyramid and leaned over her desk, clearly in thought. Her eyes widened.

"Do they know about Derrek?" she asked, her eyes full of fear.

Discord shook his head. "I doubt it. Far as I know, they think the Devourer pops up every fifty years, like clockwork, so they shouldn't be expecting it for another twelve or so. And if it were about him being a 'Hauch Von Tod,' as you like to call it, they'd be poking their noses around town or even the hotel. I don't know what they're after, but they either think it's in the forest, or they think they can get it *through* the forest."

Emmett uncovered his face and asked, "Is there anything else they might be after?"

Discord leaned back in his chair and stared at the ceiling. "Could be the copper relic, but that's on display at the Neues in Berlin, so there's no reason for them to be here. The deadlings have been spreading, but Bernmore wouldn't come all this way for a few walking corpses. Only big-ticket monster around was that big-ass cockatrice, but they didn't look like they were hunting for it." He tilted his head back down and locked eyes with Mila. "If they're looking for you, they know where you are. The Schadenfreude isn't exactly inconspicuous. I don't really know what to make of it. Is the Black Hand active at all around here? Maybe they're the target."

Mila took another sip of gin and handed the bottle to Emmett. "They haven't been, but they might be plotting something."

Emmett took a long sip from the bottle. "They're *always* plotting something."

"I'll drink to that," Discord said, taking a sip from a flask he had produced from his coat.

"What do you think we should do?" Mila asked as the bottle came back to her.

"Get Vick and Sana and meet me in the conference room," Discord said as he got up to leave. "I'm gonna go get Havok."

Mila quickly stood before he could get through the door and said, "You had better be sure you can trust him. There could be lives at stake."

Discord turned to face her and replied in a serious tone, "I trust him. We can get through this together, but we have to play every card we have. See you in a few."

He left through the door, closing it behind him.

Derrek had just stepped out of the bathroom when he saw Discord digging through his minibar.

"I'm not paying for that," he said, startling Discord and causing him to bump his head on the minibar. He sprung to his feet, one hand full of small liquor bottles, the other full of candy, with a pack of chocolate-covered almonds hanging from his teeth. He dropped the almonds, letting them land on the bed.

"They won't restock mine."

"Probably because you won't pay for it."

"Probably. You ready for crisis mode?"

"Ready as I'll ever be. Anything I need to know going in?"

Discord shoved the bottles and candy into his coat and headed toward the door. "Walk and talk—no time to waste."

"Right," Derrek said, following him into the hall.

"Mila didn't jump to blame you," Discord said as they approached the elevator, "so that's good. We couldn't figure out any reason they'd be here, though, aside from them gearing up to launch a full-on assault."

"I thought Ms. Müller ran a tight ship. How do you think they found out?"

"Dunno. We kinda came up short there on the initial," Discord said as the elevator dinged, "but we might have to put the why aside and focus on the when."

They boarded the elevator, and as the doors closed, Derrek asked, "Do you think this has anything to do with me? Can they detect spiritual energy or anything like that?"

Discord leaned against the wall opposite to the doors. "Too early to tell for sure, but since they didn't recognize what you did to that clucking lizard, I don't think so."

Derrek felt a twinge of relief as the doors opened, and the two made their way to the conference room. Discord stopped just before they came to the door and turned to face him.

"There's people in there you haven't properly met, and I'm gonna go ahead and tell you they're gonna hate you."

"Because I'm the Devourer?"

"They don't know about that—just the reaper thing. They're just really against outsiders."

"Regardless, I'm not going to sit on the sidelines. Hate me or love me, I've been welcomed here, and I'm not going to let anything destroy this place without a fight."

Discord smirked, then turned to the door.

"That's all I needed to hear," he said before leading Derrek into the conference room.

As they entered, they could practically see the tension in the air. Mila was seated at the head of the table with Emmett on her left, both wearing worried expressions. To her right, however, were two people Derrek had not formally met, a man and a woman. The man was wearing a chef's coat with his sleeves rolled up, his bearded face and toned arms covered in cut and burn scars. He recognized the woman as the same one whose name he meant to learn but never got around to and whom Discord referred to as "fangless." As he expected, they were both staring daggers at him.

"Wonderful," Discord said. "The gang's all here."

"And now that you two are here," Mila replied, "we can decide on a course of action."

The man spoke up with a gruff Belgian accent. "With all due respect, Frau Müller, why is the Hauch Von Tod present? We've dealt with the poachers before. We don't need him involved, and we don't need his filth."

Mila glared at him, and snapped back, "You seem to forget yourself, Victor. Herr Snowe is a welcomed guest, and you will treat him with the same respect you show to the rest of our patrons. He encountered the poachers alongside Discord, so like it or not, he is very much involved."

Victor opened his mouth, but the woman to his side put her hand on his forearm and gave him a look that made him stop. She then turned to Mila. "I'm sorry, Frau Müller, but please understand his apprehension. We've gotten this far by keeping our noses clean—by your behest, I might add. We let him stay, and only a month after, poachers are practically knocking at our door."

Discord interjected, "First off, it's been five weeks, bit over a month. And you sure are one to talk, Sana. Don't think I forgot about Rome." He scanned the group, then continued, "Havok wants to help, and I suggest you let him."

A beat passed before Mila broke the silence. "Well put. Herr Snowe will stay and will be allowed to help, end of discussion," she said, staring at Victor and Sana. She turned to face the rest of the table as Derrek and Discord took their seats beside Emmett. "Now that pleasantries have been exchanged, we must agree on a plan to deal with the situation at hand.

"We don't know for certain if the Schadenfreude is their target, but that is a risk we simply cannot take. Effective immediately, we will not be accepting any new guests, and all guests we currently have will be informed they will have to vacate their rooms by tomorrow at noon under the guise of emergency renovations. Their bills will all be comped, so I doubt anyone will mind too terribly much. As soon as the rooms are empty and all guests have left, we will prepare for a siege. Emmett, please take it from here."

Emmett coughed nervously and stood up from his seat. "Thank you, Frau Müller. They are likely to attack during daylight hours, when we are at our weakest, so we will need at least one person constantly manning the cameras. We have a few hundred pounds of plastic explosives in storage, and I'm sure Herr Discord can show us how to make proximity landmines to be placed strategically across the lawn. Following our cover story of maintenance, we will have plastic sheets covering the front entrance as well as the windows of the first two floors. The emergency shutters will be effective at slowing them down if and when they breach the perimeter and will buy us enough time to get to our battle stations.

"We will use the front entrance as a choke point. Herr Dupont," he said to Victor, "your crew will take point in the lobby armed with pistols and shotguns, using furniture and the steel slabs left over from construction as cover, acting as suppression while Frau Keller"—he shifted his gaze to Sana—"and the bellhops take position on the balconies, fortified with the same steel, picking them off with rifles as they enter. All the while"—he looked to Discord and Derrek—"Herr Discord, we would like for you and Herr Snowe to do whatever you can to either slow them down or take them out as you're able to do so. We only ask that you try your best to avoid damaging the hotel whenever possible."

"No promises," Discord said with his thumbs up and a grin on his face.

Derrek spoke up. "But what's the plan once this is all said and done? If the poachers do come, there's no way you'll be safe here even if we fight them off."

Everyone looked at Mila as she answered. "The White Hand has several sanctuaries across the globe, and they will serve us well until a more permanent solution can be found. The closest one is in Poland, so that will be our destination."

"I still think Norway would be a better choice," Discord said, balancing on the rear legs of his chair.

"The last thing we need right now is to be caught at daybreak," Mila said. "We can get to Zakopane in four hours, but it would take at least two days to get to Lillehammer. We may try to move there soon, but this is what we're able to do now."

"Do we have any idea when they'll attack?" Sana asked. Everyone looked to Discord.

"If y'all are what they're here for," he said, "they ought to be here sometime in the next week. They're patient, but not very. How's your food stock?"

"They're good," Victor said. "If we ration, it could last us a month."

"Wait," Derrek interjected, "if you feed off memories, how do you store that?"

Mila cleared her throat, gaining the table's attention. "As I'm sure Discord has informed you, us fangs each have a unique ability. Mine, for instance, is the ability to take memories from others and transfer them to material objects. Any fang can use these as a full replacement for blood."

"It's handy as hell," Discord chimed in. "It's the very basis of these fang's way of life. Most of the White Hand gets their fill from blood banks or willing human donors, but this way allows for a blood-free life, effectively making them totally harmless."

"Too bad the poachers don't see it that way," Sana pitched in, causing a hush to fall over the group. Discord broke the silence as he stood from his chair.

"Well, it sounds like everyone knows what they're doing. C'mon, Havok, let's go grab a drink."

"What?" Derrek asked. "There's work to do. We can't just go drink at a time like this!"

"There's nothing for us to do until the hotel's clear. Us sticking around would only raise suspicion."

"But—"

"He's right, Derrek," Mila said, standing from her chair alongside everyone else. "We have it covered. It's business as usual until tomorrow."

Derrek thought of protesting further, but it was clear there was no way he could help. He decided to go along. "All right. Let us know if there's anything we can do."

Mila smiled and silently nodded, then headed for the door, followed closely by her employees, then by Discord and Derrek, who headed for the parking lot.

"I'm telling you: I've fought sharks, and I've fought seagulls, and fifty gulls could tear a shark to shreds!"

The two were sitting at the bar of the only pub in town they had yet to leave amid a brawl, arguing over hypothetical fights and drinking their fill.

"Even still," Derrek said, "I have to side with the shark, assuming it can breathe air, of course."

Discord snapped his fingers angrily. "Dammit, I forgot he could breathe air. Gotta give it to the shark."

Derrek raised his mug in victory and watched as Discord chugged his. After finishing it, he gasped for air and coughed for several seconds.

"How is it?" Derrek coyly asked.

"You'd think it'd be better in pilsner form, but a Brewski is still a Brewski."

The two shared a laugh as the bartender came and refilled Discord's mug with, at his behest, a shot of each liquor they had in stock. After the several minutes it took to make said drink, the bartender walked away to handle the only other person in the pub.

"That looks disgusting," Derrek said. "I can literally smell it from here."

"Well, why should I just get one drink after another when I can get, like, twenty drinks' worth in a cup? It's an efficiency thing more than anything else."

"Still, I don't think tequila was meant to go with absinth."

"And pickles weren't meant to go with peanut butter, but people still eat it."

"That sounds gross too."

"It's honestly not that bad."

"I refuse to believe that."

"Suit yourself," Discord said. He took a long sip from his highly alcoholic concoction. After finishing nearly half his mug, he set it down and looked at the other patron in the reflection of the mirror behind the liquor shelves. He could tell it was a man from his large frame, but he was facing away from the bar and wore a hood and a hat, presumably to hide his appearance. He noticed the man glancing at them several times since they arrived and already had a feeling of who it was.

He threw back the rest of his drink, got up from his stool and walked over to the table the man occupied, gesturing for Derrek to follow. The man had yet to notice them until Discord grabbed him by the shoulder, prompting the man to jump and grab him by the wrist, attempting to flip him over his shoulder, but to no avail. Discord hadn't moved or reacted to it in any way.

"You wanna tell me why you're spying on us?" he calmly asked.

"Spying? Are you sure about that? He looks like a normal customer to me."

The man coughed several times, then said in a gruff voice, which he was clearly trying to mask, and an indeterminate accent, "No idea what you're talking about. I'm just enjoying a meal before I get back on the road!"

"Yeah, and I'm Lady Godiva," Discord replied, not convinced. "Now lose the getup, Jeffy. You aren't fooling anyone."

"Jeffy?" Derrek asked, very confused.

The man sighed and slowly stood up, then removed his hat and hood, revealing his bald head and bushy beard.

"Jeffrey?" Derrek asked, even more confused.

"Yeah," Jeffrey said, avoiding eye contact and rubbing the back of his head. "How're you doing, Derrek?"

"How am I doing? Why are you here?"

"Because," Discord interjected, "he's worried I'm gonna kill you or make you a monster or something like that."

"What?"

Jeffrey looked up from the ground and met Derrek's eyes. "I was worried. What can I say?"

Derrek dropped the confused expression he wore and replaced it with one of anger. "There's a hell of a lot you *should* say right about now. Maybe a 'sorry' for starters. Then I'd like to know just how long you've been following us."

Jeffrey sighed again. "You're right. I'm sorry. I never left town. I've been staying at the motel across the street."

Derrek was about to ask another question, but Discord interrupted him. "Let's all sit down and discuss this. Bartender! Three pilsners!" He took a seat at the table, sitting next to where Jeffrey was set up. Derrek hesitated but decided to sit across from Jeffrey, staring daggers at him all the while. The bartender swiftly brought them three mugs, then quickly disappeared behind the bar, which the men thought was strange, considering they were the only customers present.

Several seconds passed, filled only with Derrek staring at Jeffrey, Jeffrey nervously sipping his beer and Discord looking back and forth between the two.

"All right," Discord said, clapping and drawing the other men's eyes to him. "Let's clear the air." He turned and gestured toward Jeffrey. "First off, Jeffy here knows, at least partly, about the weird shit that's floating around. A couple of weeks back, he and I had a little chat, and he agreed to leave it be. But on the other end"—he then turned to Derrek—"Havok isn't human, not anymore, at least. It wasn't his choice, it wasn't his want, but he ended up the way he is anyway. And out of fairness"—he pointed to himself with his thumbs—"every time I go to see a movie, my pockets are absolutely stuffed with snacks I bought at a gas station. There, now everyone's dirty laundry is up to dry. Thoughts?"

The men looked at him, dumbfounded, until Derrek turned to look at Jeffrey.

"You knew?" he calmly asked.

"Seriously?" Jeffrey responded. "When I came back you were acting crazy different and had pitch white hair, how could I *not* know something was up? And how are you not human? How is that something you can just stop being?"

"It's pretty complicated," Discord said as he sipped his beer. "And we don't have a hundred years to explain it. Basically, he got the human punched out of him by a giant skeleton named Boyd."

Jeffrey looked at him like he was stupid, but after seeing Derrek slowly nod, he believed it to be the truth. After coming to that realization, he started chugging his beer and breathed deeply once his mug was empty.

"All right," he said. "Anything else I should know about?"

"The Schadenfreude is run by vampires," Discord responded, met with Jeffrey calling for another beer and Derrek staring at him with a shocked expression.

"Should he know about that?" Derrek leaned over and asked.

"He's a good guy with a gun, and we need as many of those as we can get."

Jeffrey wasn't paying attention to them as the bartender arrived with another mug, which he went straight to chugging. Once he was finished, he took a moment to catch his breath. Then, in a panic that quickly washed over him, he asked, "Did they drink my blood?"

Discord and Derrek looked to each other, then burst into laughter as Jeffrey maintained the look of panic on his face. Once the laughter died down, Discord wiped a tear from his eye. "Nah, they don't drink blood. They're totally harmless."

"Are you sure?"

"Yeah, they're good people."

"People? You just said they were vampires."

"Vamps are people too. Get woke."

"They're very accepting," Derrek said. "They want to live in peace, just like everyone else, and right now, they're in danger."

"Danger?" Jeffrey asked. "What could be dangerous to vampires?"

"They prefer the term fangs, for the record. And there's a lot of people who want to see them dead just for being who they are. We call them poachers, and we think they're going to storm the Schadenfreude, and if they do, they'll kill everyone."

"Jesus," Jeffrey said. "And they don't hurt anyone? At all?"

"Aside from self-defense," Discord said, "they're total pacifists.

But if they need to, they can fight like crazy. And they might need to pretty soon."

"Is there anything I can do to help?" Jeffrey asked.

Discord smirked. "Hell yeah, we need all the hands we can get on deck, especially Maj. Jeffrey Motherloving Reynolds! Are you packing?"

"I've got my sidearm and a few dozen rounds, not enough to fight an army, but I can try to get more."

"Don't worry about ammo. They're stocked like a doomsday prepper. What we could really use right now is intel, and you've been spying on us, gathering exactly that. I don't suppose you've seen anything suspicious around town, have you?"

Jeffrey thought for a second, then rolled up his pant leg and opened his leg, out of which he pulled a small notebook. He started flipping through the pages.

"There's some crazy political corruption for such a small village. The mayor is getting a lot of money that isn't accounted for on the budget, or his tax returns, for that matter. I think there's some kind of meth lab behind the funeral home. Not sure, though. Oh, and like eight nondescript black SUVs came through in a hurry a couple of days back. Until now, I figured it was some kind of diplomat's motorcade. Do you think it's related?"

"How long ago was that?" Discord asked.

"Hold on," Jeffrey said, looking through his notes and doing the math to figure out the date. "Looks like it was four days ago. Why?"

He looked up to see Discord, eyes wide, completely motionless.

"We need to get back," he said, getting up from his chair, pulling several loose bills from his coat and throwing them on the table. "Now."

He was already out the door when Jeffrey and Derrek realized they should follow, but as soon as they did, they scrambled out of their seats and practically ran for the door, meeting Discord in the parking lot, draping his coat over his and Derrek's motorcycles, causing them to disappear before their eyes.

"What the ..." Jeffrey said, completely dumbfounded.

"No time," Discord said. "We're taking your truck. Where'd you park?"

"Oh, the motel across the street. I walked here."

"Then come on!" he yelled as he jogged across the road followed by the other men, heading toward Jeffrey's truck, the only vehicle in the parking lot. Discord vaulted his way into the bed and repeatedly slapped the roof loudly until Derrek and Jeffrey loaded up in the cabin, started the truck and peeled out of the parking lot, leaving skid marks and smoke as they belted down the road, speeding toward the hotel.

"So," Jeffrey yelled over the roar of the engine, "what do we do when we get there?"

Discord, who was poking his head into the cabin through the rear sliding window, replied, "That depends. We'll find out when we get there."

Derrek turned to face him, then asked, "Why the panic all of a sudden? I thought they would attack in the next week."

"And I thought today was their first day in the area, but if Jeffy saw them, they've been here for a lot longer than I thought—than *we* thought. We need to warn Mila."

"Mila Müller?" Jeffrey asked. "Couldn't you just call her? That'd probably be faster than driving."

"No, the poachers might have tapped their phone lines. If we called, we'd only be ringing the bell for those jackals."

"What about the bikes?" Derrek asked. "Wouldn't they get us there faster than this rust bucket?"

Jeffrey glared at him for a brief moment before remembering that the truck was, indeed, a rust bucket, then proceeded to nod in agreement as Discord answered.

"Too loud and too visible. Plus, they'd no doubt recognize me at a glance. Not to mention their scanners would pick up any vehicle made after 2016, so this oldie goldie will fly right under their radar."

"What about that 'eighteenth gear' thing? Couldn't you just get us there right away?"

Discord shook his head. "They'd know. They scan for that kind of shit, and Jeffy wouldn't have survived the jump. This is our best option."

Jeffrey shook his head. "I have no idea what y'all are on about, but I'm with you."

"Good. That's good," Discord said as they neared the final bend, leaving the forest behind for the field upon which the Schadenfreude stood. They saw the beauty of the white and gold building silhouetted against the setting sun, slowly disappearing behind the horizon. Once the sun vanished behind the trees and the men pulled into the parking lot, they finally saw the flames.

"Shit."

Fire was roaring from a few of the windows, and several corpses and severed heads were strewn about the parking lot, along with no less than a dozen black SUVs. They all got out of the truck and looked around in horror at the damage, at the destruction brought upon the hotel, at the way the bodies were mutilated, eviscerated, and decapitated—except one, which still had its head attached, lying face down. Discord hurried over to the body and flipped it over and was shocked to see who it was.

"Choir boy?" he softly asked. "Emmett? Emmett! Wake up, choir boy! You've still got your head!" he yelled, shaking him by the shoulders, searching for any signs, only to be met with more silence.

Discord didn't stop, however, and kept shaking and yelling until Emmett finally opened his eyes.

"Herr ... D ... Disc ... Discord?"

"Choir boy! Thank the gods you're alive!"

Emmett was breathing heavily and started a coughing fit, which ended after blood spurt from his mouth. Discord looked over him, panicked, and laid him on the ground. He held his hands over Emmett's chest, and a warm amber light began to shine from his palms. After several seconds, Emmett was breathing normally and could keep his eyes open.

"How're you feeling, choir boy?"

"Probably about how I look," Emmett said, in severe pain.

"What happened to you?"

Emmett was quiet for a moment. Then he mustered up his courage. "As soon as we made it known we were closing, the black cars came. Before we could react, they stormed the lobby. There were so many of them. They brought several of us to the roof and then watched as our flesh blistered. They forced us to hang our heads over the railing and then started hacking at our necks, letting our heads ... fall ... oh, God ..."

"Goddamn poachers. Take your time, buddy."

Emmett took a moment to compose himself. "I threw myself over. I thought it would be a better death than what those monsters would do."

"Jesus Christ," Jeffrey said, looking around at the severed heads and beheaded bodies.

"Then ..." Emmett continued, "the guests ..."

"What did they do to the guests?" Derrek asked.

"No ... the guests ... they were *with* the poachers."

Discord looked at the hotel's entrance, which was broken down. The fountains were smashed, causing water to flow uncontrollably and form a massive puddle, pouring into the parking lot. The doors were little more than piles of broken glass and scraps of metal, and inside, he could see several people and even more corpses. The towering fireplace had collapsed, leaving nothing but rubble where it once stood. There were people dressed head to toe in black uniforms, brandishing firearms and machetes, as well as others simply trying to play dead. The air was ripe with the smells of fire, blood, and fear, all with faint undertones of lavender.

"Havok, Major," Discord coldly said, "get Emmett somewhere safe where he can lie down. The truck bed should do. After that, go around the building to the right. You'll see a bay entrance that goes right into the kitchen. They've probably got a bunch of fangs rounded up there for interrogation. Clear the dining hall. Save any hostages you can and kill every last one of those fuckers you see."

"What about you?" Derrek asked.

"I'm gonna tackle these bastards head on. No games. No tricks. Tonight, there will only be blood."

He reached both arms into his coat, producing Sue and Mary, then marched into the hotel, the wet glass crunching underneath his boots, until he was in the center of the room. As soon as the poachers noticed him, the several in the lobby trained their guns on him.

"Evening, fellas," Discord coyly said.

"Who the hell is this?" one of the poachers called out, attracting the attention of the rest of the people in the room as well as many on the balconies.

"Who cares?" another called back. "Just shoot him!"

"Wait!" a third voice yelled, this one from the first-floor balcony.

Discord looked up to see Bernmore slowly approaching the railing with two other poachers at his side, his rifle over his shoulder and a smug grin on his face.

"Well, well, well, if it isn't the Red Death himself. What brings you here, Discord?"

The poachers began murmuring among themselves at the mention of his name, and it was clear Discord had them scared.

"It's funny, I thought I caught a whiff of some Basilisk scat, but I guess what I was smelling was some other pile of lizard shit."

Bernmore let out a bellowing laugh that echoed throughout the lobby, grabbing his stomach as he leaned back. In an instant, he sharply inhaled and looked back down at Discord, lording over him with the same smug grin he wore seconds before.

"Your words cut cleaner than your swords, as they always have." He turned to the woman to his right and said, "I'm going back to the roof. Hold him off as long as you can and send any survivors up behind me."

The woman solemnly nodded and aimed her rifle at Discord as Bernmore walked away, entering the elevator and riding it to the roof. The other poachers put aside the fear they felt before and did the same, several of them moving to surround him.

I count thirty-eight, Sue said, heard only by Discord. *What about you?*

I got forty-one, said Mary. *Forty without Bernmore.*

Oh, I missed those two behind the desk. My bad.

"Doesn't matter," Discord quietly said. "They're all gonna die anyway."

Oooh, so grim, said Sue. *We'll let you work.*

Good luck, Mary said as she and her sister stopped talking, leaving Discord with only his thoughts, which were filled with nothing but rage.

He closed his eyes and breathed deeply, the world slowing around him as the scores of guns readied to fire. He said a silent prayer to no god in particular, as he always did before a slaughter. He opened his eyes, raised his guns, and was torn to shreds by hundreds of bullets, forcing him to the ground as his form devolved into a bleeding mess of flesh.

Several of the poachers approached his lifeless body and unloaded several more rounds into his head, heart, and gut for good measure. They surrounded him, keeping their guns aimed at him and a feeling of surprised relief washed over them as they cheered out, amazed they were able to kill this man who had cultivated such infamy within their circle.

It was when he opened his eyes and rose to his feet, however, that they realized the mess they were in. He stretched his limbs and cracked his neck, resetting several of his joints, which had become dislocated in the hail of lead he had endured as the poachers watched in horror. Some of the ones surrounding him even dropped their weapons and fell to the ground, backing away in terror. Once his body was back in place, he looked into the sea of panic-stricken faces and grinned. He spoke loudly so the poachers on the higher floors could hear.

"Let's get this party started!"

"There, how's that?" Derrek asked, having just draped a blanket over Emmett in the bed of the truck.

"Much better," Emmett struggled to say. "Thank you, Herr Snowe, and you, Herr … I'm sorry, I don't think I caught your name, sir."

"It's Jeffrey," Jeffrey said, "Jeffrey Reynolds."

Emmett smiled. "Thank you, Herr Reynolds."

"Are you going to be all right?" Derrek asked, looking around, making sure there weren't any threats around them.

"I'll be fine. Please, go help the others."

Derrek nodded and headed for the hotel, before stopping and turning back. He reached behind him and retrieved his pistol, which he had been keeping tucked in his belt after Frostbyte left. He held it by the barrel and handed it grip-first to Emmett.

"If anyone comes through, do your best to keep quiet. If they find you, don't stop shooting."

Emmett gave a forced smile as he felt the weight of the gun in his hand, then looked back up to Derrek and silently nodded as he and Jeffrey left him, going around the hotel toward the side entrance. Almost as soon as they turned the corner around the building, there was a roar of gunfire, causing them to stop dead in their tracks and press themselves against the wall. They listened for a few seconds but heard nothing.

"Do you think Discord's all right?" Jeffrey whispered.

"If I were to guess," Derrek replied, "he's playing dead right now to lure them into a false sense of security. He'll be up and fighting soon."

They waited for a few more seconds and listened as the gunfire resumed, less roaring than the first bout and slowly getting quieter as the seconds passed.

"See?" Derrek said. "Sounds like he's taking them out one by one. We should get moving."

Jeffrey nodded and followed Derrek's lead he ran alongside the wall, making haste toward the bay door. As they made their approach, they saw it had been forced open and nearly destroyed.

"That doesn't bode well," Jeffrey quietly said.

"Come on," Derrek said as he climbed the raised concrete. He reached his hand down and helped Jeffrey up.

"Why are these doors so high up?" Jeffrey asked. "Wouldn't it make more sense for them to be ground level?"

"It's so the trucks can pull right up and unload directly into the building. How do you not know that?"

Jeffrey shrugged. "Dunno. Guess I never really thought about it."

"Well, now's a good time to stop thinking about it," Derrek said as he held his hand up, signaling for silence. He closed his eyes and listened intently, ignoring the gunfire, and heard faint voices from ahead. He couldn't make out what they were saying, but he knew there were at least five.

"Get your gun out," he said as he drew his sword, holding the scabbard in his off hand. He lowered his body, keeping a wide frame as he moved silently past the boxes that stacked high in the room they found themselves in. Jeffrey followed suit, surprised at how Derrek took charge and led the way and proud of the man he was becoming.

They proceeded through the room and found themselves in a lavish kitchen, expensive-looking utensils and pristine pots and pans hung from the racks that lined the rows upon rows of top-of-the-line equipment, from stoves to wood burning smokers. They made their way across the room, deftly gliding atop the laminated floor until they reached the server window, which they slowly peeked over.

They saw the dining hall, the doors to the lobby, barred and presumably locked, the tables and chairs randomly strewn about, clearing a circle in the center of the room, where they saw the poachers. There were six standing in a circle, three of them facing inward in at what Derrek guessed to be about a dozen bound and gagged hostages, including Victor, the rest keeping watch around the room. One of the poachers looked over by the server window, but the men ducked down before they could be seen.

"Stay here," Derrek mouthed. "I'm going to flank them. Keep me covered."

Jeffrey considered protesting, but he could tell by the look in Derrek's eyes that he could handle it, so he nodded in agreement and turned off his gun's safety.

Derrek snuck back to the kitchen line, sheathed his sword, and grabbed three of the sharpest knives he could find, then slowly opened the door beside the window. It had no knob and swung both inward and outward, allowing the servers to move through it quickly, and also allowing him to pass through it with no noise. He crept his way behind several overturned tables as he listened to what the poachers were saying.

"What do you think's going on in there?" one asked.

"The fangs probably called for reinforcements. And by the sounds of it, they're putting up a hell of a fight," said a second, who had his gun trained at Victor's head.

"Even if they win the fight," a third chimed in. "We will have truly won the war if we can take out Müller."

"And what if we die?" the first asked. "What will all this be worth then, if we can't live to see a world rid of them?"

The third paused, then put down his rifle, laying it on the ground. He walked over to the first and grabbed him by the collar, pulling him in close.

"Our deaths mean nothing, but their deaths mean everything, or did you forget the oath you took when you joined?"

The first man stammered for several seconds until he finally found some words to say.

"I … no, I remember."

"Then repeat it, young hunter."

"I—"

"Repeat it!"

The first man was terrified beyond words, and continued to stammer until the third let go of his collar, dropping him to the ground. Now lording over him, the third proceeded to speak.

"'I swear, with heart and soul, with body and mind, with blood and steel, to defend humanity from the darkness they fear. I swear to give all I have and all I am worth to the pursuit of purity. And if I am unable to kill my prey, I swear to die by their hand, and I hope others will avenge my sacrifice.'"

The poachers all stared at the man on the floor as the third reached a hand down to him.

"Are you prepared to die, young hunter?"

The man on the floor summoned all the courage he had and

accepted the hand, pulling himself to his feet. Still holding onto his hand, he replied, "Yes, I am prepared to die."

The third smiled. "Good. As am I."

In a flash, the third man plunged a knife into the first's neck, sending blood gushing out onto his own face as the rest of the poachers watched, barely reacting to the violent act unfurling in front of them.

The first was doing all he could to fight off the man who held the knife as he continued to push further, twisting it slowly, and he quickly lost his strength. After mere seconds of this, the man's eyes glazed over, and he stopped fighting back, falling limp to the ground as the third ripped the knife from his throat.

"Coward," he said, spitting blood onto the lifeless body.

The entire time, Derrek had been watching, growing furious. He expected the way they treated the fangs, but to see how they treated their own, it made his blood boil.

Before the third could retrieve his rifle, Derrek sprung into action, throwing one knife after another, plunging them into the skulls of the remaining two who were pointing their guns at the hostages, as well as the one facing in his direction, as Jeffrey gunned down the remaining armed poacher, leaving only the one covered in blood, who frantically looked around at his fallen comrades, then dropped his knife and jumped for his rifle, only to find Derrek standing on it, his sword pointed toward the man.

"Stand down," he said as the man slowly reached away from the rifle, standing to his feet, staring Derrek down.

"Hands up, dipshit," Jeffrey said, his gun raised as he burst through the door, to which the man begrudgingly complied, staring quizzically at Derrek.

"The one with the reaper's touch," he coldly said. "I should have known you'd be a problem."

"Shut up," Derrek said, cutting Victor free, then moving on to the rest of the hostages.

Victor removed his gag and caught his breath, then said to Derrek, "I owe you an apology. I didn't think you would actually help us. Thank you."

"Don't mention it. Just help me get everyone untied."

"You can't stop us," the man said. "The damage is already done."

"I told you to shut up!" Derrek said, approaching him. As soon as he was within arm's reach of the man, however, he produced another knife, which he tried to thrust into Derrek's neck. Derrek caught his arm, however, and slowly crushed his wrist, causing him to scream out in agony before producing yet another knife and attempting to stab him in the stomach, leaving a shallow wound as Jeffrey reacted, unloading three rounds into his back, causing him to fall to the ground, dead.

"Damn it," Derrek said, clutching his wound, dropping to the floor. He pulled his hand away to assess the damage and found it to be little more than a flesh wound.

Jeffrey opened his leg and pulled out some gauze and bandaging. "Pull up your shirt. There's still work to do."

Derrek nodded and pulled up his shirt, allowing Jeffrey to apply the gauze and wrap the bandage around his abdomen, securing it with a bobby pin. He and Victor helped him to his feet, and Derrek took it from there as the fangs looked at Jeffrey with suspicion.

"Don't worry," he said. "This is Jeffrey. He's a friend, and he wants to help."

Victor looked him over with his arms crossed, particularly at his leg, but after a few seconds, he dropped his guard. "If you're a friend of Herr Snowe, you're a friend of mine. Thank you for your help."

"Hey, no worries. I'm just doing what any decent person should," Jeffrey said. He turned to Derrek, who he saw was pulling up a chair. "What're you doing? We don't really have the time for a breather."

"Could you just give me a second?" Derrek said, exasperated as he slumped into the chair, nearly hyperventilating. "it's just ... I've never killed anyone before. I just need a second."

Jeffrey considered pulling him to his feet, as his commanding officer had once before when he was in the same situation, but he realized he had been seeing Derrek as his superior, taking his orders, following his lead. Yet he was still that affected by taking a life. He had forgotten this was not the life he was accustomed to. He walked over and put his hand in his shoulder.

"You've got a few minutes. Could a couple of y'all help me get that door open?"

"Sure," one of them said, heading to the door alongside Jeffrey, followed by three of the other hostages.

Derrek buried his face in his trembling hands, his heart racing as he tried to steady his breathing. He barely noticed when Victor approached him.

"Close your eyes," he said. "Clear your mind and take deep breaths."

Derrek followed his advice and closed his eyes, putting every thought out of his head, and slowed his breath. He felt a wave of calm wash over him. He stayed in this mindset for half a minute, until he felt better. He then opened his eyes to find Victor kneeling in front of him.

"Better?"

"Much better. Thank you."

"No problem. I remember the first time I took a life. Even for a fang, it's a powerful thing. If I can give you any consolation, you saved a lot of lives by killing those men. You did the right thing."

Derrek put on a smile, which quickly faded. "Thank you, Victor. It means a lot."

"Don't thank me yet," he said as he stood up. "There is still much to do. Last I saw, they had Frau Müller, Sana, and Emmett on the roof. We have to save them."

"Emmett's fine," Derrek said. "He fell from the roof, but he's fine now."

Victor was surprised for a moment but relieved to hear that. He turned toward the door. "That's good to hear. We should really go, the door needs—"

He froze dead in his tracks for several seconds, apparently in deep concentration.

"What is it?" Derrek asked.

"The gunfire," Victor replied after a brief moment, "it stopped."

Derrek then noticed it too and realized it had stopped almost a minute earlier. He jumped to his feet and, alongside Victor, ran over to Jeffrey and began to help clear the door. They were soon done, and he stepped forward and slowly opened it.

Through the slowly growing crack, he saw a scene of absolute horror. Nearly every surface was drenched with blood. The floor was littered with severed heads, some cleanly cut and some seemingly ripped off, some with chunks of torso still attached. And in the center of it all, a large pile of corpses and severed limbs stood almost five feet tall where the fireplace once stood. The door was completely open by that point, and Derrek, as well as everyone behind him, were struck with the stench of blood. Even though they were fangs, it was too much for most of them, save for Victor, who didn't react at all.

Approaching the pile, Derrek saw Discord, completely dry, dragging a pair of bodies from behind the front desk.

"Oh, hey guys," he said, still dragging the bodies toward the pile, "glad you could make it—even if the party has died down a bit."

"Jesus ..." Jeffrey muttered, looking around at the carnage as he followed Derrek to the pile.

"Don't you think this was a bit over the top?" Derrek asked.

"This is the exact same thing they did to the fangs," Discord said as he effortlessly flung the bodies onto the pile. "I thought they deserved a taste of their own medicine."

"I agree," Victor said, "but you may have been a bit extreme."

"You think so?" Discord said as he picked up one of the heads. "Take a look at this and tell me if you still do."

He tossed the head to Victor, who reluctantly caught it, turning it so he could look at its face. The eyelids hung half open as the eyes themselves stared lifelessly into the distance while the jaw remained limp.

"What's the point of this?" he asked as Discord walked to his side.

Without saying a word, Discord grabbed the head by the jaw and moved it slightly, causing a set of razor-sharp teeth to fill its mouth, as well as causing Victor to drop it.

"Why would you do that?" Victor yelled into Discord's face.

"To prove a point. It's like half of what I do."

"What point? That my fellow fang was slaughtered? I knew this. We all knew this!"

Discord rolled his eyes and picked the head up by the hair, holding it toward Victor.

"Tell me his name."

"What?"

"You've been here for a long time, and I know you know the names of all the fangs that live here. Tell me his name."

"I ..."

Victor trailed off as he racked his brain, trying to remember the name belonging to the head Discord held. After a few seconds of silence, he finally said, "I don't know."

"Exactly. This head belonged to one of the poachers," Discord said as he tossed the head over his shoulder.

Victor and Derrek stood in stunned silence as the other fangs murmured among themselves and Jeffrey looked around, thoroughly confused.

"What does this mean?" Derrek finally asked.

"It means these rat bastards," Discord said as he kicked a nearby corpse, "are working with the Black Hand. You'd think they all wouldn't be so gung-ho about it, but the enemy of my enemy, right?"

Taking another look around, Derrek saw several of the severed limbs had long claws in place of fingers, and in many of the lifeless bloodshot eyes, he saw a bright yellow tint in lieu of the expected shades of blue, brown, or green.

"How could anyone turn against their own like this?" he asked as his stomach churned. "I knew they hated the White Hand, but how could they team up with the very people dedicated to wiping them out?"

"It was personal," Discord said as he approached another body and began dragging it toward the pile.

"You seem pretty sure of that," Jeffrey chimed in, still assessing the bloodshed. "What do you think could've pissed them off enough to work with the fangs?"

"Not them, it's the Black Hand's vendetta we're paying for."

Victor came to a realization. "You don't think—"

But he was cut off by Discord as he tossed the next body into the pile. "Yep, Alistair. Nobody else would come at the Schadenfreude, not like this."

Victor, as well as the other fangs, began squirming and talking amongst themselves, clearly afraid.

"This might be a dumb question," Jeffrey asked, "but who the hell is that?"

Victor, still terrified, turned to him. "Frau Müller's brother. But I thought he was dead? How could he be here?"

Discord sighed. "Mila insisted I let her decide his fate. I wanted to kill him, but she couldn't bring herself to let it happen, so she had him banished and marked up as dead. Look where that got us."

"This doesn't make any sense," Victor said as he leaned against a column just to stay standing. "Why would she lie about this to us? All these years, and he's still breathing?"

"Looks like it," Discord said, dragging yet another body to the pile. "But you know her, always wanting to give people another chance."

Victor was suddenly filled with energy. "He must be on the roof with her! We have to stop him!"

"You got that right," Discord said, putting his hands on his hips, facing the group. "Havok, you, Jeffy, and Vick head for the roof, and whatever you do, don't get too close to that pale creep. As for the rest of you, head for the parking lot and find Emmett. He's armed, so make sure you make yourself known."

The hostages headed for the entrance while Victor and Jeffrey went for the elevator and Derrek stood, wondering how Discord knew Emmett had his sidearm. He quickly shook it off, however, and stepped toward him.

"What about you?" he asked. "It sounds to me like we could really use you with what we're heading into."

Discord shook his head. "I still gotta sweep the rooms, make sure I didn't miss any poachers. I'll catch up."

Derrek could see, even through Discord's constant grin, that he was bothered about what was happening around him. With all the courage he could muster, he put on a grin of his own and reached out with a fist. "Just don't waste too much time on the minibars."

Discord laughed, then met Derrek's fist with his own. From a standing start, he leapt to the first balcony, breaking down door after door as he searched them with lightning speed. Derrek did his best to hold up his grin, but it faded shortly before he reached Jeffrey and Victor as the elevator made its descent.

"So," Jeffrey said, "what's the deal with that Alistair dude? Y'all seem pretty afraid of him."

Victor glared at him briefly before looking forward, back at the doors. "For a time, he was the leader of the Black Hand."

"I take it they're like the vampire bad guys?" Jeffrey said. This was met with another glare. "Sorry. *Fang* bad guys."

"Yes, they're the bad guys," Victor said as the doors opened and the three men boarded. He pressed the button for the roof and continued, "And Alistair is the worst of them. He wants nothing but the destruction of the White Hand and free rein over the night."

"So, you guys are with the White Hand?"

"Technically speaking, yes, but we act separately from them."

"What should we expect?" Derrek asked.

"I'm not sure. I've never met him myself. I've only heard tell of his brutality."

"Well then," Jeffrey said as he reloaded his pistol, "guess we'll have to be just as brutal. What do you think, Derrek?"

Derrek gripped the hilt of his sword tight as he watched the number above the buttons slowly rise as they made their way to the roof. He was not prepared for the carnage he had witnessed that day. Nor did he ever think he would witness anything like it. But he knew there was no turning back. He looked forward at the doors as they reached the top before they opened, and with all the courage he had, he spoke.

"We're going to save them, and we're going to take him down."

Under Jeffrey's bushy beard, he smiled. He aimed his pistol toward the door while Victor lowered his stance and grew claws from his fingers as his mouth filled with teeth and his eyes turned yellow, prepared to fight.

As the door slowly opened, the men saw a volley of guns pointed at them, unmoving as they suddenly found themselves in a standoff where the advantage was clearly not in their favor.

"Shit," Jeffrey muttered as one of the poachers stepped forward.

"Lower your weapons!" he called out.

Derrek counted twelve guns aimed at them. He knew from his training he could deflect the bullets, but he could tell Jeffrey and Victor would be in too much danger if he did that, so he slowly lowered his sword to the ground, then stood with his hands up in surrender.

"What are you doing?" Victor quietly yelled at him, his teeth and claws still bared.

"Surrendering. We can't fight them like this."

Before Victor could protest further, Jeffrey followed Derrek's lead and laid his gun on the ground.

"C'mon, Victor," he said with his arms up. "For now, this is our only option. Trust him."

Victor snarled at the poachers, debating whether to attack, but reluctantly retracted his claws as well as his teeth and slowly raised his hands.

The poachers gestured for the men to move forward, and they were led to the base of the glass pyramid that topped the Schadenfreude, where they saw Mila and Sana, their arms tied behind their backs as they stood alongside a man whom Derrek recognized as Bernmore. Two guards were pointing guns at them, and a figure with its back to them was looking down into the lobby.

The figure turned around faster than they could see, and the men were now face to face with this figure's thin, pale, emaciated face, its sunken in eyes, and its near hairless head draped in a black cloak.

"Ah," the figure said with a deep, raspy voice and a heavy German accent, "the last of Mila's lackies."

"It's about time," Bernmore said. "A lot of my men died for this. It had best be worth it."

"I assure you, it will be," the figure said. Derrek assumed this must be Alistair but saw no resemblance to Mila.

"Please," Mila called out, "leave them out of this! This is between us!"

Alistair turned his head sharply toward her, letting out a loud crack as he did, and coldly said, "You decided this when you left me to die. You left our family, and they all perished. I'm simply returning the favor."

Mila looked at the ground as Alistair snapped his neck back toward the men, fixing his gaze on Victor.

"Victor Dupont, the Belgian Butcher. I never had the pleasure of eating one of your meals, but I've heard nothing but praise sung of your culinary talents. A shame you waste it on humans." He looked to Derrek and Jeffrey. "And whatever else drags its way into this abomination of a hotel."

"Fuck you too, buddy," said Jeffrey. Alistair snapped his fingers and one of the poachers standing behind him struck him in the back of the head with the butt of their gun, causing him to stumble briefly before regaining his balance.

"There's no need for this!" Derrek called out. "We're complying!"

"I will not be spoken to like this by a filthy Hauch Von Tod! Either learn your place or you *will* be shown it."

Derrek bit his tongue as Alistair yelled at him and clenched his fists. He could tell protesting further would only serve to hurt those around him, so he decided to wait for Discord.

"Ah, the Hauch Von Tod," Bernmore enthusiastically said. "I was worried you had left with the Frostbyte party, but I suppose freaks of nature like to stick together! Marvelous!"

"Stow your enthusiasm, Reginald," Alistair said with a sideways glance. "You seem to forget our agreement."

"Last I checked, the only names on your list belonged to fangs. The Hauch Von Tod was never your prey, so to me, it seems fair game."

A brief, but tense moment passed as Alistair glared at him, until he let out a long sigh.

"Fair enough. Have your fun."

A wide smile crept its way across Bernmore's mustached face, and he let out a slow, deep chuckle. He shrugged the rifle off of his shoulder, letting it clatter to the ground as he unbuttoned his jacket, tossing it as well as his extravagant hat aside with a flourish, revealing a wall of muscle where an ocean of fat was expected to be. He stretched each of his arms across his chest, then cracked his neck as some of the other poachers nudged Derrek forward, forming a half circle around the two opposite to Alistair. He finished his stretches and reached behind his back, bringing it around with a large knife, which he pointed forward.

"Are you ready, dead blood?"

Derrek didn't reply, as he wasn't sure himself. He squared up, raising his fists and planting his feet as firmly as he could on the blood-soaked concrete. A tense silence hung in the air as the two men stared each other down, reminding him of his fights with Discord. He saw Bernmore blink, and in an instant, he was rushing toward the hulk of a man.

Bernmore couldn't react before Derrek closed the distance and plunged his fist into his gut, forcing the air to leave his body before he moved behind him. His hand throbbed after landing the hit; it was like punching a brick wall, but he could tell Bernmore felt it.

"Ugh ..." Bernmore said as he caught his breath and turned around to face him. "Nice shot, dead blood, but I've taken worse."

He moved forward, slashing at the air around Derrek as he deftly avoided the attacks. He thrusted the knife at him, but as he avoided getting impaled, he felt the air leave his body as Bernmore's knee slammed into his stomach, and an empty fist crashed into his back, throwing him to the ground. He tried to push himself up, but a firm boot to the back made that impossible.

"I've heard tell your kind were among the strongest humanoid creatures," Bernmore said, lording over him, "and until now, I was inclined to believe it. My father fought one of you once, and it cost him an arm and a leg—literally. I'm starting to think he was nothing but a drunk old liar. No matter. A kill is still a kill."

The boot was lifted from Derrek's back, but he could only get to his hands and knees before it slammed into his side and threw him several feet away. Bernmore laughed as he struggled to push himself to his feet.

"I can tell there's no quit in you. I like that. If you were human, I daresay you'd make a fine hunter. Perhaps even a—"

"Do you ever shut up?" Derrek asked as his eye glowed a piercing green.

Bernmore was surprised but quickly regained his composure.

"Like I said, a fine hunter."

Derrek rushed at him, punching and kicking wildly, trying to hit something that would do some lasting damage, all the while avoiding the oversized knife, but his fists bounced off Bernmore's muscles as though he were wearing a full suit of armor. He was getting tired, and he could feel it, but not as much as he felt the fist slamming into his gut, hitting him square in his wound. He keeled over, clutching his stomach until a hand wrapped around his neck, lifting him from the ground.

"I was so excited when I heard one of you was here, but you're proving to be quite a disappointment."

He tried to give a rebuttal, but he could barely breathe, let alone speak. Bernmore sighed and raised his knife, running the tip of the blade along Derrek's face.

"Oh well, at least your head has some value."

Derrek tried to scream as the blade cut deep into his left cheek, leaving a deep gash across his face, but all that came out was a muffled squeal and a series of coughs as his friends looked on in horror. Jeffrey called something out, but the blood rushing through his ears was too loud for him to tell what. All he could hear over the roar of his struggling veins was the deep laughter of the man gripping his neck.

He looked up at the sky as his vision began to narrow and saw the stars were out. The pain began to fade, but he could still feel the blade slowly slicing his flesh. The cold steel would have sent shivers down his spine if he could even feel anything below his neck. He thought of the nights he spent with Discord at that very spot, the conversation he had with Hadrian, the nights he spent there alone, doing exactly as he was now: gazing at the stars. They were beautiful.

Suddenly, he felt a surge of energy rush through his body while Bernmore bellowed with laughter, which was cut short by a swift kick to the chin as Derrek escaped from his grasp, back-flipped away, and knocked him to the ground. He breathed deeply as Bernmore pushed himself back to his feet and spit out the blood in his mouth.

"A strong kick—I'll give you that much," Bernmore said as he rubbed his jaw.

Derrek could breathe easy again, and although he could feel the warm blood dripping down his face, he paid it no mind, and readied himself for another bout.

Bernmore was still rubbing his jaw when Derrek lunged, slamming his fist into his hulking neck, dropping him to his knees and leaving him gasping for air. He dropped the knife and grabbed his throat in pain, trying to get a breath in until he felt a heavy punch to the side of his head, whipping him around and laying him flat on his back.

Derrek pounced, pushing his knees into Bernmore's chest as he began to repeatedly beat on his face. With every punch, his round face turned more and more into a bloody pulp; his nose had been shattered, he was missing several teeth, and both his eyes were nearly swollen shut. When Derrek was satisfied with his work, he stood and walked to retrieve the knife as Bernmore lay groaning in pain.

Derrek took hold of Bernmore's extravagant mustache and yanked the broken man to his knees, ripping half of it out as he held the heavy knife against his tree trunk of a neck. He managed to force his eyes open, and to Derrek's surprise, he was smiling up at him.

"Do it, dead blood. I failed my mission. Claim your prize."

Derrek presses the knife deeper into his neck, breaking the skin and spilling some blood as the half-mustached smile grew even wider.

"Go fuck yourself."

With those words, Derrek took the knife away from Bernmore's neck and slowly turned his back to the man and began limping toward Jeffrey and Victor.

He didn't see as Bernmore rose to his feet, his grin replaced with a murderous frown and a look to match in his eyes, but he did hear what sounded like a stampede as the mountain of muscle rushed at him and saw the look of panic in Jeffrey's face.

Before Bernmore was upon him, Derrek spun around and slashed the knife, sidestepping him as he crashed to the ground, more than half of his neck cut clean through. He turned back to face the poachers, his face soaked in blood, both his and Bernmore's, and saw fear in their eyes as their weapons trembled in their hands. One of them mustered enough courage to steady his aim, but as soon as he was trained on Derrek, his rifle was flung from his hands, clattering across the roof out of reach. Before anyone knew what was going on, the same had happened to the rest of the poachers' firearms, and they all stood in confusion for a brief moment before fixing their eyes toward where Mila and Sana were being held.

In the confusion, they had escaped their bindings, and their guards laid on the floor dead, their throats cut. Mila's skirt was splattered with blood, as was the dagger in her hand, and Sana stood by her side, her hands raised toward the poachers, beads of sweat forming on her forehead as her eyes were locked in tight concentration. Derrek had wondered what Sana was capable of, and he seemed to have the answer:

Telekinesis.

A beat passed before anyone made any moves, but as soon as Jeffrey slammed his elbow into the mouth of the poachers who struck him, it was chaos. Victor's hands were claws in an instant, and he was fighting side by side with Jeffrey against half of them. The poachers tried to draw machetes, but Victor had ripped out two of their throats, and Jeffrey had roundhouse kicked one of them out cold before they could even properly fight back.

Derrek joined Mila and Sana to deal with the other half, Bernmore's knife in hand. The ones they opposed, however, were a bit quicker to the draw, and faced them, machetes at the ready. Mila's eyes were a piercing yellow as she sprang into action, throwing her dagger clean into one of their necks, throwing the one next to the fresh corpse off enough for her to grab him by the neck, raise him into the air, and slam him to the ground, crushing his windpipe, then seamlessly retrieving her weapon. Sana had jumped toward her share, moving like an acrobat as she wrapped her legs around one of their necks, loudly snapping it before she jumped away, hand springing and flipping toward her next opponent, where she did a handstand on their shoulders before swinging downward, landing cleanly on her feet as she slammed the poacher to the ground, headfirst. He did not get back up.

That left Derrek with two to fight on his own. Bernmore has taken most of the fight out of him, but to his relief, the poachers didn't seem too thrilled about fighting him either. With all the strength he had, he brandished his knife and rushed at them, letting out a bellowing roar as he did in an attempt to scare them further. He raised the knife up high and brought it down on one who was frozen in fear, cutting through his shoulder like butter, lodging the knife halfway through his torso, which Derrek decided to abandon. He ripped the machete from the dead poacher's hand and slowly marched toward the one that remained.

The poacher had her machete raised in defense, which Derrek tested by slamming his own into it with all his strength, shattering her blade and throwing her to the ground. She scrambled back to her feet and produced a knife, but she hesitated, and before she knew it, Derrek's blade sliced through her neck, and her decapitated body fell to the ground.

He looked around and saw everyone alive and well, save for the poachers, of course, although Victor was clutching a deep cut on his arm. The group all looked at each other, making sure everyone was in one piece, but they were interrupted by the slow sound of clapping, and they all turned to look at Alistair, who hadn't moved an inch.

"Well done," he said, continuing to clap. "Now I only have one mess to clean up."

They had regrouped and now stood in a line opposite to Alistair, weapons at the ready.

Alistair slowly raised his hands palms up, and the blood that pooled around him began to move and shift, as if it were being stirred. The further he raised his hands, the more pronounced the disturbance was. The group looked on, mystified as the blood began to rise from the ground, forming countless thin, red tendrils.

"Keep your distance," Mila said so Alistair couldn't hear. "He can control blood."

"We can see that," Derrek whispered back. "But how are we supposed to fight him with claws and blades?"

As if on cue, a deafening gunshot cracked and Alistair's right shoulder exploded, leaving his arm dangling by a thin thread as the tendrils of blood collapsed into the puddle they once were. Everyone whipped their heads around to find the source of the shot, and saw Discord, revolver in hand, standing in front of the open elevator doors.

"Sup, Ali? Long time no see."

"Discord," Alistair struggled to say. "So … kind of you … to finally join us"

"You know me, always fashionably late," he said as he took his place beside Derrek, "Gnarly wound, Havok. It'll make a nice scar."

"I hope it won't be too bad," Derrek said as he cracked a smile. "I'd rather not scare everyone away."

"Scars make the man, my friend." H then grabbed Derrek by the shoulder, leaned in close, and whispered, "Hold her back."

"What?"

"You'll see."

He marched forward toward Alistair, who was still clutching his ruined shoulder. He raised his intact arm toward Discord, but it fell limp as another bullet ripped through, tearing a chunk from his arm.

"*No!*" Mila called out as she lunged forward, only to be caught by Derrek. "What are you doing?" she screamed as she clawed at

Derrek's back. He wanted to say he was sorry, but it was taking all he had just to hold her at bay. Suddenly, it felt much easier, and he saw Jeffrey, Victor, and Sana were all helping him, keeping Mila from interfering with Discord.

"So ..." Alistair wheezed out as Discord approached him, "do we continue this game of cat and mouse you love so much, or—"

He was cut off by a crashing punch to the face, ejecting blood from his mouth. He leaned back against the spotlight and tried to stand back on his feet, only to be flung back with another punch. Discord grabbed him by the collar and began wailing on him, bashing his head against the glass with every hit, gradually cracking it more and more.

"I told her to kill you," Discord said casually, still punching Alistair, "but I guess familial bonds are stronger than logic."

As he continued beating on Alistair, tears rolled down Mila's eyes while she struggled against her friends preventing her from moving. Derrek felt no joy in this, but he trusted it was necessary; otherwise, he doubted Discord would ask such a thing of him.

Discord reeled back for a heavy hit, shattering the glass behind Alistair, and toppled over the side with him, plummeting toward the lobby floor as everyone cried out in surprise.

As they fell, Discord got a few more punches in before using Alistair as a springboard, launching him to the ground while Discord rose slightly, preparing for a graceful landing.

Alistair landed with a loud crunch as he slammed into the pile of corpses. He was impaled on several bones jutting out from the mass of flesh he landed on. He writhed in pain as Discord climbed the mound, standing over him as he brandished his revolver. Alistair coughed up blood as he struggled to laugh, staring Discord in the eye as he spoke.

"You may kill me," he said, doing his best to keep his eyes open, "but this hotel will never recover. Nothing will bring this back."

"Was it worth it?" Discord asked, unloading his revolver and refilling it with fresh bullets.

Alistair paused for a moment, then managed to let out a single, "Yes."

"I sure hope so," Discord said as he slammed the cylinder back into place. "I never really had any family. Not for long enough to make any major family-splitting feuds, at least. Always just a marriage that lasted a couple of decades. Then somebody like you comes along and wipes them out just to piss me off."

Alistair laughed again. "Then you'll never know what it's like to be betrayed as I have by my own sister."

Discord fired a round into Alistair's leg, causing him to scream out in pain.

"Yeah, silver's a real bitch. And she didn't betray you. She left you to deal with your own mess. All this shit you do is your own damn fault, no matter how much you want to blame someone else."

"You're ... one to talk," Alistair said as he attempted to clutch at his leg with his ruined arms, "Look ... at all you've done. All this carnage made by your hands, and you say *I'm* to blame."

"Yeah, I killed them, but at least I own it. You slaughtered your kin. You burned your town. All in the name of the Black Hand. You consumed yourself with this pain and anger, and you blamed it all on the only person with a pulse who still cares whether you live or die. You made your bed. Lie in it."

He took aim at Alistair's head and cocked his hammer.

"Any last words?" he coldly asked.

Alistair coughed several more times, spurting blood with each hack. After finally catching his breath, he stared Discord in the eye and spoke.

"Long live the Black Hand, and may you someday perish as I have."

"I'm sure I will, one of these days."

He fired, putting a hole between Alistair's eyes as a piercing scream filled the lobby.

He turned to see Mila as she stepped out of the elevator, closely followed by everyone else. She looked around in horror at her home, the once marble-clad haven she had worked so hard to build, now standing as a monument to violence.

Discord tucked his gun into his coat and stepped down from the mound as Mila ran toward him, dagger in hand, which she stabbed upward into his chest, going under his ribs into his heart. He didn't flinch, but she didn't expect him to. She ripped the dagger out and proceeded to stab him several more times, slowing with each thrust as he maintained a stoic expression, until she finally stopped and dropped to her knees, letting the dagger clatter across the floor.

"Feel better?" he asked as his wounds closed over.

She said nothing, but she did look up at him in disgust before climbing to her feet. She walked past him toward the parking lot but made a point to slam her shoulder into him as she passed. He glanced back at her as she walked away, then shifted his gaze forward at Derrek as he approached him, followed by the rest of the group. There was a bandage over his facial wound, already soaked through.

"I know that wasn't easy," Discord said, looking at Victor and Sana as he scooped up Mila's dagger, "especially for you two. I'm sorry you had to do that."

"It had to be done," Sana said, clearly trying to remain calm. "Even after everything, he was still her brother. I just hope she can find it in her heart to forgive us."

"She will," Discord said, turning away from them and casually walking toward the entrance. "As far as she's concerned, y'all are her family. Don't know how she'll think of Havok and Jeffy, though."

"I hope she'll understand," Derrek said as he followed.

"She does. But that doesn't mean she's OK with it."

As the group exited the building, they finally understood the state of the hotel. The few burning windows had spread, and several floors were now wreathed in flames too bright to directly look at. The structural integrity had apparently been compromised, as the roof was visibly sagging. The S on the neon sign was hanging by a thread, and looked as though it could fall at any second. In the parking lot, they saw the fangs, Mila included, huddled around Emmett, who was now laying on the ground several feet from Jeffrey's truck, his wounds being tended to.

Emmett and Discord briefly made eye contact before Mila stepped between them, her arms crossed tightly.

"Leave," she sternly said.

"Just like that? Not even a goodbye hug?" Discord asked with his arms outstretched.

"This," she said, gesturing to the scene around her, "is all your fault. I want you gone, and I want you to stay that way."

"It's not my fault you let Alistair live."

Mila's eyes turned bright yellow as she approached him, and she moved mere inches from his face, even though he towered over her.

"You should have stayed," she said, each word chilling everyone around her to the bone, "or better yet, you should have actually paid an ounce of attention instead of gallivanting around the forest with a Hauch Von Tod." She turned to Derrek and said in a much more neutral tone, "No offense, Derrek. You've been nothing but courteous your entire stay."

Derrek flashed a smile but quickly faded back into the feeling of discomfort that filled the crowd.

"How the hell was I supposed to know this would happen?"

"Because you're supposed to know everything!"

She had yelled so loud that for a brief moment, the world around these people seemed frozen in place. She took a second to compose herself, then continued.

"You're supposed to know everything. You're supposed to know everybody. You're the sharpest, most capable person I've ever met, and you still managed to completely mess everything up."

Discord was silent for a moment, but before he could speak, Mila took his place in the conversation.

"You made a promise when I founded the Schadenfreude. You *swore* to me you would be here to stop these people. You promised you'd be here to protect us, and the one time we needed you, you were nowhere to be seen."

Discord gave out a long sigh, then handed the dagger back toward her, handle first.

"You're right. I should've been here. And because I fucked that up, a lot of good people died. For whatever it's worth, I'm sorry."

He wore a face of sincerity, but Mila was unfazed. She snatched the dagger from his hand, slicing his palm as she did, and sheathed it under her skirt. She turned away from him and faced what remained of her staff.

"Emmett cannot properly move in his state, so I, along with Victor and two others, will transport him to Zakopane in one of the poacher's vehicles while the rest of you, following Sana's lead, will move through the forest. Hopefully, the tint on the windows will give us the extra time we will need."

"Frau Müller," Emmett said, trying unsuccessfully to pull himself to his feet until one of the fangs assisted him. "This was not his fault."

She looked at him with exhaustion in her eyes. "Emmett …"

"We agreed to let him go, it isn't fair to blame him for—"

"Choir boy."

Emmett shifted his gaze to Discord, waiting for what he had to say.

"I screwed up, and I've got a price to pay. That's just how it is. No matter how much you protest, Mila's word is final. It's better to accept it than to just drag it all out."

"But—"

"But nothing. You've been given a command, and that's that."

Emmett looked at him for several more seconds, hoping for him to drop this stone-faced act, but he came to realize he wasn't going to. He turned to Derrek and pulled out his pistol, holding it out by two fingers on the grip toward him.

"Herr Snowe, I thought you might want this back."

Derrek was briefly surprised, as the fact he still had the gun had slipped his mind, but he quickly made his way up to Emmett and collected it, tucking it into his belt. Emmett then reached out for a handshake, which Derrek accepted. As he did, however, he heard a voice in his head.

Watch his back. He's lost so much already. I don't want for him to lose himself. And thank you for all you tried to do.

Derrek was surprised but understood it was Emmett speaking to him, based on the way he looked at him. They released hands, and Emmett flashed a smile before turning to Mila, with the assist of the fang holding him up, and following her to the closest SUV.

They had loaded up, and Mila gave a final dirty look to Discord before peeling out, speeding down the long driveway. Sana gave the men a knowing look and a faint smile before leading the rest of the fangs into the woods, heading east, leaving the three alone in the parking lot, as the building behind them roared with flames.

"What do we do now?" Derrek asked as he and Jeffrey approached Discord.

Discord was silent as he stared into the distance, fixated on the road Mila drove down. After several seconds of this, he turned back to the men.

"You guys should probably get back to the states. I've got some other business to attend to, but I oughta be heading your way soon enough."

"Seriously?" Jeffrey said, "You're just gonna dip out on us like that?"

Discord looked away from them and reached into his coat, producing a duffle bag, which Derrek recognized as his own. He tossed it to the men, and it landed at their feet.

"You've got a flight to catch, and I could only get two tickets. A buddy of mine will meet you at the gate and get your truck back across the pond, free of charge. Oh, I found your gun in the elevator, so I put that in there too."

Jeffrey stared him down until eventually realizing he wasn't going to get anywhere. He knelt down, opened the bag, and retrieved his pistol, which he placed back into his leg. He then closed the bag and slung it over his shoulder.

"All right. But I'm gonna have some questions when you make your way over there."

Discord smiled. "I don't doubt it."

Jeffrey patted him on the shoulder as he passed, making his way to the truck, tossing the bag into the truck bed before strapping himself into the driver's seat and firing up the engine.

"Are you sure you're all right?" Derrek asked with a worried expression.

Discord put on a brave face. "I'm a lot older than I look. I've gotten pretty good at compartmentalizing things like this. I've just got some answers to find, some affairs to get in order, the works. Don't worry about me."

He gave a thumbs-up. Derrek didn't quite buy it, but he could tell Discord needed some time. He opened his arms and invited him in for a hug.

Pleasantly surprised, Discord accepted and lifted him into the air in a bone-crushing bear hug, sending a shooting pain into

Derrek's stomach wound. He doubled over as soon as he was let go but quickly stood back up straight, clutching his gut.

"Oh, shit," Discord said, noticing the blood soaked through his shirt. "Are *you* all right?"

"I'm fine. One of them just had knife after knife. It's only a flesh wound."

"If you say so. Just make sure it doesn't get infected."

The two smiled and shook hands, and Derrek followed Jeffrey's lead, taking his place in the passenger seat as the motor ran. They gave a final look and wave to Discord, his flowing coat silhouetted against the roaring fire behind him. As they drove down the driveway, the hotel slowly disappearing in the rear view mirror, neither of them said a word, the silence only pierced by the steady hum of the engine and the sound of the tires running across the road.

The exhaustion hit Derrek all at once, and his eyelids suddenly hung heavy. Before he even realized it, he had passed out, drifting deep into a dreamless sleep.

Discord watched as they drove away, waving until they were out of sight. As soon as they were, he dropped his arm as well as the smile he wore and turned back to the burning hotel, greeted by a well-dressed silhouette with its arms crossed, facing the blaze.

"Mind explaining to me what the hell just happened?" he said as he approached the figure.

"I could ask you the same, Kahli."

"Don't you 'I could ask you the same' me, you interdimensional asshole. I know damn well you're behind all of this."

The figure slowly turned its head, looking back at Discord with a pitch-black eye.

"Is that so?" he asked as he turned around, facing Discord as the flames danced behind him. "Last I checked, it was you who forced my hand."

"Don't give me that Lucifer-esque backdrop guilt trip, you knew one of these days I'd catch on to your bullshit."

"Then please, enlighten me."

"After the Sumerians fell, you told me no mortal could handle hosting the Devourer without going power mad. Time and time again, you told me to trust you. You told me to have faith. You told me that every single one of them I put down was for the greater good. Bullshit, all of it."

"I never lied to you."

"I know you saw Havok. He told me about that dream of his. He can handle the power, and yet you stand there and lie to me, and then lie to me about lying to me!"

Discord got close to the figure and grabbed him by the collar of his suit jacket, and spoke sternly.

"For four thousand years, I've been doing your dirty work, blindly buying the line of crap you kept selling me. No more. I'm done."

"What are you trying to say?"

Discord glared at the man. "What do you want, a written resignation? I QUIT. I even put it in all caps for you so you can get it on all your extra senses."

"I don't think you fully understand the position you're in, Kahli."

"No, I understand perfectly. I know you can't directly interfere with mortal affairs, which is why you need poor schmucks like me to do your dance and make your moves. Now I don't know who you picked up to tip Alistair off or how you got them to persuade Bernmore, but you'd better get it through your cosmic cranium that I'll rip their heads off and mail them to you, wrapped in a dozen layers of tissue paper if you ever send any of them after Havok! Are we clear, desk guy?"

The man was unfazed by Discord's threats and casually grabbed his wrists, pulling them away from his collar and proceeding to straighten his tie.

"It's not that simple. You are bound by fate to kill the Devourer as it rises. All I've done is push you in the right direction."

"Sure, keep changing the subject. I'm sure that'll convince me."

"The Devourer is an evil beyond mortal comprehension. No one, save for yourself, has ever faced one of its hosts and survived, let alone killed one. To let it roam free, as you're attempting to do, is to put not only the entirety of earth but the very fabric of reality at risk. If you have any sense of what's good for the universe, you'll end that human's short life."

"Seriously, what part of 'I quit' don't you get? I'm not pulling any more triggers for you, and if you send any freaks my way, I'll make them deader than Humbaba."

The man sighed deeply. "I see you won't be reasoned with. Very well. Consider our work agreement terminated."

"It's about time."

"But this does not mean I will simply let all you do slide. Whatever that Devourer ends up destroying, whoever it ends up killing, just remember that their blood will be on your hands."

Discord waved his hands over himself, gesturing to his ensemble. "You've met me, right? Blood is nothing new to me."

The man's matte black eyes scanned him, eyeing him from head to toe. "So it would seem. How does it feel, then, to finally make a choice that was your own?"

"Pretty damn good, desk guy, pretty damn good."

"I'm glad to hear it."

Discord turned away from the man, as well as the towering blaze, and began walking down the path until he felt a stern hand on his shoulder.

"Before you leave, Kahli, I'd like to ask you something."

"If it's about the necklace, it's still eternally attached to my neck."

"No, not that."

"Then shoot. I've gotta meet a guy about a thing in Omaha."

"It isn't the platinum relic, you know."

Discord sighed. "Yeah, I know, but it looks cool. Are you gonna ask your question, or are we just gonna go back and forth with you knowing exactly what I'm trying to be vague about?"

He paused briefly and cleared his throat.

"Are we friends?"

Discord was caught off guard by this question but quickly turned around to face him.

"What does it matter?"

"I suppose it doesn't. We've just had this working relationship for so long, and I realized I never bothered to ask."

Discord paused as he composed his words, then, with as neutral a tone as he could muster, he spoke.

"You strong armed me into becoming the only defense against the Devourer, lied to me for thousands of years and tried to have a bunch of my friends killed, several of them successfully, as soon as I stopped following your orders. But I've had friends do a lot worse. If you want to call me a friend, it's no hair off my ass. Just cut it out with the underhanded assassination attempts."

The man smiled slightly and removed his arm from Discord's shoulder. "I'll do my best."

Without saying another word, Discord turned away from the man and started walking down the road. He didn't see as the man vanished into thin air, but he didn't really care. He reached into his jacket, producing a small device with a long antenna, which he extended as far as it would go, and a large red button. As he pressed the button, a booming roar filled the air as the charges he placed around the building detonated and the Schadenfreude came crashing down behind him, crushing the mangled bodies that lay beneath the roof, sending tons upon tons of burning rubble into the parking lot and surrounding landscape, spreading the blaze as this, the former home to so many fangs, became nothing but a flaming heap.

The flight back to New York was a long one, but thanks to the change in time zones, it was only just past midnight, relatively speaking. After the men disembarked, they collected their bags and went their separate ways, Jeffrey heading to the closest hotel while he awaited the delivery of his truck and Derrek making his way back to his apartment. They hadn't spoken since leaving the Schadenfreude, but they had a mutual understanding that their silence didn't need to be broken.

Derrek stared out the window of his cab, taking in the familiar scenery of bright lights and swarms of pedestrians flooding the streets. He thought about how many of the people he passed at the breakneck pace urban traffic moved at weren't, in fact, human. His eyes were opened in a way he never even considered before, and he had a nagging suspicion that anyone he saw wasn't who they seemed. He thought of the horrors he had seen that night and realized it could have happened anywhere at any time.

His train of thought was broken, however, when the cab came to an abrupt stop.

"Fourteen dollars, seventy-three cents," the driver said in a gruff, angry voice.

Derrek didn't say a word as he reached into his wallet and handed the man a twenty-dollar bill, then exited the cab and retrieved his bag, making his way to the door of his apartment building.

"Hey! Your change!" the driver called out through his open window.

"Keep it," Derrek called back as he entered the building.

He went to his mailbox in the lobby and found it almost completely empty, save for a small parcel, roughly the size of a brick. He wondered briefly what it could be before remembering the hat he bought online. As he made his way up the stairs, all he could think of was how the seller must have ruined the brim by cramming it into the package the way they did.

He put those thoughts aside as he reached his door, however, and focused on finding the proper key. As soon as he did, he entered his moderate apartment and was struck by the smell of dust that had accumulated while he was gone. He could see a solid layer on every surface as he made his way to the bedroom, guided by the green light of his eye. He tossed his bag into the corner, kicked off his shoes, and dove into his queen-sized bed, sending a cloud of dust into the air, which he completely ignored as he drifted deeply into sleep.

It was a loud clanging that stirred him from his slumber, prompting him to shoot upright in his bed. He listened for several seconds, holding his breath as he concentrated, and heard a faint shuffling sound coming from where he guessed was his kitchen. He silently crept out of bed and grabbed his pistol from his bag. He was surprised it made it through customs, but he supposed security was more lax for stowed luggage. Either that, or Discord called in more favors than just the truck.

He slowly opened his bedroom door, making his way through the darkness that had enveloped his apartment toward a light at the end of the hallway, where he assumed his intruder was, gun at the ready. As he reached the end of the hall, he pressed himself against the wall and peeked around the corner.

He saw a large figure moving around, digging through his fridge and pantry, apparently doing its best to remain quiet. It wasn't until he saw the silhouette of a bushy beard against the refrigerator light that Derrek decided to reveal himself.

"Why do you always have to break in?" Derrek asked, causing the intruder to jump and drop the container of butter he was holding.

"Damn it, Derrek, why do you always have to be so sneaky?" Jeffrey yelled as quietly as he could, picking up the butter and turning back to the stack of ingredients he scavenged from the fridge. Among them were eggs, no-doubt-expired milk, and grape jelly, which Derrek had no idea was even there.

Derrek tucked his pistol into the back of his waistband and walked over to the kitchen area, leaning against the counter in front of his coffee maker, away from the rancid foodstuffs.

"You might want to smell that stuff before you try and cook with it; it's all been sitting there for six weeks."

Jeffrey looked at him for a brief moment before opening the milk and taking a whiff. He immediately recoiled back and started coughing, doing his best not to vomit from the smell. He held his breath and screwed the cap back on, holding it out as far away from him as possible as he frantically looked around for a trashcan, eventually spotting it on the other side of the fridge. After he carefully placed it at the bottom of the bag, he went back to the ingredients, wondering if any of it was any good.

"I was going to clear the fridge out in the morning. What are you even trying to do?"

"Well, I *was* going to make pancakes," Jeffrey said as he pulled the trashcan around to the counter, dumping the rest of the ingredients into it, "but I've suddenly lost my appetite."

The men laughed, and Derrek grabbed his coffee pot and began filling it at his sink, starting a fresh batch of coffee with grounds he kept in the pantry above the maker. He stood and watched the pot slowly fill while Jeffrey continued rummaging around the fridge, unsuccessfully searching for anything edible.

The coffee maker gave out a short beep, and Derrek pulled two mugs out of the cupboard, filling both with the liquid energy he thrived off of. He handed a mug to Jeffrey, who was inspecting a carton of eggs before deciding not to risk it and tossing it in the trash, accepting the mug and raising it for a toast, which Derrek happily met with his own, prompting them both to take a long sip. They leaned against the counter and continued sipping their mugs silently until Jeffrey broke the silence about halfway into his mug.

"So, what now?" he asked, looking ahead instead of at Derrek.

He considered it for a moment, then answered, "Nothing's changed. Come morning, I'm going to Will's office, and I'll win Frostbyte from him, fair and square."

Jeffrey looked at him with a surprised expression. "That's what you're thinking about? I'm still stuck on the vampires."

"Just because the world isn't what we thought it was doesn't mean my goals are any different. I went to Germany because I lost our last game, and you, Discord, and everyone else there showed me everything I needed to see. I'm ready to take my seat."

Jeffrey continued to stare at him for several more seconds, taking in the seriousness in his eyes. He took another long sip from his mug and looked back forward, cracking a smile hidden from Derrek's view.

"Then here's to however many years of kickass leadership you have to offer," he said, raising his mug toward Derrek.

Derrek smiled. "We'll see how it goes," he said, and he met the mug with his own.

Derrek waited patiently in the waiting room that led to Shale's office, watching as those with appointments went in, and quickly came out. By his count, there were only three ahead of him. As soon as Shale's assistant informed him of Derrek's arrival, he made sure she turned away anyone who came for a meeting after him, as this was much more important in his eyes, but he always made a point to keep his word.

He leaned back in his seat on one of the six couches that stood against the walls as a woman opened the door and left his office, marching through the waiting room with her head held high as the next person went in, a smug-looking man with a bright blue shirt. Shale had told him once that he met with up to a hundred people a day and wanted to be sure they had ample seating while they waited. He could tell he also wanted them comfortable and could almost feel himself melting into the cushions.

He was dressed in his suit, which Shale himself had tailored for him. He rarely wore it, sporting it only on important occasions, namely, two weddings, a handful of events, and a bar mitzvah, all of which Shale dragged him along to. It was dark as night, with a pristine white button-up and a deep-blue tie, all tied together with his well-shined dress shoes, although it may have clashed with the large bandage on his cheek. He could feel the eyes of everyone waiting in front of him, nervously sizing him up. He figured they thought he was their competition in one form or another and paid them no mind, as he was no threat to them, or vice versa.

The door opened, and the smug-looking man stepped out, the smug look wiped from his face as he avoided eye contact with everyone and made his exit as fast as he could. The next appointment was called in, and he nervously shuffled through the large oak door, closing it behind him. Shale had told him once that the door was built from reclaimed wood from his childhood home, pieced together over years as the seams were sanded and sealed over, making it look like a single, grand piece of wood instead of the dozens of boards it was actually made of. He then went on to make it into a metaphor, saying something to the effect of, "With enough hard work, anything is possible, regardless of your materials' past," which Derrek thought was cliché at the time, a sentiment he still maintained.

As he stared at the door, reflecting on its metaphorical past, it opened once more, and a man walked out with his head held high; he had apparently gotten what he wanted and left the room with a spring in his step as the last appointment, apparently an intern of some kind, went in, leaving Derrek alone as he continued to patiently wait.

Before he could pick another object to reminisce over, the door opened once more and the intern hurried through, holding a stack of papers she didn't have before. With the waiting room empty, and the assistant calling Derrek's name, he made his way past the still-open door and walked into Shale's luxurious office. No matter how often he visited, the awe-inspiring view of the city below never got old. He walked past the lounge area and the well-stocked bar, approaching the grand mahogany desk, where Shale was sitting, the back of his chair turned to him as he admired the view.

"Twenty years I've had this office, and this view never gets old," he said as Derrek took a seat across from the back of his chair, eyeing the chess board set up in front of him, noticing the white pieces where on his side. "Over the years, I've watched this city grow, thrive even, from this chair. I've done my best to do my part, but, like everyone should, I know when it's time to move on."

He turned his chair around, greeting Derrek with a smile without an ounce of surprise at the reveal of neither his wound nor his hair's odd color, or rather the lack thereof.

"Think you're ready to take this chair from me?"

Derrek met his smile with one of his own. "You're on, old man."

"Then, by all means, make your move."

Derrek pondered his options and settled on moving his rightmost pawn two spaces ahead in an attempt to get his rook out early. "Did I miss much while I was away?"

Shale moved his left knight onto the field. "Aside from Hanes complaining about having nobody to dump his work on, it's been business as usual."

Derrek moved his rook behind his pawn. "I think I'll transfer him to Seattle when I'm in charge. A master of delegation should do well there."

Shale laughed as he moved his other knight, mirroring his previous move. "Don't get too far ahead of yourself. You still have to win."

They each made several moves before either of them claimed a piece, with Shale breaking out his bishop to claim one of Derrek's pawns, leaving his knight directly exposed.

"How was Germany? You look like you have some stories to tell."

Derrek didn't miss a beat as he captured the bishop with his rook, causing Shale to blink and raise an eyebrow in surprise. "Aside from Jeffrey's intense training regimen, a few scuffles at a few pubs, and the amazing food, it was business as usual."

Shale moved his knight away from the path of Derrek's rook. "But what about the last two weeks? Life isn't—"

"'Life isn't only work'—you've said it a thousand times," Derrek said as he moved his bishop alongside his rook, aimed at Shale's rook.

Shale moved his queen, aiming at Derrek's knight. "A thousand times or once, it's still true. Tell me about the other two weeks."

Derrek took the rook. "I spent most of it studying, although I did make a friend who I spent a good amount of time with. Complete weirdo but a great conversationalist."

"Friends like that are always good company," Shale said with a smile as he took Derrek's knight, putting Derrek in check.

Without taking a moment to consider his options, he moved his bishop once more, capturing Shale's queen, leaving him baffled.

"Really got me with that one," he said, figuring his next move.

"Never take your eye off your opponent. The moment you blinked was the moment you lost."

Shale looked up from the board, surprised by his words but impressed nonetheless.

"Seems you've picked up some new tricks—courtesy of that friend of yours, I assume."

"You could say that."

Shale kept looking at Derrek as he made his next move. He had almost no defenses on his king, but he was determined to put up a fight. He moved his remaining bishop to pin down Derrek's remaining knight. "Tell me about him."

Derrek moved his rook forward, taking out one of Shale's pawns and giving himself a straight shot to put Shale in check. "He likes to drink, but I've never seen it get to him. He's always smiling and quick to joke. Fiercely loyal, too; he even backed me up when some punks tried to give us a hard time."

Shale pushed back, pouncing on Derrek's knight. "Sounds like a good friend. Does he live in Germany?"

Derrek moved his rook forward and put Shale into check, pinning him down behind two pawns with no rooks to back him up. "He said he was 'technically homeless,' but he had an American accent, so I have to think he spends a lot of time in the states."

Shale took the only move he had, moving his king ahead, out of the way of Derrek's rook. "I hope you'll be seeing more of him then. A man is nothing without those close to him."

Derrek finally moved his queen and put Shale's king into check once more, again leaving only one move for it.

Shale counted his options, but he knew the only way he could win was if Derrek let him. He was brimming with pride.

"Would you do the honors?" Shale asked, putting his hands down on the table and a big smile on his face.

Derrek smiled back at Shale and moved his knight, blocking him in completely.

"Checkmate."

Shale leaned back in his chair, looking ahead at him for several seconds until he opened a drawer in his desk and produced their scorecard, updating their totals—1532 to 1532.

"Well played, son."

"Likewise. You really made me work for it."

Shale laughed. "You already won. There's no need to lie to me. I could tell from the start that I had no chance this time around, just from the look in your eye."

"I guess it has been an … educational six weeks."

"I'm glad to hear it."

Shale reached into another drawer and pulled out a stack of papers, which he went to work signing, one after another.

"I had these forms printed the morning of the last time we played. As soon as they're all filled out, you will have sole ownership over Frostbyte, including all its assets, funds, and resources. My name will be completely removed from the ongoing records, and I will no longer be involved in any company decisions, to be made public in a press release I'll set up for this afternoon."

He signed the last paper, shuffled through the stack, and slid a single sheet and a pen to Derrek, pointing the tip toward a line at the bottom of the sheet, alongside a large X.

"Sign here, and it'll all be official."

Derrek picked up the pen and found it weighing heavy in his hand. He had been working most of his life toward this moment, even if he hadn't realized it until just months prior. He looked up at the man who had been a father to him for a decade and a half and saw the warmth in his eyes, and the smile on his face, and he signed his name.

"Wonderful!" Shale exclaimed as he clapped and jumped out of his chair, then walked around his desk and gave Derrek a firm handshake before he pulled him to his feet and gave him a loving embrace.

"I'm so proud of you, Derrek. I know you'll do great things."

Even with the reaper's touch, his mouth was still curled into a huge smile.

Just then, from beyond the office door, the two heard a muffled voice, presumably the secretary, call out, "Sir, I told you, you need an appointment to go in there!"

They also heard another voice say back, "And I told you, I don't care," followed by the office door swinging open, slamming against the wall loudly, while causing no visible damage. They watched as Discord strode in, eyes fixed on Derrek.

"Havok!" he exclaimed, "I've been looking all around town for you! Took, like, twenty minutes, dragged on forever."

"You could've just called."

"Excuses, excuses."

The secretary rushed in. "I'm sorry, Mr. Shale. I couldn't get him to stop!"

Discord looked back at her, then to Shale with a surprised look on his face.

"Son of a bitch. Billy Shale, is that you?"

Shale squinted at him briefly, before his eyes widened and he started walking toward him. "Discord? My Lord, all these years, and you haven't aged a day!"

The men shook hands and shared a laugh. Shale looked to his secretary. "It's all right, Janice. He's a friend."

Janice nodded and slowly went back to her desk, closing the door behind her.

"You two know each other?" Derrek asked.

"Discord knows everybody," Shale said, letting go of Discord's hand and making his way back to his chair.

"Billy and I fought in the Gulf War together. Lost touch after he went home though." He turned back to Shale. "So, how've you been? Last I heard, you were trying to make humans live forever."

Shale gave a small laugh. "I prefer 'allow' rather than make. And as you might be able to tell by the view, the office, or perhaps the building itself, I've done rather well. And you?"

"Same circus, different clowns."

Discord noticed the stack of papers, especially the one Derrek had just signed.

"Am I interrupting something?"

Derrek and Shale exchanged a look, and Derrek decided to answer.

"I just won a game of chess and claimed ownership of Frostbyte."

Discord was stone-faced for a moment before jumping and pumping his fists in the air as the other men watched, confused.

"Hells yeah! I knew there'd be some kickass dramatic reveal! Let me guess: Billy took you under his wing, *Little-Orphan-Annie* style, and you've been working your way up the corporate ladder ever since?"

Derrek and Shale exchanged another look, and Derrek said, "Yeah, got it in one."

Discord jumped again, and as soon as he was back on his feet, he reached into his coat, producing three green bottles of beer, which he handed to the men.

"Sounds like cause for celebration. Don't you think?"

Derrek and Discord both took a seat in front of the desk, and the three men opened their beers, meeting in between them in a toast.

"To a better future," Shale said before the men drank.

Shale's face curled into a disgusted expression, and he examined the beer as Derrek and Discord chugged away at their drinks, not coming up for air until they were done.

"How can you two drink this?"

Discord let out a loud belch before Derrek answered, "It's more of a chugging beer."

Shale stood upon the podium, looking at the bouquet of microphones before him. He had only given the announcement that there would be a release an hour before, but the media had wasted no time in swarming the Frostbyte headquarters. Among the sea of hundreds of faces, he saw familiar reporters, journalists, and camera operators, several of which had once gone after him in an attempt to undermine all his philanthropic work. They all came up empty, of course, but it was always annoying when they went rifling through his trash.

He looked to his right, where several feet away, Derrek was standing, facing the crowd with his hands behind his back. Discord was standing beside him, fumbling with a puzzle cube, which he could tell was missing several stickers. He cracked a smile and turned back to the crowd and cleared his throat before gesturing to the event coordinator that he was ready.

The coordinator nodded and signaled to several people, and after confirming the cameras were ready, he began a countdown from five.

Shale did a final check of his notes, straightened his tie, and looked ahead at the main camera as the coordinator reached one. The recording began, and Shale began speaking.

"Good afternoon, everyone. For those of you who don't know me, my name is William Shale, founder, owner, and CEO of Frostbyte Incorporated, the world's leading developer of prosthetic limbs and internal organs, as well as one of the leading contributors to the largest environmental conservation charities. Over the last thirty-two years, I've done my best to make the world a better place for those who come after me, as I believe everyone should, but there's only so much one can do from a seventieth-story office.

"I called this release to announce that, effective immediately, I will be stepping down from my position and will transfer ownership and control of the company to my protégé, Derrek Lloyd Snowe."

He gestured to Derrek, who was still calmly watching the crowd. He gave a small smile and waved to the crowd as the cameras all briefly panned to him, before focusing back on Shale.

"On a related note, I would also like to take this opportunity to announce that I will be throwing my proverbial hat into the ring and will be running for the presidency in the 2036 election."

This statement was met with a roar from the crowd, producing a din of questions as everyone competed with their microphones outstretched, trying to get a comment while Derrek stood out of frame, dumbfounded at this announcement. Shale had never mentioned anything of the sort to him before then, so it hit him as a big surprise.

"I will now turn the microphone over to Mr. Snowe, and he will give a brief statement. Derrek, if you will."

He then stepped away from the podium, shaking Derrek's hand as he made his way to his place, looking at Shale with the same expression on his face until he was before the bundle of microphones, at which point he adopted a neutral expression. He hesitated for a brief moment before speaking, but after a final glance to Shale, who elbowed Discord to direct his attention to the speech, he steadied his breathing and faced the crowd.

"Hello. As Mr. Shale just said, I am Derrek Snowe. Over the past several years, I've been working closely with Mr. Shale, learning everything I could from him. I didn't know until recently that I was up for this—shall we say—promotion, but as soon as I was told, I put everything I had into preparing for this exact moment.

"There will not be many drastic changes to the way things are run at Frostbyte any time soon, as the last thing I want to do is make some naive decision from lack of experience. Over the next several months, I will be putting my all into my work, learning how to run this company as my predecessor has, then learning how to improve things from there.

"I am truly honored and humbled to be offered this opportunity, and I will not disappoint. Thank you all for your time. There will be no questions."

He stepped away from the podium toward Discord and Shale, doing his best to ignore the wave of reporters trying to get a comment from behind the wall of security officers that was set up. Once he approached the men, they were ushered inside the building's lobby, which was currently empty.

"Now *that* was a speech!" Discord said as he patted Derrek on the back. "Short, sweet, and to the point. Plus, it's gonna put all the major shareholders in turmoil. It's a win-win-win-win!"

Shale nudged Discord once more. "Any major change in leadership can have unpredictable effects on a company's share price. Don't let it bother you too much if there's a drop. You really did great out there, though. You'll do the company proud, son."

He and Derrek shared a smile and a handshake as something rang out from Discord in an obnoxious tune. He patted around his coat and pulled out an extremely outdated cell phone.

"Hold on. I gotta take this. You guys have a nice, heartwarming back-patting conversation in the meantime."

He stepped away and stood next to a large potted plant, where he flipped the phone open to answer it.

"You've reached Discord, fastest hand in the West. How can I help you?"

"Do you mind telling me what the hell that was?" a gruff voice with a Western accent replied.

"Jer Bear! Haven't heard from you in months. How've you been?"

"Cut the shit, Discord. Why the hell am I looking at the Devourer on TV right now? And why the hell is he taking control of Frostbyte?"

"Politics, man. Crazy stuff."

"Oh for the love of … aren't you supposed to be the one who deals with this?"

"I am dealing with it."

"By giving it control of the biggest corporation in America?"

"Hey, I had nothing to do with that. It's been in the works for years."

"Why is he even still breathing? You should've—"

The phone began ringing. "Whoop. Hold on. Got another call. Please hold."

"Don't you 'please hold' me, you son of a bi—"

Discord put him on hold and answered the other call.

"Discord's sarcophagi and insulated wire. You wrap 'em, we zap 'em. How can we help you today?"

A deep, monotone voice spoke back to him slowly. "So you still live, and the Devourer does as well. Why is that?"

"'Cause I didn't kill him, duh."

"Why?"

"'Cause I didn't want to, duh."

"It is your duty."

"So?"

"So it is what you must do, one must not stray from—"

The phone began ringing again. "Hold up. Got another call. Please hold."

The voice grunted in exasperation, and Discord answered the call.

"You've reached Discord's … damn it, I got nothing. What's up, Sizzle?"

"You know we have to talk about Snowe, right? I'm guessing the others already called?" a calm, masculine voice replied.

"Yep and yep. Got Jer Bear and big man on the other lines. You wanna get them together? I can get us a meeting with him so we can all work this out."

"That would be best. Get back to me with the details, and I'll make sure they don't storm Frostbyte."

"Aye aye, Captain. I'll text you the deets when I have them."

"Roger that."

Discord hung up on all three calls and went back over to Derrek and Shale, who were still carrying on with their conversation.

"And that's all you have to do to win over the board when they stand against you. Just remember to get Cheryl brownies, and you'll be golden."

"I'm no good at baking, but I'm sure I'll be able to find a decent bakery somewhere. What do you think, Discord?"

"Definitely go with Cakes and Shakes. The shakes suck, but their baking is top-notch."

"Noted. What was that call about?"

"Just some friends of mine that you're gonna have to meet soon. Maybe we could set up a meeting in a couple of days so you can be properly introduced. But enough of that for now. Billy, what's your plan? You really going through with this whole presidency thing?"

Shale smiled. "Absolutely. I've been mulling it over for the last decade or so, and now that Derrek is ready to take over here, I can go forth and give it my best shot without having to worry about all the work needed here. I know you dislike politics in general, but I do hope you'll understand this is the best way for me to be able to make major positive changes in the world."

"Now, hold up. I don't dislike politics, but I absolutely hate politicians. Those money-grubbing bigwig hypocrites do nothing but push policies that benefit themselves and harm others, especially when a goddamn businessman decides to step into politics so he can do nothing but yell nonsense, call everyone opposing him a liar, and tax the ever-living shit out of the poor and cut costs to essential services so he can line the pockets of his other fat-cat business buddies. Not you, though. You're genuine."

Shale laughed. "I appreciate that, old friend, and I hope you'll be available should I ever require your *special* set of skills."

"But of course," Discord said, reaching out to shake his hand. "No political assassinations though. I haven't done those since the Ming dynasty."

The three shared a laugh before Shale checked his phone and spoke once more.

"I must be going. My advisors are throwing a fit. I've got a list of people to meet before the sun goes down and who knows how many favors to cash in on. Derrek, just remember what I told you: keep your allies close, never compromise your morals, and above all else, do good. It's all in your hands now, son. Do your best."

He held his hand out toward Derrek, who shook it without hesitation.

"I will, and I hope you'll do the same."

They shared a warm smile, and Shale exited the building, weaving his way past the crowd as Derrek and Discord made their way back to Shale's—or rather, Derrek's—office. Derrek stood behind his desk, looking out the window at the city, admiring from a view he'd never truly appreciated until that moment. Discord poured them both a glass of Steel Barrel, handing one to Derrek as they both took a seat on opposite sides of the desk.

"Cheers," they both said as their glasses met before they took a sip and enjoyed the flavor. Discord set down his glass and stuck his hand into his coat.

"I've been working on this in my spare time for the last couple of weeks. Just put the finishing touches on her last night. Figured now's as good a time as any."

He pulled his hand out of his coat and was holding a large pistol, laying it on the table in front of Derrek, who picked it up and began to examine it. It had a large trapezoidal barrel and was much heavier than the pistol Jeffrey had given him. He could barely fit his hand around the grip. It was silver with a deep blue trim and covered in intricate carvings, depicting a series of thorny vines that seemed to crawl along the barrel, flowing in flames at the muzzle.

"It's a fifty-caliber Desert Eagle, the most powerful semiautomatic pistol ever conceived. I hopped over to Israel a couple of weeks back and picked her up. Been gradually working the carvings into it so she can affect more than just flesh-and-bone things. That baby can hurt anything from people to ghosts to gods and everything in between. I've been calling her Lillith, but feel free to call her whatever you want. She's yours now, after all."

Derrek continued to examine the gun, running his finger along the vines, getting used to the weight of it.

"I think Lillith suits her perfectly. Thank you, Discord. I really appreciate this."

Discord smirked and raised his glass toward him for another toast, which Derrek happily obliged, and the two enjoyed their drink as the sun slowly lowered in the sky, eventually dropping over the horizon.

Printed in the United States
by Baker & Taylor Publisher Services